CHILD OF PROPHECY

Divide Series Book One

Dream With All Your Senses!

CHILD OF PROPHECY
Divide Series Book One

T. E. BRADFORD

PUBLISHING THE POSITIVE
ELK LAKE PUBLISHING INC.
Plymouth, Massachusetts

Cover Design: Humble Nations and T. E. Bradford

Interior Design: Derinda Babcock

Editor(s): Linda Rondeau, Deb Haggerty

Author Represented by Hartline Literary Agency

PUBLISHED BY: Elk Lake Publishing, Inc., 35 Dogwood Dr., Plymouth, MA 02360, 2018

Library Cataloging Data

Names: Bradford, T. E. (T. E. Bradford)

Child of Prophecy / T. E. Bradford

338 p. 23cm × 15cm (9in × 6 in.)

Description: How far would you go to fit in? Another world?

Fifteen-year-old Nova Hawthorne has a unique trait that sets her apart, yet she wants nothing more than to be normal and fit in.

She soon finds out there's a very real reason why she feels so out of place in this world—she's from another one. And prophecy says she is destined to destroy them both.

Identifiers: ISBN-13: 978-1-948888-27-1 (trade) | 978-1-948888-28-8 (POD) | 978-1-948888-29-5 (e-book.)

Key Words: speculative fiction, young adult, coming of age, other worlds, family

LCCN: 2018951168 Fiction

DEDICATION

For Beans Mama and for Hector.

Please save us a seat at the table.

Acknowledgments

The time has finally come!

The time to say thank you to all of the people who have made writing the words "THE END" not just possible, but a true experience. First and foremost, to every person who has read this book, you have my heartfelt and deepest gratitude. You are who we're doing this for.

To Deb Haggerty and all the folks at Elk Lake Publishing Inc, thank you from the bottom of my heart for seeing value in my story and for taking a chance on a new author like me. You make dreams come true. To Linda Rondeau, thank you for not only helping to make this book shine, but for making me a better writer.

To Marlene Bagnull and everyone at the Greater Philadelphia Christian Writers Conference, thank you for serving God and changing lives. You are true Wardeins and Travelers of the High King.

To Jeff Wheeler for inviting me to share my story online: You set my feet along the path, demonstrated to me what truly excellent writing could be, and inspired me to keep moving. As Laura would say, "At least if you do something, you've got a shot."

To Peter Wiebe, who has endured the battles of life and come through with scars, but an inner strength forged in flame: Jesse would be so proud of you, my friend. You have my beta reader services for life. Now get writing, because I can't wait much longer to see what's going to happen next in *your* story!

To Soleil, RC, Ken, Staci, Carole, TEW, Pam, Michelle K., Michael H., Michael W. Jason, Ryan, Susan, Ed, and all of the people I met, got to know, and journeyed for a while with on Write On: I will never forget our time together there. We may have crossed the Divide to a new place, but those magical days still fill my heart and call to me.

To all of the wonderful people in RWA and especially my CNYRW Chapter: Thank you for enduring my years of growth and for all the versions of this story you had to hear over the years. You ROCK!

To Alicia who read every new and revised bit with eagerness, and to Marje, who prayed with me and for me, thank you for being my friends. You are rare gems in this world.

Now for the more personal stuff.

Mom, thank you for reading to me, always telling me how talented I was, and for giving me the gift of laughter. Dad, thank you for being a steady rock in a sometimes tumultuous world. I never once heard you complain even though life threw you many hard curves. I owe you both so much. Thank you for teaching me about God, for raising me in a Christian household, and for loving me through whatever came. I wouldn't be who I am today without the two of you.

Grandma Mason, you left this world many years ago now, but your legacy lives on. Thank you for forcing all of us grandchildren to sing and perform, even when we didn't want to. You gave us the gift of music, and I will always cherish that. I know somewhere in heaven, the angels are listening to your beautiful voice as you sing the song of the High King.

My darling husband Doug, you are the inspiration for every hero I write. Thanks for putting up with me, with having to read the beginnings to countless stories, and for challenging me to write so that even a Sci Fi reader will enjoy Fantasy. I love you beyond measure, and am so blessed to have you. God made you just for me, and I am forever grateful for such undeserved grace.

To my son, my little man, my creative inspiration: You contain the best parts of both your Daddy and I. Your mommy loves you more than you will ever know. You are my heart, and you will forever be my greatest creation and my best story.

Finally and most of all, to my Heavenly Father, my High King and the One True God, without whom I would be nothing: You have given me the gift of music and writing, and I hope they will be used to your glory.

"If I can help somebody as I pass along, then my living shall not be in vain." -- Alma Bazel Androzzo (1945)

CHILD OF PROPHECY

From whence may come the blood that holds
The elemental gifts of old
Cometh the power that seeks to bring
The end of every living thing
By choice and action freely made
Life's stones like water soon cascade
The wings of darkness stand unfurled
And seek the end of every world
So, one must stand and face the night
Else risk the loss of life and light
And for destruction to be stilled
Life's blood must then be freely spilled

—The Blood Debt Prophecy

THE STRANGER

Tiny bits of color danced in the air around Nova, fragments of the sound that had plucked her from the warm embrace of sleep. Frowning, she blinked at the clock as she registered the time. Why would there be fragments of sound at three in the morning? She tilted her head, listening and watching.

There. A small whorl of dancing orange floated in the air near her bedroom door. Orange signified a soft sound.

"Opus?" Nova whispered. "Is that you, silly kitty?"

She left the comfort of her bed and padded out to the living room. More spatters of orange floated through the air. They were coming from the direction of the sliding doors. A small, dark shape pressed against the glass from the outside, trying to get in. It had to be Opus. Something must have disturbed his nocturnal prowling, probably his enormous appetite. Nova turned on a lamp.

"Are you hungry, Op—"

The shape outside the door moved, growing before her eyes, unfolding like origami in reverse, expanding into something far too large to be a cat. The darkness shifted to reveal a man's face inside a black hood. His eyes glittered. Menace radiated from them. The shadow shifted again, and a fold rose, a pale arm sheathed inside. The lamp light reflected along the surface of something gripped in a tight fist.

Nova's scream erupted from deep in her chest, sending shards of red, yellow, and white in every direction. They crashed against the walls like waves. The figure in black recoiled, ducking as if afraid of being hit by them. Then, he turned and disappeared into the night.

"Nova?" Her mother flew into the room, eyes wide with alarm. "What is it?"

Grandpa Zeke came on her heels, white hair sticking up in all directions. One of her mother's pink bathrobes fluttered around him like wings.

"Th—there was a man." Nova saw the sound of her voice, surprised by the nearly black color that accompanied the husky, too-deep sound. "There." She could only point to the doors.

Grandpa Zeke stalked to the doors to investigate, muttering something under his breath. Nova's mother sat her down on the couch, holding her close for a moment before leaning back to look into Nova's face.

"Tell me exactly what happened."

"I heard something." Nova paused. Should she say anything more? No. She had to be honest about this, even if she upset her mother. "Something orange."

Her mother's body stilled. "I didn't hear anything."

She shouldn't have been surprised. Not by the answer or by the way her mother's lips pressed into a disapproving frown, her forehead marked with a deep crease. Nova had mentioned the synesthesia. She should have known this would be her mother's reaction.

"Yes, but you don't see sounds, Mom. I *do*." There. She'd said the words.

"Sometimes our mind plays tricks on us." The concern in her mother's voice had cooled to something more detached. "I'm sure you thought you saw something."

"Seriously?" Nova was stunned. "We're going to do this *now*? When some stranger just tried to get into our house?"

"Watch your tone, young lady."

Nova's face warmed. Fire blossomed inside her, steadily growing hotter.

"This is what you do. I try to talk, and you shut me down. You act like having a daughter who can see sounds is something to be afraid of, like spiders or heights or something. Well, I'm sorry if you're embarrassed by your freak kid!"

Her mother's eyes widened. "Is that what you think?"

Angry tears stung the corners of Nova's eyes. She didn't want to cry. She wanted to be mad. She wanted her mother to listen to her and stop pretending everything was okay when it wasn't. Hiding wouldn't make Nova's synesthesia go away. She knew—she'd tried.

"I don't think you're a freak, Nova."

These soft words pierced Nova's heart. She wanted them to be true but knew better. If her mother meant what she'd said, why did their conversations always have to end in a battle?

Her mother pulled her close again. "I never meant to make you feel that way." She pressed her lips against the top of Nova's head.

She wanted to settle into her mother's embrace, but the stab of denial in her heart wouldn't let her.

"I didn't see anyone." Her grandfather came back inside, locking the patio doors behind him.

"He was there, Grandpa."

The scene filled Nova's mind, the shadow growing, impossibly changing in a blink from cat-size to man-size.

A shiver twisted through her.

"Oh, I don't doubt that." His bushy white eyebrows crowded low over his bright blue eyes. "He left footprints."

That startled Nova. She realized she had expected there wouldn't be any sign at all, as if the stranger had been a ghost or a leftover part of her dream.

"Plus, every dog in the neighborhood is barking." Grandpa paused, sending a pointed look in their direction. "I should go after him." His normally bronze voice was the color of burned wood, stained with concern.

"No." Her mother's soft green voice sounded steady, but Nova could see the tension. The normally supple waves were rigid and hard. "Whoever he was, he's long gone by now."

"We should take every precaution," Grandpa argued.

"I know that!"

Nova flinched, caught off guard by her mother's shout. Grandpa Zeke's bushy brows climbed upward.

"I'm sorry. I didn't mean to yell." Mom's eyes softened, filled with some unspoken plea, as she looked up at Grandpa. "We stay together."

Worry and sadness warred on his face. "Mira, you know as well as I do—"

"I know, Dad. Trust me, I know." She sighed, her shoulders sagging in defeat.

"Maybe it's time to tell her."

Nova stilled, like a mouse not wanting to make the cat aware of its presence. They should definitely tell her. She had been kept in the dark for way too long.

Her mother shook her head, her gaze faraway. "It's too dangerous."

Grandpa waved his arm angrily in the direction of the doors. "And this isn't? Someone was inside the yard." His voice looked as sharp and rigid as Nova had ever seen it. "You know what that means."

What? What does it mean? Nova's heart pounded.

There was a reason for her mother's strong reaction. Nova needed to know what that reason was.

"If he's found her ..."

He? He who? Why would someone be looking for her? Unless they meant ...

Are they talking about my father?

The forbidden topic. Nova didn't just want to know who he was, she needed to know. Why wasn't he around? Was he dead? Maybe he'd taken one look at his strange child and ran, leaving them behind, broken pieces of a family scattered on the ground like shattered glass.

Nova didn't even know what he looked like.

Could this veiled conversation be about her father? Did Grandpa think he was looking for her? That he might have been here, at their house? Could that explain why they were being so secretive? But why would he come in the middle of the night?

"We'll go somewhere." Her mother's voice left a jagged trail of green pointed teeth.

"Yes, because coming all *this* way has worked."

Nova didn't understand. They'd lived here for as long as she could remember.

Her mother's eyes snapped up, shooting daggers. "I made a hard choice, but it was the right one."

Grandpa took her hand, his fingers dusted with white hairs but still strong.

"As is this one." Somehow, even in Mom's pink bathrobe, he looked wise.

Her mother seemed to deflate. "I can't." She looked at Nova as if startled to find her there. "Don't worry, honey. Everything is okay."

"Sure, it is." Nova tasted bitter disappointment on her tongue. Were they really going to try to sweep this entire night under the rug?

"We should check the yard in the morning," her mother said to Grandpa, ignoring Nova's sarcasm. "Make sure everything is where it's supposed to be."

Nova's disappointment hardened into resolve.

She had to know.

"Is this about my dad?"

The silence that followed was so deep not one speck of color showed. The room turned dark and still.

Storm shutters closed in her mother's eyes. "No."

"But you said—"

"It doesn't matter what I said."

"It does matter!" Nova forced herself to take a breath. "Mom, I need to know. I'm not a little kid anymore."

Her mother stared at her. For a moment, Nova thought she saw a glimmer of surrender in those cornflower-blue eyes. Whatever she saw disappeared as quickly as it had come, shut away behind the iron shutters of her mother's will.

"You're fifteen, Nova. I think I still know what's best for you."

"The *truth* is what's best for me." Couldn't her mother understand how desperately she needed this? "Please, Mom."

Her mother turned her face away. "I can't do this with you right now. You'll have to trust me. Everything is going to be fine."

Sure.

Sure, it was.

Nova wanted to scream at her mother but arguing would only leave them both feeling more hurt and angry.

"Fine." She was sick to death of all the secrets.

Before anyone could protest, she pulled away, storming back to her room and slamming the door hard enough to send streaks of red flying through her room. She grabbed the pillow off her bed, pressed it against her face, and loosed a frustrated scream.

If anything, her anger only intensified. They were still talking out there. She could see their voices coloring the air with bits of gray and white, like smoke drifting under the door. She hurled the pillow against the wall.

Why wouldn't they tell her the truth? She wasn't supposed to worry that some guy had tried to break into their house, but telling her about her father would be too much for her to handle? That made no sense.

None of this made sense.

Her cell phone buzzed. She grabbed it off her desk and swiped her finger across it.

U OK?

Quentin's text illuminated her face.

WHAT R U DOING UP? She texted back.

His response came back immediately.

HEARD YELLING. TXTED—U DIDN'T ANSWER. U OK?

"Nope." She wondered if you could hear sarcasm in a text.

She was definitely not okay. Not with any of this. Acid burned her guts.

I'LL B FINE.

Her phone vibrated. Nova's lips twisted into what might pass as a weak half-smile. She should have figured he'd see right through her texts. She poked the green phone icon.

"Hey, Quen."

"What happened? Should I come over?"

Warm blue-green waves washed over her at the sound of his voice.

The smile tugged at both sides of her mouth now. "No, it's okay. I'm okay."

"Are you sure? You said you were fine. I know you. You don't do fine."

Dang. He was right.

"I'm sure." *It's just that some creepy guy tried to get into my house.*

She shivered again.

"Do you need Yogi? I left him there for you."

She looked up, seeing the worn brown fur and single eye of the stuffed bear sitting on the shelf over her bed. She pulled Yogi down, clutching him against her chest and smelling the soft, clean smell that was uniquely Quentin's. Sudden tears threatened, surprising her.

"Thanks, Quen."

"Sure."

He knew something was up, but to his credit, he didn't prod. He seemed to know what she needed without her having to say anything.

"Maybe tomorrow we can meet up early for a sprint before school."

"That sounds great." And normal. Nice and normal.

A run would be exactly what she needed to clear her head. He'd used the term sprint instead of run, she noticed. He'd come to terms with his limitations but refused to let them define him. Nova liked to think she was part of the reason he'd managed to find his place in the world.

If only she could figure out how to do the same thing for herself.

"I'll be over around seven."

"'Kay. See you then, Quen."

"Later, Novagator."

Nova sighed. Best friends since they were five, they'd gone through everything together. Quentin was hands down the corniest, goofiest, silliest person she knew. She had no idea how she would have ever survived without him.

Maybe tomorrow, she would tell him what really happened. Not tonight, though. He would only worry all night. He'd have a coronary when she told him they hadn't even called the police. Quentin might be silly, but he was also very protective.

"My knight in shining armor," she said, giving Yogi a squeeze.

At least now she could go back to bed, although she might never sleep again.

She lay down, but her eyes refused to close. Something nagged at her, like an itch just out of reach. Something about what had happened didn't quite fit.

Yeah, like a stranger trying to get into my house.

That wasn't all, though. There was something else. Something she should have picked up on.

Something she'd missed.

Fabric of Magic

The fabric of magic contains three unique factors:

Creative: the power to create or add to what exists

Destructive: the power to destroy or take away

Neutral: the power to neutralize or harmonize

All living beings have at least one factor. These are called Singulars. Neutral is the most common and is an essential factor in every facet of life. It is the balance. Destructive is less common, perhaps due to the chaotic nature of the universe. Creative, as one might surmise, is the least common factor. As such, it is a rare and precious gift. From the time of inception, we are set on a course toward our ultimate destruction. The appearance of life in such a setting is possibly the greatest indication that exists of divine intervention.

Some unions between those with differing factors will result in a child being born with two factors, called Duals. This can only happen when the two factors are of equal strength and manage to align in perfect balance. For this reason, most Duals are a pairing of Neutral with one of the other factors. Creative Destructive Duals are extraordinarily rare.

There is a prophecy that speaks of a Trine—someone born with all three factors who will have power as yet unseen. There has never been such a person, although some feel the time of the child of prophecy is drawing near.

—High Wizard Ezekial, on the *Factors of Magic*

SECRETS

Nova got up and showered before Mom and Grandpa were even out of bed—one of the few benefits of not sleeping. She pulled her dark hair into a pony tail and checked her face in the mirror.

"Crud." She looked like she'd gotten punched. Dark circles underlined puffy eyes, darkening her normally light blue irises. "Nothing a little coffee won't help." Or maybe a lot.

She made herself a double.

Before she could finish draining her cup, a soft tap at the back door announced Quentin had arrived. He wheeled into the kitchen in his Z-1050 Racer wheelchair. He studied her face as he swiveled the chair in a tight turn.

"Did you get any sleep at all?" Vapor trails like blue-green ocean waves followed him.

"A little." She decided not to mention *how* little.

"Not enough," he said, eyeing the enormous container of coffee.

"Hey, a girl's gotta have at least one bad habit."

Besides, Mom hated when she snuck coffee. Right now, she needed to do something her mom wouldn't like, even if only on the down-low.

Quentin lifted one eyebrow but wisely kept quiet. Nova downed the last swallow and set her cup in the sink.

"Let's go." She wanted to be gone before anyone got up.

The warm September morning promised summer wasn't ready to give up quite yet. The sun glimmered against leaves already changed, turning them into a collage of color amid the green. Quentin no longer struggled to keep up with her. If anything, he held back so she could keep up with him. Muscles flexed as his gloved hands spun the wheels.

"You've gotten pretty good." She flashed him an evil grin. "Too bad your chrome is no match for my canvas."

He grinned back. "You speak pretty words, Nova-san, but these wheels are faster than your feet." And like a shot he was off. She tore after him.

He really had gotten good. More than good. His hands pumped easily, his wheels a blur. Actual brawn stood out where his scrawny freckled arms used to be. When had that happened?

"You need me to slow down yet?" he called over his shoulder.

Time to even the playing field a little.

Instead of answering, she swerved left, up onto the sidewalk and through the hedges, cutting across the park. A yell told her he'd noticed, and she laughed. The wind was in her hair, the sun warm on her skin, the blood pumping in her veins. Why couldn't everything be this easy? She skirted around the fountain and playground, dodging between thicker trees on the other side, and finally through the hedges.

"Hey!" She barely had time to pull up short as a flash of metal whizzed by in front of her.

No way.

She bent over, sides heaving. Quentin slowed and turned. Sweat dripped off her nose as he circled back.

"Cheaters never win."

She ignored the jibe. "How did you do that?"

He shrugged. "I've been practicing."

She used her arm to wipe her sweaty face as she sat on the curb. "You're really fast."

A hint of a blush crept up his face.

"I can't believe you beat me. You're not even out of breath."

He grinned. "Hey, you're the one who convinced me to do this."

"Nothing motivates like a little competition." Her teasing held more than a trace of truth.

"And now that I've beaten you?"

"You can dedicate your gold medal to me when you win one."

"Deal."

They sat in comfortable silence while they cooled off. Quentin wasn't one of those people who had to fill every second with chatter. She loved that about him and was amazed there were people who weren't sure how to act when they first met him. They treated him like they were afraid of how he might react to their questions. Nova loved catching the moment when they discovered the smart, funny person Quentin was. After a while, they didn't even notice the wheelchair. Sometimes, Quentin almost seemed to forget too.

"I'm glad you didn't give up."

His lips twisted in a wry grin. "You wouldn't let me."

"True." Now here he was, kicking her butt even when she'd cheated. "Brat."

She pulled up a handful of grass and threw it at him.

He laughed. "Are you going to tell me what happened, or do I have to beat that out of you too?"

She sighed. Most of the anger had evaporated with her sweat.

"I caught someone trying to break into our house."

His smile disappeared. "What?"

"I heard a noise and thought Opus might be out there. I went into the living room and saw something outside the patio doors. I thought the cat wanted in, but when I turned on the light …"

There was a monster there instead.

He cursed under his breath. "That's why I heard you scream."

She nodded, unnerved by his response. Quentin never swore.

"And what, he just took off?"

"Grandpa found footprints, so at least I know I wasn't dreaming."

As soon as she said the words, that nagging feeling hit her again. What was she forgetting?

"Did the cops get pictures of the footprints?"

Uh-oh. "No …"

He rolled his eyes. "Did they do anything at all? Man, cops are always razzing everyone for no reason, but then when real stuff happens they don't even—"

"We didn't call them."

He stared at her nearly a full minute before he spoke again. "Why not?"

She shrugged.

His hazel eyes turned a steely gray. "What if this guy comes back? What if he was dangerous, Nova?"

"I know." Her voice was barely more than a whisper. Of course, she knew. The same thoughts had raced through her head all night long. What was more important than keeping them all safe?

Quentin spun his chair around and started off.

"Quentin?" She ran to catch him. "Hey, where are you going?"

His face was taut with anger. "To the police station."

She pulled on the back of his chair until he turned to face her. "No."

"Why not?" His voice was as dark as his eyes.

"Well, for one thing, because we didn't call them last night. They're going to think something is fishy."

"Something *is* fishy."

She sighed and shook her head. "Look, I don't like it either, and I agree something is going on. I hate that Mom is keeping more secrets from me. But she thinks she's doing the right thing." She loathed the uncertainty in her voice. "Mom and Grandpa wouldn't let anything bad happen to me."

She wanted to believe that. She really did.

His face finally softened, and she turned away before he could see the traitorous tear that slipped down her face.

"I'm sorry. I didn't mean to …" His voice choked off to a near whisper.

Sweet Quentin. Sweet, tenderhearted, knight-in-shining-armor Quentin. "You didn't. Mom did. Grandpa did. Now I just need to figure out why." She pulled out her cell phone to check the time. "Crud, it's getting late. I need to clean up before school."

"We could ditch."

A laugh burst out before she could contain it. "It's only the fourth day of the year, and you want to ditch?"

"Oh, yeah. I forgot."

More laughter bubbled up. He joined her, both of them laughing so hard they were gasping. This time, she didn't hide the tears.

"Thanks, Q," she said, still giggling. "I needed that."

They both had.

The Order

A gong sounded at the precise moment the sun touched the horizon over the Adiron Mountains. Golden rays lit the grass, turning silver traces of frost into dew. Chanting filled the air. In the fields below Rifting Pass, cattle softly lowed. The heady smell of the earth rose in harmony, a symphony of the senses. Mordoon filled his lungs, letting the peaceful morning seep into him.

"Is it done?"

The question startled him, and he exhaled sharply. Cyril appeared from behind rocks like a cougar ready to pounce. Mordoon twitched as a chill slithered over him. Had they done the right thing to make Cyril their First? Ah, but the naming ceremony had been completed. There was nothing he could do now even if he wanted to.

"Yes." Mordoon continued looking out over the mountains toward the valley and the plains beyond, wanting to recapture his moment of perfect balance. Viru was a good choice. He is young and dedicated."

Cyril pursed his lips and grunted.

Mordoon hoped his words were true. He had brought Viru here not long ago, a personal selection to enrich the folds of the Order. The boy had caught his attention with his sharp questions and quick mind. His passion for the Order had been apparent. When the call had gone up for a mission into the heart of prophecy, Viru had been the first to volunteer. Mordoon's heart had both warmed and shriveled when the boy had been chosen. He was so young. Still, of all the acolytes, he was best suited. His was the strongest edah.

"If anyone can accomplish this, Viru will."

Cyril stared. "Let us hope. Failure would be *unfortunate*."

Indignation lit a fire in Mordoon's veins. "All will be as it is meant to be."

"Prophecy has already given us our path, Mordoon. A path we must follow."

Mordoon ground his teeth. Who was this man to spout the edicts of faith to him, who had devoted his entire life to the truths of the Order? How many days had Mordoon spent here, on this mountaintop, chanting the verses over and over so enlightenment might come upon him? How many nights had he wrestled with the necessity for what was to come? Cyril acted as if he made the rules to turn the universe, rather than the opposite.

"Prophecy may be a gift from the One God, but we are only men. All we can try to do is what's right." Mordoon hated the tremor in his voice. He wanted to sound wise and sure. Instead, he felt old and afraid.

Cyril's eyes burned with passion's fire. "All of the elders have agreed. The meaning is clear. Our path cannot be denied merely because we wish it to be different."

These words, at least, were true. They had all struggled with this, all wrestled with the conflict created in their souls, but the truth could not be denied. Whether Mordoon understood or not, blood had to be shed if the salvation of mankind was to be achieved.

"I also wish it did not have to be so," Cyril added, although his face was smooth and his eyes untroubled. "I wish I could turn from this path or let another carry the weight, but there is a debt that must be paid."

"But she is so young," Mordoon whispered.

"Yes, a wee lamb." Cyril replied solemnly, but a smile twisted his lips.

Creative

The nature of Creative is to build up or enhance. People with this factor are often smart and imaginative. They have a natural tendency to want to protect and defend others. They can be dramatic and sensitive, but are generally helpful and kindhearted, sometimes to a fault.

—High Wizard Ezekial, on the Factors of Magic

Indecision

"Hey, Freak. Did you finish my homework?"

Dark yellow balls of color burst around Nova like the snorts of a hideous troll, sucking away any trace of a good mood her endorphins had provided. She stared into the back of her locker and willed an escape hatch to magically appear.

No such luck.

Crappy locker.

A meaty hand closed the door. Nova yanked her head out of the way to keep it from becoming a locker decoration. She found herself staring into the muddy brown eyes of Laura Hennigan, mean girl extraordinaire and first-class bully. Nova didn't know why she'd thought sophomore year would be any different than the last three. Laura wasn't about to stop pushing her around just because they were older. Why grow up and get your act together when you could make people do whatever you wanted?

Stand up to her!

"It better be done." Laura took a step closer, her face so close Nova could feel the bigger girl's breath against her cheek. Nova heard a snicker from somewhere behind her. Laura's eyes glowed. "We had an agreement." This close, she reminded Nova of a snake, hypnotic and deadly. "But if you want to go back on what you said, I can always—"

"Here." Nova shoved the paper at her.

The only thing worse than the triumph on Laura's face was the glee.

"Ah, too bad." Laura eased back against the bank of lockers. "I was almost looking forward to seeing you stand up to me." She laughed, then spoke into Nova's ear, as if sharing a secret. "But we both know that won't happen."

Dark-yellow tendrils curled around Nova like smoke. She resisted the urge to wave her hand to clear the air as Laura turned to walk away. Nova hated that the miserable bully was right. Nova should stand up for herself. Instead she caved, just like always. Nova loosed a series of kicks on the locker that had failed to provide a much-needed emergency exit.

Ouch. Potentially broken toe.

"Miss Hawthorne!"

Crap.

Principal Weathers stalked toward her, thick black eyebrows crowding down over dark, serious eyes. Nova had only met him a few times, but he seemed nice enough. Except for when someone was doing something they shouldn't, of course, like vandalizing school property. A tall boy with dark hair and slate-colored eyes drifted behind Weathers like a leaf in the wake of a strong wind. The boy looked vaguely familiar to Nova.

"Your locker is not a kickball, young lady." Weathers inspected the locker as he spoke.

Tall Boy looked on, his face amused.

Great.

"Sorry, Mister Weathers," Nova mumbled. "It won't happen again."

"I should hope not." He glowered at her a moment longer, as if making sure she wouldn't go back on her word within the first ten seconds, then turned on his heel and walked away. Tall Boy drifted away without looking back at her.

"You okay?"

She jumped.

"Sorry, didn't mean to sneak up on you." Quentin studied her, his expression somber.

"You didn't."

"Laura again?"

"Big surprise."

"Want me to beat her up for you?"

She was being snarky, and she knew it. The compassion and understanding in Quentin's voice filled her with guilt. She tried to paste on a smile. "Thanks, but no thanks."

"Your loss." He flexed his arms. "I've got muscles now, you know."

Oh, she'd noticed. Unfortunately, Laura Hennigan was built like a human bulldozer. Though only a year older, Laura had at least three inches and twenty pounds on them, all hard as rock.

"She'd totally cream you."

He feigned hurt. "Not if I tied her to her seat first."

"She'd smear the floor with you."

"And tied one of her arms to a table."

"Have you seen the size of her head?"

He laughed. "Okay, I admit it. She does have what appears to be a very thick skull."

"And probably numb."

He nodded. "The better to bash defenseless walls with."

Nova laughed with him.

The buzzer double-rang, warning of impending lateness.

"I'll come get you on the way out," he called as he spun his chair and zipped towards the other end of the hall. "Tell Neanderthal girl I said hi."

Nova shook her head and double-timed it up the stairs, slipping in the door to her English class just as the final buzzer sounded. Luckily, Laura-the-troll-Hennigan was busy studying something on her beat-up old cell phone and didn't look up. Nova slid gratefully into her seat as Mr. Ames turned from the board and dusted chalk off his hands. In an age of technology, Mr. Ames still refused to use anything but the chalkboard to write discussion notes on. Today he'd written only one word in large, capital letters.

INDECISION

"You are in line at the bank, and you see a man pull a gun out of his pocket," he said.

The room quieted as all eyes turned to him. Those still standing slowly lowered into their seats.

"No one else has noticed yet." He looked from face to face. "What do you do?"

The room was dead silent. Mr. Ames waited.

"Get the heck out," a boy seated in the back muttered.

A few people chuckled.

"Good. A decision. Get out. That would probably be a very wise choice." Mr. Ames nodded. "Self-preservation. A natural instinct, and one of the few the human race has managed to hold on to. Anyone else?"

"Pass out?" More laughter from the class this time.

"Ah. Another common response to fear and stress. As adrenaline rushes through you and blood rushes away from the brain, your body responds by temporarily shutting down. This, however, is not a decision. It's an unconscious response."

Or maybe your body understands you need to check out. Nova looked up and caught Mr. Ames staring at her.

"Right, Miss Hawthorne?"

She hesitated. Every set of eyes in the class stared at her. "I guess."

"You guess?"

She squirmed uncomfortably in her seat.

Mr. Ames narrowed his eyes. "Do you think someone can consciously decide to pass out? Maybe control their breathing or heart rate, causing them to shut down when needed?"

She nodded.

Mr. Ames looked around the room. "Anyone else agree? Is that possible?"

"Sure," Randy Miller, one of the school's star swimmers answered. "Athletes control their breathing and heart rate all the time. People use yoga and hypnosis to do it. It's totally possible."

Now others began to nod in agreement.

"When I said passing out was an unconscious response, you *all* disagreed with me?"

Lots of nods, although some hesitated as if smelling a trap.

"So why didn't you say so?"

Silence ruled again.

"Let me ask you this." Mr. Ames walked back to his desk and pointed up at the board. "What do you think indecision is?"

"Hesitation," someone answered immediately.

"Being wishy-washy," someone else hazarded.

Mr. Ames nodded. "All good answers, but let's dig deeper." He sat on the edge of his desk. "You are trapped at the center of a maze. You know going the wrong way might get you into real trouble. Do you keep going? Go back? Or do you stand still?"

"That would be stupid," Laura, of all people, said.

"Why, Miss Hennigan?"

"Because then you're definitely not getting out. At least if you do something, you've got a shot."

"You've hit the nail on the head." He looked slowly around the room. "Indecision is the decision to do nothing." He paused to let that sink in. "We all make thousands of decisions every day. Some are less momentous than others, but each is a decision. We decide to get up every morning. We decide to eat. We decide what clothes to wear."

"Or whether to wear any at all."

The class exploded with laughter. Mr. Ames joined good-naturedly. "Okay, yes, that too. The bottom line is, we make big and small decisions all the time, yet we seem to think indecision is not a decision at all. As Miss Hennigan was so kind to point out, standing still is not doing something, it's doing nothing. So why do we find ourselves so indecisive when it comes to certain things? Why do we not want to speak up if we disagree with something someone has said?"

The class fell silent yet again.

Nova leaned forward. This was an answer she wanted to hear.

Just as Mr. Ames took a breath to answer, the door opened. Principal Weathers stood in the doorway. Nova's heart skipped a beat. Had he reconsidered letting her off so easy?

"I'm sorry to interrupt your class, Mr. Ames."

Mr. Ames motioned for Principal Weathers to come in. Behind him, a shadow materialized into a person—Tall Boy. That must be why he'd been following Weathers earlier. He'd been registering.

"This is Seth Mission. His family recently relocated to Endwell. He will be joining our fine institution and your class."

Nova groaned. Of course, after witnessing her humiliation in the hall, he'd be in her English class too. Nova couldn't catch a break today to save her life.

"Welcome, Seth." Mr. Ames said.

"All's well at Endwell," someone muttered the unofficial town slogan.

Seth gave a kind of half nod that came off as respectful but made him look totally comfortable in his own skin. Some kids would have wanted to melt into the floor. Nova was instantly jealous.

"There's an empty seat right over there if you'd like to join us. We were having a discussion about decisions."

"Thanks."

Mr. Weathers nodded and backed out, closing the door behind him.

Nova refused to look up as Seth sat down in the empty seat directly in front of hers. Thankfully, Mr. Ames seemed to be done with the interactive part of the class and started talking about various literary characters, and how their decisions—or lack of them—impacted the story.

As if making decisions was that easy. Sometimes you didn't get to decide. Life just happened. Unless you were like Laura, pushing everyone around to get your way all the time. Nova pulled out her pen and started doodling in her notebook, filling up the margins with lazy swirls and curlicues. Not only bullies like Laura, either. Sometimes people made choices for you, thinking they were doing what was right.

So easy for Mom to justify not telling Nova who her father was. Mom thought she was being protective, but her silence was her way of not dealing with the situation. Nova didn't get to choose. Her decision was made by someone else—bullying on a different level.

The bell shook Nova out of her thoughts. She looked up to find new-kid Seth turned around, facing her. He wasn't looking at her, though. He was staring at her paper. Nova looked down, not surprised to find another of her odd drawings even though she barely remembered making it. The page was covered with what looked like vines, getting thicker and more tangled as they moved towards the center of the page.

"That's really good."

At first, she didn't know what was wrong. Then she realized—no colors. Tall Boy's voice didn't show her any color at all.

As odd as her *condition* was (as the doctors referred to it), seeing sounds had become normal to her. When she was very young, one doctor had called what Nova experienced "a perceptual phenomenon." Nova had liked that doctor. She'd been much more positive about the synesthesia than most. They'd never gone back to the specialist, but Nova still remembered the term. It fit her. After all, being able to see sounds gave her an edge. Nova could see tension and sadness, happiness and peace, even anger in ways most people couldn't.

Hearing Tall Boy's voice without being able to see the color or shape was like being thrust into two-dimensions instead of three—flat and lifeless. There was no color. No shape or texture. His words were just ... words.

Was her synesthesia going away? She'd wondered before whether it could, but no one had ever been able to give her an answer. The possibility made her a little sad.

"What is it?"

She looked up at him. Did he really want to know, or was he making fun?

She tried to give a nonchalant shrug. "Just doodles."

He tilted his head one way then the other. "It's like a maze."

She frowned, her attention drawn back to her drawing. "It's more of a ... a pattern."

Now he was the one who looked up. No, he wasn't making fun. His face was totally serious. "What do you mean?"

What *did* she mean? Why had she even told him that? She didn't know him, even if he did seem familiar. Besides, she'd never talked about her drawings with anyone but Quentin. She chewed on one side of her bottom lip, unsure if she should say anything else. He seemed interested. And she supposed he was only asking a question.

"Have you ever heard music that started out really soft, then got more and more intense?"

"You mean a crescendo?"

Okay, maybe this kid wasn't so bad. "Exactly."

He looked back down at her drawing. "So, this is … what? Like a visual representation of a crescendo?"

Just that easily, he'd summed up what she'd always felt but had never been able to put into words. She had always seen sounds, represented in shapes and colors in the air. That's what synesthesia was. The doctors had explained it as a type of cross-wiring somewhere in her brain, allowing different senses to overlap or change roles. They'd made it sound like no big deal, but she didn't have to go to school with the doctors. She did have to go to school with kids who had no idea what she meant when she told them their voice looked sharp or purple.

She'd made the mistake of thinking she was normal.

That she belonged.

She'd made the mistake of letting people know who and what she was. The stigma had followed her ever since.

Being an outsider might not have affected her so much if Mom didn't freak out like she did. Her reactions only reinforced the fact that, whatever else Nova might be, she was different from everyone else. She was like a square peg in a round world—she didn't fit.

That was why, when Nova had started seeing and drawing these strange, intricate shapes, she'd kept them to herself. The only person she'd ever shared them with was Quentin. Of course, Nova had wondered if her synesthesia had something to do with them.

Now, in one sentence, Seth had put everything together.

"Look," he said, pointing to one corner. "See how these curly parts overlap? It's like they're the same shape over and over again in deeper levels." He glanced up at her. "Did you mean to do that, or did it just come out that way?"

Quentin had never noticed that. Nova didn't know whether to be excited or alarmed. "A little of both, I think."

He looked up again, and his face was so totally serious her stomach floated the way it did at the top of a roller coaster. "Can I show you something?"

She swallowed. "Sure."

He picked a brown backpack off the floor and rooted around inside, pulling out a small notebook. He flipped it open, and her heart took a sideways lurch. His page was covered in circles, linked and overlapping, making a deeper and deeper circle in the middle, and also a larger and larger overall shape. It was like looking inward and outward at the same time.

Nova's hands began to shake. She peeked at his face, but he was still studying the two pictures, comparing them.

Her heart raced, her palms sweaty and cold at the same time. This was a coincidence. Completely random. How could it be anything else? He had no way to know she had seen his drawing before. There were dozens of copies in the notebook on her desk at home. And they were in that notebook because she had drawn them at night, right after having seen the shape in her dreams.

"Woah."

Tall Boy nodded. "Yeah."

The hair on her neck and arms lifted. Nova swallowed hard. "When did you … how long have you been doing them?"

He gave a half smile. "I think I could draw before I could walk."

She studied his face, looking for a trace of deceit or mockery, but there was none. He was serious. But if he hadn't seen her drawings, then how had he managed to draw the same thing so precisely? Who was this kid, anyway?

"Everything okay in here?" Familiar blue-green waves surrounded her like a warm blanket.

"Quentin." Thank goodness. His voice and colors were still there. They washed over her like a soothing balm, draining her tension. The hair on her arms laid back down. She got up and began to shove books into her backpack. "This is Seth. He just moved here."

Seth turned around and slipped his notebook into his backpack in one fluid motion.

Slick. For some reason Nova couldn't put her finger on, the move bugged her.

"Hey." Quentin spoke to Seth but stared at her. "New, huh? Where you from?"

"Reno."

"Nevada?" Nova asked before she could help herself. Duh. She tried to cover the dumb question by slinging her backpack over her shoulder. The move would have worked except she'd forgotten to close the zipper and two of her pencils went flying. Smooth. She chased them down, determined not to trip, fall, break anything, or perform any other equally embarrassing acts.

"Nevada." Seth confirmed. "Biggest little city, and all that."

"Isn't it really warm there?" Okay, now who was stating the obvious? The question was friendly enough, but Quentin moved his chair a bit, managing to get directly between her and Seth. "Why leave all that sun for snow country?"

"It was a family thing."

Nova was overwhelmed. She needed time to think, to process. Maybe make a list. That always calmed her down.

"I have study hall in the library," she blurted.

Oh, brilliant. Like they really needed to know that.

Quentin took the cue and spun his chair in a quick half-circle, relieving her of her backpack before turning toward the door. "Nice meeting you, Seth. Welcome to our world."

If she hadn't been looking right at him, Nova would have missed Seth almost falling as he got up from his desk. His eyes went wide, and his face tightened. Before she could blink, his expression returned to normal.

"Thanks." He was all smoothness and grace again. "Catch you later, Doodles." He disappeared before either of them could respond.

"Doodles?"

Nova's face warmed. "He saw me scribbling on my notebook."

This was so stupid. She'd spent her whole life wondering if anyone else did the kind of drawings she did. When she finally found someone who did, she freaked. Or maybe she was only rattled because the drawing had been the one from her dream.

Thankfully, the buzzer went off and the moment passed.

"Come on. I've got study hall too. I'll give you a lift ... Doodles."

She tried to give Quentin a stern look, but his face twitched and then they were both giggling. Leave it to her knight in shining armor to make everything okay again.

A Father's Daughter

"We did the right thing."

Zeke looked out from under his bushy white brows. The sleeves of Mira's yellow silk robe billowed around his hands as they made patterns in the air. "Are you trying to convince me, or you?"

Mira sighed. "Me."

Zeke muttered a string of words too low for her to hear. The pattern he'd been drawing flashed once, then disappeared. After the image faded, he turned to face her. "You're beating yourself up."

She laughed, feeling the sting of tears. "I'm a mother. It's what I do."

"Mira"—his voice was gentle—"you've done what you thought was best. None of us know every answer. We only do what we can."

"What if it's not enough? He's even stronger than he used to be. I can feel it." A shiver radiated from her middle to the tips of her toes and roots of her hair. "That was no random occurrence. He's found her."

Zeke frowned, looking off into the distance. "I don't think this was his work."

"What do you mean?"

"This was sloppy. Lucien's many things, but sloppy isn't one of them. He's careful. He plans. This was almost … reckless."

"Breaking into our house is reckless?"

"Yes." His brows shot up. "Very. He finally has a chance at her, and he sends someone to her house? The place that promises to have the most protection?" He shook his head, pulling at the ruffled edges of the bathrobe. "He wouldn't have waited all this time only to waste his first opportunity."

She wanted to believe him.

"No," he said again. "This is messy. Bumbling. If I didn't know better, I'd think …"

His face paled.

Fear crept up Mira's throat like acid. "What?"

"This attempt was meant to fail."

She didn't understand. Why would he try to reach Nova, or let someone else, if he wanted the effort to fail? Why risk showing his hand? He'd have to realize they would respond.

That thought settled in her like a cold ball. He knew they would take action. They would be focused.

They would be *occupied*.

"A diversion." Her voice was a hoarse whisper.

She looked around the yard where they had spent the last several hours strengthening the wards. While what? Where was the danger? At the school? She found it hard to believe he would try anything with that many people around.

"What do we do?" Wings of panic closed around her heart, threatening to carry it away. "I have to go and get her. Bring her home."

They'd have to increase the protection wards. Maybe put some inside her room. Around her bed. In her clothes.

"I'll get my keys. Come on." She started for the house. "Should you come, or stay here and work on the—"

He wasn't next to her.

"Zeke?"

He was still standing by the fence.

"Zeke, come on!"

He stared at the wall, mouth downturned.

"Dad?"

"How long?"

His words didn't make sense. Why wasn't he moving? Nova was in trouble. She shook her head, confused.

"How long do we keep her in the house?"

"What?"

"A week? A month? How long until she's safe?"

"I don't know. As long as it takes—"

"Takes for what? For him to stop looking for her?" His eyes burned like blue fire. "We both know he'll never stop, Mira."

"Then what?" Her heart constricted. She couldn't get enough air. "What do we do? We can't give up." Her voice broke on the last word, her throat closing around the sobs that threatened to shake her apart.

He reached her in three quick steps and pulled her into his arms. She clung to him, her only rock in a raging sea. Everything was coming apart. All she'd done, all this time … all for nothing if she couldn't even protect her own child. She'd failed.

Mira cried dry tears, feeling barren, used up. "What do I do?" she rasped.

"Tell her."

She blinked, her eyes hot against the inside of her lids.

"You've done what you thought was best, bringing her here. You've guarded her and raised her. She is growing into a beautiful young woman." He lifted her chin. His blue eyes burned deep into her soul. "Now, trust her." He nodded. "It's time, Mira. Tell her."

Zeke was right.

Somewhere along the line, her mission to protect her child became a mission to protect herself. Lies had piled on top of silence. Escape had become denial. Her good intentions had slowly evolved into walls that threatened to topple in on her. She had to pull them down before her barriers destroyed them all.

"Okay," she whispered.

He squeezed her tightly, as if he could hold her together by the sheer force of his will. And maybe he could. He had always emitted a power she could feel but not fully understand. He'd never explained to her how he'd managed to cross the Divide, or how he'd found her. She hadn't asked then, and she didn't ask now. His being here was enough.

Now was the time for her to be her father's daughter.

Destructive

Because the nature of Destructive is to de-construct or to take away from existing matter or energy, people with this ability can be damaging. Destructive individuals can grow stronger by hurting others. What detracts (whether from matter, energy, or feeling) strengthens them. This is most true in those who are unbalanced (do not contain another factor in balance) and can manifest as simple selfishness or spitefulness on one end, viciousness and evil on the other.

—High Wizard Ezekial, on the *Factors of Magic*

THE DIVIDE

As much as she wanted to, Nova couldn't shake the feeling something was hanging over her, like a dark cloud waiting to unleash a sudden flurry of lightning and rain. She walked along the sidewalk, the trees and flowers a blur around her.

All the crazy things that had happened made her feel paranoid. Or maybe she felt unsettled because she'd seen a drawing straight out of her dreams. That was impossible. Right? She'd thought so, but she'd seen the image right there in Seth's notebook. There was no denying that. Maybe her dreams had been more than a random chain of events. Something she'd seen could have triggered them. Even someone else's memories or subconscious could have triggered them, if Nova had picked up on the changes in the colors and shapes of their voice. Maybe Seth had seen the same movie or television show she had, and they'd both fixated on that one image. Was that possible? What were the odds two people who'd never met before would see, remember, and draw identical images?

Pretty long odds. Almost as long as a complete stranger being able to put into words exactly what the drawing represented.

Strange.

And speaking of strange, why didn't she see anything when he talked? Where were the colors and shapes? She hadn't lost her synesthesia. The rest of the day everyone else's voice had sent lines and balls and whorls of color spinning through the air like always, so why not his?

"Penny for your thoughts."

Who was this kid who had moved halfway across the country, dropping into her school, her classroom, into the seat right in front of hers?

"Nova?" Quentin touched her arm.

Nova blinked. "Hmm? What?"

"You're a million miles away."

She bit her lip. "I'm kind of weirded out."

"That's understandable."

"It is?" She'd wondered if Quentin might be put out about Seth.

"Of course." He shook his head. "I would be too if some stranger tried to break into my house in the middle of the night.

Oh. That. She was amazed to find she'd almost forgotten. No wonder he was being so protective of her today. He wrapped her hand in his. His skin was rough and warm against her cold fingers.

"We'll figure this out."

She nodded. That was exactly what she needed—to reason through everything. Then maybe this cloud of uneasiness would melt away. "Thanks, Q. You always know what to …"

She spotted a figure in the park across the road.

Quentin frowned, then turned to follow her gaze. His face tightened.

The hunched back, head continually bobbing up, then back down, painted an obvious picture. Tall Boy was drawing. This was her chance. Nova needed to catch Seth drawing and get him to tell her more about the picture he'd shown her earlier.

"Quentin, can you give me a sec?"

He dropped her hand. "New kid?"

His voice looked wrong. The normally smooth lines were all tangled and sharp. She glanced at him. He looked wrong too. As if the muscles in his face fought each other.

"Yeah, I wanted to ask him something."

"Mind if I come along?"

His gaze was focused on Seth's huddled shape, so he didn't see her swallow quickly, which was good because she couldn't figure out why his request made her so nervous. She was being silly. Quentin had seen all her drawings. Maybe he could help her figure out how someone else had drawn the same thing.

"Sure."

Was that surprise on his face?

"Just don't call me Doodles, okay?"

He gave a little grin. That was more like the Quen she knew.

There was nothing quiet about the two of them moving through the park, the crunchy leaves already making a colorful pattern against the grass. Seth shut his book as they approached.

"What's up?" he asked when they were close enough to hear.

"Hi." Nova tried to sound cheerful. "Thought we'd stop over to see how your first day at Endwell turned out."

Seth and Quentin both stared at her like she'd sprouted a new head. Okay, so maybe she wasn't so good at playing it cool. She sighed.

"I wondered what you were drawing." If they preferred direct, she was happy to oblige.

Seth glanced at Quentin, then back at her. He nodded a little, as if he'd made a decision. "The trees," he answered. "We don't get this kind of color back home." As if proving he was telling the truth, he flipped his notebook back open.

Nova's breath caught in her throat. The colors were so perfect. They matched the color around them exactly, not only in hue, but in texture … and more. Looking at the dark red made her tongue sting, as if something hot and spicy were there, and the orange sent the smell of pumpkin and cinnamon through her. The deep greens tasted sweet and smelled clean and fresh.

Strange. She saw no colors when he spoke, yet she could taste and smell his drawings.

"I don't know if I captured the light accurately," he said.

"It's amazing." She moved her lips but heard Quentin's voice. He'd said what she was thinking.

"Really?" Seth gave Quentin a sideways smile.

Seth's smile turned into a frown. Nova thought he was frowning at Quentin, but he leaned to one side to look around behind them. "Who—"

The air exploded, invisible shock waves knocking them all to the ground. A blinding white light seared Nova's brain, and the world disappeared even though she was sure her eyes were still open. She felt her scream rasp against her throat but couldn't hear anything. Had a bomb gone off? Was she dead?

A hand circled her arm, yanking her upright.

Not dead then.

Hot breath blew in her face. "Come with me."

She heard that.

The hand pulled her again, but she dug in with her feet.

"Now!"

With her free arm, she railed at her unseen attacker … clawing, pulling, scratching at whatever surface she could find. He was not much bigger than her, but he was quick and kept her at bay while she fought. Then he yanked her in, crushing her against him.

"Stop fighting or everyone dies."

Her body froze.

He threatened Quentin—Quentin, who always helped anyone, even strangers. Quentin, who wouldn't hurt a fly. Quentin, who had already lost his ability to walk or run because of a senseless, random fluke. Anger unlike anything she had ever known before surged through her. A liquid sensation rushed in from her extremities and condensed at her core. Her fury coiled there, getting bigger and hotter, burning like the sun.

Her attacker shouted, his breath hot against her skin. He shoved her away. Nova's rage devoured the air around her like fuel, creating a vortex of fire that cascaded out of her in waves. The force lifted her arms. Liquid fire coursed along them, racing outward from her center, pouring over her shoulders and down to her fingertips. She pointed them in the direction of her assailant. She could sense him. Taste him. Then she could see him. She saw his dark eyes, wide with fear as he stared at her in horror. The air behind him rippled just before it tore, leaving a gaping hole as black as tar, as if the fabric of reality itself had come apart. The cords stood out in his arms and neck as he tried to get away, but it was no use. Nova balled up the fury inside and hurled the fire of her emotion at him. He screamed, and shards of dark red and yellow burst from his lips as he was lifted backward, hurtled into the hole in the air, and vanished.

"By the one God."

Nova heard the words, but they didn't register. She could see nothing except the licks of lightning still moving along her skin and the hole that hung in the air in front of her like a rip in the fabric of a painting, exposing what was beyond. Finally, pushing back the waves of fury that had filled her, she let her arms fall to her sides and turned around.

Seth lay on the ground, propped up on one elbow. He stared up at the gaping blackness, then shifted his gaze toward her. She expected to see something in them, fear maybe, or revulsion. Instead his eyes widened and shone, as if with …

"Nova? Are you all right?"

"Quentin!"

He was on the ground, his chair tipped over. Thankfully, it hadn't landed on him. Nova pushed it out of the way and helped him sit up on the grass.

"What happened?" He took in the scene, his gaze stopping on the strange man-sized black hole that hung in the air a few feet away. "What *is* that?"

"That," Seth said, standing up and dusting himself off, "is the hole your girlfriend just punched through the Divide." He nodded at Nova. "Quite the power move."

"What are you talking about?" He acted like she understood what had happened.

"And here we thought Threa was the only world with any magic left."

Thray-ah? Magic?

Maybe the blow had rattled something loose in his head.

He studied her face, which couldn't possibly look as dazed and confused as she actually felt and cocked his head to one side.

"What? You don't know?" He gave a half sneer.

Nova could only stare, her mouth hung open. Slowly, Seth's face changed, the sneer dropping away. His eyes widened.

"How could you …? If you didn't know, then how did you …?" He looked at the hole, then back at her.

Quentin heaved himself up into his chair. No mistaking his look. He was pissed. "If you know what happened, can you spit it out … in English?"

Like puzzle pieces, the answers she'd searched for all day finally fell together. "You know why that stranger attacked us."

Seth's eyes sparkled. "Figured that out, eh?"

"Who was he?"

"A hunter." Seth dropped any pretense. "Sent from the Order, most likely." He glanced over his shoulder. "And now that you've so handily provided a second access point, definitely not the last."

"A hunter?" Hunting what? But she thought she already knew the answer.

"Why?" Quentin asked. "Why is someone hunting Nova?"

Seth nodded. "Perceptive. Based on that little display, I assume the Order is after Nova because she's a Trine. She has all three factors. Creative, Destructive, and Neutral."

"What does that mean?" Quentin's brows lowered.

"It means, my magic-less friend, that she is the most powerful Zen to have ever been born. That, in and of itself, would attract a lot of attention, but there's also a prophecy about a Trine. Men of the Order dedicate their lives to studying prophecy." He turned back to Nova. "If they're after you, that's why."

"And what about you? Why are *you* after me?"

It could be no accident Seth had shown up at their school, in her English class.

Nova felt Quentin's stare but kept her focus on Seth. She needed to see whether his answer was an honest one.

"I was sent."

Without being able to see his words, she had to trust her gut. Right now, her gut told her Seth was telling the truth. She waited for the rest.

"I'm supposed to get you safely back to Threa and bring you to him— the one who sent me."

Nova's whole body hummed like a live wire.

"He knows about the prophecy. He can tell you how to stop the Order's hunters."

Seth paused again, but Nova could only let the silence bloom. Inside her, a ball of fear and doubt had formed, threaded with a current of excitement. At the center, a dangerous axis—hope.

Her entire being told her what came next. She didn't have to hear the words, but she wanted to.

"Your father sent me."

Nova reminded herself to breathe, to fill her chest slowly, exhaling through her lips. As amazing as this moment was, to finally confirm her father was alive and looking for her, she needed more answers. The questions piled one on top of the other.

Warm fingers laced through hers.

Quentin. Her rock.

"Why now?" This was the question that climbed atop the others. "Why wait all these years?"

"I don't think you understand. This wasn't a sudden thing. He's been trying since … well since you were born, I guess, but can't cross the Divide. Only those with Neutrals can, and he doesn't have Neutral."

"But you do," Quentin said softly, as if working something out.

Seth nodded. "I do. But there's more to it than that. You need spells to open a portal."

Quentin glanced again at the hole hanging in the air. "You sure about that?"

Seth made a face. "Not anymore I'm not."

"What now?" Nova's question brought them both back to focus.

Seth stilled. "Now we need to leave."

Quentin's eyes narrowed. "Why do I get the feeling you're talking about more than just going home for dinner?"

"This isn't Nova's home." Seth looked back at the open portal. "Through there is her *real* home."

"Wait a minute, my real home?" The world tilted dangerously under Nova's feet.

Being attacked, strange energy exploding out of her, finding out her father was looking for her ... she could handle a lot, but this was too much.

"This is the only home I've ever known," she argued. "You come here out of the blue, tell me you know my father, and you expect me to believe you, no questions asked? No way. I don't know what you're really after, but this is my home. Everything I love is here. Grandpa Zeke, Mom, Quentin, they're home."

"Don't confuse where you are with who you are," Seth shot back at her. "You can't change what's inside you. Like it or not, you don't belong here."

Hah. That was an understatement. She'd never belonged. Not anywhere. She was the oddball who didn't fit.

Nova sucked in a breath.

She had never fit. Could this be why?

"No." She shook her head, as if denial could change anything. "I belong here."

Except she didn't.

Nova's legs gave out, dumping her on her backside in the grass. She pulled her knees against her chest. Her whole body shook. Soon she would shake into pieces and blow away.

"Haven't you wondered about him?" Seth asked. "Don't you want to find out where you're from?"

He had no right to ask that question. The not knowing had torn her whole life apart. Yes, she wanted to meet her father, to answer all the questions that had consumed her for so long, but he was asking too much.

"I can't," she whispered.

The pause was longer this time. The silence pressed down like unseen hands that burned against her flesh.

"You don't understand." Seth's words slashed like a knife.

Nova glared at him.

"This hunter isn't the only one they'll send. The Order's beliefs are their whole existence. If they're hunting you, they won't stop. They'll keep coming until they find you." He glanced at Quentin. "And they won't care who gets in the way."

"Let them come." Nova said with more bravado than she felt. "I'll—"

"You'll what? Blast them all back through the Divide? There are thousands of them. You barely even understand what power you have. Do you really think you can fight them all?"

Thousands?

Seth raked a hand through his hair. Unruly licks lifted into spikes. He looked like a mad scientist. "These guys don't care if they hurt your family. If they have to, they'll hurt anyone to make you come with them."

Nova's stomach seethed like an acid lake.

"This hunter had no idea what you could do," Seth went on, "but the next one will. They'll find out what you did, and next time they'll be ready."

She would find a way to stand up to them. She had to.

"They'll come at you every way they can. You were lucky this time. They risked a day attack. What if they come at night, while you're sleeping?"

Nova's body went cold. What if they already had?

"They are devoted to their cause," Seth growled. "They won't give up. They'll come for you no matter what the cost."

Nova saw the shadow unfolding on the other side of the glass doors. What if Mom or Grandpa had been the one who'd heard the noise instead of her?

If Seth was right, no one she loved would be safe while these people were after her. Not Mom or Grandpa or anyone.

"And my father." Nova's lips were so numb. "He knows about this? He knows how to stop them?"

Seth nodded. Out of the corner of her eye, Nova saw Quentin frown.

"How does going through the hole work?"

"The Divide separates our two worlds. If you're in Threa"—Seth glanced pointedly at Quentin—"the Order won't have any reason to come here."

She caught her bottom lip between her teeth. Was Seth telling her the truth? This was all so crazy and unreal. Still, she couldn't deny what had happened the other night. Grandpa Zeke had seen footprints. There was no question someone had been there, at her house, right outside the door. If they really were after Nova, they'd follow her and leave her family alone. If she was on the other side of this *Divide*, they would have no reason to come to this side.

Quentin tugged at her. "You can't seriously be considering this." She looked at him, but her mind was a blur.

"Once we're across, they won't look here anymore." Seth's hypnotic gaze caught Nova's. "Your family will be safe."

"What about Nova?" Quentin yelled. "They'll still be after her. Who's going to protect her? I didn't see you flinging any magic around to stop that guy."

Seth turned on Quentin, eyes flashing. "In Threa we can protect her. There are spells."

"Then teach her the spells."

"Magic doesn't work here."

Quentin flung an arm toward the hole. "*Her* magic works here."

That stopped all of them. Nova looked up hopefully, but Seth shook his head. "Learning to control the magic takes time. I think … I think the fear of the moment allowed your magic to work this time but use without intent is dangerous. If that kind of power had hit *you*…" He raised his eyebrows at Quentin and let his words sink in.

The cold ball in Nova's stomach rose into her throat. Seth was right. She had no idea how to control whatever she had done. She hadn't even known she could. Power had come flying out like an eruption. She could have hurt anyone close to her without even realizing.

"At least talk to your mom and Grandpa Zeke first," Quentin said, the tension in his voice growing as he pleaded.

"There's no time!" Seth's face and eyes were wild. "Do you not understand there is a hole in the Divide right there? The Order's hunters could come through at any moment. The longer we stand here and argue, the more time they have to prepare another attack. They'll find out what she did, and they'll know they're right about who she is. They will be foaming at the mouth to get to her. No one can stop them. They will die trying."

His words reverberated through Nova's body like an earthquake. Why they were looking for her didn't matter. All that mattered was what would happen when they came.

The truth sucked the air from her lungs. She had no choice. She had to go. She couldn't let hunters come here and hurt her family, hurt Quentin. Over there, her father could protect her.

Hopefully.

"Nova, no. You don't even know him. How do you know he's telling you the truth?"

Quentin didn't understand. All that mattered was that someone was trying to get to her, and they didn't care who got in their way.

"I don't trust him."

Nova looked into Quentin's eyes, the same ocean color as his voice. "Then trust *me*, Quen."

He shook his head, his face desperate. "Seth could be taking you anywhere. How do you even know your father really sent him?"

"Lucien," Seth said quietly.

The small hairs on Nova's arms stood up. "What?"

"Your father. His name is Lucien."

Like a phantom, a memory floated up in front of Nova. Her mother cried as she hunched over a little box, the one she never let Nova look inside. Her mother hadn't seen Nova there, hiding around the corner. Hadn't known she heard her mother sob that name.

Lucien.

Quentin rolled his chair directly in front of Nova. "I won't let you."

Let her?

A spark of anger lit inside her. This was her choice, not his. She understood he was only trying to protect her. But, she wasn't a child anymore. She was sick to death of everyone treating her like a child who had to be protected and controlled.

"This is my decision."

He looked into her eyes, and she knew he could see her resolve. He wasn't going to change her mind.

"Then I'm coming with you."

"No," Nova and Seth said in unison.

She couldn't bring Quentin. He had to stay here, where he was safe. "It's too dangerous."

"Too dangerous for me, but not for you?"

His words stung, hearing the raw emotion in his voice—but his expression hurt more. She knew that look. She'd seen his eyes when he came home from the hospital, daring her to treat him like an invalid. Like a cripple.

"You'd slow us down," Seth said, his words like arrows. "I can't protect her forever. If you come, we might not make it."

Quentin flinched with each word as if they pierced him.

Nova tasted black despair as her heart cracked and broke into pieces. She didn't want him to feel like a burden, but Seth's awful words had bought them the only chance she might have to convince Quentin to stay behind. Hurting him this way was the worst thing she'd ever done. Still, seeing him killed would be far worse. She couldn't let him die.

Before he could recover, Nova stepped around him. Quentin's eyes filled with hurt and confusion, as she followed Seth to the edge of the gaping blackness. Seth nodded and took her hand. His fingers were cool and smooth. She wished they could be Quentin's warm, rough hands instead. She started to turn back, then Seth pulled her, and they fell into nothing.

THREA

A riot of color assaulted her senses.

Nova had obviously not lost her synesthesia. There was color everywhere. Ribbons and dots and whorls sprang up from the grass, threaded through the air, even lifted from the tops of the trees.

A small bird startled from the tall grass, trailing a ribbon of pale pink threaded with violet. Another bird joined it, trailing yellow and peach. The two ribbons of color wrapped around each other like a twisted rainbow.

"They're called Minstrels." Seth's voice startled her. Every sound here had color except him. "Unlike most birds, they sing together."

"In harmony," Nova breathed. The twisted rainbow was the harmony of their voices.

Nova spun in a slow circle.

She'd stepped into a painting, one with unblemished landscapes. No contrails marred the unbroken blue sky. No tall buildings interrupted the grass and trees. Being here was like stepping back in time.

Behind them, a wall of nothing paralleled trees that stretched off into the distance. Within the wall, gray and white and empty colors swirled together in constant motion.

"The Divide," Seth explained.

The Divide looked like a shifting curtain, continuous and solid except for the hole they'd come through. The rip she'd somehow made.

The forest was unlike anything she'd seen before. Huge, smooth white fingers pointed to the heavens. From the thick canopy of green, twists of pale colors eddied and rolled.

More birds?

No, that wasn't quite right. There was something different about the trees, something lifelike.

They're singing too.

Chills raced up and down her arms. The trees made their own music. She'd seen something like this once before, a long time ago, when she'd brought home from school a bean plant in a small white cup. In one night, the tiny seed sprouted into a slender stalk. Nova, excited she could actually see the plant growing, stared closely and saw what looked like movement.

Trails of green, the exact color of the stem, drifted along the stem and tiny curled leaves.

She was seeing life.

The trees before her now were ten times as wondrous.

"Welcome to Threa," Seth smiled.

All around her color swirled, brighter and deeper and more abundant than she'd ever seen at home. What had people done to Earth to make that world so dull in comparison?

"Come on," Seth said. He headed left along the ridge, parallel to the trees toward distant snow-capped mountains. "We should get moving. We don't want to stay too long in one place."

Her feelings of amazement withered.

"Hunters?"

Seth shrugged.

"I don't think they could have tracked you so soon, but we should be careful."

He scanned the tree line. There was a trace of tension in the gray depths of his eyes.

"What do we do if they find us?"

His slate eyes turned into storm clouds. "Let's hope they don't."

Great.

"Why isn't my father here?" Nova asked.

Seth tilted his head toward the opening they'd come through. "That little hole you made isn't the same one I was sent through. We were supposed to meet him near Sanoma, clear on the other side of the Great Plains."

"How far is that?"

"A few days on horseback. Maybe ten on foot."

Nova stopped short.

She'd never considered how long she might be here. "What about school? What about Mom and Grandpa Zeke? They're going to wonder where I am."

"Can't go to school if you're dead."

His words rocked her back on her heels, reverberating through her body. Seth didn't look one bit sorry. He clenched and unclenched his jaw. "And I think your mom and Grandpa Zeke will know *exactly* where you are." He spun on his heel and resumed walking.

What was that all about?

He was right. She couldn't worry about school right now. She needed to focus on keeping her family safe. Whatever was going on, she had to hope the mysterious man who'd been absent all her life would know what to do to straighten it out.

She jogged to catch up.

"Fine," she said, glaring at Seth's impassive face, "but you keep that attitude up, and I'm going to blast *you* through the Divide."

"You don't know how." His face remained stoic, although a twitch at one corner of his mouth hinted he appreciated her spirit.

"I'll figure it out," she growled. Nova didn't know whether to be furious or disgusted. She tried to remember why she'd agreed to come here.

Oh, yeah. People hunting her. Right.

As if on cue, Nova saw something moving to her right. Halfway down the grassy slope, a dark shape huddled on the ground.

"Seth," she hissed, grabbing his sleeve and yanking him to a stop.

She pointed.

Seth's lips thinned into a tight line.

"What is it?" Her voice shook with the beat of her heart as it knocked against her ribcage.

He ignored the question as he brushed past her and half ran, half slid down the grass. Nova followed, a metallic taste filling her mouth. The dark shape took the form of a body with a mop of dark hair. Seth slid to a stop, lifting his head to scan all around them, then dropped to one knee.

"Is he …?"

"No." Seth didn't look back at her. "He's not dead, but if we don't get out of here fast, we might be."

She tried to swallow past the ball of cotton wadded in her throat. They were a long way from the opening she'd created. To have landed this far away, the hunter had to have flown several hundred feet.

Seeing him now in the light of day, she realized he couldn't be more than a few years older than she was. "He's just a kid."

"He's a trained member of the Order," Seth reminded her, "and the one they sent to hunt you down."

Seth looked around again, as if making sure they were alone. Then he held his hands over the prone form.

"What are you doing?"

"We can't let him go." His voice sounded oddly defensive. "As soon as he wakes up he'll tell them where we are."

Nova's eyes tracked from Seth's outstretched hands to the stranger's chest, then back to Seth's face, which was rigid with tension.

"You're going to kill him."

She stumbled backwards, falling on her backend in the grass. Who had she allowed to bring her to this place? What kind of a person was he?

"He did try to kill all of us, remember?" Seth snapped.

"He threatened. He didn't actually hurt anyone."

"That still makes *him* the bad guy."

Nova sprung to a stand.

"No." She grabbed Seth's arm and tried to pull him away, but he was strong. Nova managed to break free enough to stand over her attacker. She put both hands against Seth and shoved. "Don't hurt him!"

"What then?" Seth shouted. "If we leave him here, we might as well hand him a knife and let him kill us right now. He found you in another world. You think he can't find you in this one?"

So, the idea she would be safer on this side of the Divide had been … what? A ruse? Nova pushed back her rising anger. She needed to keep cool until she could find her father and sort this all out. "We could tie him to a tree or something."

"Sure." Seth sneered. "Let him die of thirst and starvation. That's a lot nicer."

Crap.

He was right. If no one came along and found him, he'd still die. There was only one option, really. A bad option, but there wasn't much of a choice.

"No." Seth's voice was low and tight.

"We can—"

"No. We can't bring him. He'll slow us down. On purpose, if he can. Give them the chance to catch us."

"We'll be watching him."

Seth's chin lowered menacingly. "You think they're the only dangerous thing here? You're out of your mind."

Nova had only one bargaining chip. Seth had revealed it to her with the amount of persuasion he'd used to get her to come with him. She stared at him until his eyes finally locked on hers.

"If he doesn't come, neither do I." Her words were flat and final.

She was surprised to find she meant them. Risking herself was one thing. She was here to protect the people she cared about, not to get anyone else killed. If that's what it took, she would sit here until the Order found her and hauled her off to wherever.

Seth blinked, and she watched the small puff of surprise blow across his expression, where it morphed into something darker. Then, unexpectedly, he laughed.

"I should have figured." He shook his head. Anger brought a light to his eyes, but she saw something else there too. "You're just like your father."

There was no way to know if his words were a compliment or an insult.

"Fine. You want to bring him? We'll bring him, but you'll have to be the one who makes sure he's keeping up. I can't watch him and keep eyes out for the rest of the Order at the same time."

That seemed reasonable. All she had to do was keep their captive from running away or trying to kill them both.

Easy.

Seth pulled out two knives from the hunter's coat. They were both small but still looked sharp enough to be used as a weapon. From one black boot, Seth pulled something that looked like a piece of stone, woven into a braid. He turned the strange object over in his hands, then offered all three items to Nova.

She marveled at the smoothness of the braided stone, heavy in her hand. She refused the weapons. This strange boy, not quite a man yet, may have been carrying them for nothing more than protection. For Nova, they were a reminder she was being hunted.

Seth used vines to tie their captive's arms together. He held his hands out, palms directly over the vines, and made several small motions in the air. Nova watched in amazement as the vines slithered around the unconscious stranger's wrists and arms like snakes. They looked alive, although they didn't seem to tighten very much. When he was done, Seth sat back.

Nova couldn't help but be curious. "What did that do?"

"That was a Neutral spell, which should subdue any attempts of his to pull his hands out of the vines, or at least weaken his resolve."

The idea floored her. Beneath all the worry and fear about this strange world and its inhabitants, there was an undercurrent of wonder. What else could the magic here do?

"Come on, we'll have to make something to carry him on."

They gathered up sticks and used them to put together a makeshift stretcher.

"Help me get him on."

Seth grabbed under his arms, and Nova got his feet. She grunted with the effort to lift the dead weight. They rolled him onto one side, so they could slide the contraption underneath him. They were both sweating by the time they finished.

"He's like that braided rock," Nova panted, "small, twisted, and heavy as stone."

"Stone." Seth nodded. "As good a name as any for now."

They dragged him along for nearly an hour, taking turns pulling his unconscious form behind them. They managed the grassy slope with only minor difficulty. Once they reached the trees, the ground turned into a maze of roots, rocks, holes, and plants designed to trip them up.

All Nova wanted to do was put the stretcher down, but if she did, Seth would be ready to leave their prisoner behind—or worse, to kill him.

She focused instead on the trees around her. Here, under the canopy, she couldn't see the wisps above as clearly. Still, there were tendrils of color all around her, curling around the thick silver trunks of the trees, or drifting above them on eddies of air.

It was nearly dark when the unconscious stranger they were now calling Stone finally began to stir.

"He's waking up."

Seth lowered the ends of the tree-limb stretcher to the ground. Stone's eyes opened a moment later, widening when they landed on Nova who stood a few feet away. His body jerked backward. He stilled as he realized his hands were tied behind him. He turned to look at Seth, who scowled. Then Stone turned dark eyes on Nova. His gaze burned with a zealous fervor that glimmered like a dark jewel.

Nova's stomach clenched at the promise she saw in his stare—the promise that this battle was not over.

Neutral

Neutral is the ability to neutralize or cancel out either Destructive or Creative influences. It is the balancing factor. Neutrals have a unique ability to balance with Creative or Destructive, whether in a dual gifting, or in dealing with external forces. Neutral is thought to be the weakest of the three elements. However, because of the unique way it affects the other elements, the Neutral gifting can sometimes achieve what seems impossible.

—High Wizard Ezekial, on the *Factors of Magic*

Rescue Party

Seth was a liar. Quentin could feel it in his bones. Still, he'd managed to get Nova to believe his lies, and now she was gone. The only thing left was the crazy hole, like a reminder that something in his life had been removed.

Should he go get Mira and Zeke? They must know something about this. If that's where Nova was really from, then they must be from there too.

"Oh, man …"

The depth of that realization slowly washed over him.

All the secrets, all these years … this was why they wouldn't tell her things. To keep her from finding out. Not because Nova wouldn't *believe*. They could show her, and she'd have to believe. They'd kept the truth from her because they thought they were protecting her.

Like he was trying to do when he told her he wouldn't let her go.

"Ugh," he groaned. He closed his eyes and rolled his head back. No wonder she'd gotten angry. He'd treated her exactly like her mom had.

But now he understood what they'd been thinking. This wasn't your normal, run of the mill danger. There were people trying to kill Nova. Now all her mother's worries seemed justified. Nova had walked right into the center of the storm. There wasn't time to go get help. Every minute she was over there with that jerk she was more at risk.

Quentin had to go after her.

He rolled forward a few feet, then stopped. The hole was not level with the ground. There'd be no way to go through with his chair. If he was going to get through, he had to do it without his wheels. How would he get around without them? Worries rushed in like waves. What if he went through and the hole opened up right in the middle of a lake, or worse? And even if he got through safely, would he be able to get back? What if this was a one-way trip? He rubbed his sweaty arms.

It didn't matter. He had to go. His hands clenched on the cold metal. His heart pounded. Sweat dripped into his eyes.

"Come on!"

This was Nova. She'd go through that hole for him in a heartbeat. *Had* gone through for him. She'd known he was in danger and never hesitated. What was his problem? This was his chance. He could prove … what?

Prove he was some kind of hero? Prove he was as good as Seth?

Pathetic.

The truth was he was scared. Even if he wasn't headed into a trap, even if he managed to find some way to get around without his wheels, he might not be able to do anything to help. He might make things worse. He might do exactly what Seth had said and ruin whatever chance there was to save Nova.

Or worse.

She might have to save him.

The cripple.

"Forget that."

He refused to be that person. Nova had never let him be, and he wouldn't let himself either. Clenching his jaw, he rolled the last few feet up to the hole. A warm breeze caressed him with the smell of grass and flowers and summer.

He got as close as he could, then placed his hands at the best leverage point. He'd have to push himself out of the chair and through the hole all at once. He tightened all his muscles, rolled his shoulders, put his head down and heaved with all his might.

The impact knocked him back into his chair and left him senseless for a minute. If his head hadn't been down, he would have broken his nose. He ran his hand through his hair but didn't see any blood.

"Having trouble?"

He looked up, startled. He'd almost forgotten where he was or that anybody else would be in this world. Neanderthal girl stood a few feet away, watching him like a spider might watch a bug struggle helplessly in a web. "You've got to be kidding me." Of all the people who could have shown up, why her? "What are you doing here?"

"It's a public park," Laura growled. She glanced warily in the direction she lived before she turned her gaze toward the hole. "What is this thing?"

"You wouldn't believe me if I told you."

She frowned at him. "Try me."

Yeah, okay. Sure. Why not? This was already the worst, craziest day of his life. He may as well let loose.

"It's a hole between worlds. Nova blasted it when some guy attacked her, and now she's over there because Seth convinced her if she didn't go more people would come after her and might kill her family in the process."

Laura stared then gave a small nod. "If what you say is true, she's got guts."

"What?"

"That, or you're a raving nut case."

He waved at the hole only a few feet away.

"Yeah, yeah. I see it. So, what? Now you're trying to go after her like some knight on his horse going to rescue the princess?"

That pretty much summed it up.

She thrust her hand into the hole.

"Hey, be careful! You—" He stopped short as her hand disappeared, then reappeared as she yanked her arm back.

She stuck it in again. "Sick," she whispered.

Had he missed the opening? He reached in below Laura's hand. Only, his hand didn't disappear. Instead, he hit something solid, like an invisible wall, hard as a rock. He glanced up. Laura stared at his hand.

"Let's see what happens when we try this," she said, then reached down and grabbed his hand in hers. Before he could answer, she pushed into the hole. Both their arms disappeared. A cold ribbon of air flowed up his arm. Quentin stared at the place where his arm ended. His hand refused to move. Laura pulled back, and both their arms reappeared. He wiggled his fingers in amazement.

Laura sniffed. "We going after her, or what?"

His mouth hung open. He couldn't seem to find a way to close it, and he had no idea what to say. Why was she able to get through and not him? The fact there was a hole leading to another world hanging in the air was bad enough, but that Laura Hennigan could get through and he couldn't was worse.

So … what? Let her take him through? Bring the girl whose favorite pastime was bullying Nova with him to try to rescue her?

Nova would have a kitten.

Of course, if he didn't let Laura help, Nova might not live long enough to get upset. There was no other option. Besides, at least with Laura's help, he could go through with his wheels.

"Why?" He had to know. "I know why I want to go, but why do you?"

She glanced toward home again. "Let's just say I'm up for a change of scenery."

Her words were casual, but her voice carried a tension he could feel. He wondered what life was like at the Hennigan house, but he didn't have time to figure out her motives. Every second he lost might mean the difference between finding Nova and losing her forever.

He licked his lips. "Let's do it."

She put her left arm under his arms, grabbing the right handle of his chair with her other hand. Quentin gripped both wheels as tightly as he could. He felt like a complete idiot but supposed that would be the least of his worries in a minute. Laura turned to face the hole. Quentin looked up at her. Would this work? As if reading his mind, she glanced at him and shrugged.

Only one way to find out.

He wheeled forward as Laura pushed against him.

"Count of three." Laura said.

He was suddenly very glad Neanderthal Girl was twice as strong as every other kid in school.

They counted in unison. Quentin's heart pounded with each shout. "One … two … three!"

Quentin felt a jerk as he lifted. The chair was a dead weight under his sweaty fingers. He thought for sure he would lose hold, but then the heaviness disappeared. He floated inside a gray cloud that flowed over and around them like a river of mist. The current intensified. His chair rocked sideways and almost tipped over. Laura steadied him and dragged him forward. For one horrible second, he thought they might be trapped here in whatever void this was—trapped between worlds. Then, with a ripping noise, they tore free and surged back into sunlight.

Laura fell, her hand wrenched away from his. There was a thud as Quentin's wheels found traction and then motion. He was rolling downhill. His fingers scrambled as he tried to regain his grip. Adrenaline surged through him, leaving his mouth dry. Thankfully, his wheels tangled in long grass, and he bounced to a stop.

He sat for a moment to catch his breath, then turned back as Laura got up from her knees. "You okay?"

She nodded as she dusted herself off. Her eyes widened as she looked past him. He spun back around. They'd done it. Somehow, some way they had crossed over from one world to another.

"Where are the houses?" Laura's voice was deadpan.

Quentin scanned the tall grass in front of him. "Where are the roads?"

They were at the edge of a small hill that sloped gently down to a wide expanse. At the other end, stretching as far as he could see from left to right, was a forest. Not just a bunch of trees together like there might be in an undeveloped area, but a real forest. Tall trees so white they looked silver soared into the sky. They were as tall as redwoods, but there were no pine cones or needles. Instead, smooth, wide trunks ended in a leafy canopy that spread together to create an almost solid-looking expanse of green perched halfway to the sky.

To his left, jagged purple shadows of mountains brushed the horizon. They stood out against a sky deeper and richer blue than any he'd ever seen. His skin tingled as a ripple of emotion moved through him.

"What is this place?" Laura's voice was softer than he'd ever heard from her before.

"I think," Quentin answered, "it's called Threa."

She grunted, and her eyes scanned left and right. "Where's your girlfriend?"

"She's not my girlfriend," he mumbled, but it was still a good question. He'd half expected Seth and Nova would be somewhere in sight. How would he ever find them?

"Someone's coming."

He followed Laura's line of sight. Sure enough, a dark figure emerged from the trees almost dead ahead, like a piece of shadow breaking away from the larger darkness. Even from this distance, Quentin could tell the shape was too large to be Seth or Nova. The top resembled a head and shoulders, but the bottom was much wider and longer, with four legs instead of two. Someone on horseback, he realized, and headed straight for them. A finger of unease ran up his back. What if it was another hunter?

"Maybe we should go back."

"Can't. Door's closed."

What?

He spun around again, his eyes searching the space behind Laura.

Looking at the Divide was like looking at a solid wall of static. Nothing marred the unbroken surface. No hole, no doorway, no nothing.

Great. They'd only been here for thirty seconds, and they were already in trouble. The only place to hide was the trees, and the dark figure blocked their way. Quentin was pretty fast on pavement, but on grass he couldn't outrun two legs, let alone four.

There was nothing to do except wait to see what the rider wanted. Quentin had come here to try to help Nova. He wouldn't be any good to anyone if he chickened out and ran every time he saw something odd.

As the stranger got closer, Quentin could have sworn the man was Seth, but he was too tall. He was dressed all in black, which made the black horse he was riding look like a part of him. Laura said nothing as the man reached them, pulling his horse to a stop. He looked down at them, his gray eyes so much like the blowing void they had just come through that goose bumps broke out on Quentin's arms.

"Where is she?" The rider's voice was low but still threatening.

Could he be talking about Nova? Maybe this really was another hunter. Had Seth been right?

"Who are you?" Quentin didn't know where Nova was, but no way would he tell this man anything.

The stranger's eyes scanned Quentin, pinning him like an insect. "Where is Seth?"

A finger of hot anger clawed Quentin's chest. Why would a hunter know Seth? Was that creep in league with the people he'd told Nova were after her?

Unless—unless this man knew Seth because he'd sent him.

Suddenly, Quentin realized why the dark hair and long straight nose looked familiar. He'd seen the same features every day since he could remember. They were as familiar to him as his own reflection, maybe more. After all, he'd spent plenty of time studying them when he thought Nova wasn't looking.

"You're Lucien," Quentin said softly.

Those stormy eyes reevaluated him. Silent power radiated from them. For no good reason, other than he was afraid, Quentin had a sudden urge to spill the whole story to this man. Surely someone powerful like him could find and protect Nova better than a couple of lost kids from another world. Hadn't Seth said Nova's father wanted to find her and keep her safe?

Another thought struck him. The words were on his tongue, but he bit them back. This might be Nova's father, but there was a reason why Mira and Zeke had tried to keep her away from him all this time. In spite of their methods, they were good people. If they were afraid of this man, his gut told him he should be too. Besides, this imposing stranger didn't exactly ooze good-will.

Quentin felt a creeping sensation along the base of his skull, like insects looking for an opening. The sensation disappeared as quickly as it had begun.

Lucien's eyes narrowed. "You're a block."

"A what?"

Thin lips curled in disgust. "You have no gifting. You're powerless."

Quentin didn't know what that meant, but the distaste he heard still made him bristle. The words implied more than a lack of *gifting*, whatever that was. They implied he was powerless because he was in a wheelchair.

Lucien's eyes flicked toward Laura, still standing behind Quentin's right shoulder. "Neutral," he said dismissively, then returned his gaze to Quentin. "You would do well to go back where you came from, giftless one."

Man, this guy sure knew how to tick someone off. He needed a dose of his own medicine. "Little tough, without the hole and everything. Unless *you* can open one for us."

Lucien looked back and forth between them, then his eyes widened in surprise. "She did this." His eyes gleamed as he studied the air behind them, lips parted. "Such power ..."

For one unguarded moment Quentin could see the hunger coming off Nova's father in waves like heat shimmers off pavement in the dead of summer. Then his face closed off as if a wall had been erected.

"Where is she?"

Suddenly, and with great conviction, Quentin was glad he didn't know.

"Where is she?" Lucien's voice was thunder.

The air and ground shook. The grass danced as if blown by a powerful wind. Laura's hand brushed Quentin's shoulder as she steadied herself against him. With inhuman speed, Lucien dismounted and stood before them. He pulled Quentin off his chair until he hung in the air.

"You may be a block, but that would not stop a tree from crushing you or your bones from breaking if you fell from a great height." Though

Lucien spoke in a near whisper, Quentin had no doubt this man could make good on his threats.

"I don't know where she is."

Lucien sneered and dropped Quentin back into his chair. "I will not waste my effort on you, giftless boy. I will have her, and there's nothing you can do to stop me. Her blood belongs to me." He glanced at Laura. "If you get in my way, I will crush you both."

Casually, he lifted a foot and gave one of the wheels of Quentin's chair a shove. The chair crashed onto its side, sending Quentin sprawling. Lucien grinned at the sight. "Giftless." Then he mounted and rode back the way he'd come.

Laura held out her hand. "You okay?"

Quentin laid there, his senses on overload.

"Quentin?"

A slow grin spread over his face. He laughed at her confused look. "One good thing about getting knocked on the ground," he said, "is all the rocks."

She stared at him as if he'd cracked his head on one of them.

"They're under me," he explained, his grin widening. "And I can feel them."

He gave her a moment for his words to sink in. She looked down at his legs, then back at his face. "You mean …?"

He nodded. "I haven't been able to feel them since I was ten, but I'm feeling them now."

He grabbed her hand. Still looking a little confused, she pulled him up. Quentin's knees bent as he put weight on his legs and slowly pushed himself upright. He let go of Laura. He was standing. For the first time in more than five years, he was standing.

Then he fell over.

Quentin laughed. "I might be a little rusty."

PATROL

"He's afraid of you." Seth walked between Nova and Stone, his arms loaded with some kind of small, round fruit.

Stone's silent gaze followed her as she moved around the crowded campsite they'd made.

"You should use his fear. As long as he knows you might blast him again, he's less likely to try to kill us in our sleep."

"He can hear you, you know."

Seth glanced at him. "I'm counting on it." He dumped his armload of fruit on the ground. "Breakfast is served."

Nova picked one up, curious. Her stomach rumbled. "What is it?"

He peeled back the thick, green skin, biting into the flesh beneath. Liquid ran down his chin. He held out the fruit. "Malanqua."

Nova picked one up. The fruit was heavier than it looked. She sniffed. The thick green rind didn't smell like much. She imitated Seth, peeling the fruit like a big orange, revealing white flesh underneath. The tart, sweet smell of apples and melon filled her nose. She took a bite. Cool, crisp sweetness flooded her mouth. The flavor was bright green, red, and pink against her tongue.

"Delicious," she said around a mouthful, trying to keep from dripping.

Seth tossed one to Stone. He didn't even look as the fruit bounced off his leg.

He truly was as dark, cold, and silent as a stone. Nova wished she could understand what drove him, but he gave nothing beyond angry glares. Why should *he* be angry? Wasn't she the one who saved his life even though he'd threatened to kill them? Stone should be grateful, not angry.

"We should get moving." Seth dusted himself off. He stalked over to Stone, pushing him with his foot. "Today you walk."

Nova rolled the braided rock between her fingers. She walked over to Stone before she could rethink her decision. "Here." She held out her hand.

Stone flinched. He looked up at her, brows lowered.

"Take it."

He didn't move.

Nova thrust the stone into his hand. For all she knew, the rock was some voodoo talisman. Let him keep the thing—probably wouldn't do her or Seth any good. The sun was already out, but the canopy gave them shade—the only comfortable thing about their morning.

Seth set a strenuous pace. Stone followed in silence. They gradually pulled ahead. Despite the amazing views all around, the quiet worked on Nova's nerves. Her stomach growled after only a couple of hours. The malanqua had tasted sweet and refreshing, but she needed something more substantial. She craved protein. The occasional morning sprint with Quentin had not prepared her for this. The day wasn't even half over, and every muscle in Nova's body ached. She pushed her tired legs to close the gap that had widened between them.

"Can't we go where there are people? Get some real food?" She asked when she finally caught up.

Seth glanced at her over his shoulder. "Sure. We can stroll right up and ask someone to give us something to eat, a bed, and ignore the fact we've got some guy tied up."

There wasn't much to say to that.

Seth passed around more malanqua for lunch. The so-called food quenched her thirst but did nothing to ease her appetite. When a small group of doves burst out of the grass of a small clearing, Nova followed them with hungry eyes. Not that she'd ever be able to bring herself to kill a bird, let alone clean and butcher one. Still, the thought of a piece of hot, greasy chicken made her mouth water. She could practically smell it cooking, the tang of smoke adding to the rich aroma.

Wait.

The scent was real.

Seth met Nova's eyes and moved his head a fraction, indicating their prisoner. Nova nodded and edged closer to Stone. He leaned away from her, pulling against his restraints. She put her lips against his ear.

"You give us away, and I'll blast you so hard you'll come out in a world you've never even heard of."

Her comment had been a bluff, but the words had an amazing effect. Stone blanched, the color draining from his face.

Nova turned to see Seth disappear through a particularly dense stand of trees and brush. Should she move or stay? If someone came through that thicket from the other side of the clearing, they would be sitting ducks.

Rather than risk any noise, she crouched and pulled Stone down beside her and stared at the spot where Seth had disappeared. Shouldn't he have come back by now? Wait.

The brush moved.

Nova held her breath.

Stone tensed beside her as a figure appeared.

Seth jogged over to them in a half crouch, then whispered, "It's a patrol. Four men and horses."

Nova frowned. "What are they patrolling?" If there was a town or road nearby, she wanted to know.

Seth glanced at Stone before answering. "The landowners here send out patrols. They sometimes, uh … *enlist* people that aren't protected by another landowner." When Seth saw her blank look, he scowled and clarified. "They take people. Force them to work the land. Permanently."

Take people? What kind of crazy, psycho place was this? "People here are either slaves or slave owners? Isn't there any kind of law enforcement?"

"This is Threa," Seth said, his voice flat. "Power is the law. You either have it, or you serve those who do."

Nice. Not only were people like Stone trying to kill them for no apparent reason, there were roving bands of slavers sent out to round up anyone who was not already enslaved. Maybe crossing the Divide hadn't been such a good idea.

"Worry about the politics later. Right now, we need to find cover."

Seth was right. *Again.* "Where are they?"

"Down the hill by the stream we crossed."

The wheels of a plan began to turn in Nova's mind. "There are four horses down there?"

His brows dipped. "That's what I said."

Nova had ridden horses since she was little. Not often enough to say she was great, but she wasn't bad either. The question was, "Do you know how to ride?"

Seth looked at her like she'd sprouted a horn on her forehead. "Are you crazy? Those aren't some random strangers. They're a patrol. They train for this, plus they're armed."

"And they probably won't be the only ones we run into if we're trying to cover this entire region on foot," she hissed. "Am I right?"

He blinked, and she could see by his expression she was.

"I think we'd cover a lot more ground and be able to avoid a lot more patrols if we had our own rides. Plus, if we take their horses, we don't have to worry about fighting them *or* having them find us."

He tilted his head as if considering her idea, then shook his head. "Impossible. How would we manage to get the horses?"

Nova grinned. "We'll need a diversion."

Magic Blocked

It is said that there is no magic left in the twin world to Threa, called Earth. My own suspicion is that there is something more balanced between the two. If magic flows in Threa, then it does not seem logical that magic would be absent altogether in Earth. More likely the flow of power unfolds differently there. Some key element is missing or is blocked from that place, causing the outcome of the magic to manifest in ways yet unseen or unknown.

—High Wizard Ezekial, on the *Factors of Magic*

FAILING

The trees stood tall and silent. The grass waved, but the green fronds were lifeless. Even the air smelled wrong. Mira's heart knew what her eyes could not prove.

Nova was gone, her absence like a hole in Mira's heart

"Zeke," she whispered.

"I know."

They had to find her. If they were right, if she really was gone, there was only one place she could be, which meant there was a rift in the Divide somewhere nearby. They had to find it.

"This way." Zeke veered across the middle of the park.

Her eyes scanned the air for a telltale sign. A hole, or if it had been veiled, a ripple in the light. There was nothing. Still, as they neared the tree line, gooseflesh popped up on her arms. She stopped, turning in a slow circle. Something had happened here.

"Look," Zeke pointed to a spot a few feet away. A dark shape lay rumpled on the ground.

Her heart dropped to her feet. A part of her separated and floated out of her body, watching from above as she ran to the spot and knelt in the grass, picking up the bag and tracing her fingers over the fabric before hugging the backpack to her chest. There was nothing exceptional about the bag, except for the QD written in black permanent marker on the flap, and the fact Mira had seen the initials a thousand times before. The Mira kneeling in the grass and the Mira floating above slammed back together.

Her head lifted. "Quentin!" The shout came from between lips that had no feeling.

Was he with her?

"Please let them be together," she said, her voice ragged.

If Quentin was somehow with Nova, he would protect her. He would make sure she was all right. She had watched that boy grow up right alongside Nova. If anyone could take care of her, Quentin could.

Mira stood up, still clutching the bag, and noticed Zeke staring into empty space, his brows furrowed.

"What? What is it?"

He shook his head. "I can't get through."

"What?"

He looked back at her over his shoulder, his face tight with worry. "There's a thin spot." He motioned to the air in front of him. "I could swear there was an opening here recently."

"But now?"

"Gone. And not only that. It's as if the hole has collapsed *inward*."

"What does that mean?"

Zeke made small shapes in the air as he formed silent words. A spark jumped from his fingertips but was instantly repelled.

"It's failing."

"What is?"

Zeke's piercing glare burned Mira's soul. "The Divide," he said softly. "The Divide is failing."

She couldn't wrap her mind around Zeke's words. Nova was on the other side. There was no doubt. But how could they get to her if the Divide was failing?

"What's the worst that could happen if we open a hole?" Could it send them somewhere else? Cause them to drift like leaves on a current?

Zeke shook his head. His eyes were troubled. "We can't open a hole, Mira."

His words pierced her chest like arrows.

"The Divide itself is failing. Even if we could open a doorway, which we can't, it would be too unstable to cross. We wouldn't just be carried away, we'd be destroyed."

"No." He must be mistaken. "No. I don't accept that. I don't." She flung the pack at him. "I don't care if it destroys me. I will find a way to get to her."

Zeke stared down at Quentin's bag. She didn't care. Let him stare. Let the Divide fail. She would find a way to get to Nova or die trying.

Blood Magic

"One thing about learning to walk all over again … it's a lot harder this time around." Quentin dragged himself back on his feet for the hundredth time.

Laura sighed.

"I can do it," he growled.

"Yeah, got it the first fifty times you said it, cowboy."

He hoped his glare was menacing. Hard to be taken seriously when you looked like a newborn calf falling around in the grass.

"Maybe we should stop and rest for a while."

"You don't need to feel sorry for me."

"Suit yourself, Romeo. I'm getting a drink."

Startled, he looked up. The stream they had seen in the distance was now only a few yards in front of them. The water was shallow but ran fast between grassy banks in a gradual arc toward the trees. He'd been so consumed by getting his legs to move again that he hadn't noticed how much ground they'd covered.

Behind them, the mountains were a smudge on the horizon. In front of them, trees that had at first looked like tall, slender fingers had transformed into sprawling hands, thick and ropy at the base with white limbs splayed out in every direction. Under a canopy of green, the limbs grew sideways and even down, coiling this way and that and interlacing like a natural fence. Beneath their expansive boughs, only a few beams of light managed to seep through. The result was a silvery-green umbrella above and a seething black void below.

The scene raised the hair on the back of Quentin's neck.

Laura walked away, leaving him to get to the water on his own. He deserved that, he supposed. He gritted his teeth and urged his legs to stay beneath him as he took a shaky step. He'd been keeping up his physical therapy, but that was all about using different muscles to compensate for the ones that didn't work anymore. Now he had to undo all that. Plus, his stupid knees kept buckling.

He grabbed his left knee as it started to fold. The muscles in both legs vibrated like guitar strings. He couldn't quit. How was he going to find

Nova if he couldn't even walk two feet without falling? He finally managed to move one foot, then the other. This should be easier. Sweat trickled down his neck and back.

"You should stop now," Laura warned.

He opened his eyes. He'd made it. Grinning, he fell to his knees and dropped face first into the water. Stupid probably, since he had no idea whether the water here was even clean. There might be diseases they'd never even heard of carried on its bright, shining current.

He'd take his chances.

Quentin let the water wash away his sweat, then opened his mouth and let the cool stream wash away his thirst too. He came up gasping and laughing.

Laura shook her head, but he thought he detected a hint of a smile on her face. He rolled onto his back and looked up at the flawless blue sky.

"This is like some crazy dream, isn't it?"

"Maybe," Laura said, softly. "Or maybe this is real and everything else was a dream."

Now there was a disturbing thought. He glanced at her, but she was turned away, looking off toward the strange, hand-like trees. He wondered, not for the first time, what was going on in her life that she'd been so ready to step into another world with a guy she barely knew to follow a girl she didn't even like. He'd heard rumors in middle school about her dad being kind of a *bad dude*, but the information had never really registered. Now he wondered if bad dude was code for something darker. Maybe Laura Hennigan wasn't the thoughtless Neanderthal they had made her for. Maybe she was just a kid trying to survive.

"Don't." Laura frowned.

"Don't what?"

"I know what you're doing. Quit it. I'm not some puzzle for you to figure out."

"Okay."

"I mean it."

"Fine." A small, white cloud floated lazily in the distance. "But you're kind of confusing."

"Why? What's so confusing?"

"You spend most of your time making other people's lives miserable, then you go and do something completely altruistic."

"Al-to-what?"

"Altruistic. Unselfish. Doesn't fit your M-O. So, you know, it's confusing."

She turned to face him, her expression unreadable. "I do what I need to, okay? It's nobody's business but mine."

"Oh." He nodded. "Well, that explains it."

She rolled her eyes. "Do you always have to be sarcastic?"

"I do what I need to do."

She shook her head. "It's no wonder I never liked you."

"Yet here we are, in some alternate world, completely on our own, probably lost, and with very little chance of ever making it back home again. Assuming we survive that long."

Her laugh surprised him. All his great humor, wasted. Stark reality was what she found funny. Figured.

"You put it like that, it maybe sounds a little odd."

Indeed. "What now?"

"I vote we head for the smoke."

He followed her gaze. A cloudy ribbon drifted into the sky, coming from somewhere just inside the border of the odd forest. A small shudder worked through him. He'd been in woods before but not a full-on forest and definitely nothing like this. Still, something was burning in there. The smoke wasn't thick enough to be from a big fire. There were only a few things it could be. They'd headed in the same direction as Lucien, since he was the only lead they had on Nova's whereabouts. He'd been on horseback, so his still being this close was unlikely, but the smoke could be from his campfire.

Not that a stranger would be any less dangerous. "Are you sure?"

"No, but I don't know if we have a choice." She looked over one shoulder.

Behind them, the sky had filled with dark clouds. They boiled like angry waves, stretching from sky to ground in a terrible whirling finger. Beneath them, the grass and brush disappeared in a vortex of dirt and dust. Flashes of deep-red lightening scored the darkness like licks of flame from a tornado of fire.

"Right," Quentin croaked, his mouth drier than before he'd taken a drink. "Time to go."

He let Laura help him to his feet. Within five minutes, they reached the tree line. With one last look behind them, they plunged into the shadowy depths.

Rumbles of thunder vibrated through them like bass drums beating all around. The hair on Quentin's arms lifted. Thank goodness they made good time. Even here, in the murky depths of the trees, they were able to pick their way along winding paths of clear ground. The lack of light kept the brush growth down, which made the going easier. They could smell the smoke now, a warm, acrid scent carried on the charged air. If he'd let Laura help him right from the start, maybe they'd be somewhere safe by now.

As if sensing his thoughts, Laura moved more quickly. He was concentrating less. Instinct took over. That natural, easy feeling of legs doing what they were meant to do was like rediscovering an old friend.

He stumbled, realizing a second too late that Laura had stopped. She motioned for him to be quiet. Ahead, a dark shape loomed. They both stared. The silhouette was immense. Only the dense canopy above and the hard ropes of roots beneath gave the enormous object away as a tree. The trunk was as big across as his living room and laced with gnarled ridges like veins along the bark. The branches stretched out like arms raised in supplication to the sky.

And in the center of this fearful vision, another form came into view. Standing in the shadow of the enormous tree was a woman so short she could have been mistaken for a garden gnome, if not for hair the color of pennies. Her head swiveled back and forth, homing in on them as if she had radar.

"Well, come on," she called out. "I'm too old to bite, and storms can move quickly on this side of Elder Wood." When they didn't move, she added, "I know ye be there. And I know where ye come from. I can smell it on ye like wet on a dog." She waited a moment more. "And I've hot food."

Behind them, a crack of thunder shook the earth and made the leaves around them dance.

"I'm sold," Quentin said, nudging Laura.

"I suppose we don't have much choice at this point."

"Wise girl," the woman said, then turned and disappeared into the tree.

Quentin and Laura gasped.

"Come on now," her voice echoed from inside the tree.

Hesitantly, not sure what was more intimidating, what was in front of them or what was behind, they moved closer. A dark ridge running vertically along the trunk revealed an opening that ran behind the outer bark like a hallway. As they peered inside, the air around them began to howl. Leaves and small branches pelted them.

The storm was here.

They went in one at a time. The wind slowly faded as they followed the spiraled corridor. A soft glow lit the way ahead, and gentle warmth greeted them. Without warning, the winding entrance ended, and they stepped into the hollowed center of the giant tree. The space was easily big enough for a dozen people to move about comfortably.

The woman stood before a fire, her back to them. She was no bigger than she had appeared outside. Puffs of hair covered her head like an untamed cotton ball spun from copper. . Her feet were bare and as gnarled as the tree.

"Sit." She waved an arm without turning around.

The ropy, twisted wood formed natural seats and benches. Most were glossy and smooth from use. On the far side of the room, two of them formed what looked like a seat and desk where a fat candle burned. Behind the table, the wood was pocked with holes, each filled with a small basket or bundle. Closer to the woman, another larger indentation served as a bed, covered with spongy moss and a heap of blankets.

Quentin collapsed against one of the lips of wood. Laura sat next to him, her eyes locked on the woman.

"Let me finish the stew. We can preamble as we eat, aye?" She poked at the embers. "Yes, yes, best be done with flame ere the heart of the beast comes and blows down upon us." She carried the pot to the small table before turning to face them.

Her head turned from one to the other as if she could hear what they were thinking. She reminded Quentin of a bat—sightless, but with a sonar that was better than vision.

Where her eyes should have been, there were only indentations, as if a giant hand had erased that part of her face. Still, he had no doubt that she knew not only where he and Laura were, but plenty more. Things someone using only their eyes would not—their nervousness, the beat of their hearts, even the sweat coming from their pores. She sensed them, smelled them, and maybe something more—something unique to this place and the people who lived here. Something Nova might learn over time.

The woman cocked her head to one side. "Ye bridged the Divide, and not with magic of your own." She took a deep breath. "Ye must've followed someone, aye?" She nodded. "Aye. Ye reek of desperation and uncertainty. Ye seek her, yet ye cannot find her."

Quentin glanced at Laura, who rolled her eyes and mouthed the word *drama*.

The woman's head snapped toward Laura. "Ye should not mock what ye don't ken."

Laura's eyes narrowed. "I *ken* plenty. You enjoy this little game of cat and mouse. Surprise me, and tell us where to find her."

Quentin closed his eyes. Great. Now the lady was going to kick them out into that weird storm, and they would be toast.

A raspy wheeze, like the sound of leaves rubbing together, filled the room. Goosebumps broke out on his arms. The woman's harsh, gasping laugh pained his ears. Laura frowned as the woman regained her breath.

"I like spirit, and ye've plenty of it. Yes, I know where she is. She is led toward the North, away from us and away from he who seeks her. Deep into the heart of the Order goes the child of prophecy." She pointed. "Now do ye believe, daughter of Earth?" She grinned, not waiting for an answer, and motioned to them to come closer. "Come. Eat some. There's plenty and the storm will take the rest of the night to spend itself."

They came, hesitantly.

"How do you know?" Laura asked.

"I have no eyes, but I have sight. Inner sight, we call it. 'Tis my gifting as it was my mother's and hers before."

"And how do we get there? To the North?"

"Same way as any other. Ye walk." She chuckled as she glanced toward Quentin. "At least *here* ye do."

Strangely, the comment didn't offend him. "Yes, although I'm not as good with my feet as I used to be."

To this, the woman only nodded. She ladled out a steaming spoonful of something brown and rich into a wooden bowl and handed it to him. His stomach growled.

"Go on then, lad. Ye need yer strength." She ladled out another bowl and handed it to Laura, who scowled. "It won't bite ye." The woman cried, swatting at her. "Eat now, afore yer mouth is too full of foot and ye choke." She ladled herself a bowl. "'Tis naught but the herbs and wild mushrooms grown roundabouts, and they're better for ye than any flesh."

"Thank you." Quentin blew on the steaming liquid, then took a sip. Woodsy but not overpowering, like a beef stew minus the beef. "It's really good."

Laura lifted the bowl and sniffed the soup.

"Go on then, daughter." The woman encouraged.

"Laura."

"Hmm?"

"My name. It's Laura."

"I am Thuaat." She nodded at the tree around them. "And this is Yvin."

Quentin coughed, nearly choking. "The tree has a name?"

"Of course, man-child. Ye think I would live within the tree and not know its name? Yvin is older than the sea. He honors me to let me hide within his folds of life."

"You named it—er, him?"

She chuckled. "It is not for me to name you, or you me. Yvin whispered his name to me, not the other way around."

"You talk in riddles."

"And yet ye ken, aye?"

Although he hated to admit it, he did understand. They'd fallen down the rabbit hole. Or more accurately, jumped through.

The storm let itself be known with a howl. Quentin warily eyed the tree around them. Would Yvin' hold up to the storm? If he toppled, they'd be trapped inside. Laura eyed the tree too.

"Fret not." Thuaat patted his arm with her wrinkled hand. "The storm cannot harm us here."

"You don't think so?"

He sighed. Ever-defiant Laura. Doubting Thomas had nothing on that girl.

Thuaat inclined her head toward Quentin. "He who causes the tempest also holds it at bay. The storm cannot be where magic cannot be."

"Right." Laura nodded.

Thuaat grinned. "Spirited companion ye chose for this adventure, man-child."

"Yeah, you could say that."

Laura scowled.

"You said 'he who causes the storm.' You mean me? I caused it?"

Thuaat took a bite of her stew before finally answering. "There's not time enough to teach all of what there is, but I'll tell you as I can."

She lifted her head, and Quentin had the sudden, intense vision of eyes in those fleshy hollows. Not blue, brown, or green … but silver. And they shone like the moon.

"Magic lives here, as ye well know by now, having come after the child of prophecy. Magic is like blood and holds different factors. Creative, Destructive, and Neutral. Those with magic are generally one, or a combination of two. Those from your world are said to have lost magic. But here ye stand, having come through a barrier of magic, eh?"

Quentin shivered as he remembered his first attempt to come through, and how he'd bounced off of some kind of barrier.

Thuaat nodded. "The barrier requires Neutral, which the girl-child must have."

"But not me," Quentin said softly.

"No, man-child. Not you."

"Then what is he?" Laura asked.

Quentin gazed down at the table, feeling the pieces start to fall together like a puzzle. Lucien's words, tossed in disdain, echoed back.

"A block."

Thuaat didn't nod this time, but her non-existent silver eyes sparkled.

"I don't have magic," he said slowly, feeling the answers fall together in his mind. "I block it."

"Like a rock in the water," Thuaat confirmed. "Magic can flow around you but not through you." She waved her hands around them. "Like the storm. This is why we are safe here."

"But then how could I have caused it?"

Thuaat clucked. "Think, boy. The Divide is not merely a physical barrier, but a magical one. The magic of the Divide flows, like water. It moves. Until—"

"Until someone throws a rock in."

By crossing the Divide to come after Nova, he'd interrupted the flow of magic and caused the blackness that raged outside.

"And the Divide?" he asked, his lips feeling numb.

"It begins to fail."

Her words were like a guillotine, quiet but deadly. "What happens then? When it fails?"

She patted his arm to reassure him, but Quentin felt anything but reassured. "None can say for sure, man-child. But for true, the two worlds will once again touch, as they have not done since the dawn of time."

His fault. Just like Seth had said. Why hadn't he listened? All he'd wanted to do was to keep Nova safe, and now he may have put her in worse danger than ever. Not to mention everyone else.

"If magic doesn't work on him," Laura said, sounding unconvinced, "how come he can walk here?"

Thuaat shook her head. "Magic or no, these are two separate worlds, daughter of Earth. They do not follow the same laws." She looked at Quentin. "You were not born unable to walk, were you boy?" She asked as if she already knew the answer.

"No. I got sick from a mosquito bite. Encephalitis."

"An illness we do not have in this world."

Quentin's stomach sank. "So, if we ever—when we get back home, I'll be like before?"

"What existed there before will exist there still, but whether you'll be like before depends on you." Her silver eyes that were only in his head, twinkled and danced. "We make our own fate."

She was right. Some things in his life were out of his control and always would be. He'd accepted that truth a long time ago. He needed to focus on the things he could change.

"I have to get to Nova," he whispered.

Laura stood, her face drawn in a grimace. "Legs or no, we're not going to find her on our own. We don't even know where *we* are, let alone where she is. We need to figure out where she's going and get ourselves there."

"Lucien will get there first."

"There's nothing we can do about that."

"Actually," Thuaat said as she crossed the room to one of her nooks, "that's not exactly true."

"What?" Quentin asked, "Which part?"

She pulled something out, looked at it, then shook her head and put it back. She reached into another nook. "Ah, yes."

When she turned, she held a small leather pouch. "I told ye, boy. Ye block magic. In your world that may not mean much, but here"—she waved her arms around—"everything is magic. You have a power here that none other does."

"To block magic?"

"Aye."

"But I don't get it. How do I block something if I'm not there to do it?"

Thuaat held up a finger. "Ah. There is a spell. More ancient even than this tree, but that tells of such things. A way to use what you are. To use your blood to—"

"Woah!" Laura jumped up. "Time out. Blood? Seriously? Did you say blood?" She turned on Quentin. "Did she say blood? I think we should leave. Now."

"What about the storm?"

"You heard her. The storm can't affect you. It doesn't matter if we're here or not."

Quentin's anger started to build. "So *that* you believe, but not this?"

"Yes."

"I don't get you. You're all about taking action. But when we finally find something that could help, you don't want to do it?"

"Were you listening, Romeo? She wants to use your *blood!* No way in any universe can that lead to a good thing.

"She is right to be cautious," Thuaat said. "Blood magic is very powerful."

"But this spell can do what you said? It can keep Lucien away from Nova?"

"It can."

"And he won't be able to get to her?"

"'Twill be like two reversed magnets. They will repel each other. The magic will not allow them to be near."

Hope jumped in his heart, a twin to his fear. "Then do it."

In a flash, faster than could be possible, Thuaat was standing right next to him, her face uncomfortably close to his. Her eye hollows shimmered again.

"Be warned, boy. The spell will be tied to your blood. Your blood will feed and give it power. Be sure of this decision, for it cannot be undone."

Even in the warmth of the small enclosure, sweat broke out on Quentin's face and arms. What choice did he have? This might be his only chance to protect Nova. If he waited, Lucien might get to her before anyone could stop him. Why had he bothered to follow her here, if not for this? He swallowed. His throat scraped like sandpaper. He tried to speak but couldn't make his voice work. He nodded before he could lose courage.

"Idiot." Laura shook her head.

Thuaat emptied the pouch onto the table. There were pieces of what looked like dirt and grass, and something black, the size and shape of a toothpick. Thuaat brushed the dirt and grass into a cup of water. Then she pointed the black toothpick-looking thing at Quentin.

"A drop of blood."

He looked at the toothpick. "That's all? Only a drop?" When she nodded, he turned to Laura. "See? No knives or anything, just a toothpick."

Nervous despite his previous bravado, he rolled the toothpick between his fingers. It looked exactly like a wood toothpick, except colored a deep, smooth black. The more he looked, the darker it appeared. Swallowing hard, he pressed the sharp point to his fingertip. Immediately, a fat drop of blood welled up. He was surprised. He'd barely felt the prick.

Thuaat took the toothpick. The drop of blood hung from the tip, glistening in the light like a ruby. She dipped the sliver of wood into the cup, and the blood swirled across the water like an oil slick.

"Come," she said to Quentin, motioning for him to stand in front of her.

When he was where she wanted him, she stirred the water once more. The toothpick glistened when she pulled it out. She held it near his chest, pointed at his heart, then made soft whispering sounds, like a snake's hiss while drawing shapes in the air.

Quentin blinked. Was he crazy? He could see the shapes, as if she waved a sparkler and left a burning trail of light.

Thuaat's hissing grew louder. The pattern she drew resembled a shield. Spokes shot out in all directions. Then, Thuaat connected the shield to his chest using one long, straight line that looked like a strand from a spider web. The shield pulsed in rhythm to his heartbeat while small beads of light traveled on either side. The sight made him queasy, breathless. The room spun faster and faster. He had to stop this. What was happening?

Crud. He was going to pass out. Suddenly he felt a cool, dry hand on his forehead. The spinning stopped.

Quentin blinked. The image was gone.

Had the spell worked?

"It is done," Thuaat said, as if she'd heard his unspoken question. "The usurper has been blocked from the child of prophecy."

Quentin glanced over at Laura. She glowered at them, arms folded.

"See?" he asked, feeling only a little queasy now. "Nothing to it."

The floor rushed up to meet him as the world went dark.

Zenesthese

There are those who are born with the ability to sense power in a way that others cannot. They can see and feel it naturally. Such individuals are not only able to learn how to use magic, they are able to understand the logic intrinsically and build on what they know.

These individuals are called Zenesthese.

—High Wizard Ezekial, on the *Factors of Magic*

Diversion

Nova was nothing if not a quick learner. Watching Seth use his magic had inspired her. Still, there were four armed men somewhere down below them. She could only hope her idea would work. She crept down the slope, doing her best not to make a sound. She heard the stream and the voices of the men at the same time and crouched behind a rock that jutted out from the leaf-covered ground. She waited. If all went according to plan, at any point there would be some kind of—

Boom.

The explosion shook the ground even where she was. Horses squealed in fright as men grabbed them, their cries echoing between the trees. She grabbed onto the rock, hoping it didn't shake loose. A moment later everything stilled.

"What in—"

"Shut up." An authoritative male voice silenced the other. "Jin, Tol, go take a look."

The sound of footsteps was faint. Soon, all was silent. Nova hoped the men would walk through the same stand of brush and trees Seth had gone through earlier. He'd coated the spot in a Neutral spell meant to subdue the men and keep them from wanting to go any further. She'd asked how strong the spell could be, and Seth explained the results depended on the medium—what material he used, and what he drew the spell on. In addition to the branches, he'd drawn the spell on the ground and nearby rocks. That should at least slow the mercenaries down.

Minutes slid by. Nova heard movement and a low growl of frustration. The leader was getting restless. "You stay here," Authoritative Voice said. "Guard the camp."

Wisely, there was no argument. She also didn't hear any footsteps. When a small twig snapped, she was surprised. She left her hiding spot and quietly moved downhill. Through the branches, she saw a small fire with something roasting over it. On the far side of the fire, the fourth man sat on a log.

She waited again, knowing Seth was somewhere on the other side of the camp, closing in. She wished she knew enough about her magic to be helpful, but anything she tried now would only get in the way. A moment later, the man on the log stiffened. His eyes widened, and he fell in a heap next to the log.

Nova gasped and ran over. Seth stood up from behind the log. "What did you do?"

"He's fine. I just wiped out his energy. He'll be asleep for a couple of days."

Her head filled with questions, but there wasn't time for explanations. They had to get the horses and leave. The shouts above them confirmed the need to hurry.

Seth ran for the horses. Fortunately, they were loosely tied. He shoved Stone toward one. "Get on."

Stone glared at Seth. Nova took a step toward them. Stone flinched and let Seth help him onto the horse, looking back at Nova with fear in his eyes. Seth grabbed the lead and leaped into the saddle of another horse. Nova quickly tied the other two horses together and swung onto one of them.

She hesitated.

Seth started off, then pulled his horse around when he realized she wasn't right behind him. "Come on! What are you doing?"

This might be their only chance. She pulled her horse back toward the fire. Heavy footsteps crashed toward them, and her throat went dry. Nova held a tight rein, then kicked the horse's flanks. They skirted the fire by inches. She leaned out and snatched the stick. She started to slip but grabbed the pommel and held on, rocketing past the campsite and back around to the right in a tight U. When she looked up, Seth's gaze was fixed on something behind her. She urged her horse to move faster. Seth kicked his horse and galloped into the forest.

Nova felt, more than heard, the man who chased her. He didn't waste his breath yelling. He wasn't only stealthy, he was strong—and fast. Fortunately, he was not on a horse. When the footsteps finally faded, she risked a glance back. The man looked more bear than human. He slowed to a walk and then stopped. Even at this distance, his angry stare burned. She shivered violently. They weren't out of danger yet. They needed to put some serious distance between them and the giant they'd left behind, because she was sure beyond the shadow of a doubt he would track them down if he could.

Still, a sense of triumph filled her. Her plan had worked. They had horses. She grinned as she looked at the stick she'd grabbed.

And they had meat.

Sated and feeling more than a little proud, Nova rested her head against her arm, the flames of the fire warm against her face. Her heavy lids drooped as she listened to the sounds of frogs, crickets, and other creatures she couldn't put a name to begin a chorus. On the other side of the fire, Seth rummaged through the packs that had been tied to the horses. They'd already discovered some useful items like water and dried meat. Others, like the bows and arrows, weren't immediately useful since they didn't know how to use them well. But if they could learn, the ability to hunt game would be invaluable. At the very least, they would look a bit less like the defenseless teenagers they were.

She hardly believed she was the same person who had let a bully push her around. Why did she do that? Why had she never been able to stand up to Laura or any of the people who tried to control her? She could stand her ground for the sake of others. Why not for herself?

"Why didn't you kill those men?" The unfamiliar voice almost startled Nova into opening her eyes. She forced herself to stay perfectly still, waiting to hear how Seth would answer or if he would respond at all.

"It wasn't up to me." Of all the responses Seth might have given, she hadn't expected that one.

There were several long minutes of silence before their unwanted companion spoke again, "She could have killed them all."

"She could have killed you too, but she didn't."

This time, the silence stretched so long Nova almost fell asleep for real.

"She is not what I thought she would be."

Wow. Maybe somewhere inside his stony exterior, their captive was actually paying attention.

"No," Seth said, his voice softer than usual. "She's not."

She sensed the double meaning to his words. Was she not what he'd expected either? And how, exactly, did he know what to expect at all? Her father had never met her, so he couldn't have filled Seth in.

There was a soft rustle as someone shifted. The sounds of the night made a soft blanket around her. She wondered what color Stone's voice had made, if any. Her last thought as she drifted to sleep was of how nice it would be to see Quentin's gentle blue-green waves.

The next morning broke bright, warm, and full of promise. They headed out early, glad to be riding instead of walking. The sky was so vivid Nova could taste the blue, like a ripe berry, and feel its lightness slide down her throat. The air even smelled blue, cleaner and fresher than she'd ever smelled before. The trees, silver and majestic, towered into the sky like church spires. As the air moved between the branches, the sigh of angels filled the air around her, creating a soft light that shimmered into the sky above them. She shivered with a mix of awe and wonder, drawing her to walk beneath the towering boughs, to run her fingers over the pale bark, and feel their color under her fingers. Would it be cool and liquid like quicksilver, or warm and lush as velvet?

She felt better after having had some good food. They'd been lucky. Seth had been able to execute her plan, but it would have been better if she could have helped by using her own magic. The way he used his intrigued her.

Time to start learning.

Nova urged her horse closer to Seth's. "Tell me how you created the explosion yesterday."

He glanced at Stone, then back at her. "I destroyed a boulder."

Her eyebrows shot up in surprise. "How?"

"Rocks aren't completely solid. They have cracks, fissures, small air pockets, that kind of thing. I used Destructive to remove all of those at once, and the stone caved in on itself."

The idea seemed so logical somehow. "How did you know where the air was? Inside the rock?"

A sly smile tugged at his lips. "You like it, don't you?"

"What?"

"The magic. Figuring it out."

Something about the look on his face irritated her. "Why wouldn't I? It's something I should be able to do too, right? So why not want to understand it?"

His smile widened. "Yes, it's definitely something you can do."

"Except, I don't know all the ins and outs yet." She sighed. "Tell me again what you said about the magic, about what I am."

"You're a *Trine*." His tone sounded a little guarded.

"What does that mean, exactly?"

Seth glanced at Stone again. He shrugged, and his face relaxed. "There are three basic types of power. Three factors—Creative, Destructive and Neutral. They're the basic building blocks of magic—of life. Most people have one of the three. It's rare to have two, and those who do are almost always paired with Neutral."

"Like you?"

His smile faded, and his jaw clenched. "Like me."

"Is it ... bad? To have two?"

He barked out a laugh. "Exactly the opposite. Duals, people with two elements, are more powerful."

Okay, so there must be some other reason he didn't like being a Dual, or at least a Neutral. She decided to let it go for now. "So how many people have all three?"

"None."

"But you said—"

"Until you."

Questions crowded her thoughts for space and priority. "If there's never been one," she said, finally settling on one, "how do you know *I am* one?"

His lips twisted. "You blew a hole in the Divide. From the side that supposedly has no magic. You must have created the magic yourself. *Creative.* Then you used your power to make a hole. *Destructive.* And you nullified the power of the Divide itself to hold both sides open and push someone through. Normally, that might be able to be done some other way, but the Divide is made up of Neutral energy. Only Neutrals can go through the barrier."

His answer only added more questions to the sea of them rolling around in her mind. "You called me something else," she said, trying to remember the word.

"Zen."

"Yes, that was it."

"Short for Zenesthese. It means you can sense the magic in ways not everyone can. Some people use their gift by feel, or by using a spell to pull their gift out, but they can't create the forms themselves. Zens can use all their senses. They see, smell, hear and taste magic."

A thrill ran through her. "Synesthesia," she said softly.

Seth nodded. "It makes sense there would be a word for it. Even in a place without magic, your senses would still pick up on things others can't."

"Are many of the people here Zens?"

"Not as many as you'd think. Those with only one element have the most basic levels of magic. They can encourage plants to grow or take away someone's headache. Things like that. Having strong magic runs in families and also requires training to use the magic correctly. Some people may have strong magic but never develop their skill. So even if they are a Zen, they don't realize they are. The bottom line is that even though being a Zen is more common here than in your world, it's still unusual. There are very few who can do more than sense magic. Only the more powerful can also hear or see it."

There was an almost audible click in Nova's head as a vital piece of information fell into place. The memory of the dark shape outside her house returned. Her scream had sent shards of sound flying at the stranger, and he'd ducked. She hadn't been able to put her finger on what had seemed out of place, but now the scene made complete sense. The same thing had happened in the park. She'd seen the way Stone stared at her as she sent her power out at him, his face filled with fear, as if he knew.

As if he *saw*.

Her head whipped around to stare at Stone's back. He was a Zen! She looked back at Seth with new understanding. Maybe that explained one other mystery—a mystery of shared drawings that had seemed so strange, but only meant they could both see the magic.

"You're a Zen too."

He nodded, confirming her thoughts.

"That's how you know there was air in the rock. You could ... what? Hear it? Taste it?"

"Smell it, actually."

She let that sink in for a second.

"More Duals are Zen," Seth continued after a moment. "Those with more magic, or who are more in touch with their magic, seem to have the natural ability."

What about Stone? Was he a Dual too? Or was he more in touch with his magic than others? He'd definitely seen her magic. She had no doubt about that. Did Seth know? Could he sense if Stone was Zen? If he did, the answer must not concern him.

"The drawings in my notebook are spell forms?"

"Yes. Exactly." For the first time since they'd come across the Divide, Seth looked pleased. "Zens don't just use forms, we can create them."

Nova shook her head. "I don't see how I could create them if I know nothing about them."

"You don't, but your blood does. Your *magic* does."

"Those shapes that seem to get smaller and larger at the same time, what are they forms of? What do they do?"

"Do you remember what you said? How you described your drawing as a kind of a crescendo?"

She nodded.

"Well that's an indication of what the form does. Forms are like mathematical formulas represented in a pattern. The pattern draws what's needed, and the formula unlocks the reaction."

Mathematical formulas, patterns representing actions, the ability to see sounds—they were all linked, part of a larger whole.

Nova stood at the brink of something miraculous. Something she'd unconsciously been aware of, like a shadow in the room. Looking at the whole picture in the full light of day revealed a truth she hadn't dared to hope was true.

She wasn't a freak.

She made sense.

She fit perfectly into the puzzle—she had just spent a large part of her life in the wrong space.

WARDEIN

Shutters closed, and faces disappeared from doorways as he walked past.

They did not understand, and so they were afraid. He forgave them. He would be frightened too, if he saw someone walking past that looked like he did. His clothes were strange and threadbare, his shoulders hunched and crooked, even his gait was unusual. Yet, what they were most afraid of were the scars covering nearly all of his exposed skin. Thick, twisted ropes of tissue, some pale and others dark, made him look like a monster from childhood nightmares.

He was ugly. He'd learned to accept this price he paid.

Ignoring the closed shutters and doors, he trudged on through the village. The house he had been looking for sat back a short distance, surrounded by a garden in the front and farmland in the back. Roses of every color, shape, and size lined the path to the door. Unlike the people, the flowers leaned toward him as he passed, their petals turning to face him. He acknowledged them with a nod so slight no one would notice.

At the door, he lifted one scarred hand to knock softly.

The woman who answered looked twice her age. Dark circles curved under both eyes, and streaks of gray threaded through her once rich, dark hair. She looked up, her tired eyes taking in all of him. She didn't shrink back, although fear widened her eyes for a moment before they narrowed in a confused frown then slowly widened again, this time in amazement. Tears filled them.

"Have you come to take her?"

His smile was as gentle as his heart.

"No."

She crumbled at the sight of him. She took his outstretched hand, grasping his rough skin with no qualms. "Thank you! Oh, thank you!" She pointed toward the back of the house. "This way. Just through here."

She shut the door behind him, closing them away from prying eyes. He didn't need her to show him where to go. He knew well enough where he was needed. He passed the other doorways. She was in the last room, the one with the window looking out on the roses. Her namesake. She was so small she seemed lost on the big bed.

He knelt beside her, taking one pale hand in his. He sensed the mother behind him, in the doorway. The girl's tiny hand looked small against his own. He laid his other hand over hers, pressing gently from above and below.

He closed his eyes.

She is too young. Take this cup from her.

Warmth filled him. Light, like morning sunshine, coursed outward and filled his cupped hands, encompassing her little one. Her fingers glowed, then her palm and her wrist. The light washed up her arm. He heard the mother gasp.

Take it from her.

Tendrils of silver-white shot out from the child's shoulder, then wrapped around her chest, her legs, even her face. Inside the light, her skin glowed. He saw through her, into her, to where the girl's beautiful life force flowed like sparkling droplets of water, moving in an endless dance, until … there. The darkness coiled in her lungs, slowly squeezing the life from her.

He gazed at it.

The darkness sensed him looking.

You have no hold here. Be gone.

The darkness knew his voice and fled before a power greater than its own. The child drew in a surprised, relieved breath. The light poured into the space the darkness left behind, filling it, growing brighter until it was like the sun burning inside her, cleansing from within. Every corner of the room glowed. Nothing was left untouched.

His work was done. He opened his eyes, releasing the power, and the light winked out. On the bed, the little girl took two deep breaths, then opened her eyes. They found his. Not a trace of fear touched them.

The mother collapsed against the bed and clutched her daughter's hand. "Oh, my sweet Rose."

The girl smiled at her mother, then turned back to him.

"I knew you'd come," she whispered.

Mole's fingers twitched like whiskers next to his face. His black eyes, he hoped, were appropriately beady. He tried to wiggle his nose and was unsuccessful. That was all right. He was a good Mole. Lady would be happy with this report. *Yes, yes.* She would reward him with scraps from her own plate.

Healing was hers to command. To heal without her approval was theft. How could she take payment if someone else did the healing? And if there was no debt, there would be no one to work.

Wicked man.

Mole would tell. Lady would reward Mole. He was a good Mole.

His beady eyes watched as the man stood on the doorstep. Ugly man. The girl stood too. She was better. Mole had seen enough. He scurried away from his window, moving quickly through the single room of his house, out the back door and to the small, almost falling over shack that housed his only horse. Not a horse really, only a pony, but still big enough to eat him. Mole skirted around the animal and kept a wary eye as he saddled his ride, only getting close to the creature when he absolutely had to. He hated most animals. They tormented him. This one he tolerated because Lady had given the beast to him, so he could report to her when he needed to.

Like now.

He clawed at his face. Bad to dawdle. Bad to hesitate. Must hurry. Scurry and hurry.

Forcing himself, he led the pony out into the grass and climbed into the saddle. The pony turned to look at him, and he growled at it. Fat brown pony eyes blinked at Mole.

"Scurry and hurry," he muttered and kicked the pony's flanks.

The pony broke into a slow trot, which was as fast as the animal went but still faster than walking. Mole left town the back way, through the trees and around the small lake.

No, not a lake … a bog … it's a bog!

Lady was only a few miles away, halfway between her two nearest townships. He urged the pony to go faster. The pony ignored him. Why hadn't Lady given him a faster horse?

"You would fall off something faster," the voice in his head whispered.

The mean voice. The Geo voice.

He hadn't always been Mole. Before, he had been Geo. Lady had seen him hiding in the shadows and had known he could be useful.

"You don't look like a Geo," she'd said. Her smooth voice and red nails sent shivers up and down his back "You look like a quivering, sniveling mouse. No, a mole." She'd smiled then, a wicked, lovely smile that set him to shaking. "Mole is who you are now."

And Mole he had become. He was a good Mole.

"Rat, more like," the Geo voice nagged." You're disgusting."

"Shut it! Leave me be!" Mole slapped his face.

"Selling out friend and foe alike." The voice ignored Mole's attempts to silence it. "You deserve the hole you live in, Rat."

Mole pounded at his head until he nearly fell from the saddle. The pony looked back at him nervously. "Go away. Leave me alone," he wailed, clawing until there was blood beneath his fingernails.

The pony did a side-step and sped up. Mole laughed. The beast *could* go faster. Lady would be pleased.

"Lady, your dog is here." The guard sneered, dropping the heap of filthy clothes on the floor of the room before he backed out and closed the door.

She waited. The clothes shook but didn't move. She sighed.

"Come now, Mole. Am I so frightening?" His face lifted. "*Tsk-tsk.* You have been at yourself again."

He grinned, the sight a horror of bloody cheeks and lips over rotted teeth. "It was him, Lady. He tries to keep me from you, but I silenced him."

"Indeed." She could hardly imagine what went on inside that deranged head. Still, he was useful. "What have you come to tell me then?"

His face contorted, screwing up into a frown. "Healing," he spat from between twisted lips and clenched teeth. "Without your leave."

She felt a twinge of surprise, a rare sensation. So little happened she didn't already know about. Curiosity followed the surprise like a delicacy. "Tell me what you saw, little Mole. I will reward you for your loyalty."

"A man. An ugly man. All in robes. To the widow Morra's house. He healed the child. The one called Rose." He paused, and his eyes nearly rolled into his head. "With light, he healed her. Light like the sun." He shivered. "Foul, horrid light."

"Wardein!" She breathed in true surprise. Could it be true? She turned to one of the two guards standing behind her. "Quickly. Go and fetch Sol."

The guard snapped a fist to his heart and rushed away.

She'd heard the stories, of course. Everyone knew of them, but no one had ever seen one. Not in her lifetime. Most people thought they were mere legends. Sleep stories meant to soothe children. What they looked like, where they went, what they did, all those details varied from region to region, family to family. Only one thing was consistent. The Wardein wielded the power of the sun, a light so bright no mortal could stand to look at it.

The sound of footsteps drew her out of her thoughts as her guard returned with Sol in tow. He took in the sight of Mole on his knees, gibbering.

"What is it, my Lady?"

"Wardein, Sol. Here. In the valley."

His eyes betrayed a hint of disbelief. "Are you certain?"

"As I can be. Someone healed the widow Morra's child." She glanced meaningfully at Mole. "With light."

"Cruel, terrible light," Mole echoed.

Sol nodded thoughtfully. "What do we do?"

She tapped her nails on her chair. If the healer was a Wardein, she didn't know whether they could do anything. Still, she couldn't let him go on healing all of her potential resources.

"If I may," Sol continued, "there's something that may sway your thoughts."

She looked up at him, feeling a second stab of surprise in one day. This was like a festival.

"Word has come from the East of a fast-moving storm." His eyes carried a look she'd never seen before. "From the Divide."

She nearly lifted from her seat. She gripped both arms and forced herself to remain still as he continued.

"It's a wave of Neutral." He clasped his hands. "The Trench is spreading like wildfire."

Her lips parted. Her heart pounded. Could such a thing be true? If so, she would have more resources soon than she would know what to do with. Not only from her own region but from all over. They would seek her out. They would beg for healing as the Trench ravaged them, stealing their magic—stealing their life. They would give her anything. Ten years. Twenty. They would offer children into servitude. As long as they could get healing for their families and themselves. And she would oblige. How much phoria could she grow with ten thousand people? A hundred thousand pounds? She would be the most powerful woman in all of Threa!

Who cared about one Wardein in the face of that?

A whimper reminded her Mole was still on the floor. He stared up at her, his eyes flicking from her nails to her lips.

Revolting.

"Take him," she said to the guard who had brought Sol. "Get him some table scraps and send him home."

She had more important things to prepare for. Things were about to get interesting.

Ties that Bind

There is much study on various mediums and how they can be used, but one medium is considered too dangerous to be used by most, and that is blood.

Using blood to form a spell crosses the factors of both individuals and causes the person whose blood is used to be bound directly to the spell itself. How this bond works is not broadly known, as few have used it and even fewer studied its effects, but one thing is sure—one should be very careful about how their blood is bound.

—High Wizard Ezekial, on the *Factors of Magic*

Connections

Quentin couldn't tell anything had happened. Despite the horrific sounds that had raged, no trees lay tossed and torn, no huge branches littered the ground in the wake of the storm. Instead, the sun shone as if everything was perfect. Only the strange, tense feeling inside him gave him a reason to think otherwise.

Laura put her hands on her hips. "Which way, Romeo?"

He sighed. "You never give up, do you?"

"Of course not." Her voice sounded more serious than the question warranted. "You give up, you die." She looked at him, her brown eyes hard. "I choose not dying."

He looked away again, out at the spot where the thinning tree line met the tall grass. Toward the right, the sunlit fields glowed a rich gold. Toward the left, the meadow disappeared into a gray mist dotted with dead trees. The ground there was barely visible, but he could see enough to know what looked like grass and dirt were actually marsh and swamp.

"Great. Because I think we need to go that way."

She blinked. "Really?"

"Hey, I'd much rather take the nice happy golden road. Unfortunately, if we want to find Nova we need to take the dark, spooky swamp road." He shrugged. "Your choice."

She frowned but didn't give him any more grief. He took her silence as agreement and resumed walking. Surprisingly, the walking thing was not nearly as difficult today as it had been yesterday.

He remembered Thuaat's words of advice she had given him before they left. "It's not so much that yer body from there need remember how to work again, as that yer body from here must forget it ever couldn't. Ye ken?"

He wasn't sure he did, but at least his legs were working. As was the part about him being able to sense where Nova was.

"Yer blood is bound," Thuaat had explained, "as if a string connects you to them both. When they move, you feel the pull."

And he did. As soon as he'd left the tree he'd felt the tug.

"How do you know which one of them you're feeling? Laura asked.

Quentin looked up in surprise. You had to hand it to her, she might be pessimistic, but she paid attention.

"I don't."

She frowned but waited for him to go on.

"I feel the connections Thuaat talked about, but I can't tell which is which."

"So how do we know we're going in the right direction?"

"Right now, they both go this way."

"And when they split?"

He sighed. "Hopefully by then I can find a way to tell which one Nova is."

It wasn't much, but this strategy was more than they'd had when she'd followed him through the Divide and into another world. Besides, he couldn't think of any options.

An hour and forty thousand mosquitoes later, Quentin wasn't so sure about his plan anymore. The connection was faint at best, and the path through the blasted swamp twisted and turned, with small rises and dips that made him nauseous, like a nightmare roller-coaster ride through stinky cheese soup. Then, of course, there was the fact he couldn't see more than a few feet at a time, yet the bugs all seemed to have thermal vision.

He stumbled over a hidden rock, tripping and splashing into the murky water. His feet were already soaked from the dozen times he'd fallen before, but this time the water sloshed up over his sock and halfway up his leg. He swore and shook his leg, feeling the heaviness of wet denim as the rotted stench reached his nose.

"You okay?"

And, of course, there was Laura, staring at him like some stupid kid who couldn't take care of himself. "Great," he snapped. "Never better."

She raised an eyebrow but didn't say anything else. He shouldn't be surprised. She couldn't care less if they found Nova or not. Wasn't like she'd come with him because of how much she liked them both. No, she'd come here for her own reasons.

He pushed past her.

"Maybe we should stop to eat."

He spun around, incredulous. "In here? This place reeks. I couldn't eat in here if my life depended on it."

She frowned. "You sure you're okay? I can take the lead for a bit if you want."

Oh sure. That would suit her just fine. "I don't think so." No way would he let her take the lead. Hadn't they used his blood? He was the one who could feel where to go, not Laura—

One moment the ground was there, the next moment his foot found only air followed quickly by swamp. Thick slimy green muck sucked at him, feeling more like sand than liquid. The murky water beneath was surprisingly deep. He tried to kick back to the surface, but there was no light. No way to tell which direction was up. His fingers found only a rotted piece of wood that disintegrated in his grasp.

Panic seized him as his lungs started to burn. He needed air. He was going to drown. Bubbles slipped out his nose. If he took a breath, he'd suck in water. *Please, God, please.* He just needed to get out, to get a breath. *HELP!*

Something gripped his arm. About to scream, he realized he was being pulled up. Slime parted as he broke the surface and heaved in a rasping breath.

Thank You, God.

He blinked, expecting to see an angel all in gold pulling him to safety. Instead, he glimpsed what looked like a man covered in thick scars. Quentin blinked again, and the scars turned into twists of hair, surrounding not a man's face, but a girl's. Laura grabbed the back of his shirt and hauled him up onto solid ground. His arms and legs felt like spaghetti. All he could do was roll onto his back and breathe.

"Thanks," he said, when he could finally talk again.

"No sweat."

He squinted up at her. "Seriously."

She nodded but wouldn't meet his eyes. Apparently, she wasn't used to people thanking her for things.

He closed his eyes again and simply enjoyed being still. "My dad tried to pull me out of a mud puddle once. He threw his back out." He heard a snort of laughter and smiled. "Seriously. You're like the friggin' Hulk. Only not as green."

She shoved him, and he laughed.

"Come on, Romeo. Let's keep walking. I want out of this stupid swamp."

Agreed. He tried his legs. They were wobbly but otherwise good. "You lead," he said with a nod.

She nodded back.

He didn't know what had gotten into his head earlier. He was eager to leave the muck and bugs behind. Not to mention the stench. "I'm sorry about earlier."

She looked around, brows pulled low. "I think it's this place."

"Me too."

"But I forgive you for being such a wad."

He saw the grin and shook his head. "You're turning out to be nothing like the Neanderthal girl we thought you were."

She lifted one brow. "Neanderthal?"

"Well, come on. You do take things a bit far sometimes, what with bashing people and all."

Laura shook her head. "She likes you this way, does she?"

"Who, Nova?" He grinned. "Of course."

"For what it's worth, you two aren't exactly like I thought you were either."

He opened his mouth to respond, but a flash of light hit him in the eye. He looked up, startled. "Hey, see that?"

From a tiny part in the gray curtains, a single ray of sunlight shone. Ahead, the mist thinned. They picked up their pace, and a few minutes later they found the end of the swamp. The gray parted completely, and they were in a small valley, framed by rolling hills of green.

"Let's put some miles between us and this bog, then we can grab some lunch."

Laura's suggestion sounded awesome, and he agreed. He let her continue to lead the way. They would stop to eat, take time to rest, and get back to normal. *Then* he could break the news that the two threads pulling him had indeed split, and he had no idea which way to go.

Edah

Nova took a breath, counting to five before she exhaled. She concentrated on holding her arms steady, closing one eye and using the other to sight along her arm to the point of the arrow. Then she shifted her focus from the arrow to the blur of gray just visible on the other side of the clearing. The fat little bird had its head down, plucking at grass and roots.

You know this. It's an equation.

Her teeth tugged at her bottom lip.

Height plus velocity should generate angle. Compensate for the wind.

When she thought she had the right one she let her fingers uncurl. The bowstring pinged as the arrow launched, sailing up and over the bird by a dozen feet before landing in a tree.

"Ugh!"

The little bird looked up, its birdy eyes dancing as if mocking her, then went back to eating.

She tossed the useless bow on the ground. "It's no use. I can't do this."

Seth, who had told her as much earlier when trying to hand her yet another piece of fruit, shook his head. There was only one thing she hated more than being bad at something, and that was someone telling her she couldn't do it at all.

Nova was sick to death of fruit. Her body demanded more meat. Even with the horses, they were expending more physical energy than she was used to. Unfortunately, there were no protein bars or shakes she could whip up to give herself extra fuel.

Growling she picked the bow back up and grabbed another arrow. She tried to fit the bowstring into the little split on the back end, but the taut cord slipped off, slapping her arm and leaving a red mark. The welt made good company next to the eight matching ones that scored her skin.

"Here."

A dark hand thrust a piece of leather at her. She turned, startled, as brick-red waves curled through the air.

Stone avoided looking at her, his brows still pushed down in a frown, but he slipped the piece of leather over her forearm to cover her wounds.

By the shape she realized the covering was meant for exactly this purpose. He guided the arrow deftly onto the string.

She looked at him in amazement as he pushed the bow toward her.

"Sight," he said, nodding his chin toward the clearing where the fat little bird still marched, stuffing its face in defiance.

She was astonished he had decided to speak to her. She didn't want to break the spell. She pulled back on the string without a word. The piece of leather protected her arm, absorbing the sensations where the string brushed her skin. She held the bow steady as she sighted the point of the arrow at the bird.

"Now," a soft voice said near her ear, "do not concentrate on the arrow. Concentrate on the bird."

Confused, but willing to let him show her, she let her focus shift.

"Do not just see the bird. Sense it. Feel it."

Sense the bird? How? She watched as the hen hopped from one foot to the other, turning its head to listen for little grubs, using its beak to root them out before starting again.

Hop. Hop. Tap.

Listen.

There was a pattern.

Like magic.

"What do you see?"

"I see a dance," she whispered.

She didn't turn to look at him, but when he spoke, she thought she heard a smile in his voice. "This is the bird's Edah, its life force."

The dance was the pattern. The pattern was the magic.

"Use the bird's Edah to draw the arrow. Let the magic flow from one to the other."

She wasn't sure what that meant, but she pictured lines connecting all the strange movements. Then she imagined another line being drawn back to her, connecting at the tip of the arrow.

"When you can see the connection, let go."

She let the arrow fly. The shaft zipped neatly across the clearing.

Direct hit.

She turned in amazement. "How did you—"

He'd already walked away from her. He crossed the clearing and picked up the bird, stopping to gather her stray arrows. When he came back, he handed her the shafts but kept the bird. He knelt on the ground and gently removed the arrow from its chest. Then he placed both of his palms on the bird and closed his eyes.

"One God, we thank you for the gift of this bird's Edah you have provided for us to eat, and whose life continues the great circle."

Nova hadn't wanted to kill, but Stone's respectful prayer helped her not to feel so guilty. With sure hands, he prepared the bird. When the meat was in the pan cooking, he dug up some roots and added them. Soon a savory aroma came from the pot. He dished the food into bowls, making sure each of them got a generous portion of meat.

Seth looked impassive as he accepted a dish.

"Thank you," Nova said when Stone handed her a bowl.

Their quiet captive still didn't meet her eyes, but he gave her a small nod.

"What you did … that was amazing."

"It is nothing," he said quietly. "It is the way of my people."

And is it the way of your people to kill a girl you don't even know? Even as the thought slipped into her head, she realized the answer might be yes. He'd helped her to kill the bird after all. Maybe killing her was a gift of her *Edah.* Maybe her life would be used to continue the great circle.

Everything was so complicated. He'd started out as a nameless face, a threat needing to be stopped. Now he was a real person, with his own beliefs.

"What's your name?"

His mouth twitched. "Am I not a stone?" He glanced at Seth, who made a point to be busy eating. Stone's mouth curved upward as he shook his head. "My name is Viru."

"That was really incredible, using the magic to—"

"That wasn't magic." Seth cut in.

They both looked up, startled. Seth's unpleasant look had darkened into anger.

He looked at Nova. "You want to learn magic? Come on. Let's learn."

He stomped to the other side of their small camp. Nova didn't want to follow him, not with him behaving like this, but she didn't want to pass up a chance to learn more about her magic, regardless of Seth's attitude.

She gave Viru an apologetic look as she got up to follow, but his eyes tracked Seth, who picked up a stick and brushed his hand over a spot of dust on the ground. He drew a small round dot circled with a thin line. Then, starting at the center, he drew a line straight down, intersecting the line like an upside-down cross.

"This is the symbol for Creative," he said looking up at her.

The figure reminded her of something she'd seen before.

"Imagine it's an atom of life, and you're pulling energy out to create something more. You see?"

Goosebumps erupted on her arms. She nodded.

He erased the intersecting line at the bottom and added a line with pointed waves. "This is the symbol for fire. It's like the other but adds more. The shape displays what you want to create."

He stared at her.

Nova scowled. "What?"

"Try to push your power at the fire."

Push her power at the fire? How on earth did she do that?

"Focus. Let the image fill your mind."

She stared at the lines. She could see how they could represent the creation of fire. Pulling energy out and using the power to create those little flame-waves. But how did she make actual fire happen?

"Now feel your magic. Try to see it."

But there was no sound. How did she see magic without sound?

"Think of what you saw in the park."

She wondered if he'd mentioned the park for Viru's benefit, to remind him of what had happened. Whatever she'd done then wasn't happening now.

Frustration built, making her head throb. "I don't know how."

"Just picture it, Nova. Picture the fire."

She tried, but this wasn't like her drawings, where they just came to her when she wasn't trying.

"Concentrate."

"I am."

"Try harder. You know you can do this, you did it in the park."

"I don't know how—"

"You do. Feel the magic. Push it out."

Anger built up inside her. How did he expect her to understand?

"Come on, Nova. *Do it.*"

"I don't know *how!*" The bright orange of her words flew at him. At the last moment, they curved toward the ground where they landed on the drawing. The lines blazed orange, then red, and suddenly they were burning. There was a flash, and the entire spot burst into a bright flame, so hot she had to back up a step.

Then the fire sputtered out, leaving only a black, charred spot.

"I'm sorry," Nova gasped. "I didn't know."

Seth grinned as he looked up at her.

Nova frowned. "You did that on purpose."

"Of course, I did." He laughed. "Anger is one of the best ways to draw out your emotion, and your power." He glanced in Viru's direction. "Your *real* power."

"Jerk," she muttered. "I might have hurt somebody."

He scuffed the dirt with his heel. "Wrong medium. This was nothing but dust."

"But back in the park, you said I could have hurt someone."

He nodded. "Your form was internal. The design came from inside you. Like I said, there's never been a Trine before. Hard to know what you can do."

Seth picked up his things and headed for the horses. Viru moved to block his way.

Seth scowled. "What?"

Viru shook his head. "What you did is not right." He motioned at her. "Using anger, forcing the Edah to respond—this is wrong." He looked up, and for the first time, his dark eyes met Nova's. "A corruption of the gift."

Seth's face was dark and frightening. He tossed his head back and laughed. "Oh, come on." He rolled his eyes. "Enough with the native bit. Magic is logical. It's mathematical. The formula you use can be one thing or another. That doesn't make it evil."

A dark shape swept past her.

Nova froze.

Her eyes followed the movement as the shadow swept over a rock and through the grass, then curved back towards her. A cry from overhead drew her eyes upward. A crow landed on a tree branch. The black bird looked down at them with shining eyes and let out a caw.

There was a strange noise, like thousands of sheets ruffling in the wind. The sky darkened around them. Nova stared as a black cloud ebbed and flowed against the sky. She didn't understand what she saw. Then a small shadow split from the rest, and realization hit her. Birds. Thousands— no, there had to be hundreds of thousands of them. The noise was inconceivable. They writhed and surged like waves on a never-ending sea. The undulating mass turned, swirling toward them. Birds of every shape and size began to land in the trees and bushes, covering every branch. Little brown chickadees, huge black crows, sparrows, robins, even birds she'd never seen before.

The horses stomped and snorted as the birds swarmed like bees.

Still they came. Millions. The trees became living things. Birds covered the ground. They looked at her with glittering, stony eyes.

Maybe I shouldn't have killed the hen.

Like a switch being flipped, they went silent. Nova had never been so afraid in all her life. She looked at Seth, but he looked as confused and afraid as she was.

It was Viru who broke the spell. "Cyclorn." He spoke with a low urgency.

Seth's head snapped up. He stared at Viru. When he turned to Nova, his face was pale. "We need to get out of here."

She managed to pick up her pack amid the throng of birds. Their soft little bodies brushed her hand.

"Hurry," Seth's voice was softer this time, which frightened her all the more.

She ran. The birds swirled out of the way. The boys grabbed her and rushed her toward the horses. Nova could still feel the thousands of fowl eyes on her as she flung her pack onto her horse.

Viru leapt onto his horse. He turned to her, mouth opening to speak, but froze before the words could come. He stared over her shoulder, dread shining from his eyes. Whatever they had been running from, whatever the swarm of birds heralded, had arrived.

A cold hand wrapped around her heart. Slowly, Nova turned around.

The stallion was one of the most beautiful things she'd ever seen. Midnight flanks shimmered. Muscles twitched delicately along its back and sides. Sleek black silk draped over the curved neck, ending at a velvety nose. Eyes like obsidian stared. But what took her breath away was the object nestled between the eyes, swirling with colors like a dark rainbow. In the fairy tales, unicorns were white. This was more impressive.

Cyclorn.

"Don't move." Seth's tense voice confused her. Why would he be afraid of this amazing creature? The cyclorn was beautiful … magical.

The beast tossed its head, snorting softly. Muscles quivered, and one hoof gently pawed at the ground. The colors on the horn moved and whorled, making scenes of sunrises and soaring vistas.

"Magnificent," Nova whispered.

"Look away, Nova. Look at me."

Why on earth would she not want to look at such an incredible sight?

A flash of silvery-white flew over her head. The arrow landed in the dirt near the glossy hooves. The cyclorn reared. A horrid scream filled the air, like knives on stone. All of the stallion's dark beauty evaporated. His eyes turned flat and cold. The horn's swirling colors sucked away the light.

Something touched her arm. She choked back a scream.

"Come on!" Seth wrapped his hand around her wrist and dragged her after him.

Her legs were like lead. She wanted to run away, but she wanted to go back. She had to see the beast one more time. Instead, Seth pushed her onto the saddle behind Viru, who kicked his heels against the horse's flanks. Nova could only grab on as they thundered into the tall grasses. Behind her, the birds rose into the air with the sound of rising thunder, masking the horrible squeal of the cyclorn.

Seth raced up beside them, leaned over his horse's neck, his hand fisted around the lead rope of Nova's rider-less horse. They rode until the horses were too winded to continue.

The flames of the fire did little to dispel the chill. The echo of the birds and the memory of the sight of them all flying at once filled Nova's mind. "What was that?"

Seth misunderstood her question. "A cyclorn. They're very rare."

She shuddered. "The sound was so awful."

"The dark magic lured the beast." Viru looked at Seth.

"It wasn't *dark* magic," Seth snapped. "It was just magic." Nova looked up, drawn out of her reverie as Seth kicked at a rock. "Still, I should have realized."

She frowned. "Should have realized what?"

Seth looked at the ground as he spoke. "Cyclorns feed on magic. It draws them. The more power, the stronger the attraction."

So much for the whole unicorns being drawn to innocence and purity thing.

"With the amount of power you have, it's no wonder that thing was drawn to us. We'll have to be careful from now on."

The list of things to be careful of seemed to be mounting up.

"He was so beautiful." The image kept playing in her mind.

Viru's hand on her arm startled her. "Best not to dwell," he said. "Thoughts can be magic too."

"You have to remember things are different here. Don't trust … anything." Seth's voice caught on his words. "Lots of beautiful things are deadly. Like the beast's horn." He shivered. "I've never seen anything so black."

Nova shook her head in confusion. "But there were so many colors."

Seth and Viru glanced at each other.

"You saw colors?" The brick-red curls of Viru's voice were ridged with tension.

"Of course." Hadn't they? "It was like … like oil on water: a whole rainbow of colors, swirling and moving. I could see things. Beautiful things."

Seth studied her face with a frown.

"I don't get it," she said. "You didn't see them? I thought you were a Zen like me."

"The cyclorn's horn is different." Viru's dark eyes were mixed with sadness and compassion. "You were seeing the magic the cyclorn has stolen."

"Stolen?"

"Cyclorns feed on a person's magic." Seth's voice was heavy with meaning. "All of it."

A tremor started deep inside her. "And that destroys them?"

He looked away. "Completely." He was quiet for a few minutes before he continued. "Magic is … it's part of you. Like your skin or your blood. It's not something you can live without."

She sensed there was some hidden meaning in Seth's words. Her heart hurt to think beauty could contain such evil.

Threa was wondrous and beautiful, and also dark and frightening. How could she learn to use her magic if things like the cyclorn would be drawn to her? If someone who seemed as genuine and peaceful as Viru wanted her dead? How was she supposed to overcome that?

A nearby branch snapped. She turned, fearing more dark beasts, but saw only a man coming toward them from the darkness, his clothes barely more than rags. Worn sandals covered his feet. Beneath a dusty cowl, Nova glimpsed a face twisted with scars.

Magic Message

"You should eat something."

Nothing was working. She needed a stronger medium. What was stronger than steel? She had a diamond ring. Using such a small stone would be hard, but not impossible.

"Mira."

She looked up. Zeke stood over her, his bushy eyebrows pulled down low over his bright blue eyes. She'd always loved his blue eyes. The way they danced with laughter, even when he wasn't laughing. She remembered them even as a little girl, always watching over her. They weren't laughing now.

He knelt in the dirt beside her and took her hands, looking at her fingers. They were dirty and torn, black with the repeated efforts to do the same spell over and over in different mediums.

"Mira," he said again as those striking eyes caught hers. "Listen to me. There's nothing you can do to get through."

Tears slipped soundlessly down her face. "I have to keep trying. I have to." God only knows what Lucien would do with her. She had to find a way to protect her baby, her flesh and blood. Inspiration hit her. "What if we use blood?"

His sadness changed to thoughtfulness. "We still wouldn't be able to get through," he muttered, "but maybe we don't have to."

She could see in his eyes he had an idea. Something terrible filled Mira. Something bright and warm and filled with the potential to crush her.

Hope.

"I think I remember a passage about sending something through. Not a person, but something." His hands were strong even now, dusted with white hair instead of dark. They pulled her to her feet. "I'll need you to help me find the book."

She could do that. She could help him find his idea, and then he could tell her what they could do to get to Nova.

His room, once the den, was now more of a sleep-in library. Shelves lined three of the four walls and surrounded two sides of the bed. Even the dresser was covered with books stacked almost to the ceiling.

"What does it look like?"

He tapped his lip. "It's small. Leather. Brown or red, I think."

She went immediately to the nearest shelf and started scanning. She stopped as she realized she was flying past them so quickly she might miss the one they were looking for and went back to the beginning. This time she made a mental note of each spine. Black, black, white, yellow, green, brown—but not leather. Her eyes moved from book to book, then from shelf to shelf, first in one direction, then the other. Blue ... Red! She stopped, pulling the book from the shelf. The cover felt supple in her hands. There were symbols on it.

"That's the one." Zeke lifted the book from her hands. He switched on a small lamp, turning the pages with care. "Here. This is it."

Excitement and hope rose like buoys as she perched next to him.

"Listen." His finger traced the page. "The act requires a gap in the flow of the Divide to allow a physical form to pass through, an interruption of Neutral. However, it is speculated that for *magic* to pass through, there is no physical form. Therefore, no interruption would be required in order to pass magic from one place to the next." He looked up. "This is from the documents about the transports, when they were used to send information and messages from one region to the next."

"So ... what?" She tried to understand. "You think we can send magic through instead of us?"

"Exactly."

"But what would that do? How would we reach her?"

He looked back down. "The passage goes on to explain about the two end points. I think we need to have something to anchor her location on the other side. I'm not sure what that would be, but if we can think of something, then I think we could send her some kind of message."

The idea was still vague, but better than none at all. "Would she be able to respond?"

"I don't know. This isn't commonly done anymore." He looked at her and his face softened. "But Nova isn't exactly common either." His smile ignited her hope like a spark to tinder. "She did, after all, manage to get herself across the Divide without us."

"Do you really think she's the one who opened the hole?"

"I'm almost certain. Although I don't think she's the one who closed it."

Now that there was a glimmer, a measure of hope, the fog of panic that had enveloped Mira's mind started to clear. "Quentin."

He nodded, clearly pleased she'd had the same thought. "He's a block. He has to be. His going through must have caused a rift wave, like the water being sucked out of a harbor ahead of a tsunami."

"And the Divide began collapsing in on itself in the wake."

"The only question," he said with a careful turn of his eyes, "is where the tsunami wave is headed."

"Threa was the last side open, so the wave would have moved in that direction." She let the possibility play out in her mind. "But if Quentin really is a block, then Nova will be protected by being with him. The wave should go around them. Magic wouldn't be able to exist where he is."

"Very likely."

But not a definite. He didn't have to say the words out loud.

"What kind of message should we send her?"

"I'll work on the specifics of the spell. You work on the message."

She nodded. "And in the meantime, I'll call Dee and Richard again. Let them know this *project* the kids are working on might take longer than they thought. Hopefully, they'll be okay with letting Quentin stay here a while."

Zeke gave a half nod, already distracted by his thoughts on the spell they would need. "Let me know if you need me to do something to make them forget to worry," he said without looking at her.

"I think I can manage a little Neutral if I need to," she said, inspecting her chewed up hands. A little Creative restoration might be in order as well.

On the way to the kitchen, she grabbed a notebook and a pen. She needed to think of something short, concise, and effective. Something to let Nova know that although her mother and grandfather could not get through, they were standing by. Something to warn her to stay away from Lucien.

Wardein

There is a Holy book that speaks of people called Wardein, guardians, protectors of the people. They are said to contain a light so bright most cannot bear to look upon such brilliance. It is the light of the One God himself.

Some claim to have seen these travelers, although most have not, and many believe their existence is pure legend. One thing is certain: those who claim to have met a Wardein are easy to spot, for they are forever changed by the encounter.

—High Wizard Ezekial, on the *Factors of Magic*

THE HIGH KING

"I am far-traveled and weary. Might I sit and warm myself before moving on?"

His voice was gold. Nova had never seen anything that compared. And not just gold, but a deep, vibrant color so rich it was like looking at a river of liquid fire despite a voice so soft she had to strain to hear his words.

The stranger pulled back his hood to reveal scars covering his head and body. The thick twists of skin made him appear hunched. Even his face seemed distorted. As she studied him, another countenance shimmered under the scarred one. A face so beautiful it made her blink back tears. Then the mirage was gone, and the scarred man's lips twisted into a smile.

"*Wardein*," Viru breathed.

Seth's body jerked as if the word seared him.

The man smiled at each of them. "I'm afraid I'm just an old man on a long journey. My name is Salamain."

"Where are you headed, old man?" Seth asked as Nova laid a blanket down for him to sit on, and Viru scrambled to get him a bowl of their rewarmed stew.

"Home."

His single-word answer sent a glorious shiver up and down Nova's spine, confusing her. Why would his answer make her feel so excited and strange? Maybe she'd been enthralled with the gorgeous wave of gold flowing around him like wide ribbons, forming a robe that covered his rags.

Sidestepping the evasive answer, Seth asked, "What brought you on your long journey?"

The man looked at Seth for a long moment before answering. His eyes sparkled from inside his mask of ravaged skin. "A friend needed me."

Then he turned those sparkling eyes on Nova. "What brings you on your long journey?"

Nova felt suddenly sure, down to the roots of her hair, this man knew she wasn't from Threa at all, as if he already knew who she was and that she'd come across the Divide. Maybe even why she was here.

"A friend needed me," she answered, feeling a smile turn up the ends of her lips at their shared mischief.

The man raised a finger. "Perhaps more than one, yes?"

She laughed out loud, feeling the wonderful release her reaction brought. How long since she'd last really laughed?

The man patted her knee with his gnarled hand. "The important thing is that you are where you chose to be."

She tilted her head. "What do you mean?"

"Life is filled with choices. We all must live with the ones we make. It is important to accept this." He paused a beat. "Some never do."

Nova caught sight of Viru standing behind them, his face slack with amazement. His hands, holding the bowl of food, shook ever so slightly. Salamain turned and patted the ground beside him.

"Come. Eat with me. I will tell you a story."

Viru knelt in the dirt, handing him the bowl with reverence. The man took the dish and smiled.

"Once, when I was young like you, I went on a journey to see the High King to petition him to help our village." The gold spun from Salamain's voice, wrapping around them in waves. Even Seth sat down to listen. "We were desperate, you see, for we had no healer, and our village was overcome with a dark scourge. Not one family was untouched. Many had more than one who were ill, and nothing seemed to help.

"The High King, we'd heard, had several healers in his great city. Surely, he could spare one. When my own father fell ill, I knew I could wait no longer. I took our best horse and set out. What I didn't know at the time was the King's city had been hidden with magic for protection and did not stay in one place. No one had seen the shining gates for many years, and some said the city did not even exist. We were on our own. Best if I gave up and went to be with my family.

"But I was young and determined. I followed each rumor and trail, until one day I found myself in a great valley. The place was dry as a bone. Dust and sand blew where once water had flowed, but no more. Those who wandered in often did not come back out. I let my horse go free and walked into the valley. I followed the great stones that had once directed the path of the water, using them as markers when the air around me shimmered with heat and tried to fool my eyes. The sun drained my body of moisture.

"If I hadn't fallen onto my knees, I might never have found what I'd been looking for. There, hanging in midair, was a light that did not belong in the valley. I reached out, and my hand disappeared into the glow."

Goose flesh broke out from Nova's scalp to her toes.

"I could have turned around—could have hesitated to go forward or looked back at what I was leaving behind, but I didn't. I kept my eyes on the light, and I walked on. Though brighter than the sun, the light didn't burn. When I blinked, the valley was gone. Before me spread a lush field of green, fed by a crystal-clear stream, and beyond the field shone a city of gold.

"There were children playing and animals grazing. None of them noticed me as I passed. I wondered if perhaps I had died in the barren valley after all, and my spirit had moved on without its shell. Yet when I arrived at the great gates, the guards looked down at me. 'What business?' they asked. I tried to stand straight and look older than I was. 'I'm here to see the King.'

"I expected them to turn me away. To have to beg or convince them. Instead, they stood aside to let me pass. The guard on the left pointed toward a structure built of gold and threaded with veins of shining silver. 'There,' he said. 'Hurry, so you don't miss him.'

"I hurried up the path and into the golden hall. Two more guards were at the inner door and ushered me into a large room. On one side there was a table covered with food. People were there, eating. On the other, there was a fountain fed by a spring. At the far end of this great hall, I saw a throne covered in jewels and sitting on the throne, a man. His hair was white and his eyes a purer gold than anything around him. On his head, he wore a crown of alabaster. Light shone out in all directions. 'Come, weary traveler,' he said to me. 'What do you seek?' I found myself on my knees before his majesty. 'Please,' I asked him. 'My village is besieged with a scourge, and many are ill. We need a healer.'

"He did not quickly respond. Rather, he studied me. When finally he spoke, he asked me this. 'What would you give me in return?' I didn't understand. I had nothing. I'd left my horse behind. I had no coin or treasure of any kind. What could I give him? I had nothing but the rags on my back.

"Then I looked at my hands. They were dirty, but they were strong. My fingers were stained, but they could play a lute. My arms, shoulders, and back were sunburned, but they could carry a weight, or wield a sword. My feet were crusted with mud and dirt, but they could walk and run. Finally,

I turned my gaze back to the King. 'I have little to offer,' I told him, 'but I have myself, and that I give you freely.'

"He searched my face, to be sure I spoke true. Then he smiled—a smile like I have never seen before, nor will again. Then he held out his hand. 'I accept this offer,' he told me. 'Rise and be your father's son no longer. From this day forward, you are a son of the High King. Live in your village no longer, but dwell in my great city.' I could hardly believe his words. 'What about the ones who are sick?' I asked. 'Who will take the healer to them?' And his face shone like the sun when he said to me, 'Your people are already healed. The day I sensed you coming, I sent the healer to them.'"

The scarred man's words hung in the air around the campfire. His golden voice spun images in Nova's mind. She saw the great city, the hall, and the King sitting on his throne.

This was no mere story.

He'd said he was going home. "Are you going back to your old village now?" she asked.

"No, child." Salamain shook his head. "I left that village behind long ago. Now I am a traveler for the King."

Her breath caught in her throat. "Then … you're on your way back to the great city."

He smiled, and in the darkness, she saw again the shimmering image of another face behind the scarred one.

Salamain turned to Viru. "Thank you for sharing your fire and your food."

Viru bowed his head, and without a word he took the empty bowl.

"It is time for me to go," their visitor said.

Seth stood and dusted off his pants. "I'll fix you something to take with you." He disappeared into the darkness beyond the light of the fire.

The old man started to stand, and Viru rushed to help him. "Please," Viru said softly, "may I come with you?"

The old man put his hand on Viru's shoulder. "Your path will someday lead you to that door," he said gently, "but not this day."

Viru's shoulders drooped but he nodded.

"For now, the King has need of you here."

Viru jerked his head upward.

"A storm is coming. One unlike any this land has ever seen. Before another day is through, the tempest will reach you. Be ready."

Viru stood tall and gave a firm nod.

Salamain turned to Nova. His warm smile filled her with images of the green field and the golden city. "Until we meet again."

Like a dream, he slipped back into the night.

CAUGHT

The good news was Quentin wouldn't have to admit to Laura he didn't know which way to go. Of course, that was because he was tied up and heaped like a sack of flour in this putrid wagon. That was the bad news, he supposed.

He still couldn't believe Itchy and Scratchy, as he'd come to think of their captors, had managed to get the jump on them. He'd kick himself if his legs weren't tied to the rail behind him. He couldn't even curse, thanks to the filthy rag in his mouth. He'd be lucky if he didn't catch something awful from the grimy thing.

Laura wasn't in much better shape. Other than this gag, she was as trussed as he was.

"You idiot," Laura hissed. "If you'd kept quiet we could be planning something now." She rolled her eyes. "You can't help yourself, can you? Sarcasm just comes out like sweat."

Yes, well, he couldn't argue with her. Literally.

She took a deep breath, as if hearing his thoughts. "Okay, listen. I'm thinking these bozos will have to stop to eat soon. When they do, I think we should try to roll out of here." Her forehead scrunched together as she thought.

She either didn't see him or ignored him as he shook his head violently side-to-side.

"*Mmmff.*"

"It won't be easy, but we might be able to get close enough for one of us to untie the other one."

Was she nuts? Itchy and Scratchy may be the saddest, weakest thugs ever, but they had weapons. Guns, from the look of them, although he couldn't be sure. You don't ask questions with a weapon snugged up against the back of your head.

He pressed the back of his tongue against his throat to try and get some moisture into the right spot before swallowing.

"*Mmme cffft. Gffss.*"

"What?"

"Gffss!"

"Give it up, Romeo. I can't understand you."

He made a strangled noise not too far from real. She could be so stubborn sometimes. "*Ppww. Ppww.*" He tried to imitate the sounds of gunshots, then jerked his head toward the front of the wagon. "*Gffss.*"

"Guns?"

He heaved a sigh of relief, nodding.

"So what?"

So what? So everything! They weren't going to be much good if they got themselves killed. How could she not know that? Was she not even thinking?

"They'll have to set them down to eat."

Oh, for crying out loud. Just when he'd thought they'd been making some headway.

"Besides, if we're quiet, maybe they won't notice."

Sure. That was likely.

He didn't bother to try to talk through the gag. Laura was going to try something crazy no matter what he thought. She'd end up getting them both killed.

He was so stupid. What had he been thinking, chasing after Nova like that? Did he think he was some superhero who could fly off into the air and scoop her up? Shield her from bullets with his ego? He should have gone for Zeke. The old man might dress cuckoo, but anyone who bothered to look could see there was more to him.

Of course, knowing what he knew now about this other world business, Quentin was pretty sure there was a *lot* more to Zeke—though not certain why he hadn't noticed sooner.

More self-kicking was in order. Good thing his legs were tied up, or he'd be giving himself one heck of a beating.

Crap.

Laura was right. He couldn't turn the sarcasm off.

He closed his eyes and tried to think. He had to find a way to get them out of this. Before he suffocated for real from this wretched rag.

One thing at a time. He couldn't get loose, but maybe he could get the rag out if he tried.

He pushed at the material with his tongue, then stopped himself before gagging. This thing was horrid. Steeling himself and trying to breathe only through his nose, he tried again. The grimy rag shifted but not by much.

Okay, so pushing the cloth out of his mouth was probably not going to happen. Maybe he could push the rag between his teeth instead of behind them. At least then he would be able to keep the grimy thing off his tongue.

"Hey, Romeo," Laura whispered.

Quentin ignored her. He was busy. And he was getting a little sick of the Romeo bit.

"Yo, Q-Tip, I think we have a problem."

Q-Tip? He glared at her, but she looked beyond him. He twisted his head around to peer behind him. The wagon blocked most of his view, but between the slats he glimpsed something moving. Were those more horses?

"Hold." A loud voice shouted.

"We're on business for the Lady." The scrawny short guy Quentin had dubbed Itchy shouted back.

Horse gear jangled as the new arrivals came alongside. "You think we don't know you're Ishtar's men, you sorry sack of bones? You'd be dead already if you weren't."

Itchy gave a haughty sniff that ended up sounding more like a kid in serious need of a tissue. Quentin hoped to heaven the rag in his mouth wasn't what the guy had been using before now. He strained as hard as he could, finally working the gag between his teeth. He clenched his jaw. Most of the fabric was between his lips. If he could … push …

His bottom lip got under the fabric, and with a last thrust of his tongue the nasty thing pushed down onto his chin. *Yes!* He wiggled his jaw and the rag slipped off his face, hanging around his throat like a filthy necklace.

"What do you want with us, then?" Scratchy whined.

"To give you more prisoners to deliver."

"But we ain't got enough—"

Scratchy's whiny voice was cut off with a grunt.

"Shut up, you idiot. More prisoners mean more pay," Itchy growled.

"Besides," the man Quentin couldn't see added, "it wasn't a question."

There was a scuffling noise. Laura glanced toward the back of the wagon. Quentin followed her gaze. Two men dressed in gray dragged a woman and little girl between them.

"You have no right to do this," the woman said.

The men ignored her. One of them lifted the girl and put her into the back of the wagon. When Quentin looked at her, she smiled. She seemed calm for a girl being hauled off with her mother and handed over to the likes of Itchy and Scratchy. Her eyes were dark and warm. Quentin smiled back at her.

The woman snatched her arm away from the man holding her and climbed into the wagon on her own.

Another man in gray circled his horse around to the back, his face hard. "We have every right. All healing commits the receiver's family to ten years of service. This is the law you chose to accept when you settled within these lands."

"Ishtar was not the one who healed my daughter."

"No," the man said, "an outlaw did."

"He was Wardein."

"He broke the law." The man stared off into the distance. "You are fortunate not to be put to death for treason instead of being offered sanctuary."

"Prison, you mean."

The man's eyes narrowed dangerously. "You would be wise not to anger the one who feeds and protects you."

"Interesting form of protection," Quentin muttered.

The man's gaze flicked to him. "Who are you?"

"Well, I'm not some jerk who roughs up women and kids, if that's what you mean."

A muscle twitched in the man's jaw. He yanked his reins to the side and rode out of sight. Quentin heard horses' hooves come around the wagon, to where he was trussed to the side like a turkey.

"You are obviously a stranger here," a voice hissed from behind him, "so I will give you leniency. Ishtar's personal guards will not be so merciful."

The thunder of hooves shook the ground as the men rode off, leaving them alone with Itchy and Scratchy, who started the wagon moving again without conversation. As they bounced over the rutted ground, the woman turned to Quentin.

"Thank you," she said softly.

"For what?" He shifted a bit. "As you can see, I am not exactly in a position to help anyone."

She stared at him, her eyes sharp and bright. "You drew his attention so he would let us be."

The little girl patted his cheek with her hand.

"This is Rose," the woman said with a wider smile. "I am Morra."

"I'm Quentin. This is Laura."

The girl, Rose, looked up at Laura. "Are you his sister?"

Laura pursed her lips. "No."

"I have a brother. His name is Jacob." The girl looked down, playing with the fabric of her smock. "He and Daddy went to find me some medicine but didn't come back."

Quentin glanced at Morra. She turned and gazed out over the grass. "They must have gone very far," she said, "to be gone this long."

Rose's eyes misted.

"I'll bet they stopped on the way to pick you flowers," he said.

Rose looked up at him.

"Yep, a girl as pretty as you, I'm sure your Daddy said, 'we can't go home without flowers for Rose and her mommy.' I'll bet they're picking you a whole bucket full."

She smiled.

"I'll bet they look kind of silly, two boys carrying all those flowers."

Her smile widened.

"And the bees …"

At this she giggled—a lovely laugh. She looked like Nova when they were younger, her face all lit up and happy.

He looked up and caught Laura staring at him. "What?"

"Nothing," she said, shaking her head. "I just … that was nice what you did."

What could he say? Of all the things he'd thought would impress someone like Laura Hennigan, being nice to a little girl wasn't one of them.

Morra touched his arm as she leaned over him, and he startled.

"Hey. Stop that." Itchy yelled.

"I'm helping him to sit up," she replied, not stopping.

Something loosened. Quentin's feet dropped to the floor of the wagon like dead weights, a morbid reminder of how they'd felt before coming to Threa. Then the blood began moving, and a million tiny knives speared him. He writhed as the sensation, unlike any he had ever known, spread to his shins.

Morra gave his legs a quick, firm rub, and the pain subsided. In a few minutes, he was able to drag them in front of him and sit up, his back cracking loudly in relief.

"Thanks." He closed his eyes and leaned his head back. His neck ached from all the craning to see what was happening.

Morra looked at him, dark eyes so much like her daughter's. "You're not from here, are you?" she asked.

"No. We're from far away, actually."

"How is it you came to be here?"

His heart skipped a beat until he realized she meant in the wagon, captured.

"Itchy and Scratchy up there jumped us."

Rose giggled. "Itchy and Scratchy."

Morra shook her head. "They are wretched men, but they are nowhere near as wretched as the woman who employs them."

"Employs?" Laura asked.

Morra nodded. "They are her henchmen. Sent out to round up stragglers and travelers crossing her land." She glanced at them, sitting in the wagon seat, and lowered her voice. "She uses those who are captured to work her fields."

"Free labor." Laura's mouth twisted.

"Good help is so hard to find these days," Quentin quipped.

"Is it really a prison?" Laura's words sounded curious, but Quentin knew better. She was trying to find out whether or not they'd be able to escape.

"It's a fortress," Morra answered, smashing their hopes. "There are two walls, both manned with guards. Inside them are the fields, and at the center is the compound. That is where they will take us." Her brown eyes were somber. "These men are terrible. The soldiers are devils, but Ishtar … she is as evil a sorceress as I have ever known." She looked at Laura and back at him. "No one has ever escaped from her so-called sanctuary."

Her words hung in the air like a verdict.

Storm Wave

Nova awoke to darkness. She rubbed her eyes, peering into a dim gray light.

"Is it dawn?"

Her internal clock said it should be, but where was the sun? Something rattled the leaves next to her. She jumped. Two chipmunks darted from the undergrowth.

Nearby, Seth sat up. "What's wrong?"

"Nothing, I ..." She stared as a flash of red zipped by. "Was that a fox?" After the birds and the cyclorn, the sight of the animals made her jumpy.

Viru sat up, rubbing his face. "Did you say fox?"

Nova opened her mouth to answer, but the words died away. She stared over Viru's shoulder as three deer came into view. Two does hurried through the trees. A large buck slowed to look at their group, head raised, before darting after them.

"What was that all about?" Seth sounded dazed.

Before anyone could answer, a gray shape the size of a German Shepherd trotted into view.

"Coyote," Seth whispered.

The gray beast shied around the edges of the campsite. Nova was amazed to see two rabbits follow a moment later.

"Prey following the hunters?" Viru's voice was tinged with concern.

The three of them looked at each other, then rushed to break camp.

Salamain's words echoed in Nova's head. "A storm is coming. One unlike any this land has seen before. Before another day is through, the tempest will reach you. Be ready."

The dark, heavy sky confirmed something was on the way. Something bad. They packed up and loaded the horses, soothing them as they worked.

"We need to find shelter." Seth's voice was subdued.

"We should head for the foot of the mountains. There will be caves there," Viru said.

Seth glared at the other boy but nodded.

Nova had no idea what kind of storm this could be, but a nice mountain cave certainly sounded like a good place to ride one out. Preferably a cave they could build a fire in. The temperature had plummeted, and she could feel the chill on her skin as the wind picked up.

The horses didn't need to be urged. As soon as the three riders were on, they took off at a run, breaking out of the trees and onto the flatter plains. No sooner had they cleared the forest than Seth pulled up his horse. He stared in horror at the sky. Nova drew her horse around to see what was wrong.

She had seen storms before. Once, she'd even seen a tornado, although it had been very small and didn't stay on the ground for very long. Still, the experience had been intimidating and awe inspiring at the same time. This … this was beyond anything she had seen before. The scene before her rivaled some of the movies she'd watched with what Quentin called "awesome digital cinematography and computer graphics."

A wall of black, boiling clouds stretched from sky to ground like a curtain of darkness. Streaks of red, green, and even blue lightning pierced the shroud like lasers. They speared the ground with explosions and left craters in the torn earth. Trees, grass, and rocks disappeared into the black void. Nova half expected the four horsemen of the apocalypse to ride out, skeletal hands pointing at the world they were about to devour.

"What *is* that?" Viru's voice captured all of the awe and horror Nova felt.

"Whatever it is, it's moving fast." Leave it to Seth to be all business. "We need to go. Now."

Nova's stallion agreed. He pawed the ground and pulled its head around, urging her to move. She released the reins. The beast gave a grateful shake of the head, turning to race away from the monstrous wall moving steadily toward them.

The three of them leaned over their horses' necks and let the beasts do what instinct told them to do.

Run.

If it weren't for what was chasing them, Nova would have found the ride exhilarating. They flew across the fields, the grass a blur underneath them. The outline of the mountains they were trying to reach appeared in the distance.

Too far. They would never make it.

The wind plucked at her. Her hair whipped her face and eyes until she had to close them. Gusts tried to unseat her. She clung to the solid warmth of her horse.

The world beyond her closed lids darkened. She risked a glance back. The shadow of the storm was on them. At the edge of the wall of blackness, rocks, branches, even what looked like a thatched roof flew like paper in the wind.

Nova's chest constricted. What would happen when the storm reached them? And it would. Of that there was no doubt. She didn't know what to do. She could only think to cling to the horse and pray they somehow survived.

Something jerked at her shirt. She gasped.

"Nova! Th … must … go … way!"

Another jerk and Nova nearly lost her hold on the horse. She squinted, trying to see through the wind and dirt blowing all around her.

Viru.

He pointed frantically.

She looked but saw only gray. Only the wind and branches—wait. Was that a door? Whatever she saw seemed to be built right into the ground.

"Root cellar," Viru shouted. "Go."

Nova nodded and pulled her horse in that direction, but the stallion didn't respond. She yanked the reins as hard as she could. The horse's eyes were white with panic as he fought her. This wasn't going to work. The horse was never going to stop. Not with the storm this close behind them.

In a flash, Nova realized what she had to do. Her hands worked faster than her brain, untying the pack she was curled around. Then she was leaping, her body airborne as the wind buffeted her. She landed on the pack and rolled to a stop. Viru grabbed Seth and pointed at her. No, he was pointing at the door. She turned around and spotted it, maybe fifty yards away. She half ran, half crawled, then gained her feet and sprinted for all she was worth.

It was like running in water. She went as fast and hard as she could, yet she barely moved. The wind gusted, knocking her sideways, and she fell onto her knees. The door was still twenty yards away. The wall of blackness was nearly on her.

Hands grabbed her, lifting her and propelling her forward. More hands on the other side. The three of them hurtled together for the door. She didn't see who opened it. She could barely see anything. They were flung inside, and the wind slammed the door behind them with enough force to crack the wood. Nova groaned, feeling grit between her teeth as she rolled onto her side on the dirt floor. Behind her, Viru grabbed bags from a stack along one side and moved them in front of the damaged door as a blockade.

"Will it hold?" She moaned.

"I don't know." Viru gasped. "The frame is built into the ground and hillside, so … hopefully."

As if in answer, the wind rattled the door. Thankfully, the blockade held.

Nova pushed herself across the dirt until her back met something solid. Barrels lined the back wall. She crawled between two of them, wedging herself in as deeply as she could. Around her, the small room slowly disappeared as a deeper darkness settled in. The sound of the lashing wind stilled for a heartbeat.

"It's here." Seth's whisper was like a pin drop in a moment of silence.

Then there was an unearthly moan as the storm arrived, and the world around them blinked out like an ember.

Sanctuary

She was possibly the most beautiful woman Quentin had ever seen. Hair the color of the summer sun flowed down her back in soft waves. Eyes a mix of light blue and violet were framed by long, thick lashes. Her nose was small and straight, and her lips were a perfect pink bow. The only thing to mar the image was the cruel sneer on those bow lips and the coldness that radiated from her periwinkle eyes.

Fingers tipped with long, sharp nails gripped his face and turned it one way then the other.

"Interesting," she breathed. "What are you?"

One could only assume she was overcome with his manly charms.

"I am a Quentin," he said with as much dramatic flair as he could muster.

A frown flittered across her brow before disappearing. "I cannot read you."

"No need. I am an open book."

Next to him, Laura sighed and shook her head ever so slightly. He could only assume she was, as usual, somewhat disagreeable to his choice of responses.

"I assume you're Ishtar, the lady we have heard so much about."

One of her delicate brows quirked upward. "Oh? You have heard of me?"

"Oh, yes. Your name is spoken in many circles."

"And what, exactly, do they say in these circles?"

"That you are a very powerful person," Quentin answered truthfully.

"A wise answer for so young a boy."

"Ah, but I am no ordinary boy."

Her eyes narrowed. "No, you are not."

She turned and glided more than walked to stand in front of Laura. She gave her the barest glance. "Weak Neutral," she said before moving on.

Quentin didn't bother to correct her, although Laura was anything but weak.

She stopped in front of Morra, and Quentin's stomach clenched.

"You thought to avoid payment for the healing of your girl?"

To her credit, Morra didn't look the least bit intimidated by Ishtar's demeanor or her beauty. She stared boldly into the other woman's eyes.

"I did not seek out this healer. He came of his own free will."

"Yes. I know." Her bow lips turned down in a frown. "Wardein. The folk of legend. The legion of the High King. The travelers." She shook her head. "Where is your Wardein now? I do not see him here to stand with you." She waved her hands to either side.

Morra didn't answer. It was obvious their beautiful jailer wasn't really looking for an answer. This was her stage, and she was giving a fine performance all on her own.

"The payment for healing is ten years from all family members. Since your husband and son are not found, I will add their payment to yours. Your daughter and you will work my fields for twenty years." She gave a sickening smile. "A fair price, I think, for the life of a child."

Morra smiled down at Rose, who bravely smiled back up at her mother. "I would pay any price for my daughter's life."

"Excellent." Ishtar clapped her hands together, and a guard quickly came forward. "Take the girls to the dormitory."

He snapped a bow and motioned for the women to move in the direction he indicated.

Laura gave Quentin a quick glance before turning to follow. Quentin wasn't sure, but he thought maybe her glance said something like, "Don't do anything stupid."

If they got out of this, they were going to need to work on her trust issues.

"Come, boy." Ishtar waved her clawed hand at him without turning around to see if he followed.

She led him away from the cart and up the steps of an enormous white square building. Columns lined the entire front side, reminding him of the Lincoln Memorial. Beyond them, two large doors opened to a room the size of his high school gymnasium.

"I guess slavery pays well," he muttered.

"What's that?" Ishtar turned sharply.

"Nothing."

This lady was a real hoot. Right out of a book on villains. Too bad this was not a book he could close and put away. He was stuck here, in her world, and in her so-called sanctuary. Hopefully they'd manage to get out of this unscathed, although the more he saw, the less hopeful he became.

The room was sparsely furnished, although he noticed the walls were covered in what looked like tapestries. Scenes of girls dancing, men hunting, and sword battles stretched in all directions.

A painting adorned the wall near the doors on the other side. The portrait was done with remarkable detail.

"Do you like it?" Ishtar purred.

He thought the painting made her look lovely. Gentle. Compassionate. "It doesn't do you justice."

Her smile was predatory.

They went out the door and continued down a hall, turning into an opening that revealed a flight of steps leading down. Quentin got a very bad feeling in the pit of his stomach. "Can I ask where we're going?"

"To visit a friend of mine."

"Does he wear a leather apron and have lots of ugly tools?"

Ishtar's laughter surprised him. The sound was clear and honest, the opposite of its owner. "I assure you, Sol does not wear any aprons. I doubt he's ever held anything uglier than a dinner fork."

Quentin could only hope she told the truth. She motioned for him to go ahead. Not that he had anywhere else he could go.

The lower level was darker. To his surprise, fires gave the area a warm feeling. Instead of a torture chamber or dungeon, he found a library. Rows upon rows of books surrounded the large space as far as the eye could see. And in the middle of the room there were several long tables. A solitary figure sat at one and looked up as they came down.

"Lady." He waited for her to acknowledge him with a small nod of her own. Only then did he look at Quentin. "A guest?"

"Yes," Ishtar said sitting down in one of the chairs. "A puzzle for you."

He quirked his head to the side, then came to stand in front of Quentin, looking him over like a prize pig at the county fair.

"He's a block."

Ishtar looked up in surprise. "Truly?"

"Well, I could have told you that," Quentin grumbled. "I've had several people tell me recently."

She ignored him. "How can that be?"

Sol's eyes glanced at him again, and Quentin thought there was something hidden in them. Something guarded.

"He's come through the Divide. I rather suspect he caused the storm."

Now, it was Quentin's turn to look up in surprise. "Storm?"

"Yes," Ishtar answered, staring at him from under her eyelashes. "It passed here two days ago. It's fortunate my people have such a talented protector. That gale was a rare and terrible beast."

He wondered if the irony was lost on her or intentional.

Then, as if a curtain was stripped away, her face changed. The catlike features hardened. She turned to Sol. "I want you to find out where he's been, how he came, and why he's here."

"Yes, Lady."

"You have my leave to do … whatever is necessary."

Ishtar walked away but paused beside Quentin and leaned toward him. "And yes," she hissed, "slavery pays quite well, as you will no doubt help to prove."

A small shiver of fear wormed its way through him. He'd underestimated her.

She slanted him an evil smile, then whisked herself back up the stairs, leaving him to worry what his newest captor had in mind.

Susceptible

Like any other part of the body, magic is susceptible and can be impacted by things outside the body, such as other magic, even in the form of a plant or organism.

Snare Weed uses a creature's magic to capture it. Felinius can corrupt or alter magic when touched and can kill if enough is ingested. Such plants are well known, and children are taught at a young age to avoid them.

Organisms can be much more dangerous, since they cannot be seen or easily avoided. The most fatal illness is the one that drains a body of its magic. If left unchecked, the disease rages through the individual, leaving only an empty husk with no essence of life remaining.

This illness is known as the Trench.

—High Wizard Ezekial, on the *Factors of Magic*

The Trench

Something was in here with them.

Nova closed her eyes and tried to squeeze herself into an even smaller ball. Outside, the storm raged, ripping, tearing, and crashing. Inside, there was cold and darkness, and a sense of something else. Something *apart*. The knowledge crawled along her bones, burned behind her eyes and sucked at her muscles, as if she were being tasted, sipped, and drunk. In its wake there was a vast emptiness. A cold deeper than the dank, frigid room. Black ice.

Nova felt her mind slip away into a void.

Where were Seth and Viru? Were they here? She was lost. Alone. Quentin. Where was Quentin? She needed him here. He would protect her from this. He would find her. He always did. *Always.*

The cold fingers moved inside her head.

They were in her brain.

They moved like tiny eels, burrowing and slipping into the deepest parts of her. They touched her soul, biting and ravaging.

She was empty.

Seth cursed. He paced. This wasn't part of the plan. He didn't know what that freak storm was or where it had come from, but he knew what he was seeing.

"She's burning up." Viru's dark eyes were filled with worry.

Nova was sweating, her body burning with fever. She moaned and thrashed, as if battling something within. Seth had seen this before:

Red hands, clutching his. The skin permanently marked from her years of scrubbing floors, clothes, and bedding. She was a washer-woman. A strong Neutral, yet consigned to bending at the feet of others. The feet of the wealthy. The powerful.

Still, she'd kept her dignity. Somehow, despite what she was, she was regal. Her body was strong but lean. Her face unmarked by time. Her eyes soft and gentle.

Until now.

Now they were underscored with dark wedges, her body unable to take anything in. No sustenance. No water. Her energy drained away like a trickle of water. Everything drained, even her magic. The essence of who she was, sucked away.

The Trench.

He was no healer. He'd done the only thing he could think of. He'd gone to his father, the man who had abandoned them completely, and begged.

"Yes, it's a terrible illness," his father had said.

Seth could tell he was not interested in helping. Anger filled him. Rage at his helplessness. How could this man have cared enough about his mother to bed her but not enough to help her? How could anyone be so cold?

Heat filled him, radiating to the tips of his fingers where it danced like electricity. His father's head lifted, his eyes following as the light moved across Seth's hands.

"This?" Seth yelled. "This you're interested in? You can't rouse yourself that my mother is dying, but this you see?" The flickers of light had intensified with his anger. Bolts of white-hot lightning moved up and down his arms.

His father smiled.

As if he enjoyed the torment … as if the entire display was all fun and games. Seth's rage coalesced, and he slammed his arms together. The magic launched from his fingertips like a tree trunk of fire, blowing a hole into the wall next to his father's head.

How had he missed?

His father turned and studied the hole, his fingers tracing the edges. Not blown, Seth realized, but eliminated. Removed.

Destroyed.

"Well, I see you have a little of me in you after all." The smile was back, and it made Seth want to throw up. "Do you have Neutral also?"

Confused, Seth nodded sharply. What did this man care what factors he had? He'd abandoned his family.

"Then perhaps you'll be of use to me after all."

Use? "I don't understand."

"You want me to help your mother?" His monstrous eyes glittered like stones. "I'll agree on one condition."

"What condition?" He'd do anything.

"Bind yourself to me."

The air was stolen from his lungs, leaving his chest to cave in as he slowly imploded. Bind himself? To the man who had left them like garbage in the street? Commit his magic and his fate to the man he hated more than anyone else? Lock himself into servitude with no way to escape? How could he say yes?

How could he say no? His mother would die.

He saw the triumph on his father's face. He knew Seth had no choice. If he said no, he'd as good as killed his own mother.

"How?" He hated the broken sound of his own voice.

"Blood sigil." His father flicked a hand as if it were nothing. "It's a simple spell."

He closed his eyes, defeated. "When?"

"Now, of course."

What? But how would he—

"I'll see your mother gets to the healer once the spell is done. Come boy, give me your blood."

He'd pulled out a small but lethally sharp knife. The strange lighting in the room made the blade look red already. As if his soul had already been carved out of his chest.

How he hated this man.

He winced as the knife pierced his palm and was dragged in a small pattern across the skin, leaving a crimson trail.

"Your blood to mine," his father intoned, "your magic to mine … your life to mine." His eyes were black with greed. "From this day forward, I will be your teacher. Your Maester."

He used the ancient word. A shiver twisted Seth's body.

"Yes, Maester."

"I require your obedience."

Seth's mind rebelled. His thoughts screamed he would never do this, but he could not speak words against the man he was now bound to.

"You will train with me and learn all I require of you. You will execute my will as I command. Your magic will only be used for my purpose and not your own until I release you or until you die."

The words were bitter in his mouth. "Yes, Maester."

At least his mother would live. At least his sacrifice had saved her. There was that to soften the blow.

Except he'd forgotten one thing.

His father… his Maester … was a liar.

The monster of a man had never even bothered to put up a pretense. As soon as the binding had been completed, he packed them up and left Seth's mother to die alone in a cold and empty house.

Seth looked down at the dirt floor where Nova lay, her head thrashing back and forth, her face flushed.

"The Trench," he whispered.

"What?" Viru's face mirrored his fear. "Are you sure?"

Seth nodded, an empty feeling sweeping through him. "I've seen this illness before."

"Then we must get her to a healer."

Anger, sudden and fierce, filled the emptiness. "How? We're in the middle of nowhere. There are no healers out here." He slid down the wall to sit on the cold, dirt floor.

"She'll die if we don't."

Seth didn't answer. He was all out of answers. Nova was going to die, just like his mother. Her death and everything Seth had done would be for nothing.

He stared as Viru, his face pinched in a scowl, moved around the room pulling things from shelves, breaking things apart, and binding things together. Whatever he was doing, Seth didn't care.

When Viru finished, he picked Nova up and laid her on a cloth he'd stretched between two pieces of wood. Beside her, he placed three bundles of food. Only once he was at the door did he turn around and look at Seth.

"Are you coming?"

Seth watched without a word as Viru waited for several long minutes before pulling Nova away, leaving Seth alone in the cold, dark room.

Instructions

Short.

Concise.

Effective. That was the key. Getting a useful message through. If they were able to make a connection, how long would they have? Seconds? Maybe a couple of minutes? What could she tell Nova that would help and protect her within such a small amount of time?

Okay, Mira. Start with what you'd say if you had all the time you needed.

Her hand shook as she held the pen.

Nova, it's Mom. I love you. I hope you're okay. I'm so sorry I didn't tell you sooner, but you are in grave danger. Please believe me.

She paused to take a deep breath.

The reason I came across the Divide with you was to protect you. You need to understand. We were both so young. Your father, Lucien, was so eager and full of passion for life, for magic, for... everything.

For *her.*

At the beginning, that's what it had boiled down to. Lucien had not simply loved Mira, he'd adored her. When he'd stared at her with those fathomless gray eyes, she'd seen the intensity of a firestorm raging. His passion had sent shivers through her. Yes, sometimes he rushed things, but she could forgive him for his desires. She could forgive him anything when he'd held her, his hands tracing lines of fire over her skin.

But the same flames fueling his passion could cause a wildfire to rage out of control. Before long the same eyes that had captivated her became windows to a frightening inferno. And she knew who had fanned those flames.

Cyril.

Lucien's closest friend. His mentor. Or, as Mira had often thought of him, his *tor*mentor. He'd seen Lucien's intensity and fanned the flames with tales of power. At first, Lucien told her everything.

"Just think, Mira." His eyes glowed with childlike excitement. "Think what I could do if I found the ancient text with forms from all the oldest and most powerful Duals the world has ever seen."

"What would you do with it?" She'd asked, innocent herself. Would he build her a grand house, with rooms for all the children they would have? Would he fly her away to a place so beautiful even the birds sang of only beauty and love? A place where nothing would ever intrude on their solitude?

"Anything, Mira. I could create spells to increase my power tenfold. I could find new ways to use mediums and bind their power. Think of it. I could become the most powerful Dual in all of Threa!"

Those eyes she loved so much filled with a feverish light. A drunken fire. A fire so hot could ignite everything in the vicinity, burning all to ash, and consuming them both.

She'd shivered then, and she shivered now remembering the stranger he'd become.

But something happened, and his passion turned to darkness. I was afraid of that darkness. I was afraid of him. So, I ran. I ran as far and as long as I could, until I came to a place where I couldn't run any further.

The Divide.

Even then I felt him searching for me. Searching for us. He knew somehow, even though I never told him … I was pregnant. He was in my head, and I could feel him closing in. I did the only thing I could think to do. I fled to a place I knew he couldn't follow.

I crossed the Divide.

He's never stopped searching for us, Nova. For you. And I'm afraid of what he'll do when he finds you.

She stopped there, unable to continue. Drops dotted the paper, and she raised her hand to her face, surprised to find tears. Even after all this time, he affected her strongly. If only she could have kept him from changing. If only her love had been enough.

But it wasn't. Her inner voice turned hard. *Now stop sniveling and find a way to help your daughter.*

Futility threatened to overwhelm her. There was no way to condense it all down. No way to make Nova understand how light could spiral into darkness so gradually, one didn't even notice until you were lost. No way to express how worried she was that if Nova found her father, she would put her very life in danger.

Mira searched for something to capture those feelings.

Clutching the notebook and pen to her chest, she wandered down the hall to Nova's room. The door was closed. That was her fault. She'd created a wall between them with her fear and her lies.

Oh, Nova. I'm so sorry.

If only she could have the chance to start over. Nervous, she twisted the knob and opened the door. Immediately her eyes welled with more tears. Nova was everywhere here. From the shelves of books, to the neatly arranged desk, to her bed where Yogi sat, one sad eye hanging by a thread staring at her as if asking where his friends had gone.

Mira picked the old bear up and pressed it against her chest, along with the notebook and pen. She sat at Nova's desk. Nova's sketch pad sat in the center of the blotter. Both were at perfect right angles.

A small laugh bubbled out. *Only Nova.* Most kids her age had rooms covered in dirty clothes, old food, and goodness only knew what else. Of course, most kids didn't do a lot of things Nova could do. Like her drawings. Mira flipped absently through the sketch book. They were so beautiful. Obviously, not telling her about her magic had done little to dampen her natural ability. Mira had occasionally drawn figures, but some of Nova's were so intricate they looked more like art, each one exquisitely unique.

Unique.

Mira stilled. She wiped at her eyes and looked again. "Drawings are unique."

Could they send Nova a drawing? One picture to tell her everything they needed her to know?

Mira jumped up, excitement flowing through her.

"Zeke!"

She grabbed Nova's sketch pad and ran down the hall. Zeke reached the door at the same time she opened it, her lavender robe flapping around him like fluffy wings.

"What is it?"

She thrust the sketch book at him. "We can send her a picture. A picture can say a lot more and is faster than writing a letter. This could work."

Zeke opened the book, and his face paled. "What is this?"

"Nova's sketch book. Haven't you ever seen inside before?"

He flipped to the second page. "No. I haven't."

"But she keeps the pad right there on her desk."

"I don't generally go into young ladies' rooms without asking, Mira."

"Yes, but … she never showed these to you?"

He glanced up sharply. "Did she show them to you?"

"Of course." She stopped. "At least, I think so." Had she? Had Nova ever shown her the drawings? Or had she peeked at them when she was cleaning?

"Mira." A strange tension edged Zeke's words. "These are spell forms."

A surge of unexpected pride warmed her. "I know."

"They're not like anything I've ever seen before."

Why did he sound so surprised? "Well, they're unique. They're Nova's."

He looked back down at the book, flipping to a third page, then a fourth. "Yes, but these forms are more than mere spells. They're fractals."

"But that's not unheard of, right? Using mathematical formulas?"

"Mathematical formulas are rare but not unheard of. Using fractals? I've never seen anything like it. They look like … music."

Music?

Zeke would know more about fractals than she did. Mira had always loved magic but not like Zeke. Not like Lucien, either.

"These feel dimensional." He looked up again, and this time his eyes were bright. "And they give me an idea."

His excitement leaped between them like a bolt of electricity. She followed on his heels as he crossed to his desk where the small book they'd found earlier lay amidst scattered pages.

"If these are what I think they are, we can do more than send a message." Zeke was a flurry of activity, shuffling and reading, then flipping through the pages of Nova's book. "I think we can send her instructions."

Mira put a hand on his shoulder and pulled him around. "Slow down. What do you mean, instructions? Instructions for what?"

He held both her arms, and a smile curved his lips. "Instructions for a spell."

Q and A

The burn in Quentin's arms changed gradually to an agony more intense than he'd have thought possible. In spite of the pain, his eyelids drooped, and his arm muscles jerked.

"Careful," Sol said from his spot at the table, still concentrating on whatever he was doing. "The contents of the jar may not kill you but will certainly do damage."

As if Quentin didn't know. Sol had demonstrated his point well enough. If one drop of the gooey flesh-colored liquid could eat a hole through paper, no doubt something equally horrible would happen to his body.

He forced his eyes to refocus, blinking away drops of sweat that threatened to run into them. His muscles were stronger than they had been, thanks to the training he'd done with his chair. His arms had done the work his legs used to, though they weren't used to this kind of position or strain. His shoulders screamed in protest.

Sol looked up. "It's amazing, isn't it? Most people think you have to resort to barbarism to inflict pain, but there are a number of non-harmful ways to do the same thing. I think you could use a break." The chair scraped back as the man stood and walked toward Quentin. "What do you think?"

Quentin had a million answers. Good ones, too. Instead of giving voice to any of them, he nodded.

Sol smiled. "Excellent."

He plucked the cement jar from each of Quentin's hands, placing them carefully into a small alcove in the wall. Then he motioned for Quentin to sit at the table.

He complied, shaking his arms to get the blood flowing again. Pins and needles assaulted him from shoulders to fingertips.

Sol sat down opposite Quentin and steepled his fingers. "As you've probably realized by now, we can do this the hard way or the easy way. I'd much prefer a civilized conversation. Less time consuming and generally just as productive." He probed Quentin with a piercing stare. "Do you think we can do that?"

Quentin thought the pretentious jerk could stuff his civilized conversation up where the sun didn't shine. With a growing admiration for his own restraint, he again decided not to voice his thoughts and simply nodded.

"Good." Sol smiled. "Let's start with something easy. Why are you here?"

Great travel deal for vacations in alternate worlds. The answer popped into his brain. Probably not a good response. "Someone brought me here. I didn't have a lot of choice in the matter."

Sol shook his head. "Evasion wastes our time and makes me want to provide you with additional encouragement."

What next? Hanging upside-down?

"You may think I have lots of productive methods to inspire you, but the truth is Ishtar is the innovative one, not me. She uses her creativity in ways most find unique and generally very distasteful." He made a sour face. "I tend to skip over all that and get right to the heart of an issue if I can. Most people require quite a lot of convincing on their own. Introduce a few of the people they care about to the mix and their willingness blossoms nicely." He gave a half smile. "Let's let your friends get the sleep they need and handle this amongst the two of us. Yes?"

He didn't mean just Laura, either. He would bring Morra and Rose into this.

"I came here to help my friend."

"What kind of help?"

"Protection."

"From what?"

"I don't know." Which was, essentially, the truth.

Sol tilted his head. "You can't think someone needs protection but not have at least an idea of what you're protecting them from."

Quentin didn't like to be angry or negative. Still, his frustration and fatigue clumped together into a ball of anger that sat in his belly, leaking heat through his extremities.

"From people like you, for one thing," he said, clenching his jaw to keep from yelling.

"People like me."

"Yes, people like you. People who don't seem to care about anyone but themselves and don't mind hurting whoever stands in their way. Egotism— this whole place is full of it. It's like a disease."

"So why did your friend come here, if this world is so terrible?"

One of Quentin's eyes began to twitch. "She came to make sure nobody else got hurt. Not for money, power, or to make some poor slobs slave in a field. She came to help people. To protect them."

Because that's who Nova was. She was the least selfish person Quentin knew.

"Protect them from what?"

Sol's question drained some of Quentin's anger, and he realized he'd let the guy get into his head. He needed to step back from the edge of the cliff he'd been so easily led to.

"We're not sure from what. Some guy attacked her."

"Some guy."

Quentin nodded. "Never saw him before. If there was any chance he'd hurt someone else trying to get to her, she figured she should come here."

"And you chased after her."

Quentin's face flushed. "I guess I did."

"You love her?"

His ears began to burn. "Yes."

Sol nodded, apparently satisfied with this answer. "How did you get across the Divide?"

"Laura. The girl who was with me when we got here. She saw me making an idiot out of myself and helped me out."

Another nod. This was getting easier. At this rate, maybe he would be able to get some sleep before sunrise after all.

"One last question," Sol said. "Where have you been since you came here?"

Quentin shook his head, confused. "I don't know the names of the places—"

"Describe them."

"We were in a long field when we came through," he said. "Then the storm blew up and we tried to outrun it. We took shelter in a forest. Once the storm had passed we went through a swamp and into a small valley. That's where Itch—er—the men who captured us were."

Sol's eyes glowed like twin lamps. "This forest you took shelter in, what did the trees look like?"

And just like that, Quentin knew.

This man knew about Thuaat and about the blood magic she'd used. This was a test.

"They were strange. Huge and twisted. Like fingers. There was a woman living inside one. She let us take shelter with her."

"What was her name?"

More tests. "Thuaat."

"And she sheltered you?"

He nodded. "She fed us. She told me what a block was. That's how I knew."

Sol nodded slowly. "Thank you."

Quentin felt a surge of relief. His adrenaline was nearly depleted.

"I knew, of course, about the blood magic." Sol admitted. "I could sense it."

"I know."

"We've had a good talk. I'll send you back now so you can get some rest."

Quentin's relief was short lived. "*Then* what?"

Sol smiled. "Then we'll see what other questions Ishtar would like you to answer."

His words were chilling, but Quentin was too tired to care.

At Sol's command, a guard came to escort him. Quentin went without complaint. When the guard led him into a dark, smelly building and tossed him into an open doorway, hard enough to send him sprawling, Quentin didn't so much as glare in the man's direction.

He was more tired than he'd ever been.

"Quentin?"

His eyes flew open. When had he shut them? "Laura? Is that you?"

There was a scuffling noise. Someone bumped him. "We didn't know where they'd taken you. Are you all right?"

"Fine."

He could sense her skepticism though he couldn't see her face in the darkness.

"Really. I'm okay."

Silence. Had Laura fallen asleep? His own lids drooped.

"That was a good thing you did," she said, her tone surprisingly agreeable.

"Which?"

"Protecting them."

He didn't have to ask who. "Anyone would have done the same."

"No." Her voice was soft but unyielding. "No one else I know would have done what you did. I wouldn't have. Not before, anyway."

Warmth bloomed inside him, chasing the coldness and tension away. "Well then, I'd say you haven't been hanging out with the right people."

He took her silence for agreement, and let his heavy lids slide closed. He drifted off almost immediately. The last thing he heard before sleep claimed him completely was her whispered response.

"No, but that's going to change."

Singularly Destructive

Individuals born with only one factor are known as Singulars. If that one factor is Destructive, they are sometimes called Singularly Destructive, a term not merely descriptive but also an indication of the potential for someone who is particularly troublesome or troubled.

By its nature, the Destructive factor can cause the nature of a person to turn dark and violent and can affect thought and personality, leading to a pattern of greater and greater harmful behavior. The behavior can also leave the individual open to increased influence by those around them. They are prone to pessimism and fear and can be drawn very easily into depression or even mental distress. If enough negative influence is asserted, a Singularly Destructive person could be injured beyond repair, demolished from the inside-out.

—High Wizard Ezekial, on the *Factors of Magic*

Mole's Plan

She was here. He'd seen her with his own eyes. His own beady little mole eyes. They saw everything. That was what Lady said. "You see," she'd told him, "that is your specialty." Yes, he saw. He watched. They'd brought the mother—*filthy traitor*—and the child with her. The girl who had been healed. And that wasn't all he saw. The man's light stained her. The man Lady had called *Wardein*. The others couldn't see the light. No. They were blind. Mole saw. The Wardein's light filled her like a disease. Clung to her skin. Leaked out in trails.

Mole curled deeper into the pile of hay. He hated barns, but this end was empty. This end he'd claimed for his own. His hidey-hole.

Slipping away from the guards had been easy. They didn't really care. Lady would care. She had told them to send him home, but he'd heard her man, Sol. He'd heard about the storm. Home would not be safe. Lady would be safe. So, after he had filled his belly and crammed as much food as he could into his clothes, he'd slipped away into the long shadows. There hadn't been many places to go. He couldn't stay in Lady's house. No, no, no. Mustn't do that. Couldn't go to the place where the others were. Where the child was. The only other place was the barn.

Mole hated barns.

You belong in a barn with the rats. Filthy vermin. You belong with your own kind.

"Mama," he moaned, clutching at his head. Why wouldn't she let him be? He was grown now. Not a boy anymore. He was no rat. He was a mole. Lady's mole.

That shut Mama up. She didn't like Lady. Lady gave him something Mama never had.

A purpose.

He scuttled into the barn. The smell nearly made him scream.

Like before. Just like before.

He buried his head under his arm, and huddled there, shaking.

But no, this was now. This barn wasn't falling in. No bats hung in the rafters. There was a wide aisle. Somewhere farther down, horses nickered to each other, snorting as they flicked their tails at the flies.

Mole slowly uncurled, putting his hands near his mouth. His mole eyes and whiskers told him what he needed to know. This end of the barn was empty. The stall nearest him had some hay in a corner. No flies clouded over the pile of straw.

Hurry and scurry. Mustn't stay out in the open too long, or they'd find him. Better to hide. The hay would keep him warm, and the barn would shelter him from the storm. Mole hurried into the empty stall.

Found you a hidey-hole, did you? Geo's voice whispered. Sometimes Geo was mean. Always he was disgusted. But sometimes he was okay. Like now.

Yes, a hidey-hole. That was what he had. A nice, warm little hidey-hole. He'd stayed there all that night and all the next day, eating the food he'd hidden in his clothes. He didn't have pouches in his cheeks, but he could stash just fine without them. When the storm had arrived, blasting the ground and shaking the foundations, Mole had huddled in his hidey-hole knowing Lady had protection over the sanctuary. He hardly shook at all, and the voices were quiet. Mole felt almost … peaceful.

Until the wagon had arrived.

He'd been out, foraging for some food. His stash was depleted. There were some berry bushes, but he needed more. He'd been about to sneak into the kitchens when he'd heard the shout.

Curiosity had held him in place as the inner gate opened to let the wagon through. It rolled past the barn, up to the front steps of Lady's court. Lady had come out to see, as the men unloaded the wagon.

Then he'd seen her.

The child.

She smiled at the man who lifted her down, and that was when Mole saw it. Pouring from her. Beaming out from her eyes and from her smile.

The light.

His light.

The *Wardein*.

Mole turned to spit in the grass beside him. His beady eyes watched the girl move to stand by her mother, leaving a trail of the infectious light in her wake like a fungus.

Lady hadn't even looked. Couldn't she see the blight?

No. That was Mole's job.

He had seen. He had watched as Lady looked over the others, then had the guards take the woman and child away to the building where the others were kept. Thankfully, none of the light had gotten on Lady. She was clean. For now.

Food must wait. He'd scurried back to his hidey-hole. Back to the safety of the barn and the dark cave he'd made for himself in the old, dusty hay. The hole was a good place but not safe from nightmares. The dreams had stolen in like wraiths, filling his mind with twisted pictures.

Now, with the dawning sunlight, he knew. Mole would have to protect Lady. The guards would not. They couldn't see the child was contaminated. Even Lady didn't see. No one could see but Mole.

His stomach growled.

Food first. Then he would think. And plan.

He wasn't a good thinker—not anymore, but this was important. He must not let Lady be tainted by the awful light. The child's terrible, poisonous light.

Mole had to find a way to put it out.

Allies

Everything burned. Nova's arms, her legs, her stomach … her brain. Fingers scratched inside her head, leaving trails of fire and ash. She wanted to scream, but she was trapped in a void. She couldn't open her eyes. All she could see was inside, and the burning was inside. The trails where the pain razed her were filled with a hellish blue-white—the color of agony. The burning fingers gouged wounds into more than her flesh. They ripped into her soul, dripping out more than blood. Dripping out the essence of who she was. Her Edah.

The lines blazed.

They shifted.

They were changing. Moving with purpose. They left behind an image.

A pattern.

The fiery image of a face staring into a face. Nose to nose. Only more than a face. Something else. The lines were more. They were …

Mirror.

"Mom?" She could have sworn she'd heard her mother's voice. She strained to listen, but there was nothing more.

Everything was quiet.

With a start, she realized she could see something green.

Was that grass?

"Nova?"

She hadn't even known her eyes were open, but now she looked up and found a face hovering over her.

"Seth?" Her voice was a cracked whisper.

"No. It's Viru."

Viru? Her mouth was dry. She licked at her lips. "Where's Seth?"

"You're sick. I'm taking you to a healer."

Yes, she was definitely sick. She felt hollowed out inside.

"Where?" She croaked.

"There should be a landowner nearby. Those men, the patrol we took the horses from. They look for wanderers to bring to the landowner who hires them."

She should understand, but his words washed over her like waves, leaving her dazed and slightly nauseous.

"There would be a healer there."

She could only nod. If he was right, maybe someone could help her. If not, maybe she would die. She felt like she might die.

Viru sat on the ground beside her. He put a water jug to her lips, holding the back of her head with one hand to help her lean forward.

The water was as cold as ice.

Colder.

It poured over her dry tongue and down her hot throat, quenching the fire and ash inside her. She took another swig, rinsing her mouth before swallowing.

"How are you feeling?" he asked, when she leaned back.

"Awful."

He nodded, as if expecting this answer. Then he looked away. Such an odd person. Nova wasn't sure what to make of him.

"Why ... are you helping me?" Speaking was an effort.

He frowned, as if surprised, then sighed. "You must understand," he said as he plucked a few blades of grass and contemplated them. "I was raised not to question the teaching of my master. Prophecies are like diamonds. Hidden in layers of matter, unclear until polished, rare gems of great strength and light." He paused, as if figuring out how to say what came next. "I did not think there was any other way to view the things I'd been taught."

He glanced at Nova, and she sensed sadness in him.

"There is only one thing I know better than prophecy and that is the truth of the One God, the High King, and the Wardein, his travelers. His messengers." Shame filled his face now as well. "That one would visit us, would share a meal and a story ..."

He shook his head. "You could not be what I was told. He would not have asked me to protect you if you were."

Technically, Nova thought, he hadn't said those words, but she wasn't about to question. Better to have an ally than an assassin. "What made them think this prophecy was about me?" she asked him instead. Talking drained her, but she wanted to understand.

"It is simple," Viru said, as if she'd missed some point. "Prophecy speaks of a Trine. There has never been such a being. Until you. You are the only one."

She supposed that made sense, if she truly was a Trine. Was she? Seth had seemed convinced. Viru, and apparently, Viru's master believed. Nova wasn't so sure. Why was she the first? With all the people in this world and all their magical power, why would there have never been a Trine before? What was so special about having all three ... what did Seth call them ... factors? And if she had them, why couldn't she feel their power? Why couldn't she use her gifts?

Why would Mom have hidden this from me?

The thought of her mother triggered a memory from her fever dreams. There had been an image, and then she'd heard her mother say something. What was the word?

Nova's mind refused to think clearly. She needed more sleep, but she was afraid to close her eyes. Afraid of the searing pain as something crawled through her, cutting into parts of her she shouldn't be able to feel.

Viru chewed on a piece of dried meat. "You should try to eat."

She shook her head. Eating was not an option.

He dusted himself off. "Then we'll keep moving. The sooner we can find a healer the better."

When he left her line of vision, she saw the trees. They really were quite beautiful. She wished she could touch them. Feel their silvery branches. Let the breeze from their leaves cool her head.

Her eyelids were like stones, too heavy to hold up.

The trees whispered as sleep reclaimed her.

Mirror.

Creative Destructive

Creative Destructive Duals are very rare. Without the balance of Neutral, there must be a nearly exact level of power in both a Creative and Destructive individual to create this pairing, and even so, the strength of the inherited gift must also be equal. Otherwise one of the two factors would outweigh the other, leaving only one factor remaining.

When such a thing does manage to happen, the outcome is an individual with the power to both create and destroy and who is without the balancing effect of Neutral. The result is a person of great power and even greater ambitions.

—High Wizard Ezekial, on the *Factors of Magic*

Lost

All his planning, all his deception would all be for nothing if she died.

"Hah." Seth laughed in the darkness of the root cellar.

That would be a joke on everyone. Prophecy said nothing about the Trine dying of a stupid disease. The Order had devoted themselves to finding her and killing her before the prophecy could come true, yet here she was dying without any help from them, and who should be trying to help her but one of their own. This was a twist he never would have guessed.

Neither would his Maester.

Lucien.

He had no idea. No clue. Here he was—so powerful and so hungry for more—and his treasure was slipping right through his fingers. How long had the man planned and waited, watching her? Studying her? At first, he hadn't let Seth so much as peek. Then, when he'd decided to send Seth to retrieve her, he'd begun to let Seth watch also. As training. To ensure Seth wouldn't stand out in her world and would be able to deceive her.

If only the fool had known.

Lucien would never have guessed his precious daughter, his Trine, dreamed in magic. That she had a book filled with spells unlike anything anyone had ever seen before.

Except for Seth, of course.

He'd watched her when Lucien was too busy to do his own spying. Seth had seen her wake up from a nightmare and turn over in bed, grab her book, and sketch out a picture unlike anything he'd ever thought was possible. Once Seth knew about them, he took care to study them until he could reproduce them. Understand them.

Use them.

Lucien had let him watch Nova, so he could deceive her, and instead Seth had used what he'd learned to deceive Lucien. A twisted irony. There was no way Lucien would have known. How could he? The very idea of a Trine was shrouded in myth and legend. No one knew what such a person would be capable of. No one would have guessed that without having been exposed to magic, without knowing she had power, she could create spells that would change existence.

Like the one Seth had used to undo the binding.

He could still remember seeing the drawing for the first time. Looking at the form sent thrills racing through him. He'd studied carefully, sketching the spell over and over until he had a perfect reproduction. Even Nova herself was stunned when she'd seen his finished product, thinking someone else might share her dream.

Little did she know.

Once he'd realized he could undo the binding, that he could be free of his wretch of a Maester, his mind had latched on to what was possible. What he could do.

Seth's plan was a thing of beauty, really. Simple, yet intricate. Lucien was so arrogant, so full of his own power he never saw the truth right in front of him. He'd reminded Seth over and over of his purpose. Of what was expected of him. Of his place in the grand design. While all the time Seth was using the map Lucien laid out to circumvent his Maester.

Fool!

Only now who was the dupe? Nova was gone. She was going to die. And all for nothing.

Seth folded his hands over his head. If he couldn't have what he wanted, at least he could find some comfort in the fact Lucien wouldn't have what he desired either.

Nova was lost to them both.

The snort of a horse brought Seth's head up in the darkness. He could hear grass being torn from the ground. Careful not to make a sound, Seth stood up. Nothing indicated others were present. One of the horses must have come back after the storm.

He went to the door and peeked out.

Nova's stallion. Well, not hers really, but the one she had ridden after they'd taken them from the patrol. Those brutes were probably still searching for them.

Seth could see the grooves cut into the soft dirt from the travois. Viru had headed back the way they'd come. Stupid, or genius? They'd been one, maybe two days ahead of the patrol, and on horseback, so maybe three days walk would find them.

Was Viru's plan to let Nova be captured so she could be healed? It seemed likely. The only question was whether Viru would let the men capture them both. He thought not. Viru would try to avoid capture so he could rescue Nova later. Once she was healed.

"Oh, Stone." Seth shook his head. "You devious thing."

The horse tore up another mouthful of grass, looking up at him.

Seth grinned. He could be devious too. Oh, yes. Scheming was what Seth did best. Lucien had taught his student well.

Found

"What happened? Did our message get through?" Mira's eyes met Zeke's.

He looked tired. She'd never seen him look so tired. He'd always been old to her, a child's view of her father. She'd never noticed the wrinkles on his hands and face. The creases time had etched there. And now, the worry that clouded in his eyes.

"I don't know," he said softly.

He was lying. Her father never lied. Fear balled in her belly. She couldn't bear not knowing. "Tell me."

She hid nothing. There was nothing left to hide. If her baby was hurt, if she was in trouble, Mira would die trying to save her. If her baby was lost … then so was she. Her heart would not go on without Nova.

"I think," Zeke said slowly, as if puzzling through a problem, "our connection to her wasn't complete. She wasn't fully aware of us."

"Maybe she was sleeping."

"Maybe." He pulled on the sleeves of Mira's favorite yellow chiffon housecoat. "If she was, I think she woke up right before we lost the connection."

There it was again. That hurtful little nugget of hope. "If she heard us, maybe she saw the image."

Zeke shook his head, and the nugget disintegrated. "Even if she did, I don't think she understood." He pulled Mira into a hug. "We'll try again. Nova's strong. She'll be all right."

Mira had to believe he was right. She had to.

"Dad," she said, her head snuggled up against his chest, "why do you wear my robes?"

She felt him look down at her.

"Hmm. Well." He cleared his throat. "I suppose I'm just old fashioned."

"How is that old fashioned?"

"Well you're much too young to remember, but the older wizards believe what one wears can impact the magic performed."

Her brows scrunched in confusion. She opened her mouth, but he continued before she had a chance to voice her question.

"It's like the medium. What substance you draw the spell in can impact the strength. If the user can see the magic, if they can sense and feel it, they can affect the outcome. Colors can make a difference in how the magic feels. A wizard can wear a specific color to enhance the way the magic will work."

The power of color almost made sense in a strange kind of way. Nova saw sounds in color as part of her magic. But wearing women's robes?

"Are you sure you don't just like them?"

He chuckled and squeezed her tighter. She smiled, her face pressed against the side of him. What would she and Nova have done without him all these years?

"How did you find us?" This was the question she'd been burning to ask him for many years.

The day he'd shown up, only a few days after she'd left Threa, had been both the worst and best day of her life. Lost and alone in a world completely foreign to her, she'd given up looking for someone who would help her. She'd sat under a bridge and watched rain drip down around her. Pigeons cooed and flapped and left droppings everywhere. Even a dog had shunned her, coming close only to grab a scrap and give her a growl as it took its prize and ran off. When she'd seen Zeke appear through the drizzle, she'd thought he was a mirage until he took her hand, pulling her up.

He was always pulling her up.

"I didn't find you," he said now, his voice distant as he remembered. "A witch woman did."

Mira had heard of witch women. Instead of learning magic and the science of herbs and minerals in the traditional way, they were taught by their mothers and grandmothers. They were said to live in the giant Elder trees.

"I had heard there was one who knew a way to find someone. To trace them. When you disappeared, when I couldn't find you, I sought her out."

Mira couldn't imagine the worry she'd put him through. "I'm sorry."

He gave her shoulders another squeeze. "Don't be. You did what you needed to do to be safe. That's what's important."

"What happened? How did this witch woman find me?"

"She cast a spell to let me feel where you were."

She frowned. "Even through the Divide?"

"Yes." His voice was strained.

166

She looked up at him. His eyes shifted away from hers. "Dad, what did she do?"

"Oh. Um, well … like I said. She cast a spell."

"What *kind* of spell?"

"A blood spell."

"What?" The blood drained from her face, leaving her lightheaded.

Blood magic was an ancient, archaic form of magic. Not many knew enough to use such power, and few risked doing so. Using blood for spells linked you to others in dangerous, sometimes deadly ways.

"Don't fret, Mira. I knew what I was doing, and so did she."

"What did the spell do, exactly?"

"It connected us."

And there it was.

Fear leached the heat from Mira's extremities. "You're bound to me?"

"And to Nova. You were pregnant."

Both of them? "So, if something were to happen to one of us …"

"Now, stop." He pulled her away from him and looked down at her. Beneath his bushy white brows, his eyes were filled with tenderness. "I'm your father. If something were to happen to one of you, the result would be the same whether we were linked or not."

"Oh, Dad." She understood—she did—but the knowledge still tore at her heart. He'd joined his life to theirs. That was how he knew Nova wasn't dead. Probably how he sensed something was wrong. "And this link led you to us?"

He nodded.

"Did she know, do you think? The witch woman?"

"Know what?"

"That I was across the Divide."

He paused. "I don't know." She could almost hear the wheels spinning in his head as he considered the possibility. "Maybe."

Somehow, Mira thought the witch had known. Witch women were not like everyone else. To use the blood magic was no small thing. They were powerful, yet they lived outside of normal society. Seldom did they even associate with others. When they did, there was always a reason.

"Who was she?" Mira asked. "What was her name?" She glanced back up at him.

His eyes were far away, remembering another place and time. "Her name was Thuaat."

The Light

"What is this stuff, anyway?"

The sticky green leaves clung to his pants, his socks, even the laces on his sneaks. The plants looked for all the world like pricker bushes, but that couldn't be right. Surely Ishtar would not be stockpiling prisoners to work the fields for a bunch of weeds.

"It's called Phoria," Morra said from her spot a few feet away.

Rose held the basket while she pulled off the leaves with no white left on them. Her arms were covered in the sticky leaves as well.

"Is it food?" Laura asked, thwacking the wooden hoe they'd given her into the ground and yanking it back attached to a twist of ivy.

In Laura's hands, the gardening tool made Quentin nervous.

"No," Morra answered, wiping one sleeve across her brow. "The plant is smoked." She raised one brow as she looked at them. "To enhance one's senses."

"No way," Laura lowered her head, eyes wide. "It's a drug? What's that make us? Free labor for the local cartel?"

"Momma," Rose whispered.

Morra glanced toward a guard who had wandered their way, then bent back to her work. Quentin and Laura took the hint and got back to work as well. Quentin's job was to pull off the small white berries from the bushes. He'd filled the sack hung over his left shoulder. They'd only been at this an hour, and he was already tired, sore, and covered in sweat, among other things.

"You there," the guard's gruff voice sounded from behind them.

The girls kept working, but Quentin stopped and looked back. The guard stood a few feet away, his face red from the heat and the sun. He had a load of weapons and ammunition strapped to him, and Quentin figured standing out here all day wasn't much fun for the guard either.

He frowned at Quentin's scrutiny. "What's with all the chatter?"

Quentin held up both hands, palms out. "Hey, man, I'm only trying to make sure we do this right."

The guard grunted. "You must be new here."

"Just arrived."

"Well, listen up. While you're out here, you work. You don't talk. If you're not doing things right, someone will let you know. Got it?"

"Yep." *Jerk.*

Quentin turned back to resume his work, but the guard apparently had other ideas. He pulled Quentin backward, ripping the pack off his shoulder. The white berries spilled out onto the ground.

"Aw, look what you did," the guard said with a sneer.

He was looking for trouble. No matter what Quentin did this wasn't going to end here. When a small hand appeared on the guard's right wrist, they were both startled. Rose looked up at the guard. He stared back at her as if in a trance.

"Please," Rose said, her sweet little voice like tiny bells in a meadow. Even the birds and wind seemed to hush at the sound. "Let us be. Wouldn't you rather be in the shade getting cool than out here in the hot sun?"

Quentin could swear he saw a glow spread from the girl's hands to the guard's wrist, flowing up his arm like a current. The glow disappeared before he could be sure.

The guard blinked, then looked up at the bright, cloudless sky. "I'm getting out of this sun," he muttered. He glared at them. "Back to work!"

He shook off Rose's grip and stomped away.

Quentin could only stare. He didn't even know what to say, which was unusual for him.

"Come, Rose." Morra certainly didn't seem surprised.

Quentin glanced at Laura, who stared back at him before checking to make sure no one else had observed them. She nodded at the berries still littered on the ground.

"Work now, talk later."

He nodded at her. "*Comprendo.*"

He knelt in the dirt and scooped up the berries. Rose was still standing where the guard had been. When Quentin squinted up at her, she grinned and turned back to her mother.

Quentin shook his head. He must be seeing things. Maybe the drug plants were making him hallucinate. He swore she left glowing footprints in her wake. He reached to touch the ground. All he felt was dirt, but a warm tingle spread up his arm, through his shoulder and across his back. He shuddered.

Quentin examined his fingertips. Nothing was there. He looked again at Rose and her mother. They were busy working. Laura faced the other way. No one saw a thing. Maybe nothing had happened at all.

Yet he couldn't explain the fact that all his soreness, not only from today but from yesterday's torment, had melted away like clouds in a summer sky.

Zen Creation

While the use of spells can be learned, the creation of spell forms requires the ability to not only sense the magic, but to understand what the power will do. This combination of natural ability and learned discipline is necessary for the successful implementation of new spells. Ability without discipline can be extraordinarily dangerous.

—High Wizard Ezekial, on the *Factors of Magic*

Nova's Heart

No matter how he tried, Quentin couldn't sleep. Whatever little Rose had done to him out in the field today had caused an interesting side effect. Since leaving the swamp and the valley, he'd felt the link to Nova and her father split into multiple directions. The problem was, he didn't know which he should follow.

Until now.

Suddenly, he was very aware of which link led to Nova. The invisible wire was alive, thrumming with energy. He not only felt the connection, he felt the unique differences between them, and Quentin was very, very worried.

Something was wrong with Nova. She was frustratingly close, yet with every passing minute he sensed her drifting away. How was he losing her when she was so near?

He turned over on the hard floor.

"What is it?" Laura's voice drifted out of the darkness.

"We need to get out of here, that's what." He was more edgy than he should be, but he couldn't help it.

He heard Laura turning over. "Something's wrong." She stated.

He bit back the first angry retort that jumped to his lips. This wasn't her fault. Instead, he growled and rubbed at his face. "I think so."

He sorted through the series of questions Laura might ask him next. What she said surprised him.

"What is it about her?"

He frowned into the dark room. "Huh?"

"You came all this way for her. You risked everything." Laura paused. "I mean, I know you like Nova and all, but why? What makes her so special?"

Quentin tried to swallow. His throat had gone dry. He hadn't told anyone this, not even Nova. If Laura had said anything else right then, he might not have answered, but she stayed quiet and the words made their way through the fog in his brain.

"When I was ten, I got really sick. I remember my neck and head hurt, and I couldn't eat anything. My mom didn't know what to do for me. She took me to the doctor, but he said I just had the flu. There wasn't much to do but let it work its way out."

He remembered that night, how the ride home tortured him. His whole body hurt. His head hurt so bad he thought his brain would explode.

"I got a lot worse on the way home, so my Mom turned us around and went to the hospital. They told her later that was the only reason I didn't die."

The next week felt like a bad dream—hazy and dim. He remembered only snippets of doctors, nurses, and his mom who never left his bedside.

Man, he really missed his mom and dad right now too.

"What did you have?" Laura's voice was subdued.

"Triple-E."

Most people in their neck of the woods knew the term. Eastern Equine Encephalitis was the reason summer nights on the river included extra strong insect repellent or screened-in porches. For the kids his age, the extra precautions had been another inconvenience to complain about. He'd never thought a mosquito bite could make someone so sick.

"The good news was I didn't die. The bad news was I was paralyzed."

Quentin remembered coming out of the fog of fever and pain. He felt so strange, so still. It had taken him a while to realize his stillness was more than being weak. He couldn't move his legs at all. Not until he'd looked at his mother's face, did he understand how bad things were.

"Everything changed. I was mad. *Really* mad. I wanted to run and jump and play. I wanted to keep being a normal kid. I didn't want to be in a wheelchair. The first time they tried to put me in one, I threw a fit. I tried to knock the thing over." He snorted. "Those suckers are wicked hard to knock over. I managed to push the chair a few feet before I fell on my face." He paused, remembering. "I saw something for the first time that day. The worst thing. The thing that made me wish I'd died instead."

"What?" Laura whispered.

"Pity." He shook his head. "I saw the pity. Poor little crippled boy."

How he'd hated that. How he'd hated *them*.

How he'd hated himself.

"I didn't want to go home," he said when he could finally continue. "I didn't want to see anyone. Especially Nova. We'd been best friends since forever. I didn't want to see the pity. Not from her."

He remembered that day so clearly. A smile covered his face. "When Dad pulled out that wheelchair, I saw Nova running up to the car, and I wanted to hide. I wanted to yell and scream. When she opened the door, I thought she would say something horrible like 'Oh, Quentin,' or 'I'm so sorry.'"

When he paused, Laura took the bait. "What did she say?"

"'Don't expect me to let you win just because you're new at this.' Then she grabbed the wheelchair and spun it around a little. 'You really think you're gonna be faster than me just 'cause you have wheels now?'" He heard Laura's chuckle and smiled in the darkness. "It was the first time I laughed since I got sick. I thought she'd treat me like I was going to break, but she didn't. She pushed me. Even when I was ready to quit. *Especially* when I was ready to quit." He blinked, and his eyes misted with the memory. "I'd always known she was a good friend, but that was when I started to realize what she was really made of." He swallowed. "That was when I learned her heart."

Minutes passed, and Quentin wondered if Laura was going to say anything more when he heard her shift. "You really love her, don't you?"

Nova had challenged him. Pushed him. Even yelled at him from time to time. "Yeah," he answered truthfully. "I do."

More silence followed. He could almost hear her thinking about what he'd said.

"So how come she isn't like that with everyone?"

His lips twisted. "You mean, why isn't she like that with you."

"The first time I met her, she yelled at me for picking on some kid— some little princess who dropped her books. Most of the time, this girl was completely obnoxious, always showing off the pretty shoes her daddy bought her. Man, I hated that kid. But right then, Nova comes along and yells at me. Grabbed the girl's stuff right out of my hands. I thought, okay, so she's got guts. But as soon as the kid was gone, she caved, like what she'd done was all for show or something."

Quentin rolled his eyes. "You really don't get it, do you? Nova's great at defending other people. That's who she is. She wants to save the world."

"Then why the complete turnaround?" Laura seemed genuinely confused.

Anger simmered. "You're here, in this world, and you have to ask? Nova thinks she's broken. She didn't know why she was so different or why her dad wasn't around. When you ragged on her and called her a freak, she believed you because she's afraid it's the truth."

This time the silence dragged. There'd be no more questions.

Quentin turned his head, even though he couldn't see Laura lying there. "The only reason she came here was because she thought everyone else would be in danger. Her mom, her grandpa ... me ..." He took a deep breath. "She's got more guts than most people I know. She just doesn't know it yet."

And now, when they were so close, something was wrong. Stretched out on a cold stone floor, Quentin could only hope he could find a way to reach Nova before time ran out.

The Song of the High King

"Don't touch her!"

Nova recognized the sharp, commanding voice. How did she know that voice? Threads of dark blue drifted into view like ribbons floating on the breeze. She could see the trees beyond, but they were hazy. Fuzzy. Not quite real.

Was she dead?

"She has the Trench."

Ah, there was a word she'd heard before, whispered in the darkness. The name fit. She felt hollowed out like a trench, as if someone had furrowed out a long gouge where her insides had been, leaving her empty and torn apart.

"What do we do?"

This voice was new. A weak, watery-brown curl of color like smoke drifted around her, dirty looking against the muted green of the trees. A speck of color stood out against the rest of the green and blue background. Something high up and not quite clear. A smudge.

"Pull her on the pallet."

"Are you sure we shouldn't just leave her? She looks pretty far gone."

"No." Commanding Blue-Voice had a hard edge of black. "She'll live. Then, she and I can have a little chat."

A deep shiver tried to work through her. Like a sneeze that couldn't work its way out her body refused to respond. She should be afraid, but she was too tired. There was nothing left. She was drained. Blue-Voice could do what he wanted.

The landscape tipped and spun, causing the world around her to blur, like being on the Tilt-a-Whirl at the county fair. Up and down, round and round, faster …

The blur, the smudge, flashed by.

Spinning, rocking …

There it was again. Waving now.

Seth? No. Viru?

Why was he up in the tree?

Swirling, blurring, rushes of color blended into a giant blender of motion.

Too bad I don't have my sketch book.

A tear trickled down one cheek. If only she could be home in her bed, her mom putting a cold washcloth on her forehead, Yogi tucked under one arm.

Quentin.

"Careful," Commanding Blue-voice cut into her. "Keep her steady. We're almost there."

If only Grandpa were here. He could help her. He would protect her. Grandpa Zeke pretended to be a crazy old man, but she knew better. She knew his eyes, and they were clear. Sharp. He saw.

He lied. Just like Mom.

Yes, they'd lied, although she kind of understood now why they had. Wouldn't she have lied to protect someone from all of this? Wasn't that why she was here? Or was there more to it? Was she using that as an excuse? A strange thing, the line between protecting someone else and protecting yourself. Maybe she'd only wanted to believe she'd followed someone she barely knew into a world she didn't know at all to protect Quentin and her family. The truth was, she wanted to know why her father had finally come looking. Why not before? Didn't he want to know her?

Was she really so bad?

She wasn't a freak. Not here. Here, she belonged. She fit.

Except …

She had no idea how to really use all the stuff inside her. Seth had managed to trick her into letting her power out. Viru had called that a corruption of the gift, but how else could she make her magic work? Anger and fear seemed like the only things strong enough to draw it out.

Draw.

If only she could sketch for a while. Maybe she'd find some way to capture the thoughts and emotions. If only she could take the feelings and mold them. Blend them. Change the colors. Change the …

Tune.

A faint sound of music drifted past her. Someone singing.

A girl.

Behind her eyelids, Nova could see the sound. Gold, like the traveler's voice, sang to her soul. The sound drifted with her, filling the void inside her with light.

As if in response, a rainbow of colors seeped out of her, along the bottom of the trench. The colors ran together, filling the bottom of the hole like a river running through a dry riverbed, cooling her, soothing the scorched places.

"Gron." A voice shattered her thoughts. "What is this?"

A woman's voice, sharp and pink like the stuff Grandpa drank when his stomach was upset. Jagged shapes and jarring color.

"It's the Trench," the man with the brown voice said.

"Yes, I see that."

"She managed to steal our horses," Commanding Blue-Voice said. "I thought you might find her interesting."

In the silence between voices, Nova strained to hear the music again, but the golden sound was gone. The rainbow waters inside started to drain.

"We'll have to hurry. Go and get Sol."

"Yes, Lady."

Now the voices tangled.

Nova left the web of sounds above her, diving inside to work on the rainbow river. The music had been helping. If only she could get the sound to come back. The golden light had soothed her and called to her soul, drawing the magic out. Without anger. Without fear. The magic had poured out of her like water.

"Put her on the bed."

Living water. Edah. Nova breathed in, picturing the gold and calling to the rainbow inside her. What was in her flesh was already gone. What had been in her veins was gone too. All that was left was what was in her bones. In her soul. She spoke to that fragile tendril of magic. Called to her power.

Sang to it.

From deep inside the trench that consumed her, the water trickled out. Rainbow colors.

Yes.

Deep, rich, vibrant colors. *Her* colors. Nova was seeing her own color for the first time, and she was all of them. Laughter and the song flowed through her. The trickle became a stream, and the stream a waterfall.

"Sol, what's happening?"

"I can't …" A man's voice. New. Different.

Nova wrapped his bright color up with her own. Blended them together. Let his magic strengthen what was already there.

"She's healing herself."

"That's not possible."

Sharp shards of black and silver tried to cut through, but Nova pushed them off. She flicked away the distracting pink too. The woman was nothing here. Not now. Not with power coursing through Nova like a flood. The liquid rainbow filled the cleft inside, restoring all that had been lost. Power poured through her veins, flooding every fiber of her being.

A bright light filled her.

In the center of the light, a face.

Salamain?

Yes, Nova. I'm here.

Am I dead?

Not even close.

Wonder filled her. *I did it, didn't I? I used the magic.*

Yes, child.

It was the music.

The song of the High King.

The refrain was so beautiful. So achingly, perfectly beautiful.

Now what?

Now rest. There is still much to do.

Nova sighed, the light inside her shining out, washing away everything except peace. As Salamain's face faded, she drifted toward sleep. Real sleep.

"What in all creation was that?" a faint voice asked as she drifted away.

There was only silence in reply.

"What was that song you were singing?" Quentin asked.

Rose smiled up at him. "The song of the High King."

He smiled back, but his brows twitched. "High King?"

"Mm-hmm. I sang it for her."

He glanced at Morra, but she was working two rows over and had her back to them. "For your mom?"

"No, silly. For the girl." He glanced at Laura, but Rose shook her head. "The one they brought."

Something fluttered in the pit of Quentin's stomach.

"She was sick," Rose explained, "but she'll be okay."

"D-Did they help her?"

"They tried," Rose giggled. "She didn't need them. She healed herself already."

It was possible, right? He could feel Nova more strongly now than ever. She was very close. Could she really be here?

"She saw you in her dreams," Rose said, her voice suddenly shy.

Quentin's world slowly wound down to a stop. "She did?" His voice was barely a whisper.

"You, and her mom, and Grandpa Zeke. Everyone she loves."

Vaguely, he heard shouting. One of the guards turned, startled as Quentin raced by. Quentin didn't care and he didn't stop.

Nothing would stop him now.

Fever Dreams

Nova woke from her fever dream to an image of Quentin beside her. How real he looked.

She could almost believe he was really here, warm from the heat she generated, damp curls framing his cheeks and forehead. He was all that was good and familiar in her life. It was so easy to remember all the times they'd spent together growing up—birthdays blowing out candles, Christmas mornings laughing and tearing open gifts, days spent poring over good books or interesting blogs, endless summers spent talking and dreaming together. How had she ever left him behind?

She could see him so clearly, his dark lashes impossibly long, soft breaths stirring her hair. Quentin. Her best friend. Her knight in shining armor. Her fingers ached to trace the small crease between his brows, the one that only appeared when he was worried about something. How had she lain beside him so many times without ever kissing his soft lips? She couldn't stop herself from taking advantage of the dream. Slowly, tenderly, she pressed her lips against his. They were soft and warm, just as she'd imagined they would be. They even tasted like him, a subtle mix of earth and honey. If only he were truly here. As sleep pulled her back into its depths, she vowed she'd never miss another chance to let Quentin know how much she cared for him.

She didn't want to let go. This was a sweet dream. When she woke, she would be alone again, and he would be gone. But sleep was insistent, and her weakened body could not resist. Nova's eyes fluttered as her dream faded into darkness.

Sunlight pulled her back from the depths into awareness. She could feel the heat on her face and arm. Not damp heat, like her fever, but dry warmth. Nova groaned softly, cracking her eyes open. A jolt of shock flashed through her.

Quentin?

Was she still dreaming? He looked the same, yet different.

He looks older.

Her stomach gave a deep, hungry growl. The gnawing pangs of hunger clawed at her middle, and she needed to pee. But if she wasn't dreaming, then Quentin was really here. How could that be possible?

His eyes fluttered open, and she gasped. He smiled at her.

Not a dream. He was here.

"How?" She grabbed his hand. It was solid. "How did you ... how can you ...?"

Instead of answering, he grabbed her and pulled her into a rough hug. All the smells of him, the feel of his arms, even the way she fit into them was right. This was home.

Quentin was home.

Nova wanted to laugh and cry at the same time. But how could this be? How had he gotten across the Divide? How had he found her?

In that moment, she didn't care. She only cared he was here. His arms held her tightly, as if he'd never let go.

"You're crushing me a little," Nova said with a laugh.

He released her enough to look down, studying her face as if trying to believe she was here, that they were somehow together. The emotion shimmering in his eyes was almost her undoing.

She looked away before he could see her traitorous tears. "What is this place?"

His arms tightened a fraction. "Don't worry about that right now." The ocean colors of his voice rolled over her. She'd never seen anything more wonderful.

"But how did you get here? How did you cross the Divide?" A flash of anger sparked. "You crossed the Divide." She pushed to arm's length. "Quentin, you could have died."

Quentin grinned, but his smile was guarded. "Danger is my middle name."

"Sebastian is your middle name."

His eyes quickly scanned the room. "For crying out loud, don't let anyone hear you say that."

She sighed and laid her head against his chest, smiling at their old, familiar banter. "However you managed to get here, I'm glad you are."

"Like anyone could have stopped me," he answered, and the gruff, steely sound of his voice was new to her.

He'd changed.

They'd only been apart for what? A week? Yet, in that short span of time, they'd both been altered.

No matter. What mattered right now was that he was here, lying beside her. He'd survived whatever had gotten him here, and he was okay. They'd both weathered the storm.

The storm.

The Trench.

Nova leapt off the bed, vaguely surprised she was strong enough to move that fast. "You shouldn't be here. I'm sick, Quen."

He shook his head.

"Yes. Yes, I am. And it's contagious. You can't touch me."

He reached for her.

"No, don't!"

"Nova," he leaned over and caught one wrist, pulling her to him before she could escape. He captured her face with his hands. "It's okay. You're not sick anymore."

He was right. She felt strong. The place where she'd been hollowed out was gone. Filled. The memories of the song and the rainbow water came back to her in a rush. Her gaze met his. What she saw in his eyes surprised her.

"How did you know?"

He leaned back. "It's a long story."

One that would apparently have to wait, because at that moment the door at the far end of the room opened, and an oddly familiar figure strode toward them. Nova frowned. Why did she know that walk?

Quentin groaned.

But Nova stared at the beefy arms and blonde hair she knew all too well. Shock rooted her in place.

"What are *you* doing here?"

Laura Hennigan's dark-brown eyes flicked down to the bed. "Didn't have a chance to tell her yet, eh, Romeo?"

Romeo?

Wait. Tell her? She turned to Quentin, who buried his face in his hands. "Tell me what?"

"Look, I don't mean to ruin the class reunion," Laura said, the yellow ocher of her voice spinning out like a noxious fume. But we need to cut it short." Her eyes were locked on Quentin. "If they find you in here, they'll probably toss us all in a hole somewhere."

Nova's anger flared like an inferno. Her hands balled into fists. She was not going to stand here, and let Laura Hennigan of all people tell them—

"Hey," Quentin jumped off the bed and grabbed her arms. "Easy, Nova. She's on our side."

Nova's initial shock was nothing compared to the tsunami that hit her now. Quentin stared, eyes wide and uncertain. She stared back, her gaze drawn downward.

At his legs.

That he was standing on.

The room tilted.

"Woah."

Two sets of hands grabbed her, guiding her back to the bed and sitting her down. She realized one of the sets belonged to Laura and shoved them away. A whole parade of emotions marched across Quentin's face, not the least of which were guilt and shame.

Nova wanted to be excited. She wanted to scream and laugh and dance for joy. Quentin was standing.

And standing right beside him was the bully who had made Nova's life miserable. Who he'd apparently brought here with him. The person who had tormented her, day in and day out. The one who'd called Nova a freak.

"There's no time to explain now," Quentin said as Laura moved to a window and looked out, keeping her body in the shadows. "We have to go, but I'll come back. I promise. Please, just rest."

His mouth turned down, and with a start Nova remembered how she'd pressed her lips against his, thinking she was dreaming that he was there. No wonder she had been able to feel the softness of them so clearly. To taste him. Had he been awake? Did he know? The heat of embarrassment crept into her face and crawled down her neck.

Laura glanced at her, and Nova turned away before her guilt could give away her secret.

How could he have done this? He'd always looked out for her. Protected her. Now he'd brought, to the only place where Nova had a chance to fit in, the one person who hated her most.

He'd betrayed her.

"Nova," his voice cracked.

He had to know what she was thinking. What she must be feeling.

Footsteps vibrated from outside the room. Laura moved back the way she'd come, pulling Quentin after her.

"Come on, Romeo. You can fix things later. We need to go."

"I promise I'll be back," he called. "I'm not letting you go again."

Then he was gone.

The hollow inside Nova was deeper than ever before. How could Quentin have done this? Hot tears welled up, pouring out all of her joy and rainbow colors onto the cold, hard bed.

Symbols

Spell forms are comprised of symbols. Often these symbols represent something physical, such as a person or place. While the belief may be that the symbols are what control the outcome of the magic, the true driving force is actually the belief of the one using the magic. If they believe the symbol represents the physical, they will produce the necessary power. If they do not believe, the spell will be powerless. Form without faith is devoid of power.

—High Wizard Ezekial, on the *Factors of Magic*

Sharp Tooth

Tainted.

No one else saw, but Mole saw. He watched. He knew what had happened. How the girl had grabbed the soldier's arm.

She'd *infected* him.

Now the light clung to the soldier, worming into him like a parasite. The soldier left the barracks, headed across the gravel. The contamination was worse already.

Spreading.

Growing.

But Mole was ready. He knew what he was supposed to do. He hadn't been sure at first, but then the sign had happened. As soon as he'd found the talisman, he'd known. The object was meant for him. Left for him purposely, to make sure the outbreak was contained. The soldier couldn't be allowed to pollute anyone else.

So, Mole waited. He could be good at waiting when he wanted.

You must not want to very often.

He batted at his ears. "Go away!" Mama's voice was the worst voice. She had gotten louder lately. When he was here, in the barn.

Well, whose fault is that?

"Yours, Mama. Your fault."

Act like a rat, live like a rat.

Mole bared his teeth in the darkness. They were only flat little squares, not nice pointy teeth, but exposing them made him feel better.

Don't you look at your Mama that way. Do you need another lesson? Is that it?

No. No more lessons. He was done with lessons. Mole smacked at his face with his palms.

"Get out. *Getoutgetoutgetout!*"

He was a grown man now. He didn't have to listen to her anymore. He squeezed his eyes shut, pounding on his head with his fists. A sound made him look up. A rustling, sighing sound that made his whisker fingers shake. He shouldn't have opened his eyes, but he did.

"Daemon!" He flung himself backward, shoving with his feet until his back came against something solid.

The apparition floated toward him, face contorted. Black hair threaded with dull gray drifted like seaweed in the tide. Mottled lips twisted. Her eyes had always been awful—blue and cold as chips of glacier ice. Oh, how those eyes could glare—but this was worse. This was so much worse, because now those eyes were milky and dead. Filmy muck writhed like mucus over the blue orbs, and still they glared. Glared and shined with a cold light.

I know what you are. The Banshee screamed.

He cowered, shaking.

You think you can fool me, but I know.

Drool slid down his chin. Not again. He couldn't stand it. "I banished you." He howled.

My baby died. You think I didn't know? My baby died, and you took his place.

There was no other baby. Never. Just him.

You ate him. You ate him, and you took his place.

Glowing eyes of daemon fury flew at him, reaching for his soul.

You can't hide from me. I'll find you, and I'll kill you for what you did.

But he had hid. He'd become the rat she always accused him of being. He'd stayed, still and quiet, waiting and waiting.

And she'd come for him. Oh, yes. She'd come to finally kill him. To claim back the heart she said he'd stolen. Only she'd waited too long. He wasn't a little rat anymore. He was older. Stronger. Maybe not like other boys, but strong enough.

Stronger than her.

She'd been surprised. He remembered. Her angry glowing eyes had flown open wide. He'd seen her fear, and her terror had exhilarated him. No more beatings. No more being locked in the barn. No more rat.

Mole jumped up, and the apparition stopped moving. Eyes went wide. Yes.

She flew back, away from him. Away from his strength. He followed. She wasn't getting away this time. He was no rat anymore. He was a mole, and he had at least one sharp tooth. She flew away from him, and for an instant, her image hit something solid and shimmered. She had nowhere to go. She was trapped.

Mole bared his teeth. He lunged at her and buried his one sharp tooth as far as it would go. "I killed you already." His scream echoed. "I killed you. I killed you already."

Her image flickered. Behind her face, another face appeared. Mole tilted his head in confusion. She looked the way she had when he'd been little, when there was still softness in her as she hummed and rocked him … before she'd changed. Then the image of his mother evaporated like smoke and was gone. In her place was the soldier.

Mole yanked his hands back, raking his fingernails down his face. He'd had no choice. She would have killed him.

You had to. Geo's voice now. Not mocking but not nice either.

You had to kill her, and you had to kill him. They were tainted.

Yes. Tainted.

The soldier had been infected. Even now, his face slack with shock as he slid slowly to his knees and then to the floor with Mole's sharp tooth still stuck in him, the light seeped from him to pool on the floor, rising in tiny specks into the air above him.

Mole jumped back.

He mustn't let himself be corrupted.

No, Geo's voice crawled through his head. *You chose darkness. You chose it the day you killed your mama.*

Yes. Darkness was better than the wretched light—the light that seared his soul and choked him. The light that showed him who he was. He hated the light. He was a mole, through and through.

And with the soldier dead, there was only one vile light left to put out.

Willing

"Mom? Grandpa Zeke? What are you doing here?"

They didn't answer. How strange. Nova reached out to touch her mother's arm. The image dissolved.

I'm dreaming.

She wished the vision had been real. She wanted so much to be able to see them, but they were gone. The dream changed. She saw her notebook on her desk, opened to one of her drawings. The pattern was familiar, yet not. The sketch looked like one of her drawings but doubled. Twin versions laid side-by-side on the paper. She'd never drawn anything like that.

Then a finger appeared and pulled half the image away.

Mirror, Mirror.

The words whispered in her brain. What did they mean?

The mirror changed direction, and instead of reflecting her drawing, the glass reflected a face.

Nova gasped.

Her eyes opened to find the empty bed where she'd slept. She wished Quentin was still there, and their earlier encounter had been nothing more than a dream. But what had transpired had been all too real.

"I see you're well."

Nova spun and stumbled, nearly falling to the floor before she righted herself.

"Easy. Easy," The man standing there held out a hand to steady her.

His yellow hair and toffee eyes were unfamiliar, but his voice wasn't. She'd heard it before. "Who are you?"

"My name is Sol. I'm a healer."

Like an echo, the sound of voices came back to her.

"Go and get Sol," a woman's voice had said.

And later, "Sol, what's happening?"

"She's healing herself." That had been this man's voice.

"I don't need healing," Nova said carefully. Should she trust him?

"You're right. You don't." The way he spoke made him sound mysterious. As if he was trying to solve some great puzzle or equation.

"Where am I?" Nova asked.

"This place is called the Sanctuary, although some have used other names."

A straightforward answer. So why did she see the curves and bends in his earth-brown colors that indicated something hidden in his voice?

"How did I get here?"

His forehead creased as he looked down. "How much do you remember?"

He was hedging.

"I remember a storm," Nova answered truthfully, "and feeling like something was inside me, eating me alive."

Sol nodded.

"After that my memory gets fuzzy. There were voices, but they seemed far away."

And the music. The singing. There was that too.

"When they brought you here you were hot with fever," Sol said, as if confirming.

"How did I get well?"

Sol leaned forward. "I was rather hoping you could tell me."

Nova's heart fluttered hard and fast like the wings of a bird.

"We tried to heal you," he said, his words soft but intense, "but we couldn't." He stayed that way a moment longer, leaned toward her as if he were a jaguar waiting for her to move before he pounced. Then he leaned back. "Now here you are, no fever, no sign you were ever sick."

"Maybe I just got better."

"No one just gets better." His voice was serious, and his shoulders sagged. "Not from the Trench."

"Then you tell me what happened," Nova challenged him, half hoping he had an answer for her. She needed to know if her suspicions were true.

"The Trench drains a person's magic," Sol said, as if giving a lesson. "The very energy that powers an individual is torn away, leaving nothing but an empty hole. That's why they call this sickness the Trench. Once a person's magic—their essence—is drained, the body starts to die. Creative magic cannot grow what is no longer there. Neutral cannot balance what is gone. Destructive cannot destroy what has already been annihilated."

She remembered the feeling of being hollowed out. Of the vast emptiness left inside her like a wound. She shivered, realizing how close she had come to dying.

"Ishtar is Destructive and Neutral," Sol went on. "I am Creative and Neutral. Only together can we heal this particular disease. One to destroy and hold at bay the Trench itself, and the other to restore and balance what was lost." His eyes burned as if a fire had been lit inside them. "Healing requires all three factors."

Could she have used all three to heal herself?

"Where did you come from?" he asked, his voice fierce and urgent. "Are you a …"

A noise echoed from outside the door. He didn't move, but his gaze shifted to the side. Listening. Sensing. Then he was up and out of his chair, hurrying over to her bedside and leaning close.

"Quickly now," he whispered. "Lie back and pretend to be asleep."

The door creaked open. Heart pounding in her chest, Nova closed her eyes. She heard soft footsteps approach.

"Is she still sleeping?" A woman's voice. The other voice she remembered. The one some called Lady, and who Sol called Ishtar.

"I think whatever happened drained her."

There was a moment of quiet.

"What exactly *did* happen, Sol?"

Nova thought the woman's voice held more than a trace of distrust. Why? This was her man. Her healer. Why wouldn't she trust him?

"I wish I knew." That, at least, sounded like the truth.

Ishtar must have thought the same. "We need to find out."

Twin points of flame ignited on Nova's skin. She wasn't just being looked at, she was being looked into. *Invaded.*

Like white blood cells called to defend against infection, streams of rainbow-colors flooded toward the spot inside her, blocking the probe. The burning stopped as the cool waters of Nova's magic surged, filling her skin and her senses.

Ishtar grunted. "I can't sense her."

"Nor can I," Sol said.

"Put her to work with the others but watch her closely."

"As you wish."

The sound of retreating footsteps filled Nova with relief. When the door closed, she let out a long, slow breath and opened her eyes, preparing for another round with Sol, but he was gone. The room around her was empty.

Why had he protected her? Or had he? Maybe he was saving the information for himself. She didn't know what to believe.

If only Quentin …

The thought died before she'd even completed it. How could she trust Quentin when he was here with the person who had tormented her most? Maybe she should leave. Find a way out of here now.

She sighed. Her heart knew better. She couldn't leave. Not now. Despite everything, Quentin was her best friend. Whatever had happened, she owed him a chance to explain. Though that would not make his betrayal easier to swallow. He'd better have a mighty good reason for having Laura here and for being here himself.

Now what? Sit and wait? Nova hated waiting. Patience was not one of her virtues. She sat on the bed, trying to think everything through. Where were Seth and Viru? What had happened to them? Did they have the Trench too? How had she gotten to this place they called the Sanctuary? Had they brought her? She didn't think so. The fever dreams were fuzzy, but she thought she remembered strange hands pulling her along, and for some reason she remembered seeing Viru in a tree.

An hour later, as the sun began to lengthen into long shadows, she still had no answers.

At the far end of the room, the door opened. For a foolish moment, Nova thought Quentin had come back to rescue her. A smallish woman dressed all in white walked into the room. She had dark hair but light green eyes. She smiled at Nova as she came near.

"You're awake." The woman said. "Lady will be so pleased. Are you hungry?"

Nova's stomach rumbled.

"Excellent. Follow me. I'll see you have some food. You'll begin work tomorrow, if you're well enough."

Nova couldn't help herself. "Work?"

The woman nodded patiently. "Of course. Everyone who is healed must work. That is how we repay the Lady."

Ah. So that's how things worked here. No wonder Quentin had looked so odd when she asked where they were. They were prisoners, forced to stay and work here whether they liked it or not. They were slaves.

Herself included.

"Come," the woman said. She headed back the way she'd come, leaving Nova to trail after her.

All else aside, she needed to see what this place looked like so she could start planning a way to get out.

When the woman led Nova across a wide room and to a set of double doors, the sight beyond them stopped her cold. All around them, as far as she could see, there were fields. In those fields, hundreds of people worked, sweating in the sun, harvesting and tending some kind of crop. The reference to 'work' made so much more sense now.

Between the steps of the building and the edge of the field, there were dozens of guards. They wore silver and red uniforms and had weapons harnessed to hips, shoulders and legs. However these weapons worked, the guards were well-armed.

"Come," the woman said again when she noticed Nova had stopped walking.

She waited until Nova came down the steps, her jeans and sneaks feeling oddly out of place, then resumed walking. The woman headed toward a round building tucked away at the edge of the field. As they neared the building, Nova heard sounds that reminded her of the gym back in school. The squeak of people walking, the bangs of things being moved around, and the hum of voices. The woman swung open a door, and Nova saw the place was a cafeteria. The smells of meats, breads, and the mineral tang of vegetables wafted through the opening.

The woman motioned for Nova to go ahead. "Go and eat. When you are done, ask for Emyl. She will show you where to go next."

And with a quick duck of her head, the woman hurried away.

"That wasn't strange at all," Nova muttered.

"She's a willing," a voice said next to her.

Nova turned. An older woman leaned against the wall, waiting for a turn to pour something that looked like water into a cup. She had light green overalls on, and her face was sun-kissed but still looked young in spite of the gray threaded through her long braid.

"As in, she doesn't owe anything but stays here anyway." The woman shrugged. "Don't understand why anyone would want to be within a hundred miles of here if they didn't have to be. Willings like her, they feel guilty."

"For what?"

The woman barked out a laugh. "For not being us." She motioned for Nova to follow her. "Come on. I'll show you where the vittles are."

She led the way through a field of tables to a long buffet at the front. As they walked, the woman glanced behind them. When they finally reached the buffet, the woman leaned close. "Are you Nova?" she asked softly.

Nova swallowed her surprise and nodded.

"I'm Bell. Friend of Morra's. She and her group said to keep an eye out for you. They should be along any minute. Grab some food and head back over by the door where you came in. Sit at one of the tables in the back, behind the water service."

Bell melted into the throng of moving people and disappeared.

Someone bumped into Nova. "Move it already," a man growled. "We ain't got all day."

Nova quickly stepped to the side as four others followed behind the man, eyeing her as if she were "a thumb in a bowl of fingers," as Quentin's mother liked to say. She'd never quite understood the reference until now. She wished they could be back home, having a normal conversation and a normal meal instead of here.

She gave a surprised laugh. Did she really just think of home as normal? She'd spent her entire life feeling out of place there, yet here she was in the place where she actually fit, and she was longing for her old life.

Nova picked up a square white tray and followed the group that had jostled her. They moved around the table clockwise, picking up whatever looked appealing. Nova saw a variety of meats, settling on something golden brown with a rich, sweet smell. There were small hard loaves of bread and what looked like cooked spinach. Malanqua, of course, but she'd had enough already to last a lifetime. She opted for a smaller, round kiwi-like fruit.

She waited in line for a cup of water before finding the table Bell had pointed out. All of the tables on this side of the room were empty.

"That's why we picked them," a little girl chimed, skipping toward her. The girl looked over her shoulder at a woman who walked behind her. "She's here."

Quentin burst around the table and pulled her into a hug. Seeing him like this, not just standing but so full of life, she could forgive him everything. It didn't matter how he'd gotten here or even that behind him Laura made her way to the table. All that mattered was they were together.

Quentin was somehow, impossibly, here. Of course, he'd come after her. She would have done the same for him. *Had* done the same for him, really. How could she stay angry when his face was buried in her hair, and his arms crushed her to him like he would never let her go?

When he finally eased his grip, he turned and smiled. "Everyone, this is Nova. Nova, this is Rose, and her mother, Morra."

"We already met," Rose said, sitting on a chair and happily wiggling her feet.

Nova looked at the little girl, confused. "We did?"

"Oh, yes," the girl said, nodding. "You might not remember, though. You were asleep." She smiled proudly. "I sang anyway."

Nova vaguely remembered hearing a voice from within her fever dreams. A song. Threads of gold spun through her memory.

Rose nodded, although Nova hadn't said anything. "The song of the High King."

Mirror, Mirror

As it turned out, Emyl was more than happy to let Nova choose to bunk with her friends. The wisp of a girl, barely more than a teen, seemed relieved to not have to figure out where to put another person. When Laura stepped in front of Nova and said they had room for another person in their quarters, the girl had swallowed and nodded so hard, Nova worried Emyl's head would pop off.

"Yes, yes, that's good," she'd said, her hands fluttering about like birds. "Nova can work the fields in your section. You can give her one of the extra baskets."

Then Emyl hurried off as fast as her legs could carry her, looking back over her shoulder as if expecting Laura to give chase.

"Poor thing," Nova said softly.

"Poor nothing," Laura sneered.

"She's just a kid." Nova couldn't help but defend her. "You can't expect a girl her age to know what to do in a place like this."

"You're younger than she is." Laura's statement hung in the air as they all looked after the retreating figure.

"She's right," Morra said, her face mirroring the sadness in her voice. "She made a choice to be here."

"Then she's a …" What had the woman called them?

"Willing," Morra said with a nod. "They think being on the wrong side will get them something, but you can't bargain with evil."

Morra was right. As, to Nova's astonishment, was Laura.

"This Ishtar person isn't likely to let us go then?"

The others shared a serious look.

"No," Morra answered as they walked toward the bunk house. "This is how Ishtar obtains her power. From selling what others reap. Some are willing to pay good money for Phoria. Money is power. Ishtar's built an empire on the crop, and she's not likely to let go of her control without a fight."

"Then we'll have to find a way around her."

"Now there's a statement I can work with," Laura said with a grin.

Nova wasn't sure how to feel about the two of them agreeing.

When they walked into the building, all other thought ceased. The sheer noise of so many people together in one place was overwhelming. Morra patted Nova's arm, as if understanding. Rose, apparently unaffected by her surroundings, skipped down the hall ahead of them, waving at people and stopping to talk with some of the other children.

By the time they reached their small room at the end of an endless number of hallways, Nova was completely turned around. "How do you find your way back here?" she asked, feeling like a mouse in a maze.

She stared at the small room, barely large enough for them to all fit, even if they slept side-by-side. There were rolls of blankets along one wall. No furniture. Not even a chair. Everyone sat on the floor, except Rose who climbed into her mother's lap.

"Rose and Laura can both find their way around without a problem," Quentin answered.

Nova glanced at Laura who shrugged. "I've always been good with directions."

That probably helped you to find the people you wanted to pick on.

Nova gave herself a mental shake. She needed to focus. They had to figure out how to get out of this place. Being stuck here meant not finding her father and not figuring out how to stop Viru's Order from trying to kill her. Every moment she lost was another moment when an assassin could show up. Or a whole army of them. She shuddered to think what would happen then.

"What's our first move?" she asked.

Quentin leaned forward, resting his elbows on his legs. "Do you think you'd be able to do what you did before? You know, open a hole?"

She stared at him, confused.

"I know it'd probably be hard, but if you could make another hole, we could walk back through and be home."

"What about Morra and Rose?"

"I thought they might come with us." His neck and cheeks began to redden. "I figured your mom and Grandpa Zeke could get them back where they belonged."

Nova took a moment to digest Quentin's suggestions. What he said made sense. They knew how to cross the Divide. Otherwise they wouldn't have ended up on the other side to begin with.

"Too dangerous," Nova said, shaking her head. "I don't know enough about what happens or how making a hole works. Rose and Morra could end up trapped on the other side." Or worse, in between. Something told her the void they had stepped through was not a good place to be stuck in.

Morra smiled. "Don't you worry about us."

"Daddy and Jacob will come to get us," Rose added with a confident nod.

Nova wasn't about to let them stay here to wait for that to happen while the rest of them took off.

"Next option?"

Quentin's face tightened. "Don't dismiss the idea, Nova. If we can get back—"

"What about the people trying to kill me?" Anger sparked inside Nova's chest, warming her face. Did he not understand why she'd come here? What she'd been trying to do? "They're not going to stop just because we go back. Did you forget about that?"

"No, but—"

"I have to find my father. He's the only one who might know how to stop them."

Something washed across Quentin's face, and he looked away. "You don't even know him," he said so softly she barely heard the words.

Shock filled her. What was he doing? Was he trying to help her or not?

"That's part of what I'm trying to fix," she snapped.

His face flushed. "All I'm saying is what if he's not what you imagined? I mean, there's got to be a reason why your mom didn't talk about him, right? Maybe she was trying to protect you."

"Protect me? She *lied* to me." All of the emotion Nova held in check for so long threatened to burst out. "There are people trying to *kill* me. And if Mom, or Grandpa Zeke, or *you* get in their way, they'll kill you too! They don't care. They've been taught to believe I create some kind of horrible danger just by existing. Everything they believe requires them to kill me before some disaster can happen. You don't think that's more dangerous than meeting my father?"

She was embarrassed to find hot tears had welled in her eyes, and she turned away before anyone could see them fall.

Quentin was at her side in an instant, his arms wrapped around her.

"I'm sorry," he said softly. "I didn't mean it like that. I'm sorry."

She didn't understand. What was everyone thinking? Why couldn't anyone seem to recognize the danger they were in?

"I wish your Grandpa Zeke was here," Quentin murmured.

With his words, images from Nova's dream flooded back—Mom and Grandpa pointing at her pictures, her drawings, duplicated on the pages of her notebook. Grandpa Zeke had never seen her drawings. Yet, in the dream, he pointed at them as if he was telling her something about them.

"It wasn't just a dream," Rose piped up.

Nova's blood drained to her feet. "Wh … what?" She wiped her face and looked up.

"What you saw," Rose said, tilting her head. "It wasn't a dream. I know. I have them too."

"You have what?"

"Visions." She grinned. "I saw the nice man before he came to heal me. The one with all the scars. I knew he was coming." She looked up at her mother, who smiled and kissed the top of her head.

"What makes you think I have visions?"

Rose's face smoothed, and in that instant Nova thought she glimpsed an angel. "We've both been touched by him," the girl explained.

Such a simple answer, but goosebumps rose all up and down Nova's arms in response. Could the child be right?

"If I wasn't dreaming," Nova murmured, "how did they …?"

Quentin stared at Nova. "Tell us what you saw."

"I saw Mom and Grandpa Zeke." She glanced at Quentin, and he nodded for her to keep going. "My notebook was open, like someone had turned to a specific page." The pattern had looked so familiar. "I saw one of my drawings, but the pattern was doubled."

Mirror, Mirror.

"Then someone pulled half the image away, and I saw …"

"What?" Quentin whispered.

"She saw herself," Rose said. "Like in a mirror."

"Mirror, Mirror." Nova echoed. The words weren't random, they went together.

Like a name.

"Can you draw the form you saw in your dream?" Morra asked.

How odd that she would call Nova's drawing a form. "I think so."

"We need to get her some paper," Quentin said.

"No." Rose shook her head emphatically. "She needs a mirror, silly."

Something rushed through Nova, filling her up. Was it possible? Hope thrummed through her veins.

"Wait here," Morra said, scooting Rose out of the way. She hurried out the door, leaving it ajar.

The rest of them sat in silence, as if aware something, some *event* was happening. When Morra reappeared a few minutes later, she clutched a small round mirror in her hand.

"Here," she thrust it at Nova. "You can use this."

Nova set the mirror on the floor, feeling suddenly nervous. What if she couldn't recreate the pattern? What if she broke the mirror? She didn't even know whose it was. If—

"It's all right," Morra said with a smile. "Go ahead."

Rose cuddled back into her mother's lap. "I would help," she said with a serious look, "but I can't stay in the lines very good yet."

A chuckle of laughter bubbled up inside Nova, soothing her frayed nerves. She looked down at the mirror, then closed her eyes and tried to remember exactly what the drawing had looked like. The pattern rose out of her thoughts as if waiting for her. Repeating lines, each individual one lay end to end with the next, like pickup sticks.

"But do I draw one or two?"

"One," Rose answered confidently. "The mirror will make the other one."

Nova gasped. Rose was right. The mirror image was exactly that—a mirror image. She opened her eyes, suddenly sure of exactly what she had to do.

She pulled the mirror up to her face and breathed until the glass was covered in condensation. Then she quickly traced the image from her drawing into the vapor. Time seemed to stop. The edges, which had already started evaporating, halted. The image froze in place and began to burn. Sparks of color ran along each line of her drawing like the fuse on a piece of dynamite. When the last one lit up, the whole image flashed, both into the mirror and above it.

"… think she's done it," the familiar voice filled the room. Nova couldn't believe her ears.

The light shining above the mirror grew. In the middle of it, a face appeared.

"Nova? Nova, is that you?"

Nova's lips went numb. "Mom?"

"Oh, thank God, Nova!" Her mother's face was covered with tears. "Are you okay? Are you hurt?"

"I'm fine." She grinned. "I'm good."

"Here, let me see, Mira." Her mother disappeared. What Nova saw next in the light made her heart leap for joy.

"Grandpa Zeke!"

His brows were pushed low over his eyes, but even in this odd mist-light she could see them sparkle. "You figured out the spell, did you?"

"With some help from my friends," she answered with a laugh.

"I knew you could do it." Her Grandfather's proud smile warmed Nova's heart.

Quentin gave her a huge squeeze.

"Now listen to me," Zeke said. "You can do the Mirror, Mirror spell on any reflective material, but the surface has to be able to create the second image to work."

Nova nodded.

"Good. Next thing you need to know is the Divide is failing."

What?

In the background, she could hear her mother's protests.

"No," Zeke argued. "There's no time for that. She must know." He focused on Nova. "You mustn't try to come back through. Not yet. It's far too dangerous."

He paused to make sure Nova nodded.

"We can't get through either, so we'll have to try to help from here."

"Okay, Grandpa."

"Tell us what's happening. Where are you?"

Nova swallowed. Man was her Mom about to freak. "We're in a kind of a ... a sanctuary. A woman, Ishtar—"

"Ishtar," Grandpa Zeke bellowed. "That she devil. What's she done now?"

He knew her?

"She heals people with the Trench," Nova explained, "but then she makes them pay by working in her fields."

"The Trench? Nova, are you sick?" Her mother's voice echoed.

"Not anymore."

Grandpa Zeke stared at Nova. A knowing smile tugged at his lips. "Ishtar healed you?"

An answering smile tugged at Nova's lips. "No, I healed myself."

"That's my girl." His smile widened into a full grin.

Nova swelled with pride. It grew when she heard her mother give a whoop in the background.

"Now," Zeke said, back to all business. "Let's figure out how to get you out of there."

Inner Sight

Zenesthese, individuals who can see magic, are rare. Moreover, there are some who can not only physically see magic, but who have the ability to look inward and expand their sight outward on a metaphysical plane. This ability is called Inner Sight, and as implied, requires one to look inward in order to be able to see outward. When this ability is achieved, the seer will have vision far beyond normal physical sight.

—High Wizard Ezekial, on the *Factors of Magic*

LUCIEN

"Found you."

Lucien's eyes narrowed in the darkness. He reached out with one hand, locating the small volume without looking. He wasn't about to take his eyes off the rippling image.

He watched as they communicated.

"How unlike you, Zeke," he said, his voice a little more than a whisper.

Such a powerful wizard should know that sending magic through the Divide required a starting and end point. He should know such a thing would pinpoint Nova's location like a dot on a map.

"Such a foolish mistake."

Lucien focused on the image of the girl with the dark hair and vivid blue eyes. The eyes were Mira's, but everything else in her countenance resembled Lucien. He liked that his daughter looked like him. She had his strength, too. Of that, he was sure. Her power might be buried under whatever Mira and Zeke had taught her, muted by living in a world where magic did not thrive, but she had too much natural ability to be totally affected. Her gift would have bled out of her at every chance.

Interesting choice of words—*bled out of her*.

Lucien wished things didn't have to be the way they were. Seeing her real power in action would have been interesting.

No. He mustn't let himself be distracted. Not now. Not after coming so far. She had been created to fulfill a destiny, and her destiny was his to claim. He could not step back from the brink. Not when all the power of the Trine was within his grasp.

The idea filled him, the width and breadth of his future swelling inside him. Gone was the boy he had been, strong but always seeking something more. Lucien Gray would be the fulfillment, the embodiment of power. Glory was within his grasp. All he needed to do was go and claim it.

As if in synchronization with his thoughts, the communication ended. The water in the stone bowl stilled and went dark.

The time had come.

Still clutching the small book in his hand, he pushed up from the table and strode purposefully to the door, pausing only to pick up one additional item.

The barn only held one horse—his favorite. The young stallion was spirited but no match for Lucien's hand. Rather like Nova. His pack was already prepared in anticipation. He slipped the object into it, then tied the pack onto the back of the saddle and led the black horse out into the rain. He pulled his cloak around him and leapt on, startling the stallion into a quick run. He let him have his head. Shining black hooves pounded the mud, spraying dirt in all directions.

Lucien made certain his cloak covered the pack, ensuring the small mirror packed inside would be protected. If they made the same mistake again, Lucien would be there to intercept their little chat.

Time for Nova to meet her father.

CYRIL

Mordoon enjoyed the silence of the moments just before sunset when the last rays of the sun spread a carpet of fire along the ground. This day, with Cyril at his shoulder, the carpet looked more like blood spilling out over the normally serene valley. The sight filled him with dark foreboding. Viru, one of his most promising young acolytes, had not come back from his mission.

"She's turned him," Cyril accused.

Mordoon refused to believe. He had raised Viru like his own son. The boy was devout. He would not be so easily swayed from all he had grown to know and believe. Not unless something so powerful had happened that Viru's very heart had changed. Or unless, as Cyril continued to assert, the girl had somehow corrupted him.

All of his life, Mordoon had believed completely in the teachings, in the prophecies. But recent events filled him with unease. Was his faith lacking? Did doubt hinder him from seeing the truth? Or was this unrest something more?

"We must send another," Cyril said from behind.

"We should give Viru more time," Mordoon argued. "It's only been—"

"No."

The simple word sent shards of ice through Mordoon's bones. Cyril had given more than an answer. He'd given a command.

"Prophecy says—"

"I know what prophecy says," Cyril snapped. "The Order was built on prophecy. Do you so easily forget your oaths?"

Mordoon's face heated. "Of course not."

"We must not lose focus. What we do, we do to protect the future of mankind. Every mother, every child. We are the only hope for all of them."

Mordoon had always believed this to be true. The prophecy had seemed so clear. One child, one powerful child, who had to be stopped before bringing about *the end of every world*. The prophecy said life's blood must be spilled. There could be little doubt of the meaning. He had studied the ancient words and believed their truth for the entirety of his life.

Why did his heart betray him now?

"Who were you thinking to send?" He was giving in too easily, but what else could he do? Cyril was right. He had given his oath.

"One will not be enough. We must send more."

A cold ball formed in his belly. How many must be sacrificed to this task? Was this truly the will of the One God? He must pray on this, but there was no time.

"How many?" he asked with a tongue devoid of moisture.

There was no answer.

Mordoon turned, but Cyril had frozen in place. His eyes were distant and unfocused. He was looking inward, Mordoon realized, seeing something far from here. This was what intimidated the others so much. Cyril had inner sight. He could see people and places from great distances inside his head by pushing his magic outward. The ability was impressive and frightening. A slow smile spread over Cyril's face. The cold ball in Mordoon's stomach grew.

Cyril turned to Mordoon, eyes blazing. "All," he answered. "All must go."

Mordoon struggled not to fall onto his knees. "All?"

"Fate has revealed her to me." His voice was like the rasp of claws. He turned, walking quickly back toward the monastery, forcing Mordoon to jog to keep pace. "We will go and claim her before she can escape. We will have her blood once and for all."

The viciousness in Cyril's words brought Mordoon to a stumbling halt. Cyril walked on, unaware Mordoon no longer followed.

Mordoon trembled. "May the One God help us all."

Cyril gathered his things quickly. There was no time to waste. If he had noticed the communication, Lucien had undoubtedly noted it as well. Perhaps not in the same way, but the man was too driven to overlook such an important thing.

Cyril should know. He'd taught the boy everything he knew. Lucien had been nothing but an eager child when Cyril had met him and taken him under his wing. Granted, a child with strong magic and a rare Dual combination. There were so few Creative Destructives. Without Neutral to limit him or to balance him, turning Lucien's power to his own design had been simple.

The only hindrance had been the woman, *Mira*. Cyril had used every tool in his arsenal, every trick and every move to cajole Lucien's heart away from his young bride.

But the boy had always been hungry for power. His thirst for control was his greatest weakness. Cyril had exploited this need ruthlessly, and Lucien had given in, as Cyril had known he would. Oh, how he'd enjoyed sending his puppet dashing about on mission after mission, finding tidbits Cyril had left scattered about. On one of those trips, Lucien had found the most delicious tidbit of all.

"You did well," Cyril whispered to his memory of Lucien. "You did better than I ever imagined you could."

Of course, what Cyril hadn't imagined was that Mira would flee on the very day he had finally convinced Lucien of her treachery. She had slipped away, taking the promise of the future with her. She had hidden in the one place she knew they could not go. Across the Divide. And in so doing, she had fulfilled the very prophecy she had sought to escape, if unwittingly.

She had been outside of his grasp, but he'd felt the tremor in his soul on the day the Trine was born. He'd been planning ever since.

Now, finally, the destiny he'd designed had come back through the Divide and stood within his reach.

The time had come to claim it.

Colors

"What color am I? What color am I?" Rose jumped up and down in excitement.

Nova had to laugh. Waiting was horrible but seeing the excitement and joy on Rose's face helped ease the tension. They had decided to get to know each other better as a way to pass the time until Grandpa Zeke could come up with a plan to get them away and out of danger.

Nova had explained her synesthesia, which Morra nodded and called 'Zen' as Seth had. When she'd talked about being able to see sounds, Laura had asked her to clarify. "How does it work? What do the sounds look like?"

Nova had looked for some sign that Laura was making fun, but she seemed serious enough.

"When people talk, I see colors and patterns in the air. Some people's voices look smooth, others are choppy or sharp. Sometimes the pattern changes when they yell or get emotional."

"Do different people have different colors or do they all blend together?" Rose quipped.

Nova was startled by the girl's insightful question. "Everyone has a color or shade different from anyone else's."

At which point, Rose had jumped up and run over to her, piping her eager request to know what color she was. Nova couldn't help but like the girl. She was so sweet and a little weird, which reminded Nova of herself as a child.

"Your voice comes out like a soft ribbon," Nova explained, trying to describe what she saw in a way the girl would be able to understand. "It's wavy, but not too much. And you're special because you have two colors. They sort of weave together when you talk."

Rose's eyes were wide with wonder. "What are they?"

"One is pure white," Nova paused as the girl sucked in a deep breath. "The other is gold."

"Like his." Rose sighed happily.

Nova knew she meant Salamain. "The two colors together are very pretty. Almost as pretty as you."

Rose giggled. "What color is Momma's voice?"

Morra smiled. The glint of curiosity in her eyes was unmistakable. "Hers is silver."

Nova had experienced a lot of colors in her lifetime, but the ones on this side of the Divide made the ones she'd known before pale in comparison. They were richer, more vivid, as if they were more real. Or perhaps understanding what they were had made them more tangible.

Rose seemed duly impressed with the color assigned to her mother. "What about Laura?"

Nova's cheeks heated. She'd always thought of Laura's color as horrible, an accurate depiction of the kind of person she was. She didn't want to answer, but how could she not? They were all looking at Nova eagerly.

"Yellow," she said finally.

Rose nodded sagely. "Like the sun," she said, "and the light that makes things grow. That's 'cause you're so strong, Laura."

Laura flashed the girl a half grin but said nothing.

"What about me?" Quentin asked.

She elbowed him. "You know your color. I told you ages ago."

"It hasn't changed at all?" For some reason, he looked uncomfortable asking. Almost shy.

What was that all about?

"No. Your voice is blue-green with deep curls, like ocean waves. The shape and color together are very soothing …"

She trailed off, afraid she'd said too much. Her face was on fire.

Quentin cleared his throat. "What about Rose's light? Do you see that too?"

"Her light?" Nova got the feeling he was intentionally changing the subject.

Quentin nodded, as if he'd asked a silly question. He gazed around the room, the lines in his forehead growing deeper. "Don't any of you see Rose's light?" He turned to Laura. "You did. You saw it with the guard in the field."

Laura nodded, and relief filled Quentin's face.

"She glowed when she touched the soldier. The one in the field."

"After he left, his footprint glowed a little too."

Laura quirked an eyebrow. "I didn't notice."

"When I touched it, the pain in my shoulders went away."

His voice trailed off, and he swallowed, glancing at Nova nervously.

"Wait," Laura said, frowning. "I thought you were a block? I thought magic didn't work on you?"

Quentin stared at her, blinking in surprise.

Rose giggled, pulling all their gazes to her. "That wasn't magic, silly. That's the light of the High King."

"What do you mean, honey?" Morra asked.

"When the man healed me," Rose said. "He used the light. He filled me up." She grinned. "Sometimes the light leaks out a little."

Morra's lips parted with wonder.

"Salamain." Nova said, remembering how wonder had filled her as he'd recounted his story of the High King at the campfire. "His name is Salamain."

Rose smiled a secret smile. "I call him a different name," she said, "but that's him. The man with the scars."

"Wait," Quentin broke in, "scars?"

Nova nodded. "He's covered in them."

Quentin didn't say anything more, but he looked like he'd seen a ghost.

The last light of day started to dim. Already the room was so dark they could barely see each other.

"I'll try again in the morning to see if Mom and Grandpa have any ideas," Nova said as they spread out, trying to get comfortable with nothing but thin blankets to cushion the hard floor.

"Be careful," Rose sighed, as she closed her eyes, her head against her mother's chest.

The back of Nova's neck prickled. What did she mean? Rose was a sweet girl, but there was more to her than met the eye. Being touched by Salamain had changed her somehow. Her sleepy words sounded like a warning, but of what?

Nova's thoughts were cut off as Quentin laid his blanket beside hers and stretched out next to her. His arm found her in the growing darkness and pulled her close. She rolled gratefully into the circle of his embrace, leaning her head on his chest and listening to the sound of his heartbeat as she breathed in the familiar smell of him. If she closed her eyes, she could almost imagine they were still kids, having one of their regular campouts in the yard, sleeping under the stars.

Except his skinny arms had become harder, and her head had to be farther up now to lie on his chest. The realization made her feel strange inside. When he pressed his lips to the top of her head, a swarm of butterflies took flight inside her stomach. What was this? Why did lying beside him suddenly feel so different?

I kissed him.

Heat flushed her face and neck. She was grateful for the darkness in the room. Had he been awake when she'd pressed her lips against his? Wouldn't he have said something by now? Did the fact he hadn't meant he didn't know or that the kiss was no big deal?

Nova sighed. Kissing Quentin was definitely a big deal to her. When his hand gently pushed the hair back from her face, tingles zipped through her. Without warning, she wanted him to kiss her. She wanted to explore his soft lips. To feel him intentionally press his mouth against hers, both of them knowing it was no dream and—

With a gasp she pulled herself back, trying to cover the sound with a fake yawn. What was she doing? This was Quentin. Her best friend since they were little. What would he think if he knew what was going through her head?

She turned away, resting her head on Quentin's arm instead of his chest, hoping he couldn't feel the pounding of her heart. She hoped he wouldn't think she was angry, turning her back to him. A moment later he dispelled any fears as he pulled her closer. Being comforted was nice, but it was also torture. She felt strangely warm and nervous in a good way.

How was she ever going to sleep?

She looked around at the bare walls of the room, picking out faded features in the darkness. She thought she saw eyes staring at her from the direction of Laura's blanket, catching the barest light still in the room, moving over the shapes of her and Quentin pressed together. Then the eyes blinked and disappeared, leaving Nova unsure whether she'd really seen anything at all.

Patterns

While symbols within spell forms represent the physical, patterns are used to affect action. Such patterns are often mathematical, in the form of equations. The more complex the mathematical formula, the more complex the spell. Thus, many spells require detailed renderings or more than one user in order to be successfully implemented. However, equations have limited ability to measure against and apply to non-linear objects. The symmetry and grand design of the universe cannot be fully captured in a standard equation.

—High Wizard Ezekial, on the *Factors of Magic*

Backup Plan

Safely hidden in the shadow of a large tree, Lucien watched the shapes pass him, the light from their torches flickering and leaping. He was not their prey, but they were headed in the same direction, here for the same reason. This was going to present a problem, although not his only problem or even his biggest. Still, he marveled at the number.

There had to be five hundred men.

This was no small hunting party. This was a force. They had not come to search or to abduct. They had come already knowing where she was, and they were here to force her to return with them.

Lucien sighed in the darkness. Yet another setback. Only one person could be responsible. He searched for the familiar face among the others. The arrogant fool wouldn't be able to resist being included. Not now. Not when his prey was so close and penned in.

The last flank made their way over a small ridge and down the hill beyond, backlit by the half moon. At first, Lucien thought perhaps he'd missed the man—that he'd slipped by on one end or the other unnoticed. No. There were two more shapes coming after the others, trailing behind. One was old, slightly bent from age and walking slowly by necessity. There was no mistaking the other.

Cyril, my old friend.

The two men stopped, standing together at the top of the rise and looking out over the group ahead of them.

Once I was in awe of you but no more.

Cyril had taught him. Mentored him. Shown him everything Lucien had wanted so desperately to see, but the Blood Debt Prophecy had changed everything. He still wondered vaguely if his friend had known about the prediction and planted the book containing the passage in his path on purpose.

Possibly.

Probably.

Cyril might be one of the most powerful people Lucien had ever known, perhaps one of the most knowledgeable, but Cyril lacked the combination of factors required to fulfill the prophecy. Unlike Lucien.

Cyril was nothing if not cunning. He'd recognized Lucien's potential. Cyril was the ultimate puppet master, pulling the strings until everything fell together exactly as he wanted.

But sometimes the student outgrew the master.

Lucien's stallion snorted. Cyril turned, hearing the sound *or sensing it* and knowing what it must mean. His eyes scanned the trees, but he could not find what he was looking for. Even Zen as he was, he could not sense some things. Lucien had learned long ago how to hide himself.

In acknowledgment or in defiance, Cyril raised one hand in greeting. Then he turned and followed the rest of his men into the night.

Lucien bared his teeth.

Cyril wasn't responsible for the invisible force holding Lucien at bay, preventing him from reaching his destination. This was someone else's doing.

The block.

He should have taken care of both the other-world children when he'd found them. Somehow, the boy had managed to use his block blood to keep Lucien from Nova. Even for someone with Lucien's power, blood magic was difficult to overcome. He could not easily break such a covenant. Not yet, at least.

Still, there were other ways. His cunning mentor had taught him well. Never leave anything to chance, and always have a backup plan.

Lucien ran his fingers over the small mirror.

Nova would want to contact her mother and grandfather again. The girl was on her own—frightened and captured. By Ishtar, of all people. She would no doubt use the spell again. When she did, he would be ready.

If he couldn't go to Nova, he would bring her to him.

Hidey Hole

He huddled in his newest hidey-hole. It was good. Better than the barn with its daemons and blood. This one was perfect for a mole. So much better with rock overhead. The solid mound covered him and hid him. No animals to mock. Best of all, from here he could see the side of the field where the child and her companions worked.

From here, he could watch.

This hidey hole had been a sign confirming he was on the right path. The light must be purged, and he must be the one to do it.

Mole wiped his sharp steel tooth against his leg. It was already clean, but sometimes he could see the stains anyway. That was how she tormented him by not letting him go, even though she was dead.

You can't be rid of me so easily ... her whisper was a viper's hiss.

Her voice was fainter here though. The stone muted her. Mole laughed. He laughed and laughed until his mole whiskers twitched.

Careful, the other voice warned. *Don't lose control now. Not when you're this close.*

He had to make sure this time was not like before. She'd won that time. Mole had killed her, but she'd still beaten him with her whispering and her torment. He gave himself a hard slap. He had to stay focused on his purpose. He couldn't let the daemons get him. He grabbed his head and rocked back and forth, his body crouched into a ball.

He was Destructive. Many times, when Mama had driven him to the brink of what he could stand, he'd let out his frustration by destroying something. Pieces of furniture, a barrel, and even small animals all felt the brunt of his rage. As he grew, he graduated to bigger animals. Getting rid of her should have been simple. He'd aimed his magic at the places where she hid, where she crept about and seeded his mind with her cruel voice, loosed his Destructive with the same ferocity he'd used to kill her the first time. How he'd longed to carve her out of him. To burn her away to ashes for good.

All he could remember now was the pain.

In his hidey hole, Mole moaned.

The pain had been terrible. Agony. Fire searing his head and racing through his body, exploding out of his eyes. He couldn't stop. Didn't want to, if he could be rid of her, if he could finally gouge her out of his head. Instead, his mind had split. Horrendous pain blinded him as he heard the ripping, rending sound. His brain was torn in two. He'd screamed, and screamed …

He was no longer Geo. He didn't know who he was for a while. He had only known pain. Pain and voices. Terrible, long days of agony. He remembered darkness, but not a good darkness. The pain was still there. The burning, searing pain like a hot brand on his skull.

And in the darkness, the voices.

Not just hers now. His too. Geo. The other him. Another voice to add to the noise constantly battering at him. He'd wandered, eating anything he could find, unsure of whether he was even still alive. Until the Lady had found him. Found him and named him. Her men had wanted to kill him, but she had said no.

She was his salvation.

His purpose.

His Lady.

Now he was only Mole. He was better as Mole. He was a good Mole. He could hurry and scurry, and he could watch.

And now he would save his Lady the same way she had once saved him. He would protect her from this scourge the healer had brought, the one the child now carried. He would make sure his Lady could not be touched by the awful light.

Dawn was only a few hours away. Mole stopped rocking and huddled back in a corner, the rock against his spine. He didn't need to sleep. Not now. Not this close to the morning. Tomorrow would bring the people back to the fields. The child would be close, and he would watch and wait for his chance. His sharp tooth would sink into flesh once more and douse the light that threatened to break loose before it could infect anyone else.

Tomorrow, Mole would bite.

Blood Debt

Nova woke in the darkness, her heart pounding from the dream. Something coming for them. Something dark and horrible, waiting to pounce. The feeling of danger wrapped around her like a thick blanket, closing her in like a trapped moth, smothering her.

Trembling, she shifted out from beneath Quentin's arm. It was still dark. Probably just an hour or so before morning. She didn't want to go back to sleep.

Carefully, she picked up the small mirror she'd left against the wall and padded across the room to the door. She didn't want to disturb the others from their sleep. They had all been through a lot and needed rest. Rest and peace. She slipped into the hall, shutting the door as softly as she could behind her. She wanted to see the early morning sky. Feel the night wind caress her face.

She wandered through the maze of hallways, hearing the occasional sounds of movement from behind closed doors. She hurried away, not wanting to intrude on their privacy, and found herself somehow at the entrance. She braced herself, letting the building lend her its strength as the night wind blew away the shreds of her dream and soothed her.

The warm smells of food cooking already wafted from the cafeteria. They must have to start early to feed so many. Ishtar's business was certainly booming.

Nova made her way toward the building, pretending to be an early riser headed for breakfast. The few guards who were out ignored her. They knew she couldn't escape.

Instead of going inside, she slipped along the far wall, where the night shadows were the deepest, and sat on the grass. The trees danced and whispered, and the moon peeked out from behind the clouds.

Nova pulled out the small mirror.

Would the time be the same at home? Didn't matter, she realized. Mom and Grandpa had probably never gone to bed. Not with what was going on. They'd promised to come up with a plan to get Nova and her friends out.

She closed her eyes. The pattern was clearer now that she'd used it once. Quickly, she breathed on the mirror and drew the form. Like before, the condensation on the mirror froze into place. The lines burned away, and the image burst into the mirror and up into the air. This time instead of light, there was something else—something that looked like ... fire.

"I've been waiting," a voice said softly. "For so long."

Nova frowned. A prick of fear ran through her. There was no color to accompany the sound. She could see someone. Black hair and dark eyes peered at her from a familiar face.

Her face.

Nova's breath caught in her throat. Was this possible? Was the moment she had waited for her whole life finally here? How long had she wanted this? How many nights had she wished for this moment?

"Who are you?" She wanted confirmation, wanted proof.

"You know the answer already." His eyes burned as they took her in. "You have her eyes, but you are certainly my daughter."

Nova couldn't speak. Her tongue was stuck in a mouth suddenly and completely dry.

"You have my countenance," he said with something like pride, "and my power."

So many questions crowded her mind at once she felt lost in the midst of them, unable to pick any single one out. They fluttered around in her head like birds, wings beating against her skull.

The face in the fire grew somber. "You are in grave danger. Have you been told?"

"Seth," she whispered, her throat filled with ash and dust.

The muscles in his face twitched. "Where is he? Is he with you?"

"No. We ... got separated. I was sick."

"Did he tell you about the prophecy?"

He didn't ask about her being sick. Didn't he want to know if she was all right? Wouldn't he at least ask?

"Seth said *you* would tell me."

The face nodded. She couldn't bring herself to call him her father, even in her head. She wanted to, but something held her back. Maybe it was the flames behind him or the way he had taken her by surprise, but she couldn't. Not yet.

"You must come to me so we can talk."

"Where?" She was so confused. "How?"

"You must find a way out. I cannot get to you." His face clouded with anger. "I am blocked."

"What?"

"Blocked. By the boy. The one who came after you."

"Quentin?" How could Quentin be blocking him? None of this made sense.

The angry look shifted to concern. "He is, by his nature, devoid of magic. He blocks the flow of it. He's used this to block me."

Shock filtered through her. Was that possible?

"Such a spell requires blood magic," he answered as if he could hear her questions. "He would have had to use his own blood. His *block* blood."

His eyes bore into hers, their intensity frightening.

"I would have come regardless," he said softly, "but doing so would have killed the one the spell was tied to."

Shock turned to horror. Nova's body went cold. Had Quentin really done something that could get him killed? And for what? To keep her father from reaching her? Why would he do that?

Quentin's words from the night before echoed back to her. "All I'm saying is, what if he's not what you imagined? I mean, there's got to be a reason why your mom didn't talk about him, right? Maybe she was trying to protect you."

Maybe Quentin was trying to protect her too.

"Oh, Quentin, what have you done?" she whispered.

"You must find a way to come to me, before it's too late."

"Too late?" She was beginning to feel like an echo.

His eyes burned like twin flames. "The Blood Debt Prophecy is even now being fulfilled. The storm has swept the land, and the Divide is failing."

She remembered running as the storm chased behind her. Grandpa had told her the Divide was failing. Could what he was saying be true?

"You must not blame yourself."

She looked up, startled.

"The boy followed you because he cares for you." Nova winced as his soft words cut her. "You couldn't have known. They never taught you. You had no idea that by crossing to this world, by giving the block a reason to follow, you caused the disruption of the very flow of life. As the prophecy says:

From whence may come the blood that holds the elemental gifts of old;
Cometh the power that seeks to bring the end of every living thing.
By choice and action freely made, life's stones like water soon cascade.
The wings of darkness stand unfurled and seek the end of every world.
So one must stand and face the night, else risk the loss of life and light.
And for destruction to be stilled, life's blood must then be freely spilled.

"You are the child of prophecy, Nova. You hold the elemental gifts of old. By your choice to come here and the boy's action freely made to follow you, you fulfilled it."

"No."

"The proof is clear. The truth cannot be denied."

Why was he doing this? This wasn't how meeting her father for the first time was supposed to happen. She'd imagined this day so many times. In her dreams, he sometimes pulled her into his arms, welcoming her back. Other times he ran, afraid to face her. Never in all her imaginings had there been anything like this.

Quentin's words echoed. "You don't even know him."

This couldn't be right. None of this could be right.

"Quentin would never ... he wouldn't ..."

"Ask him then." Lucien's voice was hard and cold, stabbing her, piercing her heart. "Ask him what blood magic he performed. Ask him what happened when he came after you." The man in the mirror leaned toward her, and she found herself wanting to lean away. "This storm, Nova, this event, *this* is what will cause the destruction of all the words. The Divide is all that has kept them apart and intact. When *the Divide* ends, *everything* will end."

Nova hurled the mirror away from her. The light shining out from the glass cast a glow on the tree branches before the mirror crashed to the ground sending shards of glass in all directions. She pressed her hands against her mouth. Sobs wracked her. He had to be wrong. Maybe that hadn't even been her father.

She crumpled to the ground. She couldn't deny the truth. His face was familiar because she'd seen his features in her own mirror every day for as long as she could remember. She was his daughter without a doubt. And if he was telling her the truth about that ...

"Hey, you okay?"

Only the fact that she was already breathless kept her from screaming. She peered into the darkness. Of course. Of all the people who could find her like this, the girl who had been her tormentor would be the one to show up. Nova swiped savagely at her face and nose. She refused to let Laura Hennigan see her at her weakest moment.

"I'm fine," Nova growled.

"Sure, you are." Laura held out her hand. "Come on. Let me help you up."

Nova took the hand, wondering how often the limb had been used to support someone rather than knock them down. Nova stared into the brown eyes she had always avoided.

"What?" Laura asked.

"Did Quentin do something to block my father?" she asked bluntly, not bothering to soften the question. "Did he do something with his blood?"

Laura was as still as a statue.

"You should ask *him*," she said quietly, but the answer was written all over her face.

Destructive Neutral

Destructive Neutral Duals can be an interesting combination. The volatile nature of Destructive can be brought into balance by the calm, collected aspects of Neutral. This mitigating factor often provides the ability to produce positive results from an otherwise negative individual. The ability to remove or detract is not in and of itself bad, and can in fact have desirable impact, such as extracting infection or sickness.

However, Neutral individuals can also be detached, indifferent, even unemotional. These traits in combination with the combative, militant and sometimes deadly nature of Destructive can produce results that are quite disturbing.

—High Wizard Ezekial, on the *Factors of Magic*

SHATTERED

Breakfast was about as awkward as could be. Nova stared at her plate, unwilling to look up and see Quentin's confused, nervous face. She couldn't stomach another round of glances between the others, and she especially couldn't stand to see Laura's thoughtful concern.

She just couldn't.

She pushed food around her plate. What would Viru think? The boy who had crossed worlds to kill her so she couldn't do exactly what she'd done? The one who had changed sides and protected her? What would he think when he found out Quentin was here? Nova had set off the chain reaction that could destroy them all, just like his prophecy predicted.

Thankfully, the guard announced they should report to work. Nova picked up the basket Morra had given her and shuffled out the door behind the others.

The sun blazed, already blasting heat even at this hour. Nova's shirt stuck to her body, and for the first time, she wished she had something other than jeans to wear. They weighed her down and chafed against her legs and waist.

Someone pulled her to a stop.

She looked up, expecting Quentin and surprised to find Laura staring at her. "What do you want?"

Laura raised a brow and tilted her lips. "Easy, killer. I only want to talk."

Nova decided not to say anything at all.

"Look"—Laura gazed off toward where the others had stopped—"I know you're mad. I would be too. Just … just give him a chance to explain, okay?"

Nova's anger boiled up hot and fast. "Why should I? I trusted him. He knew how much finding my father meant to me. He knew, and he betrayed me anyway. What could he say to explain that away?"

Laura's face tightened. "Listen, little miss know-it-all. We met your father when we first got here. All right?"

Shock filtered through her. "You *met* him?"

"He was waiting there when we crossed over, and he was ready to eat us alive to get to you. It was pretty freaking apparent he wasn't looking to have a nice family chat. Maybe what Quentin did wasn't the right decision, but he didn't know what else he could do to protect *you*. He had just found out he could walk, we had no idea where you might be, and this crazy storm was pounding everything. He could have done nothing at all. He could have just cowered in a corner like a baby, but he didn't. He made a choice. So just deal with it, Princess."

"How?" Nova whispered. "How do I deal with it? How do I pick between my father and my—my friend?"

"Nova?" Quentin called, and they both turned as he came toward them.

Laura leaned in, her face strangely conflicted. "You hurt him, and I'll kill you." She stalked away, shoving past Quentin.

Nova could only watch in disbelief. Did Laura Hennigan actually feel …?

"Hey," Quentin said, jogging over. "Let me carry that."

He reached for her basket, but she jerked it away. His confused look made her want to cry all over again.

"What is it?" he asked. "What's wrong?"

How could she answer him? He was the same boy she had shared every dream and every wish with since they were little kids. He was the one who had comforted her when everyone else had made her feel bruised and abandoned. He had crossed the Divide to save her. How could she question his motives?

He squeezed her hand. "Look, I'm sorry."

She twitched. Did he know? Had Laura told him?

He wiped his face. "I know last night might have been too much, the way we … the way we were all snuggly, but …"

He trailed off and looked down, his face a brighter red than his sunburn could explain.

Nova wanted to laugh and cry at the same time. He thought she was angry about him cuddling with her? When all she had wanted him to do was hold her even tighter?

"Listen," he said, and his voice was hoarse. "I wasn't going to tell you, not here, but you have to know. I can't risk having something happen to one of us and you not know." His voice broke on the last word, and Nova's heart broke right along with it.

232

She'd blamed him, but this whole mess was her fault. She was the one who had run off without any warning to goodness knew where with someone she'd barely met. If she hadn't gone, if she'd waited and talked to her mom or grandpa, all of this might have been avoided. Instead, she put everyone she loved in danger with her stupid attempt to protect them.

Now … now if she followed her heart and went to her father, she might kill the one person who had always been her closest and best friend.

"When I came home from the hospital," Quentin said, still looking down, "I thought my life was over. Not being able to walk was about the worst thing I could imagine. Then the pity started. I hated it. I hated the nurses letting me get away with things because they felt sorry for me. I hated Mom and Dad for being so nice to me and always crying and hugging me. I hated all of it. I wished I'd died instead."

A lump filled Nova's throat. "Why didn't you ever tell me?"

He gave a sad little grin. "Because when I came home there you were, challenging me to races and pushing me around, and giving me crap." His smile widened. "You didn't pity me."

"Of course not." Why would she? He was still Quentin.

"You saved me," he said, and the look on his face was more serious than she'd ever seen before. "That's when things changed for me," his grip on her hand tightened. "You'll always be my best friend, Nova. No matter what. But for me, it's more than that."

The world had stopped and was holding its breath.

"I love you, Nova." He looked up, and their gaze met. When she saw his eyes brimming with emotion, her own tears began to fall. "I have for a long time."

She'd thought she was the only one who felt more than friendship, and here he was waiting for her to catch up.

"Do you … do you think you could ever feel that way about me?"

Couldn't he tell? Couldn't he see her love every time she looked at him? "I …"

How could she say yes? Telling him she felt the same way might put him in even more danger or even get him killed. She'd come here to protect everyone, and look at where they were now. No matter what she did, she would hurt him. Her broken heart shattered into dust inside her chest, leaving her hollower and more desolate than the Trench ever could.

"I can't," she whispered.

She couldn't bear to see Quentin's crushed hope. When he let go of her hand, she wanted to die. She wanted to run and hide. To crawl into a hole and never come out again.

Then they heard the screams.

They spun in unison, but Nova reacted first. Her legs moved before her head even registered that the high-pitched shrieks shattering the morning came from Rose.

DARKNESS

At last, he had her. The light would be put out. If only he still had his sharp tooth. He'd jabbed his only weapon into the girl's mother to make sure she couldn't stop him. She'd fallen away, no longer a threat.

The girl's screams echoed through the still morning air.

Mole hissed at her, clamping his hand over her mouth.

The girl's companions ran toward him. He needed to get away. He pulled her back toward his hidey hole. The rows of Phoria gave them some cover. If he could get her inside, he could finish her before—

"Ouch." He yanked his hand away from her mouth. "You bit me!" His middle finger welled up with blood.

"Mommy!" She screamed, kicking at him. "Laura! Nova!"

There were no guards nearby. The sun was too hot for them. They were hiding in their own little hidey holes, staying cool. The ones that braved the heat were far away, back near the buildings, too far to hear the screams.

He turned with a growl, half carrying—half dragging the child. The wall was so close. If only he could—

He was tackled and grunted as the ground pounded the air from his lungs. He locked his arms around the child to keep her from getting away, muffling her face against his clothes.

"Let go of her," a voice snarled in his ear.

Don't listen, Geo breathed in his head. *You must hold onto the child. You must put out her light.*

"Cursed light." He squeezed harder. "Hateful light."

"Laura," the child gasped against him.

She was fading. His plan was working.

Fists found his face and shoulders. Mole laughed. These blows were nothing. He'd done worse than this to himself.

"Laura, move," another voice shouted.

With a sudden release, the weight left him. The blows stopped. He cracked one swelling eye to see the girl who had tackled him looking back and followed her line of sight.

The other friend, the one who'd had the Trench, stood a few yards away. Her feet were planted apart, hands pushed out towards him. Across her fingers, light danced. Rainbow light like colored lightning, sparking and flashing. The girl's dark hair danced as if blown by a gale-force wind.

Mole felt afraid.

Coward, Mama's voice screamed in his head. *Fight her! Kill her!*

He was not a coward.

She wants the child, Geo's voice joined in. *Don't let her have the child.*

He wanted to tear at his face. To claw and make the voices leave him be, but he had to keep hold of the child. He couldn't let go.

A clap like thunder shook the ground. A blinding wave of light pulsed out, washing over him. He rolled backwards over his head. Everything was upside down. He hit something solid, and a flash of pain ignited in his shoulder. The earth around him shook and buckled.

Thou shalt atone for thy sins. Mama's voice cried like a harpy.

"Nooo!" Mole clapped his hands over his ears, squeezing his eyes closed.

Get the girl, Geo's voice cried. *You've lost her.*

Mole opened his eyes, but the world was wrong. Grass was on his right, sky on his left. He saw feet running. Two sets—one big, one small. Beyond them, standing like a statue, his mother turned burning eyes on him. Eyes filled with the light. The child's light.

She'd infected his mama. Righteous fire burned in eyes that should be dead.

Terror washed through him. He kicked his feet, pushing with his hands against the dirt, but he was already up against the wall.

"No, Mama," he begged.

He could feel her heat burning into him. Searing him.

"Please!"

Tears and drool wet his face.

"Don't hurt me."

His mother stood, her arms raised to the heavens, burning in her righteous fire. As her heat melted into him, he saw the broken part of him apart from the rest, torn away, but still there. The part he had destroyed. Geo. The Mole part was disintegrating beneath the blaze of her holy fire.

He looked up, remembering every good and bad time. Every beating. Every berating. Every terrorized moment of his life.

He looked up, and he remembered why he'd killed her.

"I hate you," he whispered, and the light in her eyes flickered uncertainly. A scream ripped from his throat. "I killed you already!" He launched himself toward her letting loose his Destructive power. He flung his hatred at her, teeth bared.

A ball of darkness raced toward Mama, rolling through the air. He would do more than kill her this time. He would destroy her completely.

His mother's image rippled, and he stumbled. Behind her face, there was another. The girl with the rainbow sparks. Her wide eyes watched his ball of Destructive magic roll toward her with growing horror. Yes, kill her too. Kill her for hurting him and taking the child. He backed up step by step until his back was against the stone wall. Destroy them all.

The ball of darkness had almost reached her when another figure jumped into the path. The Destructive fire hit, crashing against the figure like a wall. Instead of tearing into the blended image of his mama and the dark-haired girl, the sphere of dark magic spun in midair. Smoke rolled from the orb until a hand reached out to grab it. The girl who had tackled him stared down at the darkness in her hands. She looked up, and Mole saw the fury burning in her eyes. She pulled her arm back and hurled the Destructive ball. Mole watched in horrid fascination as his own magic came for him. The air in front darkened, and a trail flowed in its wake. He cringed, but the blast missed him and crashed into the wall.

Mole grinned with glee. He would destroy *all* of them. They would be sorry. He would kill the child and take the light from them one by one.

What were they looking at? They stared over his head. Mole looked up and understanding filled him as the slab of wall thundered down.

At last.

Then he joined the never-ending darkness.

Arrival

Nova stared in shock at the legs and feet that poked from beneath the rubble of fallen wall. Quentin stood frozen in front of her. He'd somehow managed to keep the magic from hitting her. She owed him her life. Laura panted and shook her hand as if she'd been burned by the wretched dark ball of magic. Laura had thrown the mass of dark magic like a baseball. Nova owed her former bully her life as well, she realized.

Laura turned, her face twisted and wet with tears. Was she crying? Shock thrummed through Nova. Quentin put a hand on Laura's shoulder and said something to her. She nodded, wiping at her chin. There was more to the girl Nova had always thought of as her own personal bully. Much more.

Then a small wail reached her ears. *Rose.*

The girl was huddled over a prone shape in the grass.

"Morra!"

Nova ran to the two of them, falling onto her knees in the grass. Morra was face down. A wicked-looking dagger lodged in her back near her shoulder blade. Nova's hands shook as she felt for a pulse. A faint but steady beat brought a sob of relief to her lips.

Quentin and Laura reached them.

"She's alive." Nova drew Rose into a reassuring embrace.

"We have to get her out of here," Laura said.

Nova looked up into the face of her former nemesis. "That was great … what you did back there."

Laura grinned. "Not so bad yourself, Princess."

"The guards are coming." Quentin sounded as shaken as Nova felt.

"What do we do?" Laura asked, but she wasn't looking at Quentin. She was looking at Nova.

Nova looked around, feeling as though she had woken from some terrible dream. To their left, the inner wall gaped. A whole section had been destroyed. Beyond, the outer wall sagged. A jagged hole had been blasted clean through the stone, leaving an opening the size of a wagon, but even as she watched small rocks and chunks of stone rained down from the now unsupported section above.

The wall was going to give.

Would it hold long enough for them to get through? She glanced down. Could they carry Morra?

Nova shook her head. "It's no good," she said. "We have to take her back."

"What do you mean, back?" Quentin shouted. "Those guards will—"

"What they'll do doesn't matter." Nova's firm answer silenced him. "If they can help Morra, nothing else matters We can figure everything out later."

Quentin's face clouded with a mix of emotions she couldn't even begin to identify and mostly didn't want to. She didn't want to know how deeply she'd hurt him. To know would only make the wound in her heart that much worse.

"Here, let me."

Nova jumped, staring in surprise as Sol knelt on the grass beside Morra, laying his hands against the small of her back below the knife. He closed his eyes, brows furrowing together.

"Go get one of the carriers," he turned and shouted over his shoulder. The guards raced to do his bidding.

Sol put his hands on either side of the dagger. Quentin gently tugged Rose into his arms as soft, dancing light played along Morra's back and shoulder. Sol turned his head in Nova's direction, his eyes still closed.

"I need your help," he said softly.

"How?"

"Put your hands near mine," he instructed.

She did as he asked, and watched in fascination as rainbow threads drifted from her hands, mingling with the light coming from Sol. The bright fusion blanketed Morra. Slowly, as if a living thing, the dagger began to quiver. The vibrating blade slowly extracted from the wound, like a stinger drawn out with mud. The light filled the puncture in its wake.

Morra took a deep, shuddering breath.

Soon only the knife's tip stood on her skin and then dropped into the grass. Sol deftly used his fingers to draw more of the threads in and around the laceration, weaving them like sutures. When he finally lifted his hands, a patch of color covered the small dark hole in Morra's skin. Gently, Sol turned Morra over.

Her eyes fluttered open.

"Rose," she moaned.

The girl rushed to her mother's side, putting her little hand on Morra's cheek. "I'm here, Mama."

Morra ran a shaking hand over her daughter's face and arms as if not quite able to believe she was all right. "You're not hurt?"

Rose shook her head.

"We need to take her inside," Sol said as the guards arrived with a stretcher and moved Morra on to it. "Her wound is closed, but she's lost a lot of blood. She'll need time to heal."

Nova nodded, and the guards hurried away. Sol scooped up Rose and hurried after them.

"What about us?" Laura's voice was heavy with meaning. "What do we do?

Nova looked back toward the wall. Any thoughts of escape were quickly extinguished. Through the hole in the outer wall, shapes drifted, moving like smoke. A horde of men poured through, running straight toward them. A guard from between the two walls moved their way, shouting something to the advancing horde. They cut down the guard and kept coming, their faces alive with a zealous light.

The Order.

Those who had been hunting for the Child of Prophecy had finally found her.

Nova looked at Laura. "Run."

Creative Neutral

Creative Neutral is, in most cases, a positive combination. The Neutral factor lends a balance to the dramatic and sensitive side of Creative, while the Creative factor lends an optimism and drive to the sometimes uninterested or lazy side of Neutral. As with anything in life, there can be exceptions; but Creative Neutral is generally an optimum pairing, and one that often produces powerful individuals. Such clever and imaginative people, enhanced with patience and even-handedness, have produced some of the brightest minds of our time.

—High Wizard Ezekial, on the *Factors of Magic*

Lair of the Beast

Quentin raced with Nova and Laura as the horde chased hot on their heels. Ahead of them, Sol turned and shouted. Guards appeared from either side, running to stop the invaders. Quentin and the others didn't pause to look back. They followed Sol as he raced up the steps of the main building with Rose in his arms.

Then suddenly, he stopped. Ishtar, more beautiful than ever in her anger, stood in the center of the room. The men carrying Morra continued past her without looking back.

"What's happened?" Ishtar's gaze was as sharp as her words.

"We're under attack." Sol looked back over the fields.

Workers screamed and ran in all directions. The guards tried to stem the flow of invaders, but they may have as well tried to stop a river. They flowed over and around the guards as if they weren't even there.

Ishtar's face darkened. She glanced at the group following Sol, her gaze landing on Nova. Sol reached out with his one free hand and grabbed Nova's wrist. "Don't worry, I'll keep an eye on this one."

Ishtar looked at Sol with narrowed eyes. "I'd like a word once all of this is taken care of."

Quentin stepped to the side as Ishtar came to stand in the open doorway, eyes flashing as she took in the scene beyond. Then her beautiful face began to change. A black wave issued from between perfect, blush-colored lips stretched wider than should be possible. The stain grew like a dark curtain, spreading outward, slamming into the invaders. Instantly they were burned to ash and dust.

The terrifying scene turned Quentin's insides to water. Tearing his gaze away from the carnage, he followed the others into the lair of the beast.

Sol hurried them across the large room to a side door that opened to a long hallway. At the other end, the men with the stretcher disappeared again. Quentin caught a glimpse of beds lining the room on the other side and knew where they were going. Nova had filled one of those beds not long ago.

"Stop!"

The others drew up quickly.

Sol took a few more steps before he turned around. "We can't stop here."

Quentin stared at the man who had tortured him. "Why should we trust you?"

Sol's shoulders drooped. "You have no reason to, really."

Darn straight.

"You have to understand. The people who come here are genuinely sick. There is no way to prevent the Trench. It's a wretched way to die. Ishtar's motives may be wrong but saving people isn't." Sol rubbed his face. "By being here, I can help heal people, and by pretending to be an ally, I can try to prevent any lasting harm."

"You tortured me," Quentin shouted, his face hot with anger.

"Did I wound you?" Sol asked point blank.

Holding the weights had been excruciating. Still, he hadn't suffered any real wounds. Just sore muscles.

"No, but if I'd dropped one of the jars—"

Sol huffed. "Harmless goop."

"I saw that goop burn like acid."

"A trick designed to fool you. You had to think you were truly in danger. Otherwise, Ishtar may have sensed my deception." Sol gave a grim smile. "She may not be able to heal, but she can certainly destroy."

"You pretend to be in league with her, so you can help people?" Nova asked, sounding dubious.

At least she wasn't buying into this good guy routine.

Sol turned to her. "I am Creative Neutral, and Ishtar is Destructive Neutral. Without her Destructive factor I would be able to heal many things, but not the Trench. For that, all three factors are required, which means no less than two people." He paused, his eyes like lasers. "Unless you're a Trine."

In the dimness of the hallway, Nova met Quentin's stare. He understood the question she was asking him. Could they trust Sol?

"It's okay," Rose whispered. "He'll help us."

Sol turned to look at the girl in his arms, and she put one of her hands on his shoulder. Sol gave her a soft smile before turning back to Nova. "I knew what you must be as soon as I sensed what you were doing. How you were healing yourself. I could sense all three factors."

There was an explosion from somewhere outside.

244

"We must hurry." Sol's voice was urgent.

"We're trapped." Quentin could taste the bitterness that tinged his voice. He wondered if this was what Nova's Synesthesia was like.

"No. There's a way out." Sol moved down the hall toward the door.

"What?" Nova echoed Quentin's surprise.

"Tunnels," Sol said as he opened the door.

He put Rose down. She ran into the room, hurrying to the bed the guards had transferred Morra to. Sol turned back to face them, holding the door.

"There are tunnels under the Sanctuary," he said. "I can get you out."

Quentin turned to Nova. This was her call. Something clouded her eyes. Sadness? Grief? Whatever he saw vanished too quickly to be sure. She turned and hurried after Sol. As Quentin watched her stride away from him, he had the overwhelming feeling she was slipping through his fingers, trickling away like water in the desert.

In spite of everything, in spite of hearing her say she couldn't care about him the way he did about her, he couldn't bring himself to lose her. Not like this. Not yet. When he'd come home from the hospital, he'd been ready for his life to be over. Nova had taught him he could stand tall, even while sitting in a chair. She'd helped him become a fighter, and he would never stop fighting for her.

Motioning for Laura to move ahead, he trailed after her, hoping they weren't walking into a trap.

Sealed

Nova looked out one of the long windows of the infirmary, her arms wrapped around her middle as if she could keep everything inside her from spilling out. The sun had nearly reached its zenith, but not even that burning ball of light could hide the glare of fires. The other buildings were burning. Maybe this one too. Screams echoed through the thick walls. Nova flinched with each cry.

These people were dying because of her.

All she'd ever tried to do was help people. She hated to see anyone hurting. How had her life come to this?

"Saving the world a little less fun than you thought it would be?"

Nova turned, half expecting to see a mocking smile, but Laura's face was serious, even compassionate.

"A lot." Nova gave her own sad smile and turned back to the carnage raging outside.

"My Dad's a real jerk," Laura said softly, "but he is right about one thing."

"What's that?"

"You can't build a house with a marshmallow."

Nova glanced at Laura's reflection in the window.

"He was determined us kids wouldn't end up soft." She gave a small snort of laughter. "He managed that for sure. None of us are soft. Some of us"—Laura's jaw clenched and unclenched before she could go on—"some of us got so hard we broke." She looked up, meeting Nova's gaze in the window. "I thought I had to be so tough no one could ever hurt me, not even him."

A lump formed in Nova's throat.

"For what it's worth, I only picked on you because I thought there was more to you. You were different."

A freak.

"I'm sorry for how I treated you. I ended up just like my old man." Her eyes shone. "But I wasn't wrong about you." She poked a finger into Nova's shoulder. "There's metal in there. I saw it. Don't let everything strip you down until that's all there is." Laura glanced back toward Quentin. He sat with Rose who knelt beside Morra's bed. "He really does love you, you know."

Nova's throat tightened. "I know."

"Don't you love him back?"

There was no stopping the hot tears that brimmed and streamed like burning liquid down her cheeks. "I love him too much to get him killed."

Laura stared at her in silence for several moments. "We're not so different, you and me," she said finally.

Nova noticed Laura's double meaning. She was happy there was someone else who saw how amazing Quentin was and who would do anything to keep him safe. He deserved friends like that.

"I like marshmallows," Nova said.

Laura looked like she was about to choke. She let out a bark of laughter. "Yeah, I guess they're okay. They're better once they've been cooked, though."

"Oh, smores …" Nova's mouth watered at the thought.

Laura grinned. "Forget that. Give me some Krispy Treats."

They laughed together for a moment before the sound of explosions and screaming reclaimed the mood.

"Laura, if … if anything happens, take care of him, okay?"

Laura studied Nova, then gave a firm nod. "I got your back."

A door opened, and Sol bustled in followed by two other men carrying a stretcher. One of them was older, but he looked strong enough to best most men half his age. Though no longer wearing the silver and red uniforms, they were clearly guards.

"Time to go." Sol flicked his gaze from the windows to the door at the far end of the room. He pointed to Morra and motioned to the men. "You two get her."

Quentin picked up Rose and followed the men as they carried Morra.

Sol looked at Nova. "Ready?"

"As I'll ever be."

He led them away from where they'd entered, out into a back corridor and down a short flight of stairs. The building shook as a series of explosions echoed from outside. Small stones and dust rained down on them.

"Who's winning?" Laura asked.

"No one," Sol answered cryptically.

He led them to a door half hidden behind a pillar, then down another, longer set of stairs. The walls here were cold and damp, as if the earth behind them tried to seep in. When they reached the bottom step, a heavy wooden door blocked the way. Sol pulled a key out of his pocket. He put it in, but the lock refused to budge. He frowned and wiggled the key. Finally, it gave with a faint snick of sound. The heavy door opened. Beyond it, a passage disappeared in darkness.

Sol pulled a lantern off a hook that jutted from the wall. He drew shapes in the air with his fingers, and a flame ignited the wick. He handed the lamp to Quentin. "Lead the way."

Quentin set Rose down and glanced at Nova. How different he looked now than he had only a few days ago. His eyes pleaded for something she couldn't give.

"Go ahead," she said. "I need to talk to Sol for a second."

Quentin's eyes hardened. In their depths, a gate slammed down, locking his emotions away from her—locking his heart. He turned and headed into the darkness.

Sol motioned for the men carrying Morra to follow. Rose trailed alongside. Laura gave Nova another long glance, then strode ahead with purposeful steps.

Sol looked at her, his brows raised.

"I'm not coming," Nova whispered.

"You can't stay. You'll be killed. It's—"

"I know what I'm facing." Nova held his gaze until he looked away. She glanced back the way they'd come, remembering the faces of the men as they'd raced toward her across the field above, wanting her blood. "I can't let anyone else die."

Sol took her hand. His face was filled with kindness. "Are you sure?"

How could she have missed his true nature before? "I am."

"Then may the One God be with you and keep you in His arms until we meet again."

"Take care of my friends." She took a deep, shuddering breath as she looked into the gloom, wishing she could see their faces one more time.

Sol squeezed her hand. "I will."

He slipped into the darkness, pulling the door behind him. The lock fell back into place, sealing her decision.

I nto the Fire

The devastation made Nova want to weep.

Fires burned all around. Everywhere she looked, there were fallen men and women. Mothers and fathers. Brothers and sisters. All of this devastation was because of her.

At the bottom of the steps, Ishtar stood with arms flung wide, unleashing wave after wave of dark Destructive power. Nova could see why the Willings had come to the Sanctuary. Ishtar may be treacherous, but her power was strong. The attackers still swarmed the fields, though there were far less of them than there had been.

A figure emerged from the smoke. Something about him made Nova's skin crawl. His eyes glowed in the haze covering the field. Ishtar turned, flinging a wave of her power in his direction. The destructive magic washed over him, and Nova waited to see him disintegrate like the others. But he walked on.

Ishtar lowered her arms. "For what reason do you invade my land?"

The man didn't answer.

"I am the master here." Rage laced her words.

The man lifted his arms. Between his outstretched hands, the atmosphere cracked and split apart. Devoid of light, the growing chasm absorbed everything around it, sucking in smoke and air. Even the daylight bent and disappeared into the dark abyss. It whirled and pulsed like a living, breathing thing.

Nova huddled in the doorway. A cold wash of fear swept over her. The air crackled. Ishtar lifted her arms in defense, and what Nova saw turned her fear into terror. Ishtar's hands shook.

Then Nova heard the tumult.

A banshee screech like a thousand knives all scraping on stone. Like a thousand voices joined in a chorus of devastation. Nova pressed her hands over her ears, horror filling her. Who was this man?

Ishtar released her dark power, pushing out a wall of darkness that slammed into the man. The widening fissure sucked the Destructive magic into its vacuous maw. The man's eyes burned. His face contorted as he bared his teeth in a horrid smile. Lifting his hands over his head he pulled his arms back, then heaved forward. The void rushed through the air, eating everything in its path. One of the attackers didn't move aside quickly enough. He shrieked as the chasm sucked him in.

Ishtar loosed a guttural scream, flinging up a wall of magic as a shield. The fissure struck it and tore the wall apart. Ishtar's scream stretched and grew. Nova couldn't look away. She watched in horrid fascination as Ishtar's body began to come apart. Molecule by molecule her form began to shatter and smoke, as if she bled shadows. The pit drew the shadows in, sucking them down its gorge. Ishtar threw her head back as dark smoke seeped from her eyes and mouth. Like water on a painting, the lines and colors of her body ran and smeared, bursting into droplets. The chasm drank her in.

A loud clap boomed over the field.

Nova looked down. The man had slammed his hands together. The terrifying abyss instantly collapsed and disappeared. What was left of Ishtar fell into a heap on the ground like an empty shell.

Slowly, Nova pulled her hands from her ears, her face wet with tears. Her body was soaked in sweat. The man with the glowing eyes turned his gaze on her.

"Child of Prophecy," he whispered, and yet his words filled the Universe.

Nova's body trembled as if she were hot with fever. She could barely stand. This was how it had to be. She knew that, but how did she face this … this *creature*, for surely, he was no ordinary man. From behind him, another shape emerged. This one was bent with age. He looked up at Nova with weary eyes.

"It is time."

"No!" The shout startled Nova as much as the old man.

A dark shape hurtled up the steps, coming to a stop in front of her, arms spread wide.

"Viru?" the old man shouted in surprise. "What are you doing?"

"You cannot harm her." Viru yelled. "The prophecy is wrong."

He shook his head. "It is not wrong, Viru."

"It is. She was visited by the Wardein. She is—"

"The Divide fails."

Silenced, Viru shook his head in disbelief.

"The storm that raged across the land was the first sign. The Divide is coming undone."

Viru glanced at Nova. She could see in his eyes he did not want to believe the old man. She wished she could tell Viru what the man said wasn't true. But she couldn't. Instead, she forced her legs to move forward.

"It's true." Emotion choked her.

She turned to face the old man. She couldn't bear to look at the other man's burning eyes. "I freely give myself to you. Do what you must to stop the destruction."

The old man nodded.

Nova turned to Viru. "I'm sorry."

He studied her, his face a mix of emotions. "Then I will go with you."

She wanted to say no, to tell him to run to safety like the others. Instead she said nothing, grateful not to be alone. With Viru beside her, she walked slowly down the steps of Ishtar's hall into the waiting clutches of the men below.

Portals

Portals are passages created for the use of travelling between physical locations quickly. While they can be made using either Creative or Destructive energy, they must also employ Neutral.

Portals generated with Creative magic are like entryways, with either end becoming a focal point. In contrast, portals made with Destructive magic are designed to negate the distance between two points. Both produce similar outcomes, and both require Neutral not only to counterbalance, but to subdue the current of magic that flows through and between all things.

—High Wizard Ezekial, on the *Factors of Magic*

Maester of Deception

"No!" Lucien slammed his fist against a rock, barely aware when the stone cracked in two from the thunder of his magic.

This wasn't supposed to happen.

He paced furiously in the small clearing. His horse stomped nervously and shied away.

He'd revealed too much. He should have cajoled her instead. He'd thought fear would drive her to him. Instead, she had given herself over to the Order like some lamb offering itself for slaughter. Did she think her sacrifice would matter? That she could singlehandedly fix the Divide?

Yes, he realized. That was exactly what she thought. Just as the men of the Order did.

"Fools."

All of them. They had all been duped by the master of deception.

Cyril.

How many times had Lucien fallen for the same trickery? Too many to count. Half-truths and lies mixed together to create a potent brew of misconception. Cyril had orchestrated this moment perfectly. Perhaps he had even orchestrated Lucien's role, allowing him to set the net while Cyril waited to pull the catch away at the last moment. Now, he had his hands on the greatest prize of all.

Nova.

Her Trine blood would be Cyril's to use. *He* would fulfill the prophecy. With her power he would be unstoppable.

"I was the one who created her," Lucien seethed. "My blood made her. My seed brought her life."

He turned his palms out toward the trees on the opposite side of the clearing and unleashed a torrent of power. The trees burst into flame, burning with an unnatural speed. Explosions rocked them one after the other. Behind him, Lucien's horse reared at the sounds. Lucien didn't hear the horse's screams. He didn't feel the heat of the flames or the concussion of the explosions. His own cry was all he knew.

"HER BLOOD BELONGS TO ME!"

All his planning would not be in vain.

The power of the Trine had been built by him alone and he alone would claim her blood. No one else could be allowed.

No one.

Candles in the Dark

Quentin sat in the darkness, his arms wrapped around his knees. The dark, depressing room seemed fitting. He'd failed. He'd managed to let her go again, and now there was no way for him to get to her.

Nova was gone.

On the other side of the room, Sol tended to Morra. His two large guards sat quietly, resting from what couldn't have been an easy trek even with their huge arms. They'd walked for at least two hours.

"How far do these tunnels go," Laura asked, her eyes tracing the contours of the dirt walls and timber braces.

"Hundreds of miles," Sol answered. "They were used in the time of the great wars to transport people and supplies."

"Where will we come out?"

Sol glanced back at her, his eyes shifting to Quentin's. He knew what they were asking. He said something softly to Morra before walking toward them. In the middle of the room, he squatted down, rubbing his hand against the dirt floor. Then, he used his finger to draw a large shape.

"This is the region of Kota," he said.

Quentin and Laura both came closer to see.

"Kota stretches from the Panean Sea to the Arta. The Divide runs here." He drew a line along the left side, stretching across the land and off on either end into whatever was beyond. Then he drew a cluster of small *x* marks, creating a swath parallel to the Divide. "This is Elder Wood. You'd have had to come through there at some point."

"Where is the Sanctuary?" Quentin asked.

Sol's finger moved to a spot on the far side of Elder Wood. "Here, in Eldervale." Then he drew several small spoke-like lines running out in various directions. "These are the tunnels. We're in this one." He pointed to one that ran Northeast. "I brought us here because it will take us to the least populated area. One far from the heart of the Order."

"The Order?"

Sol nodded grimly. "The men who attacked."

"The men who have Nova." Quentin's hope guttered like a candle in the wind.

"They are a group dedicated to prophecy. They study and train the acolytes from childhood in the prophetic beliefs."

"And where is the heart of the Order?" Quentin didn't want to see what his heart already knew.

Sol drew several upside-down *v's* at the top of the Elder Wood, making a crescent shape that swung in a half circle. "These are the Jatae Mountains. Or as we call them, the Jagged Teeth." He drew a line from left to right. "The Mizrah River. Further north, the Adiron Mountains." He pointed to a spot in the center of the Adiron Mountains, making a small *x*. "This is the heart of the Order."

Quentin traced the distance across the drawing from the tunnel they were in all the way to the mountains. His hope snuffed out. There was no way they could get from one to the other in time. He couldn't be sure of distances from the crude drawing, but if the distance from the woods to the Sanctuary was any indication, the span was more than could be traveled in a week. Maybe more than a month.

"This place has magic," Laura growled. "Haven't you come up with a faster way to travel than by foot and horseback?"

Sol gave her a sad smile. "Not without attracting unwanted attention. I suspect the Order was drawn to Nova when she used her magic. If we used magic, we'd be spotted as well."

Laura scowled.

Quentin felt lost. He had no idea what they could do. "I wish Zeke were here," he said sadly. Even Nova's mom. Either of them would know what to do right now.

"Zeke?" Sol asked.

"Nova's Grandfather. Zeke."

Sol's eyebrows lifted. "Do you mean the High Wizard Ezekial?"

Laura and Quentin shared a glance.

"I've always known him as Zeke," Quentin said, a strange flutter in the pit of his stomach.

"It would make sense," Sol muttered half to himself, "that a child so strong would be of his lineage." He looked at them, his eyes intense. "What does your Zeke look like?"

"White hair, thick white bushy eyebrows …"

"And he's kind of weird," Laura added.

"Weird how?"

"He dresses strange," Laura said, her face going red.

She'd been one of the kids to make fun of Zeke, whispering about his odd habits.

"He likes to wear Mira's robes," Quentin explained with a half grin. Zeke was an odd bird, that much was true. "His daughter's name is Mira. Nova's mother."

Sol's face lit with excitement. "Then it's true. Nova is the granddaughter of the High Wizard Ezekiel." Sol looked from Quentin to Laura. "If we could reach him, he could certainly help us."

"He's in my world," Quentin said, "on the other side of the Divide."

"Ah," Sol said, deflating. "And with the Divide failing ..."

"He told us." Rose piped from across the room. She sat cross-legged on the dirt floor, watching them. Her eyes were bright even in the dark room.

Sol turned to look at her. "How could he have told you?"

"Nova talked to him," Rose said proudly, as if Nova were her sister. "She used the mirror."

"A spell," Laura clarified.

Rose nodded. "Yeah, a spell."

"Could *you* recreate the spell?" Quentin asked Sol, almost too afraid to let his hope reignite.

"I don't know." Sol rubbed his face. "I don't know the pattern or which factors she used to activate the magic."

"I can show you," Rose piped. "I'm not good at drawing, but I remember things."

"Of course, you do," Sol said with a wide smile.

Quentin's spark of hope fanned into a small flame.

"We need a mirror," Rose said.

"Or anything reflective." Morra's voice was barely a whisper.

The others crowded around her, glad to see she was awake. With a knowing smile, Rose took her mother's hand.

"I don't have a mirror," Sol said with a frown, "but the Casca River is near the tunnel opening. The clear water would work like a mirror." He looked down at Morra. "Do you think you can manage a bit more?"

Morra's lips curved as she squeezed Rose's hand. "I'll be fine." She glanced at the two burly guards. "It's not like I'm walking."

"Then let's get a move on," Laura said. She dusted herself off. "We're wasting daylight."

The Wilds

Beyond the bars of the cage, an amazing vista opened, unlike anything Nova had ever seen. The men of the Order of the Light, as Viru had explained they called themselves, had made quick work of regrouping. By nightfall, they had already crossed a vast body of water, according to Viru called the Casca River. Like a tour guide, he explained that the trees on their left were Elder Wood. Now she could see mountains looming ahead of them, their blue-white peaks poking into the clouds, some even disappearing beyond them. One soared into the sky above the others. Seeing the incredible majesty was like getting a first glimpse of Mount Everest.

Viru focused instead on the place where the trees grew denser and the mountains appeared to meet the forest. The closer they drew, the more tense he became.

"What is it?" Nova asked, clearing her throat from the dryness.

Even this early, the sun beat down harshly. Even with a blanket tossed over a portion of the bars above them to keep them from frying, the heat was oppressive.

Viru looked at her, his face taut.

"The Wilds," he said, as if that answered her question. He licked his lips. "You must be certain not to touch your magic while we are near this place. There is much danger."

She squelched her desire to laugh. "As compared to the end of all life as we know it?"

Viru frowned. "Until that happens, we cannot live as if the end will come."

He was right, but she couldn't bring herself to feel optimistic. The prophecy was clear. She was a prisoner, and she was likely heading to her own execution. It was pretty hard to feel hopeful. Still, he had become a prisoner with her to keep her from being alone, an amazing and brave thing for him to do. She shouldn't punish him for his sacrifice.

Nova swiped her forehead. A sudden thought struck her. "What time of year is it, Viru?"

His eyebrows raised in surprise as he gestured toward their surroundings. "Can you not feel it? This is the beginning of Solstice."

"Solstice?"

"The time of the sun."

"We call it summer," she said, but her mind was stuck on the fact he'd said 'beginning' rather than end. School had started. This should be the end of summer, not the beginning. Maybe seasons weren't the same here.

Or maybe the Divide separated more than space.

She felt a thrill at the possibility, but then the wagon jolted over rough ground. She banged her head against the bars of her traveling prison, and the thrill faded. She tried to ignore her discomfort. Soon none of this would matter.

She watched, lulled back into silence as the mountains came closer. The ground turned harder. Where the wheels of the wagon pulled up bits of dirt, the color was an orange-red like clay.

"Those are the Jatae," Viru said, sweeping an arm at the lofty peaks. "They are some of the tallest mountains in all of Kota."

"That's what this land is called? Kota?"

"Yes. This region spreads from the Panean to the Arta Seas. I was born in Nurandaar, a valley surrounded by the Jatae. Normally to get there, we would skirt the mountains across the great plains." He pointed off to the Northeast.

"This is a shortcut?"

"Yes. There is a pass at the foot of the Jatea that will take us farther North to Rifting Pass in the Adiron Mountains. The Adiron form a ring with a valley at the center. This valley is the seat of the Order."

"How did you end up in the Order?"

Viru smiled, perhaps the first time she'd ever seen him smile. The expression made him look even younger.

"When I was a boy, Mordoon came to Nurandaar. The elders of the city planned for his arrival. There was to be a large celebration. A feast. Dancing. A great ceremonial hunt. Mordoon entered ahead of schedule, unannounced, arriving on foot. No one realized he was there. Instead of going to the hall of elders, he came to the school. He asked to take our class outside, and we spent the afternoon learning about trees and bugs."

Nova was surprised. "Trees and bugs? Not prophecy?"

Viru shook his head. "One must learn about the life and world around us before trying to understand what prophecy has to say about them."

The way Viru spoke of the Order made them sound like monks.

"You joined so you could study trees and bugs?" Nova grinned to show him she was teasing.

Viru laughed. This was for sure the first time she'd ever seen him laugh. The color of his laughter was a rich, bright maroon. She liked this color even better than his normal, more serious tone.

"I joined because I had a dream that night," he said, still smiling. "I dreamt I was visited by a Wardein, a traveler of the High King. He told me I must learn all I could about life, and the Order was where I should start."

Nova's heart skipped a beat. "Salamain?"

"I don't know. All I could see was a shadow surrounded by light, but I knew this was more than a dream. What I saw was a vision." He looked down. "My family didn't believe me. They didn't want me to go." He looked back up, his gaze distant. "But I knew I had to. The One God was calling to me."

"You went back with … with Mul—"

"Mordoon. Yes. He became my teacher."

What Viru had done for her took on a new significance. Not only had he been willing to stand at her side and possibly be punished for his choice, he had gone against his teacher.

"You're very brave, Viru."

He looked at her with surprise. "As are you."

Nova shook her head. "I'm not brave. I'm afraid of everything. I'm afraid of who I am, of what I can do. I'm even afraid of what I'm doing right now."

"Doing what you are not afraid of is nothing. Doing what fills you with fear is brave."

She let his words sink in. "Then I agree. I'm being very brave."

They laughed, but the echo of a long wail stilled them. The sound reverberated through the air around them, seeming to come from all directions at once.

"What was that?" The hairs on Nova's arms lifted.

Viru's gaze seemed tense. "The Wilds."

"When you said the name before, I thought you meant a place."

"The Wilds *is* a place." He turned to look at her, and his eyes were as dark as she'd ever seen them. "Named for the creatures who inhabit it."

She swallowed hard. "We're going there?"

"We'll only skirt the edge," he said, "but in Nurandaar there are stories of people who have disappeared from as far away as the Jatae valley, never to be seen again."

"How do they know these creatures caused the disappearances?"

He lifted his chin toward the point where the trees and mountains met. "They heard the cry."

Emotion in Magic

Beginners in magic will often find the most difficult thing to learn is how to use their power. Drawing the magic out of oneself goes beyond the mere drawing of a spell form. It comes from within the individual. Accessing that well of power and drawing the magic forth requires learning, patience, and practice.

Some feel that the use of strong emotions can help to trigger this ability. However, this is considered by most to be an unclean method, as the user of magic cannot fully understand what they are doing nor control the outcome.

—High Wizard Ezekial, on the *Factors of Magic*

Faith

Darkness had already descended when they arrived. The Casca River stretched in front of them like a black ribbon against the landscape. None of them had accounted for the fact they needed daylight in order for the water to reflect clearly.

"What about the moonlight?" Quentin asked. "Won't that be enough?"

Sol shook his head. "The spell needs more light."

Laura scowled. "Won't the ripples cause some sort of problem?"

"They might." Sol whispered to the two guards who had carried Morra, and they hurried away into the darkness. "If they can find anything else in time, they'll bring it here."

"And if not?" Laura's soft question carried a heavy weight.

Sol shook his head helplessly.

Again, the last bit of hope Quentin had to find Nova was stripped away from him. How could they reach Zeke if they couldn't do the spell? Every moment took Nova further away. He could feel the cord that bound her to him stretching thin. Would their bond disappear altogether at some point, too distant to be felt? At some point, his connection to Nova had become a comfort, a way to know she was okay, that he was still with her in some way even if not directly.

"I need a minute," he mumbled, leaving the others as he walked through the tall grass.

He saw them glancing after him with worried expressions, but he needed to think. The bank of the river rose up ahead of him, a small incline before the slope down to the edge of the water. A single tree clung to the lip, like a lone survivor. Though small, the branches were covered in dark fruit. Quentin circled the tree until the river flowed in front of him, then sat and leaned against the smooth bark.

A crescent of moon poked out from behind a cloud. The grass beside him glowed in the temporary light. He ran his fingers along the green blades. The memory of sitting next to Nova after their race and having her throw grass at him filled his mind. Her laughter echoed.

Quentin clenched his fist, tearing the grass away by the roots and heaving the handful toward the water. "How could you do this?" His sudden swell of anger surprised even him. "I found you. How could you leave again?"

But his anger went deeper than Nova's leaving.

She'd left him the first time because she wanted to protect everyone, even herself. This time she had willingly gone back to the people who were trying to kill her. She wasn't protecting herself. She was sacrificing herself.

Martyr. The word rang bitterly in his head.

"It's not such a bad thing, you know, to be a martyr."

Quentin's back slammed against the tree. Beside him sat a smiling stranger, his face twisted with scars.

"Who—how did you—"

"Peace, Quentin of Endwell. I am no threat."

Quentin stared at the scars, realizing he'd seen them before. "I saw you once, in the swamp."

The man's eyes seemed to sparkle. "I go where I am needed."

"Who are you?"

"I am called by many names, but you may call me Salamain."

Quentin looked back at his friends. They were huddled around a small fire, oblivious to what was going on.

"Why are you here now?"

"I am needed."

"For what? There's nothing you can do here. Nova's the one who needs someone. They're going to …"

The thought was too terrible to continue.

"You must have faith."

"Faith?" A sad, bitter smile tugged at Quentin's lips. "How can I? I can't even help her."

Salamain sighed. "Have you ever seen a chick being born?"

What did that have to do with anything? "I don't see—"

"They must poke a hole through the shell with a beak barely bigger than your pinky nail," he went on as if Quentin hadn't spoken. "Their small, fragile body, still wet with birth, must find a way to break through the shell and burst free." He turned to look Quentin in the eye. "If you are not there to help, how is it that the chick is still born?"

Quentin's mouth popped open, but he had no response to that.

"Faith," Salamain said, holding up a finger, "is in knowing that even without your help, each chick will find its way. Faith is believing they were created to do this and made with the strength to complete their task."

He could do nothing to stop the swell of anger inside him. "Am I supposed to have faith that Nova is strong enough to *die?*"

Hot, angry tears spilled down his face.

"In the darkest moments of our lives, we must cling to the light."

Salamain's face was so kind and his voice so gentle. Quentin wanted to believe the man, to cling to some hope they could still find a way through this.

"I don't know how."

When everything had seemed lost before, Nova had been the guiding light in his darkness. She was his hope.

"You must believe," Salamain said, placing one scarred hand on Quentin's shoulder. "Believe that the hope you found in her, the hope she wants to share with the world, will bring about something bigger than anything you can imagine here and now."

Quentin wanted to believe. He really did. But he wasn't sure he could still feel hope in a world without Nova.

"I don't know if I'm strong enough," he whispered.

"Funny thing about strength," Salamain said as he looked at the water. "Sometimes you have to let yourself be weak in order to find it."

A fish jumped somewhere, making a splash. Quentin watched ripples spread on the water's surface.

"I don't understand," he said looking back, "how do I …"

But Salamain was gone. The hairs on Quentin's neck stood up. He looked down the bank and around the tree, but there was nothing. Not even an indentation in the grass where the man had been sitting.

"You're losing your mind," he whispered to himself. Even as he said the words, he knew they weren't true.

His shoulder was still warm where Salamain's hand had been.

"You must believe," he'd said.

Quentin wanted to have faith like that.

"Trust me, Quen." Nova's words from the park came floating back to him.

Trust.

Faith.

Hope.

They were difficult words. Harder than he'd ever thought they could be. He looked at the moonlight on the water and wondered if God was really up there watching him.

"If you're there," he whispered, "I'm trying. I'm trying to have faith. Just help her, okay? Help us both."

Quentin didn't know what else to say. For now, that would have to be enough.

LOST SOULS

Nova stared into the darkness, fear thrilling through her. All around her, the men were asleep, even Viru. How could they rest? Unearthly moans sounded all around, drifting on the night air, the ghostly harmony a terrible song of doom and despair.

Nova stared into the thick black between the trees. They were camped too close. The Wilds were here. Even as the realization hit her, she saw a strange, glowing shape drift from the darkness. An eerie blue glow moved toward her. Inside the glow, something moved. She had to get away, but she was locked behind bars.

The blue glowing form floated closer, gliding over the grass. In its wake, everything froze. The bushes, the trees, even the blades of grass were coated in ice, reflecting the spectral light. In that light, Nova saw a form. The creature's mouth stretched impossibly wide. Hands reached out from between the gaping lips, seeking escape. Fingers hunted something to grasp. A chorus of voices called for help. For salvation. Together, the voices rose in discordant strife, louder and louder, creating the wail carried on the wind.

The cries of lost souls.

Nova moved as far away as she could, until the cold hard bars pressed into her. The wraith came closer. She could see some of the hands were large, others small. Too small. The banshee reached the side of the wagon and pressed its face between the bars. The arms reached out, elongating and reaching for her, stretching—fingers moving like pale white worms.

Then suddenly, dark shapes swarmed them. A familiar sound drowned out the wails.

Birds.

Nova stared in horrid fascination as they covered every branch, every inch of ground, every bar of her cage. They stared at her with dark, foreboding eyes. Then as one they exploded upward.

She knew what came next. The dark beast stood behind the wraith, sleek and elegant. Its black eyes stared, calling to her like limpid pools. Between them, the swirling colors danced up and down the single horn.

Cyclorn.

Understanding filled her with cold dread. The lost souls of The Wilds were what was left of beings after their magic had been stolen by the cyclorn. The glowing-eyed wraiths were the empty shells, longing to have their lives back. Their music. Their color.

The cyclorn reared, hooves pawing the air. Then he came down and stretched his long, arched neck close. Nova tried to speak but nothing came out. The cyclorn touched the wraith with its terrible horn.

A scream erupted from within—a scream with many voices. Nova pressed her hands over her ears, but there was no escaping the noise. The horn darkened, and the colors swirled up and down as the light of the wraith began to dim. Echoes of light left a glowing trail in the air. A pattern that dissolved slowly inward. A pattern of theft and destruction.

She knew this design. She had drawn it before.

Tears wet Nova's face. Tears for the lost souls. They had been stripped, and now they were being eaten by the monstrous beast who stole the remaining essence of life from the helpless beings that were not even beings. The pattern of destruction blazed. The spectral, grasping hands turned black, falling into ash. They were gone. The lost souls had been devoured.

"No!" Nova's scream wrenched her. She sat up violently, her head spinning.

The fading sun left a faint orange glow against the mountains. In spite of the light, the air had turned cold.

"Nova?" Viru sat nearby, his arms wrapped around his knees. "Are you all right?"

She looked around, disoriented. Men were eating, setting up tents and cleaning.

"A dream," she said, her heart still pounding against her ribs.

Viru nodded. "It is the nearness of the Wilds."

"I ... I saw—"

A horn sounded, and every head turned.

The men who had been eating hurried to toss the last of the food into packs as everyone else rushed to the horses, cinching harnesses and calling instructions. They scurried like mice.

"What's going on?" Nova asked.

Viru frowned. "I don't know. We should be stopping here for the night. Something has happened."

Nova rubbed her arms. She couldn't shake the feeling of horror that followed her from her dream. She was almost glad when she was jolted back and forth as the wagon moved over the ground. She wanted to be away from this place.

Viru shouted something in another language, startling her. A man hurrying alongside them looked over and yelled something back, his face a scowl. Viru replied, the lilting words sounding like a question. The man threw up his hands, then waved to another man, who tossed him a pack. The man running alongside shoved the pack between the bars and hurried away. Viru grinned.

"Here," he reached into the pack and pulled out a blanket, holding it out to her.

The material was coarse and scratchy but thick. Gratefully, she wrapped the blanket around her bare arms.

"Aren't you cold?"

Viru shook his head. "I have lived in the mountains all my life. I am used to the cold."

She huddled beneath the rough material, trying to get warm. "What did you say to him?"

Viru grinned again. "I reminded him our ways teach we should always help others, even those who are against us."

Nova couldn't help but smile. "He didn't seem to like being reminded."

The horn sounded again, and Nova saw the men urging the horses to move more quickly.

"It is Cyril who blows the horn," Viru said, his voice full of obvious distaste.

"Which one is he?"

"He is the one who destroyed the Lady of the Sanctuary."

"Ishtar." A chill that had nothing to do with the cold filled Nova. Ishtar had been a greedy, selfish woman, but the man who had killed her was no man at all. He was a devil. "He is wicked."

To her surprise, Viru nodded in agreement. "His words do not always follow our teachings," he said, frowning. "He is too hungry. Too filled with thirst for things beyond him."

"Why do you follow him, then?" He was obviously the man in charge.

Viru looked at her, and she saw sadness in his brown eyes. "They are afraid of him."

That, at least, was a truth she could understand.

"At first, his ways were our own. He had a way with prophecy greater than any we had seen. He became our First." Viru paused, remembering. "Then the madness began."

He turned to her again, and the intensity in his face frightened her.

"That is why I tried to stop them. To protect you."

"But what about the prophecy?"

Viru shook his head. "No. There is something wrong with our understanding."

Nova remembered Lucien's voice as he recounted the prophecy to her. "The words seem pretty clear. I'm the one with the blood of old, and I came here of my own free will. That's why Quentin followed me, and that's why the Divide is failing. It's my fault."

Viru shook his head. "There must be something we have failed to comprehend. Prophecy is often vague and easy to falsely interpret. Perhaps we have interpreted something incorrectly. There must be a way to—"

Horn blasts sounded from all directions. The men and animals ran, even the horses pulling the wagon. Nova and Viru were jolted against the bars as the uneven ground bounced them. They grabbed hold of the bars, bracing themselves as the men of the Order fled through the fading evening light.

Nova's gaze was drawn to the trees and the dark places between them. In those pools of blackness, Nova saw lights dancing. Blue-white lights. They glowed and drifted.

And there were thousands of them.

Her hands clutched the bars, knuckles white. Not a dream, *a vision of the truth*. The Wilds were exactly what she had seen. They were wraiths. The lost souls of those drained by the cyclorn.

Viru scanned the area for something ahead of them. "Look." He shouted to be heard over the noise of the men and horses.

Nova craned her neck to see, glad to pull her eyes away from the trees and the drifting ghosts. Ahead, something flashed. Two figures stood on either side of an opening, arms waving people through. The opening resembled a chuppah and was made of twisted sticks woven together to form an arch.

Nova's eyes widened as a man rushed into the opening. With a flash of light, the man was gone.

"A portal," Viru yelled.

"A what?"

He looked at her. "The portal to Rifting Pass. We will soon be home."

The reality of her looming death fell on Nova like a weight. This device would bring her to the place where she would face her end. She had barely lived, and now she was going to die. Alone. In a land far from her home and the people she loved.

Mom. What would her mother do when she found out?

Grandpa Zeke.

This would destroy them. She may have thought she was coming here to save the world, but she couldn't. Her mother and grandfather would be alive—saved from destruction caused by the failing Divide—but they would be devastated. What was she doing? What had she been thinking? Did she really believe she could fix this on her own?

One by one, the men ahead of the wagon, some on horseback, others on foot, ran under the arch and disappeared.

The old man, the one Viru called Mordoon, stood on one side of the arch, waving his arms frantically, urging people to hurry. Cyril stood on the other side. He had eyes only for Nova. They burned with malicious glee, sending chills up her spine. Cyril had been the one searching for her, the one who had sent Viru across the Divide and into another world to capture her, and she had walked willingly into his clutches.

She gripped the bars, dread eating at her insides like voracious moths as the wagon hurtled toward the portal. The horses were lathered, their eyes rolling and white. Nova could taste the scent of their terror, heavy on her tongue. Then the wagon thundered beneath the twisted branches, and a blinding light filled the world.

WARDEIN

Lucien glared at the portal.

He'd missed them by mere minutes. Cyril was clever. Lucien would give his old friend that much. He must have sensed Lucien gaining and decided to speed up the trip a bit.

He would not let this happen. Cyril was not going to take what was his.

Lucien stalked toward the portal. Stealth was no longer an issue. He didn't care who knew he was coming. There was no one in the Order he feared.

"I wouldn't do that."

Lucien spun on his heel. A strange man covered in scars stood on the path behind him, leaning on a wooden staff. Where had he come from? "Who are you?"

The man gazed at him serenely.

"What is this, some sort of trick? Did Cyril put you up to this?"

"This is no trick, Lucien of Millwind."

There was a name he hadn't heard in ages. He'd left behind the village where he'd been born years ago. There was more to this man than met the eye.

"How do you know me?"

"I know what you intend. You cannot go after her. You must not."

Lucien took a step closer. "Who are you to tell me what I can and cannot do, old man?"

The stranger was not intimidated. "I am who I am."

"Crazy old buzzard." Lucien turned away.

He didn't need this nuisance. He needed to get to Cyril before the fools of the Order could do anything stupid. He stepped toward the portal, but a hand pressed on his chest. He looked down in amazement. Thick, twisted scars roped across the skin, running up the man's arm like veins.

"You will go no further." The stranger's eyes were firm and his voice steady. "Turn aside."

Lucien slapped the hand away. "Or what?"

The old man said nothing.

A laugh rose in his throat like bile, spilling out. "Move," he growled, "or I will move you."

A sudden thunder filled the air. "Leave this place, Lucien, son of Lorian, son of Griven."

Lucien's eyes narrowed. He raised his hand, but before his fingers could weave a pattern, the old man slammed his staff against the ground. A ring of gold roared outward, slamming Lucien to the ground. Still reeling, he lifted his arms, weaving magic. He would blast this fool into oblivion.

Lucien's magic struck and washed over the old man without impact. "Impossible!"

Still, the old man merely gazed at him serenely. Around him, the air took on a faint glow.

"Wardein," Lucien hissed with an intake of breath. "But Wardein are a myth."

"Do I look like a myth to you?"

Filled with anger, Lucien struggled back to his feet, his hands shaking. "I am not afraid of you."

The man gave a wry smile, the scars pulling at his skin. "Who are you trying to convince?"

This was not happening. Lucien bellowed and charged at the old man. If magic would not work, Lucien would take him down with his bare hands.

The old man passed his hand through the air in front of him. Lucien ignored the move. He would not be distracted. He would—

All thought ceased when his body encountered something solid. An invisible wall stopped his forward momentum. He heard something crack and pain seared through his head and right shoulder. The impact flung him backwards. He landed flat on the dirt, dazed. He blinked, unable to breathe. Fire filled his shoulder, and blood trickled down his face from his nose. As he looked up, a face filled his vision. He tried to scramble away, but a spear of pain held him in place.

"Know me, Lucien of Millwind." The old man's voice boomed louder than thunder. "I am a traveler of the High King. I command you to leave this place and return to your home. Remain there for a fortnight hence."

Lucien felt his body move. He looked down and saw with horrid wonder that the old man had one finger beneath him. With his single finger, the traveler lifted Lucien to a standing position. Fire raged through Lucien's damaged body.

"You will not receive healing from these afflictions. They will be a reminder to heed the voice of the High King and his travelers."

Lucien cradled his right arm against his chest.

"Go."

He spoke this single word—nothing more—yet Lucien's body responded. He turned and limped to his horse. The beast stood calmly as his hands grabbed the reins. Once he was mounted the horse began to walk. Lucien looked back, ignoring the pain the movement caused him. The path behind him stood empty.

The man with the scars had disappeared as if he'd never been.

Discipline of Magic

Discipline is needed for those seeking to truly master the use of magic. Power requires not only energy but a controlled, steady conduit able to contain the flow and focus its outcome. The use of power without discipline is like trying to harness a storm. Education, method, preparation, and practice are tools that provide those with power a way to truly manage and strengthen their gift.

In truth, those who truly seek to learn the ways of magic never stop studying or training. Learning is a life-long endeavor.

—High Wizard Ezekial, on the *Factors of Magic*

Bound

"Help him!"

Laura turned to make sure Sol was coming. Her heart pounded as he dropped to his knees in the grass where Quentin was on his side, curled into a ball, arms clenched over his stomach.

"Quentin." Sol put a hand on his back. "What is it? What's happened?"

Quentin moaned.

Sol felt Quentin's forehead, pulling his hand away with a frown. "There's no fever."

"What's wrong then?" Her mouth was dry.

He shook his head. "I'm not sure."

Morra and Rose sat up from their beds on the other side of the fire.

Rose rubbed her eyes. "What's wrong with Quentin?"

"We don't know yet," Sol answered as he examined Quentin's arms and legs.

Laura watched anxiously. She wasn't used to feeling like this. She hated being helpless. Worry dug at her gut.

She could remember when she and her brothers were still small, the times she'd spent lying in bed with her eyes pressed shut, hoping against all odds not to hear her father come home. If they were already asleep, he might not bother to come all the way upstairs. He'd yell at Mom instead, and she'd scream back for a while, then he'd escape her by going to bed. But if anyone was still awake …

Some nights, Evan had to pee. He couldn't help it. He was just a kid still. Unfortunately, the only working toilet in the house was downstairs. If her father came home to find Evan downstairs, a riot was likely to break out. Then she'd have to press her hands to her ears and try not to let her father hear her crying. That was a fast way to a bad night.

"You gotta learn to shut up," her older brother Jack would say. "Evan can take care of himself. You gotta learn to take care of yourself, or you won't make it."

She didn't know for sure if he was right. Evan was still pretty small to take care of himself. He cried a lot for a boy, which just made their father even more ticked off. Still, Jack had managed to survive the bad years, so he must know something she didn't.

She'd taken his advice to heart. She learned not to care. Don't let anyone hurt you. That was how she had survived. Except she hadn't really. She'd avoided some beatings, but she'd also become someone she didn't like.

Nova had always rubbed her the wrong way, defending everyone like she was some kind of guardian angel. Laura had never really noticed Quentin. He was just Nova's sidekick. Where Nova was, Quentin was. That was why Laura had followed Quentin when she saw him in the park. That, and Monday was bill day. Bill day was always a bad day in the Hennigan house.

Without any warning at all, an opportunity had presented itself. A chance to escape not just the day, but maybe everything.

Maybe even herself.

Now look at her. She'd gotten soft. Jack would disapprove. She'd let people in. Heck, she'd done more than that.

She cared.

Quentin gasped. Laura's stomach lurched. His eyes opened, and he grabbed her arm.

"Lucien," he whispered. "Almost … got to her …"

Understanding washed over Laura like an ice bath. "I *knew* that witch was trouble. You should never have let her do the spell."

Understanding dawned on Sol's face. "Blood magic?"

Laura nodded. "She used Quentin's blood to block Nova's dad from getting too close to her."

Sol's face drained of color. "She *bound* him," he whispered.

"What?" Laura asked, fear rising in her throat. "She what?"

"I knew she'd done something, but I didn't realize …"

Laura was going to smack him if Sol didn't tell her what was going on.

He looked up at her, his eyes wide. "Thuaat bound Quentin to Nova and to Lucien. She used him to do more than merely provide the block—she created the form with his blood."

Dread formed a cold, hard ball in Laura's chest.

"If the spell is somehow broken"—Sol looked back at Quentin who was panting on the ground, his face covered in sweat—"he dies."

"He *dies?*" Laura shouted her fear.

Her ears were hot, and her head was about to explode. She was going to find that witch woman, and she was going to wring her wobbly little neck.

"S'okay," Quentin squeaked between pants. "It's okay now."

"For now. What if Lucien tries something again? What if next time he succeeds?"

Quentin closed his eyes. He was afraid, but he didn't care. If his dying would help his little girlfriend, he was willing to risk his own life. It was all so stupid and pointless.

Except it wasn't. Because Laura wasn't sure, but she thought maybe she wished someone cared about her that way. She wished someone cared enough to risk their life for her.

The fear on Quentin's face washed some of her anger away. She looked at Sol. "Is there anything you can do? Can the spell be undone?"

Sol shook his head. "Blood magic is very powerful. Few even know how to use such ancient magic."

"Great." There was nothing she could do. Blast Quentin and his noble intentions.

"It's okay," Quentin whispered again, only Laura knew this time he meant something completely different.

"It's *not* okay, you idiot," she growled. "You think she wants you to die? Why do you think she came here to begin with? To save your butt!" Laura shook her head. "Between the two of you, I don't know who's denser."

Quentin stared at her in surprise.

"What, you didn't know? Oh, come on." She rolled her eyes. "You're two of the most clueless people I've ever met."

Quentin's face contorted. Dry, wheezing sounds came out of him. Her heart skipped a beat. Then she realized he was laughing. Relief flooded through her.

He was going to be all right.

For now.

CHOICES

Nova sat alone in the darkness of the cell. Tears dripped from her face, falling silently onto her knees as she huddled on the dirt floor.

Gone.

Her home, her family, her friends ... even her hope. They had stripped her of everything. Now she was going to die in some forgotten place, and no one would even know. She'd searched the room frantically for anything shiny, anything that might make a reflection. There was nothing. Not even a puddle of water. She was alone and filled with despair.

"I've waited a long time for this."

Nova gasped. In the dim light beyond the bars of her cell, a set of eyes glowed. Nova scrambled away until her back was pressed against rock wall. A body slowly materialized from the shadows. Hands clasped behind his back, he cocked his head to the side.

"Did you know I was the one who created you?" His horrible smile was full of malice. "Oh yes. Lucien may have sired you, and your mother may have birthed you, but I ... I was the one who imagined you. Who knew you could exist. I was the one who whispered into Lucien's ear what he might do. I birthed your possibility."

She followed him with her eyes as he paced in front of the bars.

"He was so thirsty for power, your father." He shook his head. "It was almost too easy. I knew of the prophecy of course. All I had to do was dangle the idea in front of him like a piece of gold. He was only too eager to snatch it up."

Looking at his grin was like looking into the mouth of a shark.

"Every bone I tossed him, he gobbled up. He begged for more. He dug and ran and panted after his treasures." He gave a little laugh. "Such a good pet."

Nova couldn't keep her silence. "If he was such a dog, why didn't you sire me yourself?"

He gave her a sidelong glance. "I didn't need to. I had a lapdog to do the work for me."

"No," Nova said softly. "I don't think that's the reason at all."

She didn't know everything about the magic yet, about the different factors, but she knew some things.

"I don't think you *could*."

His face hardened. She'd struck a nerve.

"You didn't have what it takes, did you?"

He whirled, his eyes twin lamps of fire. "I have more than you'll ever know, mongrel pup of a pathetic dog."

Fear wormed through her. She'd seen what this man had done to Ishtar, but something inside Nova had shifted. She wasn't the same person she'd once been. She wasn't the freak she'd always believed she was. She was also in a cell waiting to die, alone, her back against a wall.

Nova had nothing left to lose.

"You didn't have what you needed, so you had to find someone who did."

His eyes narrowed dangerously.

Nova drove her point home. "You're the one who's pathetic. You couldn't even do what a dog could."

His fingers clenched the bars, and she saw dark smoke wisp from them.

"Brave words for a child about to have her life blood spilled out like water."

He'd told the truth then. Her death was how the prophecy would be kept from unfolding. Her blood would fix the failing Divide.

"At first light," he said softly, his voice like the hiss of a snake, "as the sun touches the horizon and the land is painted with its rays, your life will be spilled for all to see. You'll be drained until you have nothing left. You will be left an empty husk."

Nova shuddered but refused to give him the satisfaction of a sound. He stared for several long minutes, then sighed when a response failed to come.

"You're as stubborn as your father," he said finally. "Shame you'll never actually get to meet him."

Nova flinched at the reminder Quentin had purposely kept them apart.

"A block," Cyril mused, tapping one fingernail against the steel of a bar. "Such an unusual thing to have here. It's a pity he wasn't filled in on the details of his little *contribution*."

What was he talking about? How could he know about that?

"Oh yes," his grin was back. "I know many things, little pup. I know about your friends, and I know what the witch woman Thuaat did. I see these things."

A finger of dread worked its way up her back. She didn't like where this was going. He was too happy.

"Funny thing about blood magic," he said, as if sharing a secret. "It binds the provider to the spell in more ways than one." He nodded, agreeing with himself. "If the spell is broken, he dies." He shrugged. "If Lucien were to reach you, your friend's life would end. Simple as that."

Lucien had been telling her the truth.

"But there's more." Cyril's smile widened. "If something were to happen to our Lucien, something that were to say, cause his *demise*, the blood bond would cause their fate to be shared."

Horror flooded Nova's veins.

"You see," He stretched the revelation out, savoring her anguish, "if *you* die, your little block dies too." He clapped his hands together happily. "Isn't that lovely? Just like a fairy tale. So romantic." He pressed his face into the space between the bars. His smile became a leer. "Together for eternity."

Then he whirled and disappeared back into the shadows. Nova listened but didn't hear anything more. Unable to hold back the tears, they tumbled down her cheeks.

Everything she'd tried to do had been for nothing. She'd come here, fought the Trench, even given herself up to be sacrificed to protect the people she loved. Now Quentin was going to die anyway, and his death would be her fault.

Her despair grew with the deepening shadows. The moon was setting. Sunrise was not far off. In a few hours she would be dead, and so would the boy she had only just discovered she loved. Nova buried her face in her hands and let her tears flow.

They were all she had left.

Papa Noel

Ripples danced on the water.

"Softer," Rose instructed.

Sol did as she said, his finger skating over the water, barely skimming the surface.

Rose held out the flat rock for him to see. Her drawing, done by a finger dipped in mud, was beginning to dry. Flakes drifted down.

Sol studied the image. He smiled. "I think I've got it."

Rose nodded.

Sol traced the shape as if drawing just above the water rather than on it.

Quentin's breath stuck in his throat. Sol moved more quickly, and the lines began to glow. They didn't spark and burn as Nova's had, but the glow slowly intensified until each movement created an afterimage like the tail of a sparkler. There was a sudden flash, and light split into the water below and the air above.

Sol had done it!

Quentin searched the light, looking for Zeke's face.

Nothing.

"Where are they?" Laura asked.

"I don't see anything," Morra said softly.

"It has no anchor," Sol said, shaking his head. "I was afraid of this."

"What?" Quentin felt lost. "What do you mean? What anchor?"

"Nova's spell was directed to where Zeke and Mira are by something inside her. The spell allows the communication, but the end points have to be anchored by something."

"It's like trying to make a phone call without a phone number," Laura said.

Sol frowned. "We need something to link us to where they are. Some way to infuse their location into the spell."

"Do you have anything from home?" Laura asked Quentin.

He jammed his hands into his pockets, but they were empty. "Nothing," he said. "What about you?"

She shook her head.

"How did Nova anchor the spell?" Quentin asked. "Did she have to have something physical, or did she just think about home?"

Sol looked pained. "I don't know."

As a group, they all turned to look at Rose. She looked back at them with wide eyes and shrugged.

"Can you leave the portal open?" Morra asked.

Sol looked at her. "What do you mean?"

She nodded toward the glowing form and the light glowing above and below. "That light you made. It's a doorway, correct? Can you leave the door open?"

"For a while, I think. Then the spell would begin to fade."

"I just thought if you could, maybe Zeke can find us." She looked at the others. "Maybe we don't have his *number*," she used Laura's example, "but he might have ours."

Sol nodded. "It's the best we can do for now."

He backed away from the edge of the water, leaving the spell suspended. The magic pulsed and glowed like a lamp.

"How long until the image fades?" Quentin couldn't pull his eyes away.

"A couple of hours maybe." Sol put his hand on Quentin's shoulder, reminding him of Salamain. "If this doesn't work, we'll keep moving and try the spell somewhere else tomorrow."

Quentin tried to smile. Optimism was harder knowing Nova might not have until tomorrow.

The group of them sat on the bank and watched the sun slowly rise.

"I like Nova's grandpa," Rose sighed softly.

"How do you know him?" Sol asked.

"I saw him when Nova did the mirror thingy," Rose answered. "He's funny looking. Like Papa Noel."

"Papa Noel?" Laura asked, incredulous. "You have Christmas here?"

Rose frowned. "What's Christmas?"

Laura frowned right back at her. "Who's Papa Noel?"

"It's just an old legend," Morra explained. "Papa Noel brings the snow in winter. He's a snow elf."

"In our world, we call him Santa Claus," Laura said. "Our legend has elves too."

"Oh," Morra said with a shake of her head. "Elves are no legend. They're quite real, although they haven't lived here in Kota for hundreds of years."

"Where do the elves live now?"

At Laura's question, Quentin turned to look at her in surprise. She raised one eyebrow at him, as if daring him to comment.

Morra drew a shape in the dirt that resembled the one Sol had drawn in the tunnel. Then she drew a line running along one side, going off beyond the edge of the shape at both ends.

"This is the Divide," she said. "Above Kota is the Arta. It's a vast body of water." She pointed. "Somewhere in the Arta where the Divide meets the top of the world, that is where the snow elves are said to live."

"North Pole," Quentin and Laura said in unison. They both laughed.

"Go figure," Laura said.

"Figure what?" The gruff voice caught them all by surprise.

The light over the water above the spell grew as an image filled the air.

"Zeke!" Quentin shouted. He looked at the others. "We did it."

They erupted into whoops of joy.

Zeke stared from under his bushy white brows. He did sort of look like Santa Claus, Quentin thought with a laugh. Zeke's gaze shifted from face to face, squinting as if he was having trouble seeing the man clearly. "Sol Breven, is that you?"

Sol gave a small nod. "High Wizard Ezekial. It's an honor to speak with you again."

"I remember a skinny lad running errands," Zeke said, "yet here you are a grown man."

Sol smiled. "Somehow you have not aged at all."

"Hah!" Though more like a shout, Zeke's snort was as close to a laugh as Quentin had ever heard from Zeke.

Then he moved as if someone poked him from behind. "Yes, yes, we have important things to speak of. Where's Nova?"

The smiles and laughter died.

Zeke's image grew grave. "What's happened?"

"The Order has her," Sol said. He exchanged a quick glance with Quentin before looking back at Zeke. "She went to them," Sol said, his voice thick with emotion, "willingly."

"What?" Zeke roared. "And you let her do this?"

Sol dipped his head slightly, but his eyes never wavered. "She knew what she was doing."

Even through the spell, Quentin could see Zeke's face was tinged with red. His jaw clenched and unclenched, and his bushy eyebrows twitched.

"Yes," he said finally. "I suppose she did." His eyes snapped up. "Still, we must rescue her. Goodness only knows what those fools will do if left to their own devices."

"There's more," Sol said, and his voice was tense. "The Order … they have a new First."

If possible, Zeke's brows lowered even more. "Who?"

"Cyril."

The name hung in the air like the emptiness after a crack of thunder.

In the background, Quentin heard Mira sob.

Then Zeke leaned in, his eyes ablaze. "Listen closely. Here's what we're going to do."

Mediums

The medium is a critical part of spell forms and of magic in general. It is the material used to create the design (such as sand, wood, stone, etc.), and the mechanism that regulates the amount of power. If too much energy is channeled through too weak a form, the results can be explosive. If too little energy is channeled through too broad a form, the results are ineffective.

In addition to providing the spell form with strength, the medium also designates a binding between the user and the magic. The stronger the medium, the more magic required from the wielder to execute, and the more powerful the outcome.

—High Wizard Ezekial, on the *Factors of Magic*

PROPHECY FULFILLED

Nova couldn't see the sun, but she could see the lighter shades of blue where the sky already began to lighten. She stared upward, wondering if this would be the last thing she ever saw. A bird flew high above her, a speck of darkness against a deep blue background. She could smell flowers in bloom. The breeze was cool and fresh.

The day was so beautiful, she could almost forget her back was pressed against a wooden beam. The wood spanned a marble basin set in the center of a clearing, surrounded by hills into which rings of long stone benches had been carved. Each ring rose higher along the hillside than the one before, giving every level a perfect view. She wondered vaguely if the ancient coliseums she'd read about in school had looked something like this. The men who lined the seats now were dressed like monks, with simple brown robes and sandals. They were somber and silent. She was unsure whether their silence was better or worse than if they had taunted her with shouts.

She had tried not to look at the stains on the wood when they'd tied her to it, and she was doing everything she could not to imagine what was about to happen. The reality would be bad enough. She tried to push the images and thoughts of pain and death away.

The man who had tied her to the beam stood beside her, his hands clasped behind his back. Nova saw the glint of steel.

"People of the Order of Light," a voice rang out.

Though he didn't sound as angry as he had a few hours ago, Nova recognized the voice.

"Before us lays the child of prophecy," Cyril called. "She faces the judgment of the world for setting destruction into motion. We have witnessed the text come to life. We know the Divide fails. What is the judgment?"

"Death." As one, the men of the Order spoke her sentence. Their voices rumbled across the hills and from the mountain tops.

"She chose to cross the Divide into our world, bringing those who did not belong," Cyril's voice continued. "And in their wake the magic of the Divide issued forth as a dark cloud. Through choice and action freely made, as was foretold, so did destruction sweep across the land, carrying with it a wave of the Trench. The wretched disease has struck down many. These are the signs that prophecy has been fulfilled. The child of prophecy brings the destruction of *all* the worlds. What is the judgment?"

"Death."

Hot tears streamed down Nova's cheeks, into her hair and down her neck. She hadn't wanted to cry. She'd wanted to be strong, to face this with bravery, but she wasn't brave. She wasn't strong. She was just a kid who wanted to see her mom and her grandpa and to hold them one more time.

"Prophecy tells us one must stand to face the night. That for destruction to be stilled, life's blood must be freely spilled. Her death is the only way to stop what has begun. Her blood is the only thing that can heal the Divide and avoid the destruction of all life. Stand now and protect the life you hold dear. Affirm the prophecy and uphold the law! What is her sentence?"

"Death."

"I'm sorry," Nova whispered. The prophecy was true. Her foolish choice had brought her here. If she hadn't crossed the Divide, Quentin would never have come, and the storm of destruction would never have been unleashed. The Divide would not be failing.

"As your First, I declare ..."

Nova heard murmurs break out in the crowd as his voice trailed off. What was happening? The man beside her stared across the field, hands unclasped, and she saw for the first time the dagger meant to end her life.

"How did he get in there?" A voice asked.

Others joined in.

"Who is that?"

"What is he doing?"

She craned her neck to see. The sides of the basin rose too high, and her bonds were too tight.

Everything quieted. The crowd's murmurs stilled. Even the wind seemed to hold its breath. Footsteps approached, followed by the thud of something hitting the soft ground. Then, she saw him.

His face blurred and tripled as tears poured and sobs shook her body. He turned to her, gentle and somehow beautiful, despite the thick and twisted scars.

Salamain.

"Peace, daughter."

His words were meant for her alone, his gold wrapping around her like a cloak. Instantly, an amazing peace filled her. The fear subsided. Her heart quieted. He lifted a wooden staff, then raised his arms into the air and faced the men of the Order.

"Who will speak for you?" His voice rang across the clearing, louder than she had ever heard.

"I am their First," Cyril shouted. His voice trembled with rage … and fear.

"No," Salamain answered firmly. "You speak no longer."

His staff hit the ground once, and a ring of light flashed outward. There was a commotion. Nova couldn't see what was happening.

"I … I will speak for us," a wobbling voice called.

Nova knew this voice also. This was Viru's teacher. The old man who liked bugs.

"I require your name," Salamain commanded.

"I am Mordoon," he answered, and Nova could feel even from her prone position he was trying not to show his fear. "We require your name as well, stranger."

"I am known by many names," Salamain answered. "I am called Salamain. I am a traveler. I am a son. I am who I am."

There were gasps all around. Nova saw the man next to her gape, his face growing pale. He dropped the dagger.

"Wardein," he whispered. Then he dropped to his knees, and Nova could no longer see him.

The rustle of motion and whispers of "Wardein" filled the air around her. She didn't need to see them to know every man of the Order had dropped to their knees before Salamain.

"What you do here today is accursed."

There were more gasps. Cries and moans filled the air.

"Master," Mordoon croaked. "We seek only to fulfill the prophecy. The Divide fails. There is no avoiding what must be done."

"Killing this child will not heal the Divide."

The moans turned to wails.

"But her power…"

"All power flows from the one true source. There is no power but through him."

"How then?" Mordoon cried. "How do we avoid the destruction? The prophecy is clear. Life's blood must be freely spilled."

Salamain slowly lowered his staff.

"Blood will be freely spilled this day," he said softly.

"No." Mordoon's moan made Nova shiver. "No, Master. We cannot."

"If you will be saved, you must be willing to accept my blood." Salamain's eyes met Nova's. "This is the only way."

Nova's peace shattered. This couldn't happen. "No," she whispered. "It's my fault. I did what they said. I—"

"But the girl is the child of prophecy," Mordoon argued.

Salamain brought down his staff with a sharp crack, and the earth trembled. Men began to shout and scream. Salamain brought the staff down again, and the trembling stopped.

He looked at all of them, his gaze moving slowly from left to right. "I serve the creator and the fulfillment of *all* prophecy."

The High King!

Nova's heart leapt with joy despite her overwhelming sadness.

"Only this gift, freely given and not taken, will restore what has been broken. *This is the only way.*"

Salamain turned to the man huddled somewhere beside her who had been prepared to end Nova's life. "Release her."

The man was instantly on his feet, cutting through the bonds that held Nova to the wooden beam. She sat up, her body shaking. Around them, the men of the order knelt on the ground, foreheads pressed to the dirt, arms extended in supplication.

Only Mordoon stood, and his head was also bowed.

Nova looked at Salamain. He smiled, and the air before him shimmered. His scars vanished. His beautiful, gentle face glowed with love and light.

"But I'm guilty," she whispered, unable to find her full voice.

He nodded. "All are."

Hot tears flooded her again. "I don't want you to die."

He reached out his hand. She moved to the edge of the basin, and he cupped her face.

"Fear not, daughter. Death is not the end of life."

Then strange hands pulled her out of the basin and away across the field.

Cyril, a cruel sneer across his face, silently pointed at the four men with him and then at Salamain. The men, clearly distraught, looked between them.

Salamain leaned forward and laid his staff on the ground.

"No," Nova cried, her voice strangled with grief.

Cyril pushed one of the others away and moved to Salamain's side himself, grabbing him and shoving him toward the basin. Salamain fell against it.

"No, leave him alone!"

The hands dragged her, too strong for her to break free. She heard a door open. She saw the men lift Salamain and put him on the beam. Cyril had the dagger in his hand, lifted high. Then she fell as she was thrown into the dirt and the door slammed shut.

"No! No!" She scrambled back to her feet, leaping for the door.

It wouldn't budge. She pounded on the thick wood. She grabbed the bars in the small opening near the top, straining to see.

On the table, Salamain was still. Blood dripped from the dagger and cascaded over the wood, pooling into the basin beneath. A dark understanding of the stone bowl's use filled her, as did a deeper grief than anything she had ever known before.

He died for me.

She alone was to blame. For everything. Yet, he'd sacrificed himself.

For her.

Nova pressed her forehead against the bars, squeezing her eyes closed. She didn't want to remember him this way. She didn't want to see him lying there, dead because of her. This amazing, gentle man.

Salamain.

A light flickered against her eyelids. Against her better judgement, she opened them. Her breath froze in wonder. Sparks of golden light lifted into the air like flakes of snow, spinning and shining brighter than the sun. The sparks swirled and grew larger, filling the sky like golden clouds, spreading in all directions. The light filled the valley. Men covered their faces. The brilliance was too great to behold. Tears streamed from Nova's eyes, but this time they were tears of wonder. The golden light flowed across the mountain tops and slowly formed a wall that ran from the heavens to below her line of sight.

The Divide, Nova realized. *I'm seeing the Divide.*

Looking was enough to make her go blind, yet she knew she wouldn't lose her sight. She'd been permitted to see this miracle ... this gift from Salamain.

Death is not the end of life.

All along the wall, light poured into cracks. Broken places reformed. The Divide was restored. Then with a final flash, the light vanished. The vision of the wall faded away. The valley seemed dark in its absence, although the sun still rose behind the mountain peaks. Nova looked back at the wooden beam and gasped.

Salamain was gone.

"It is finished," Mordoon said to the men. "The Divide is restored. Prophecy has been fulfilled."

RESTORED

Quentin stared at the curve of twisted wood. It looked like a huge upside-down horseshoe. "This is the portal?"

Sol nodded. "It's exactly as he told us."

"Will it work?" Laura's trembling voice held the same doubt and hesitation he felt.

Sol hefted a small rock in his hand. He looked at them, then turned and tossed the pebble into the opening. There was a flash, and the rock disappeared. Sol turned back to them. "Yes."

Morra came closer, her smile tinged with sadness. "This is where we leave you."

Quentin searched her face. "Are you sure?"

She nodded and squeezed his hand. "We're not meant to come with you. The rest of this journey is yours to make." She tried again to smile. "Besides, our men are returning. We must get home before they find us missing and worry."

"How do you know?" Laura asked.

"I saw them," Rose said, her face lit with a huge grin. "In my dream."

Laura smiled as she squatted in the grass to meet Rose eye to eye. "Well, then, I'm sure it's true."

Rose giggled. Then she wrapped her little arms around Laura. Quentin watched, fascinated, as the hardened bully blinked, startled, then put her arms around the little girl.

"Take care of Nova," Rose said as she pulled back.

Then she turned and launched herself at Quentin. He went to a knee to catch her, giving her the tightest hug he could.

"If I had a sister, I'd want her to be just like you."

She pulled away enough to plant a kiss on his cheek before running back to Morra.

Morra turned to Sol. "You look after them well, healer."

He put a fist to his heart and gave a half bow. "You have my word." Then he turned to Quentin and Laura. "We'll go through together. If the portal doesn't take us to Rifting Pass, at least we'll be together, and we can try again."

They nodded.

There was nothing left to say.

They lined up in front of the portal. Quentin glanced through the opening. He could only see a long stretch of field on the other side and wondered what else they would find when they stepped through.

"Together," Sol said.

They grasped hands and stepped.

There was a flash of light. Quentin felt a slight resistance, but Sol and Laura's grip on him was firm. They pulled him through. The flash of light dissipated, and a blast of cold air greeted him. Tall mountains stood to either side.

They'd made it.

The sun peeked from behind the mountain tops. Rays of light splashing the land with red and orange. A long gradual decline led into the valley below. At the center was a large stone building and beyond, the top of a wall or fence of some kind.

"We must hurry." Sol moved quickly along the grassy slope.

A crack resounded from the valley, echoing across the mountains. A blast of light erupted.

"Nova!" Quentin shouted.

They broke into a run. They were not even half way there when the ground heaved and began to shake. Laura fell to her knees, and Sol crouched beside her.

"Earthquake," he shouted.

A moment later the shaking stopped. No, Quentin thought. This was more than an earthquake. He looked toward the valley but could see nothing. Where were the men of the Order? Where was Nova?

Sol helped Laura up and they moved again, more carefully this time. Running wouldn't do any good if someone fell and broke a leg or an ankle.

Quentin outdistanced them. He heard Sol call but didn't stop. He couldn't. He needed to get to Nova. He had to find her.

Someone shouted in the distance.

"Nova?" There was no way she could hear him, but he yelled her name anyway.

Something was wrong. Dread filled him.

There was a wrenching tear. Quentin's belly filled with pain. He stumbled and hit the ground. Sol and Laura reached him and knelt beside him, but their gazes were glued on something else. Gritting his teeth against the pain, Quentin looked up.

Gold snow filled the sky. Sparkling gold snow. Only instead of falling, the cloud of snow moved from the ground to the sky, lifting upward in a vortex of golden light that slowly filled the heavens. Quentin watched in wide-eyed amazement as a blazing portion of cloud split off and came toward them like the finger of God.

"Quentin," Laura breathed, but she could say no more, and he could not respond.

Sol and Laura stared as the finger of gold twisted down to where Quentin sat, wrapping him like a blanket. A pulsing warmth filled him. A soft sense of wonder widened his eyes. The pain was gone.

The sky was alive with the flowing river of light. They watched together as the swirling mass passed over them, over the mountains and Rifting Pass, coming slowly down to form a long wall. Jagged cracks and broken sections became visible, only to be filled by the light.

"The Divide is restored," Sol breathed, his voice filled with wonder and with horror.

Quentin touched his ribs. The pain was gone, as was the connection to Nova.

No.

He couldn't move. His legs were as useless as they had been before coming through the Divide. They refused to respond. He sat, stunned and immobile.

Nova couldn't be dead.

"Look," Laura said softly.

A shape emerged from the valley, moving quickly toward them. Sol stood up, stepping in front of Laura and Quentin. A defensive position, Quentin thought. But it didn't matter. Nothing mattered anymore. Not if Nova was gone.

The shape came nearer. A man. No, Quentin corrected himself, a boy. Dark hair and dark eyes took them in.

"You're looking for Nova?" he asked.

Laura looked at Sol.

"She can't be dead," Quentin whispered.

"No," the dark-haired young man said. "She is not. They have released her."

"What? How do you know? Who are you?" Sol grabbed the boy's arm.

"I am Viru. I am … a friend of Nova's." He smiled ruefully. "Now."

Recognition slowly washed over Quentin. "You," he said, the memory coming into focus. "You were the one in the park."

Viru nodded. "Yes."

"You tried to kill her."

"No, I was sent only to retrieve her, to bring her here."

"Then how are you her friend?" Laura growled.

"Nova found me when she and Seth came across the Divide. They brought me with them. We … shared a long journey. I came to understand she was not what I had thought."

"Where is she?" Quentin's fear and frustration outweighed any anger. "You said she's been released. Is she okay? Did they hurt her?"

Viru shook his head. "I did not see her before they released me, but they would not harm her. Not after what happened."

"What did happen?" Sol urged.

"Salamain," Viru said, his face a mix of wonder, sadness, and joy. "Wardein. The traveler."

"He was here?" Quentin asked.

Viru nodded. "He fulfilled the prophecy." Viru looked at each of them. "He died in her place."

CHILD OF PROPHECY

Nova walked with her arms wrapped around her middle. She had no idea where she was. They had let her out, freed her to go on with her life, and shown her to the front gate. A lush grassland spread out from the foot of the mountains, but Nova had no idea where she was or how to find Quentin and the others. She put one foot in front of the other, eager to be away from the Order and all that had happened. The world around her was a blur, and only partially because the tears would not stop coming.

Salamain.

Her heart ached for him. How could he have given himself to them like that? She was guilty of everything they said. He knew the failing Divide and all of the destruction it had caused was her fault, and he'd died for her anyway. She'd never known anything like that before. Yes, her mom loved her and Grandpa Zeke loved her, but this was different. Salamain didn't care if she was broken. He didn't care what she'd done wrong. He'd sacrificed himself without hesitation, healing the Divide and setting everything right. Still, without his kind, gentle face, the world seemed darker.

Somewhere nearby a horse nickered. Nova blinked, wiping her tears. Her stomach growled, and she gave a little laugh. It was good to feel hungry—to feel anything. Her life would go on, thanks to the gift she'd been given.

"If only I deserved his sacrifice."

"Now there are words I'll agree with."

Nova spun around with a gasp. "Seth?" She frowned in confusion but took a step toward him, glad to see any familiar face. "What are you doing here?"

His face looked funny.

"I saw them take you, and I followed them," he said, but he still didn't look right. His face was … angry.

Did he know what had happened? "Salamain," she whispered. "They killed him."

Hot tears filled her eyes. She felt like she would never stop crying.

"Good riddance."

His comment took a moment to sink in. "What?" Nova stared at him, trying to comprehend.

Seth laughed. Not a good laugh. The sound was dark and wrong.

"I said good riddance." He waved his hand. "Ugly old man, with his strange stories and his stupid High King this and High King that." Seth raised one dark eyebrow. "Honestly Nova, I don't know what you ever saw in him."

Anger welled in her like a storm. "Take that back."

He shrugged. "Whatever. You can fall for that stuff if you want."

"Fall for it? You act like it's a bunch of garbage. He *died* for me." The tears burned as they fell. "He did nothing but care about everyone. I caused everything they said I would, and he still took my place." She shook her head. Nothing made any sense.

"How do you know?" Seth asked, and the anger in his face was so familiar. "How do you know he wasn't tricking you into thinking that so he could get you where he wanted you?"

"I know because I saw what they did to him." Nova said, trembling. "I saw him die."

Seth sneered. "You saw me, but you didn't figure out who I was, did you?"

What was he talking about?

He shook his head. "Oh, no, you were too busy being Nova, the Trine. The perfect girl. The *Child of Prophecy*. You were always the right one, while I was the one who did all the work."

"What are you talking about?" Seth was acting as if he'd lost his mind.

He ignored her. "I did everything he said. *Everything*. I watched you. I learned the spells. I was *just* as good as you, but did that matter? Of course not. I never mattered. Not to him. I didn't have what he wanted." He gave a bitter laugh. "That was all you, *Sister*."

His words hit her, but didn't register, didn't make sense.

"You were the one with the right combination. The right factors. The right blood. You were all he ever wanted. Me? I was the mistake. The experiment gone wrong."

Slowly, Seth's words started to sink in. Nova stared at him. She remembered seeing him in school that day, thinking he looked vaguely familiar. His dark hair, the lines of his face … but they hadn't been familiar enough. Not back then.

Not before she'd finally seen what her father looked like.

Seth watched her watching him, and his eyes widened. "What, you didn't know? You didn't figure that out?" Suddenly he was right in front of her, his face twisted and horrible. "Yes, that's right. He's my father too. You're not the only precious offspring of Lucien the Great and Terrible." He gave a miserable laugh. "There are lots of us."

Lots?

"He had to keep trying, after all. Had to get the combination of factors just right so he could create his little Trine. But first, there were lots and lots of us failed attempts."

"Oh, no." The awfulness of what had been done washed over her.

Everything clicked into place. Why her mother had never talked about Lucien. Why he wasn't around but had been looking for her. Why he'd seemed so intense when he'd spoken to her. He hadn't wanted to reunite with his long-lost daughter.

He wanted the Trine he'd created.

And if that wasn't bad enough, she wasn't his first attempt. How many were out there? How many children had he fathered in his hunger to create a Trine?

"Oh, yes," Seth growled.

Her mind was numb. Sadness overwhelmed her. The pain took her by complete surprise. Her eyes rolled up, catching a flash of Seth standing close, a rock covered in blood in his hand.

"But he underestimated this mistake," she heard him say before the world went dark.

Finally. Seth watched the precious chosen one fall to the ground.

"Where are you now, old man?" Seth asked the empty air. "I'm here with your precious Trine. She's not dead. Her precious blood is still intact and ripe for harvest. And who's here to collect it? Me. Your mistake. Your second best."

He turned Nova over, yanking her arms behind her and tying them up good and tight.

"But I won't be second best much longer."

He left her there, trussed, and went to fetch his horse. Then he grabbed her under the arms, hauling her up until she was slung over the saddle.

"Wow, that looks really uncomfortable," he laughed.

He carefully climbed onto the saddle behind her prone form. He knew where he had to go. Thankfully, the place wasn't far away.

"You failed, Father," Seth said as he pulled his horse around to the East. "You failed, and I'm the one who will claim her blood and her power for myself."

He kicked the horse's sides, urging the beast to a full gallop.

Seth's time had finally come, and he was eager to claim the destiny that should have been his.

Edah

Magic exists in all living things, an energy that flows like lifeblood. This is the essence of each person, each animal, each plant. Without the spark of sentience, there would be no vitality. No vigor. The Edah is the spirit of who we are. The soul made flesh.

The breath of life.

—High Wizard Ezekial, on the *Factors of Magic*

Stolen

"Someone else is coming," Viru pointed.

Quentin, the feeling finally returning to his body after finding out Nova was not dead, was able to stand up with Laura's help. He dusted himself off and turned to see two figures hurrying toward them.

They came from the direction of the portal.

One figure was smaller than the other. For a confused moment, Quentin wondered if Morra and Rose had followed them for some reason, but as the figures drew closer he could see neither one was a child. He squinted.

"Yes!" He gave a whoop of joy and started running, leaving the others behind. Finally, reinforcements were here. "Zeke! Mira!"

Mira held her arms out, and he ran into them, grateful to be wrapped in a familiar hug. Then she was holding him away.

"Quentin?" Her gaze moved down his legs, eyes wide.

"No Triple-E here," he explained.

Zeke nodded. "Of course. I should have guessed."

Quentin couldn't help but laugh, even though they still needed to find Nova. "I couldn't have guessed any of this," he said, wiping away happy tears.

Mira's face was still lined with worry. "Where is she? Where's Nova?"

"I think she's headed toward the Mizrah," a voice behind them said.

The others had caught up.

"They freed her before we arrived. She would have gone from the front gate."

"Sol!" Zeke shouted, clasping the other man by the arm. "You've grown into a man."

"Thank you for taking care of the children," Mira added.

Sol glanced back and forth between them. "I was happy to help," he said, "but I don't know if I would call them children."

Zeke nodded. "Agreed. But let's talk as we go. We need to find Nova."

Viru lead the way, skirting the monastery and arena where the men of the Order were still reeling from all that had happened. Shouts could be heard from the building, calling for a change in leadership.

They stopped at the front gate to look down the sloping path, each set of eyes searching, but there was no sign of Nova.

"Come," Sol said. "Let's—"

"Wait."

They turned to see someone hurrying through the grass.

"Mordoon," Viru said, rushing to help the old man who was clearly struggling.

"Wait," he said as he reached them.

He held out his hand as he took several deep breaths.

"One of our seers," he said between gasps, "you must ... get them. Nova ... taken."

"What?" Mira's face paled.

Zeke took a step closer. "Who took her? Where?"

Mordoon's eyes widened as he looked at Zeke. "High Wizard."

"Yes, yes," Zeke waved a hand. "Just tell us where she is."

Mordoon nodded. "One of our seers had a vision. A boy. He has her on a horse."

"A boy?" Viru asked, his eyes looking off into the distance.

"Yes. A dark-haired boy with gray eyes."

"Seth." Viru's whisper sent shivers up Quentin's arms.

"Seth? Why would he take her? Is he trying to find us?"

"No," Viru said, shaking his head. "Something is wrong. When I left him, he was not himself. When Nova became ill, he would not come. He would not help. Why would he take her now?"

"Seth said Lucien sent him," Quentin said, his heart feeling like a block of stone in his chest. "Maybe he's taking her to him."

How could they have been this close, only to have her snatched away from them?

"Then we must get to them before that can happen." Zeke turned to Mordoon. "Did your seer say which way they were heading?"

"East, across the Northern edge of the Great Plains."

Zeke squinted into the distance.

"Not to Lucien, then." He said thoughtfully. "I know of only one place of any consequence in that direction. The cave of dreams."

"Viru, go and fetch six of our best horses."

"Six?"

The old man smiled at him. "You must go as well. It is only right."

Viru flashed a smile, then was off and running.

"The least we can do," Mordoon said with a slight bow, "after all that has happened."

"I should think so," Zeke answered, his face stern. "She is my only granddaughter you know."

Mordoon cleared his throat nervously. "We did not know," he croaked, "but it would not have ... we did not ... we only did what we did because we thought—"

Zeke placed his hand on the old man's shoulder. "Thankfully, you have seen the error of your ways. Have you not?"

Quentin thought he liked this side of Nova's grandfather.

"Yes, High Wizard." Mordoon's face was red, but to his credit he met Zeke's eyes. "We have."

Viru appeared in the distance with two others, trailing six horses.

Zeke nodded. "Then perhaps the future of the Order will be brighter than its past."

"We can only hope," Mordoon agreed.

Cave of Dreams

Nova's head throbbed in a steady rhythm, as if someone had drummed on her temples for hours. A horse snorted, and Nova realized she wasn't too far from the truth as the hooves continued their steady beat.

She tried to move her hands, but they wouldn't budge. Her shoulders ached. Her wrists were scraped and raw.

She was tied up.

"Have a nice nap, little sister?"

Seth. The memories flooded back to her in a rush.

"Where are you taking me?" Her voice sounded thick, and her throat was dry.

"Oh, it's a fun place. You'll find it very special, I think." He gave a dark laugh.

She tried to turn to look at him, but a sharp pain stabbed the back of her head. "Why are you doing this?"

"What? Riding a horse? It's more fun than walking."

"I'm not Lucien. I didn't do those things to you. I thought we were … I thought we were friends."

He laughed again. "Friends? The chosen one and the mistake?"

She shook her head, quickly regretting the movement as a wave of dizziness rolled through her. "I thought I was a mistake too. My whole life. I thought I was a freak."

"You were on the wrong side of the Divide."

"I got picked on. Bullied. Nobody would tell me the truth about who I was or why I could do the things I could do. I thought I was broken."

She'd gone her whole life without fitting in. She'd made the rash decision to come here, not knowing what she was doing, just for the chance to find somewhere she belonged.

"Oh, poor Nova!" She flinched at Seth's retort. "You got picked on. So, what? You had a mother. Mine was taken from me. By *him*. While you were busy feeling sorry for yourself, feeling sad because people didn't explain why you were different, I was busy being a slave because I wasn't different *enough*."

His words were harsh, but he was right. She did have a mother who loved her. She had Grandpa Zeke and Quentin. She had a lot more than some people had. Why was she constantly feeling sorry for herself? There were a lot of people who were worse off than she was. She was actually pretty lucky.

Something bright filled Nova. A soft smile curved her lips. She wasn't lucky, she was blessed. She had taken things for granted before. No more. She'd been so wrapped up in what she was going through she hadn't stopped to consider what was going on all around her, but that could change. Somebody died for her. She would never be the same again.

Yes, things would definitely change.

"You're right," she said softly.

Surprisingly, Seth had no response.

"I'm sorry."

He was quiet for a few minutes. The horse slowed. Had he changed his mind? Was he going to let her go?

"I don't want your pity," he growled as he pulled the horse to a stop.

No. He wasn't going to let her go. Not now, not ever. He was going to go through with his twisted plan, born at the hands of their twisted father. But a new purpose filled Nova. The fear was gone.

When Seth pulled her down from the horse and she finally got a look at his angry eyes, she felt only sadness for him. "Lucien shouldn't have done those things to you," she said.

He twisted her around, shoving her. She stumbled but managed to steady herself as she neared a rock formation. A dark opening appeared behind one of the large boulders. A cave.

"What is this place?"

Seth laughed as if pleased by the prospect of her fear, but she wasn't frightened. She was fascinated. The cave thrummed with power like a live wire. The rocks shimmered, as if they had their own magic embedded inside them.

Stepping into the gloomy opening was like walking into the Divide. Power flowed around them like water running through the air. Nova stifled a gasp.

There were colors here. *Rainbow* colors.

Seth shoved her again. "Keep moving."

The rock floor sloped down steeply.

"Nasty, isn't it? Sorry about that. I know it's probably not to your liking. Too dark and wet and smelly."

She disagreed but didn't say anything.

"I would have picked a prettier location, but this place is more than meets the eye."

She couldn't agree more. This cave had far more than met the eye. The colors pulsed along the walls of rock. They coursed through the air and danced along her skin. The pain in her head and shoulders eased, and she squelched the urge to shout for joy.

Then the walls opened up, and Nova found herself standing in a cavern. Waves of color soared, crashing off the walls and reverberating like music. She was reminded of her drawing with the crescendo, the lines getting smaller yet gaining more strength. She stared in absolute wonder.

"Welcome to the cave of dreams," Seth said with a flourish. "Not much to see but lots to do."

Not much to see? How could he not see this? He was Zen too, wasn't he? How was he not seeing the amazing vortex of colors that danced through this place? How could he not at least *feel* the power?

Instead of looking above them, Seth fixed his gaze at the floor. He pulled a knife from somewhere and carved a shape into the dirt. A familiar shape emerged—one she recognized—a shape she herself had drawn. She frowned. She'd seen this shape recently.

"What are you doing?"

He didn't look up. "I'm taking what's mine."

Lines overlapped inward, collapsing on each other.

Destructive.

Rainbow sparks danced along the drawing. She wondered if he could see them but thought not. This was her spell form, not his.

"Be careful, Seth."

This time he looked up with a savage grin.

"Recognize this, do you? He snarled. "I'm a quick study."

What did he think this form was? What did he think the spell would do?

The image of the cyclorn, his awful horn touching the wraith as he fed on the lost souls, burned in her mind.

Taking the magic of others like a vampire.

Stealing power.

This was what the plan had been all along. This was why Lucien had wanted a Trine. Not to create her or to use her, but to steal the power for himself. He'd used Seth as a pawn.

I'm the one who will claim her blood and her power for myself. Seth's words echoed. He'd double crossed Lucien.

Seth wanted Nova's power for himself.

"Oh Seth, no." He didn't understand. He didn't realize what he was doing.

The rainbow colors danced around him like a storm. He didn't stop. If anything, his strokes became faster. More determined. More brutal. Understanding settled on her like a cloak.

Destructive.

Creative.

Neutral.

She was the only one who had ever used all three factors. No one knew what they could do together. Even when she'd used her combined magic, she'd done it without true awareness, her subconscious forming what her conscious mind didn't yet understand.

Until now.

"You can't wield all three," she cautioned again, but he was lost to her.

He crouched on the floor, knife in hand. Furiously, he reconstructed what he'd seen her draw. The image she had created. The rainbow colors grew denser in the air around him until she could barely see him.

When Seth stood up with the knife still clutched in his hand, she knew what he intended. He'd once told her the strength of a spell depended on the medium. He grabbed her hands roughly, pulling them close and pressing the point of the blade into the heel of her left palm. She watched, mesmerized, as a drop of ruby red fell through the swirling colors in the air and landed dead center on the form.

A brilliant, blinding light flashed. Seth's grin was feral as he released her.

"Now, it's my turn!" He screamed.

"Yes," Nova said sadly, remembering Salamain's face as he'd smiled at her. "It is."

He frowned at her words, but his eyes were drawn to the spell. The spell didn't ignite slowly, as the mirror spell had. Instead, the form was consumed all at once. The rainbow colors in the room flooded to the design, creating the shape in the air above the floor. As the Neutral collapsed inward, the Destructive was unleashed. Blackness formed at the spell's center, devoid of color, devoid of light. This blackness moved toward Seth.

His eyes widened. "No. It wasn't supposed to work this way," but his protests were lost.

Destructive magic covered Seth like a blanket of darkness. Through the cloak of blackness, Nova watched as Seth's mouth opened in a silent scream. Despite everything he'd said and done, her heart ached for him. She remembered being hollowed out by the Trench. She knew what it felt like to have your magic stripped away like flesh and bone, leaving you empty inside. Only Seth had brought this on himself.

Head thrown back, eyes wide and mouth open, he looked as the wraith had, except there was no lost soul trapped inside. There was only Seth. Whittled down and stripped bare.

Nova looked down at the spell form. She remembered the horrid way the cyclorn had used this magic, and the terrible lost souls the beast had created. There was only one medium more powerful than blood. The lines might be on the dirt and stone, but the true nature of the spell was drawn from another medium.

This spell was drawn in the magic itself.

The rainbow colors surrounded her as the Destructive collapsed, and the true nature of the spell unfolded. This time, there was no blackness. This time when the spell ignited there was only the pure light of creation. The Edah.

The essence of life, shining like the light of the High King.

Creative magic pulsed like a star, blanketing Seth. The darkness was wiped away. The light sank into him, pouring over and through him. Where once he had been desolate and withered, now there was life and light. Where he had been purged, he was reborn.

Death is not the end of life.

Salamain's gentle words caressed her, bringing tears to her eyes. Not sad tears, but tears of joy. She was only beginning to understand.

The light of the Creative magic pulsed through Seth, taking on a rhythm. She heard him gasp. He blinked, taking in a deep, ragged breath. He sank slowly to his knees, smearing the lines he had drawn. He was like a newborn. Here, but not yet fully aware. She let him be so the magic could finish its work.

Behind his prone form, a soft light bounced off the cavern wall. Nova looked up, her eyes widening. A slow, happy smile curved her lips.

"I knew you'd come," she whispered.

Salamain reached out and took her hand. His fingers were warm. Solid. Full of life. He cupped her cheek as he had before, and she leaned into him, letting her tears flow.

"You're really here? I'm not dreaming?"

"Death has no place in the City of Gold," Salamain said with a smile of his own, "and I am a traveler of the High King."

"I'd like to meet this High King of yours."

"Someday, but not today. You have gone through the fire, but you have come out the other side stronger for the trial. You are a rare and precious gem."

She put her hand over his.

"Will I see you again?"

"I go wherever I am needed," he said with a sparkle in his eye.

"Thank you."

He nodded once and then he was gone, leaving only the warmth on her skin.

Nova looked down at Seth. He still knelt on the floor, but he was breathing regularly now. He looked up at her, blinking.

"Where am I?"

Nova smiled. "You're with me."

HOME

Quentin pushed his horse as hard as he dared, but still he couldn't keep up with Mira. She perched over her mare's neck as if part of the animal. Together, they flew like the wind. He couldn't blame her. She must be frantic. His own stomach writhed with worry.

What was Seth up to?

"I knew I shouldn't trust him." He let the wind take his words.

There was a commotion up ahead. Mira had stopped, leaping from her horse and running toward what looked like a large rock formation sticking up out of the grass. The rest of them arrived moments later.

"This is the place." Zeke jumped down like someone half his age.

He hurried toward the rocks, the rest of them scrambling to follow.

Quentin's heart pounded. All he wanted was to see Nova and know she was all right. There was a shout. Mira had stopped at a dark opening. What was happening? She backed up a step, and sweat broke out on Quentin's arms.

Mira stepped to one side as two forms emerged from the darkness.

"Nova!" He couldn't contain his shout.

Mira swept her daughter up in a hug.

Quentin ran on legs that felt like spaghetti, outpacing the others. He tried to take everything in, but only one thing registered: Nova was here. She was alive. He swept her into his arms, crushing her against him. She hugged him back fiercely.

"Are you hurt?" He pulled her away, his eyes trying to examine every inch of her to make sure she wasn't injured.

She laughed and cried at the same time. "I'm fine. I'm okay."

Mira pulled both of them into a hug.

Then Zeke was there. His strong arms wrapped around all of them.

Nova rested her head on Quentin's shoulder. This was where she belonged. Where he belonged. This was right.

They were slow to let go, basking in the fact they were finally together again. Seth stood to one side, staring.

"What happened?" Quentin gave Seth an angry scowl before turning back to Nova. "What did he do?"

Nova glanced sadly at Seth before turning back to the rest of them. "He tried to use one of the spells I'd drawn," she explained. "He didn't realize."

"Didn't realize what?" Zeke asked.

"Anything. What the spell would do, what the form meant, how the magic would work. He didn't understand, because he could only see the magic from one perspective. He couldn't see the Creative. The cave was dark to him."

Zeke studied her, his bushy brows moving up and down as he absorbed her words.

"Seems we have quite a bit to talk about," he said finally.

Nova smiled as Mira squeezed her.

"Does this mean we have to go back?"

The others turned.

Laura looked almost embarrassed for having spoken.

"I'm afraid so," Zeke answered. "In spite of Mira's excellent use of a memory neutralizing spell, Quentin's parents are frantic. All three of you have been written up for excessive absence, and the local police are getting more than a little curious."

Laura swallowed. "What about my parents?"

Zeke's brows stilled. "I'm afraid I haven't heard anything from them."

She nodded as if she'd expected this answer, but her relief was stained with disappointment.

"What happens now?" Quentin asked. "We just go back and pick up where we left off?"

"How do we even get through?" Laura added. "Won't Quentin cause the Divide to fail if he goes through again?"

Quentin's stomach clenched. He hadn't thought of that.

"Never fear," Zeke said. "We can wrap you in a bubble of Neutral for the crossing."

Nova stared at her Grandfather. "A bubble of Neutral?"

He nodded sagely. "It's like two negatives making a positive, my dear."

Mira rolled her eyes at him. "Like wearing my bathrobes makes you more powerful?"

That made them all laugh.

Zeke turned to Sol. "Thank you for all you've done."

Sol smiled. "It was an honor."

"I think we'll meet again, but for now we really should get them home."

Quentin noticed Zeke didn't use the word children this time. A hand touched his. He looked over to find Nova leaning close.

Her forehead was scrunched with worry. "Are you sure you'll be all right? Going back? The way things are … over there?"

"My chair." He'd completely forgotten. "I left it near the Divide."

"That shouldn't matter," Zeke said. "We can go back to the moment before you came through, and your chair should still be there."

Quentin squinted. "Wait. Won't we still be there too?"

Zeke shook his head firmly. "Not possible. You can't be in two places at once. We're moving to a specific point in time, not to the physical—"

Mira placed her hand on Zeke's arm. "It will be all right. He knows all about how the Divide works … apparently."

Zeke had the grace to look a bit guilty. "Yes, well …"

"Don't worry, Grandpa," Nova said. "We'll have time to talk everything through when we get there." She turned to Quentin again. "You're sure this is okay?"

He gave her a wink. "Don't expect me to let you win any races."

Nova's smile was radiant. "You really think you're gonna be faster than me just cause you'll have your wheels back?"

Nova had never been so happy. So complete. Everything was back to normal. She had Mom, Grandpa, Quentin, even Laura.

"What's going to happen to Seth?" She looked at her newfound brother.

Sol cocked his head. "I could use an apprentice."

Zeke nodded. "I think that's a good idea."

"Then, it's time we got ourselves home," Mira said.

Except, Nova thought, that world wasn't her *only* home now. Maybe, just maybe, she had two places where she belonged.

AFTER

Nova stared into the sky, watching as a cloud drifted slowly against the blue background. The white curves reminded her of a bird. She was transported back to the clearing with the bow and arrow against her cheek, Viru speaking from just behind.

Do not just see the bird. Sense it. Feel it.

She remembered the sense of wonder as she realized its movements were a pattern. That they were the bird's magic.

This is the bird's Edah, its life force.

All of life was a pattern.

"Nova," Quentin's voice was soft and sleepy.

"Mmm?"

"Do you ever miss Threa?"

She smiled. "All the time."

"Do you think we'll ever go back?"

She noticed his use of the plural. "I hope so."

She understood Quentin's desire to go back. She could only imagine what he felt being able to get up and around without having to hold onto something or someone. Using his legs to run again must give him an incredible sense of freedom.

Nova unwrapped her arms. Soft fur brushed against her skin. "You wanna hold Yogi?"

Quentin looked at the stuffed bear, taking in the weathered fur, the scraggly ears and the damaged eye. "No," he said softly, "I think Yogi will be okay without me."

Nova felt a soft pressure in her chest. "Are you sure? He's a little worse for wear these days."

"I'm sure," Quentin answered, voice firm. "He knows being strong isn't everything. He's okay being a one-eyed bear. He was made well." There was a pause. "Besides, he has you."

Warmth spread through Nova like honey—slow and sweet.

"I think he'll be just fine."

Nova found Quentin's hand and laced her fingers through his, the rough skin familiar and right.

"I think he will too."

About the Author

T. E. Bradford is a writer, singer-songwriter, cancer survivor, and proud wife and mother. Born and raised in Central New York, she will tell you her parents gave her the two best tools in her arsenal by reading to her and raising her in a Christian household. In spite of the long CNY winters, she continues to live there with the husband God created just for her, and the son who is her forever best story. In her heart, she feels her gift of writing is a little piece of magic, and that it is both her privilege and grandest adventure to find new ways to stretch a hand out to touch the wonder of this vast universe God created.

Made in the USA
Lexington, KY
27 September 2018